BLOOD STANDARD

"The action is fast-paced, the characters well drawn, the settings vivid and the hardboiled prose quirky in the manner of a writer who cut his teeth on horror and poetry."
—Associated Press

"Laird Barron has so much fun with this character, who admires Humphrey Bogart's take on Sam Spade and tosses off one-liners that bring the spirit of Dashiell Hammett into the twenty-first century."
—*The News & Observer* (Raleigh, NC)

"Massive, scarred Isaiah is a thug's thug, but he's also a well-read student of mythology. He's indifferent to stab wounds and generates righteous mayhem in his quest. Fans of violent crime fiction will love this one and will be eager to hear more from Isaiah."
—*Booklist* (starred review)

"Barron is one of the most talented voices in contemporary fiction. . . . If you mixed together the best violent portions of the John Wick movies, the almost inscrutable nature of vengeance as it is dealt with in Greek mythology, the tension and darkness that has always characterized Barron's horror writing, and the sine qua non elements of all best-selling thrillers, you'd only begin to approximate what *Blood Standard* has to offer. The rest of it is worth discovering by reading it, which is something you should do as soon as possible."
—*PANK Magazine*

WORSE ANGELS

LAIRD BARRON

G. P. PUTNAM'S SONS

New York

PUTNAM
— EST. 1838 —

G. P. PUTNAM'S SONS
Publishers Since 1838
An imprint of Penguin Random House LLC
penguinrandomhouse.com

Copyright © 2020 by Laird Barron
Penguin supports copyright. Copyright fuels creativity, encourages
diverse voices, promotes free speech, and creates a vibrant culture. Thank you
for buying an authorized edition of this book and for complying with copyright
laws by not reproducing, scanning, or distributing any part of it in any form
without permission. You are supporting writers and allowing
Penguin to continue to publish books for every reader.

The Library of Congress has catalogued the
G. P. Putnam's Sons hardcover edition as follows:

Names: Barron, Laird, author.
Title: Worse angels / Laird Barron.
Description: New York : G. P. Putnam's Sons, [2020] |
Series: Isaiah Coleridge
Identifiers: LCCN 2020013628 (print) | LCCN 2020013629 (ebook) |
ISBN 9780593084991 (hardcover) | ISBN 9780593085004 (ebook)
Subjects: GSAFD: Noir fiction. | Suspense fiction. | Mystery fiction.
Classification: LCC PS3602.A83725 W67 2020 (print) |
LCC PS3602.A83725 (ebook) | DDC 813/.6--dc23
LC record available at https://lccn.loc.gov/2020013628
LC ebook record available at https://lccn.loc.gov/2020013629

First G. P. Putnam's Sons hardcover edition / May 2020
First G. P. Putnam's Sons premium edition / April 2021
G. P. Putnam's Sons premium edition ISBN: 9780593085011

Printed in the United States of America
1   3   5   7   9   10   8   6   4   2

For Jessica M.

Out of the window,
I saw how the planets gathered
Like the leaves themselves
Turning in the wind.

—WALLACE STEVENS

The other was a softer voice,
As soft as honey-dew:
Quoth he, "The man hath penance done,
And penance more will do."

—SAMUEL TAYLOR COLERIDGE

PART I

VALLEY OF THE HORSES' HEADS

CHAPTER ONE

A blood moon glowered over the Catskills as I climbed out of the hole. I glowered back, imagining claws and fangs and muscles bursting through my clothes the way it happened for Lon Chaney Jr. on moldy old *Wolf Man* posters. Nothing doing. I remained plain old Isaiah Coleridge, but that was probably bad enough. Werewolf movies were on my mind, for various reasons. Earlier that evening, I'd commented on the topic to my girl, Meg.

Freudian as all get-out, she'd said. *Good guy on the surface, woman-and-sheep-ravishing beast on the inside. Those faux-romantic posters where the werewolf—in pants!—carries an unconscious gothic heroine in his arms? Not like that. He—it—dragged the woman by her hair. Blood drooled from where the roots tore free. Her shinbones gleamed in the moonlight . . .*

You're ruining everything, I'd said. *Why do horror movies always preface the main story with a curse that began years, if not decades or centuries, in the past? Does evil need to steep like a tea bag before it can manifest?* Didn't get an answer, but one of Meg's enigmatic smiles, as if to say I needed to pay more attention.

"Every rock in the state of New York is in this god-damned hole." Lionel Robard tipped back his safari hat. He leaned on a pickax. It was chilly; steam rose from the sweat on his brow and his matted hair. Rawboned and sinewy, he was built for marathon bouts of hard labor. His Monte Carlo's headlights were on so we could see what we were doing, like a pair of resurrection men in a graveyard after the world had gone to sleep. He needn't have bothered, what with all that nickel-plated moon-light spilling through the mist and the trees.

I wiped my face and popped the top of a beer.

"The wages of sin are digging rocks when you go to bury your ill-gotten treasure." I eyed the inky shadow of a man crouched near an Austrian pine. The longer I peered, the more closely the shadow-man resembled a stump.

Last year, we'd snatched a bunch of money from the secret cache of a notorious murderer romantically dubbed the Croatoan, since deceased. North of one and a half million dollars. Held it and waited. First, to see who might creep in from the woodwork searching for the loot, and for us. Second, because the bills were minted in the 1960s and '70s. Changing that filthy lucre into con-temporary currency without tipping off the authorities, or other Wrong People, presented a challenge. Our best bet was to launder the trove via one of my underworld connections at a substantial cost and the risk of alerting the aforementioned Wrong People; in this case, the Albany mob.

I kept other items from the Croatoan's cache. Tools of murder, documents, and videocassettes, chiefly. These were buried too, although closer to home in my own backyard. I was tempted to destroy these evil mementos. Yet, what if I needed them one fine day? *That* possibility stayed my hand.

Sinister home videos and killing knives weren't the issue right then. One and a half mil was the issue. Lionel had proven a good sport so far. He wouldn't, couldn't, stay cool forever. Prudence and temperance weren't his watchwords. The Marines taught him other skills, other bellicose virtues.

Thus, here we were in the sneaking hours, burying the money once again (we'd originally stashed it near home and then decided a lonely plot in the hills was wiser) with an eye toward a more permanent solution and only the gods knew when that might be. I set aside a portion for a sample, should a sample become necessary. We sweated a hunter or hiker stumbling across our handiwork and leaving an empty pit for us to find later. Farfetched, yet eminently reasonable to our minds—which spoke volumes about the state of those minds, I suppose.

"I vote we quit pussyfooting around and cash in our chips," Lionel said as we made ready to lower the sealed containers. "The German? He could handle this weight."

"The German isn't safe. His partners were pinched in a sting. The Feds will have him under a magnifying glass."

"I hadn't heard. Who, then?"

"Japanese liaison to the U.S. government might be our ticket. Former liaison. Sonny loves America and Elvis. Three years stateside near Graceland as a teen. I stayed with him in Tokyo when the Outfit sent me over on business. Elvis memorabilia out the wazoo."

"Rhinestone suit?"

"Rhinestone suit."

"Isn't he with the yakuza?" Lionel said.

"Sonny provides equal opportunities to all criminal gangs. I have to be careful. He likes me, but we aren't bosom buddies. He makes one call and we're boned. These ex-diplomats aren't loyal to anybody."

"Man, whatever gets us paid."

"The loot isn't going to evaporate."

"*We* might."

Touché. My left hand trembled. In the dim, and not so dim, past I'd broken it, had muscles torn, the fingers dislocated. Healed, all healed, yet the nerves were weakening, the rubber bands of sinew and tendon losing their snapback, and no matter how many racquet balls I crushed daily, or spade-loads of dirt I shoveled, the status quo slipped and my hand quivered when it grew tired and it grew tired ever more quickly.

"Hold tight a bit longer. I'll ask Meg for help."

"You ready to take it there?" he said. "You loop her in, this gets real."

"She's a research genius. Be peachy to know what we're dealing with." Detective license in my wallet notwithstanding, my girlfriend was the brains in the relationship.

"Kinda your job."

"I'm too busy getting punched in the face."

He hefted a stone and chucked it onto the pile.

"Does the origin matter? Gotta figure it's blood money, pure filth, the veritable root of evil. Get it laundered, problem solved. Who cares where it came from as long as we know where it's going?"

Any counter I threw at him would be weak.

"Blood money tends to carry a curse. I don't want to get bitten in the ass down the road."

"Brother, we were screwed the moment we walked into the madman's lair." He dropped his cigarette butt and commenced digging again. "Go read one of your books on mythology. Any of them. Curses get stronger with time. Dumping it for whatever we can get is the smart play."

"The smart play is to douse it in gasoline and strike a match."

He laughed as if I were making a joke.

Increasingly, there were moments when I wished heartily that we *were* capable of making the smart play. Just once.

■ ■ ■

Nature has everything plotted to a gnat's ass. Her vast blueprint overwhelms our ability to fully comprehend the true shape of reality. We glimpse points of intersection, we hear phantom notes on a cool autumn breeze, but seldom apprehend the greater symphony at play.

The day after we relocated the money, I sparred a few rounds with the regulars at the Deadfall Gym in Kingston. The Deadfall didn't help me improve my skills; it slowed their degradation. I'm strong and have fought enough to acquire an arsenal of nasty techniques. Fighting isn't a static art; it mutates rapidly, endlessly, and for every offensive tactic, there's a defense or a counter. I gave better than I got, and while sparring isn't really combat, to put it bluntly, I'd slowed. Somebody drilled me with a flying knee, applied a guillotine choke, and cranked my neck; somebody else hooked me behind the ankle and flung me headfirst onto the mat. The crash rattled the gym's metal garage door. Also got a complimentary dented nose in the bargain. Rub-some-dirt-on-it-and-walk-it-off type of damage.

Food for thought, these sessions, coupled with the aforementioned weakness in my left arm. Proof positive my problems weren't localized; they were systemic. I'd withstood copious measures of physical punishment in my days with the mob. The physical abuse quotient only got worse since I began sticking my nose into folks' business as a detective. Hospital visits and medical bills accrued. MDs tsked and clucked over my collection of injuries and chronic ailments. They passed around X-rays and CAT scans with the enthusiasm of kids trading baseball cards. The upshot being, my bones and muscles ached in the morning; neither hand was quite so steady

at the range, and I squinted to read fine print. I did my
level best to outwit and out-grapple Father Time; in addition to sparring at the Deadfall, I religiously committed to physical and mental exercise, which included
jogging, swimming, and weights. Daily I completed
crossword puzzles and played chess matches against the
computer and valiantly argued philosophy with Lionel
and Meg. I read a book a week.

Regardless, the slippage couldn't be ignored, only en-
dured.

■ ■ ■

Homeward bound, downtown rush hour, I waited at a
red light. A couple of frat bros in the oncoming lane
jumped out of a Saab to harangue a guy in a rattletrap
Chevy. The frat bros jeered abuse and pounded on the
Chevy's door; its driver slowly emerged. He required
some time because there was a lot of him to unfold from
the cab. Six-six and two-fifty, easy. He wore grungy
work clothes and an orange safety vest. His hairy arms
dangled near his knees. I didn't get a clear look at his
expression and didn't need to. His posture spoke volumes. Reminded me of the deceptive laziness of a grizzly several heartbeats before it decides to charge.

Obviously, the punks had never seen an angry bear or
heard death call them by name. The bright orange vest
was a pretty clear metaphor. DANGER. KEEP OUT. BE-
WARE OF DOG. MINEFIELD. They weren't reading the
signs of impending doom.

More yelling ensued, coupled with threats of a beating. When this didn't resolve the matter, one of the bros decided to raise the stakes. He poked the construction worker's chest. The big guy palmed the kid's face and slammed him into the pavement. The other bro wisely beat feet toward his own car. My light turned green and I didn't catch the end of the melodrama. Or perhaps that *was* the end. The dude pronated in the intersection was bound for somewhere on a stretcher.

Once I'd gotten home and sipped a tall whiskey, I considered the implications. It's no evolutionary mistake that men default to stupidity and aggression. No accident that they overestimate their capabilities, recklessly court danger, and are reliably delusional regarding the hazards involved. Nature greases the gears of progress with blood. I'm a believer in omens and auguries, except by different names—pattern recognition and quantum entanglement. Reality is a frequency, time is a ring, and gravity bleeds through a membrane that cocoons this universe from its neighbors; cells gently colliding within an infinite superstructure.

Which is to say, I'd scaled a mountain summit and instead of finding a wise man in a cave, Death looked me in the eye and winked. Guru Death compelled me to consider my allotted span in less than romantic terms—the phases of an animal's life cycle. Maybe that's the reason I'd recently obsessed over werewolf movies. The popular legend of the lycanthrope featured a surcease of mortal weakness. Werewolves shrugged off disease and lead. They shunned personal responsibility, and that might've represented their most attractive quality. Loping through a night forest, howling in bloodlust, and doing what comes naturally without remorse.

■ ■ ■

Since my ouster from Alaska, home was a cabin on a sprawling farm-slash-commune near the rural outskirts of New Paltz. I enjoyed the abiding quiet of Hawk Mountain Farm at night, after the tourists who came for the sweat lodge or the meditation circles or the folksy seminars drifted away and the animals were dreaming in the barn. I yearned for the scent of green bark after a hard rain and the rush of wind in the trees. Darkness was truly dark on the edge of the forest—a security lamp hanging from the barn center beam and the porch light of the main house up the hill floated in a void. On those occasions when a storm knocked out the power, we were instantly transported to an epoch of peasants who took shelter behind barred doors, praying for sunrise when all the beasts withdrew into the forest.

I savored it because I knew change was inevitable. Much sooner than later, Meg would demand a gesture of commitment, and that gesture would entail wholesale changes by yours truly. She and her son, Devlin, wanted me to move in. Or I assumed they did. They loved me and my faithful hound, Minerva. We'd edged around the subject and watched it grow into the proverbial elephant in the room. Even I couldn't feign obliviousness forever.

Lionel inhabited a shack not far from mine through

the woods. He acted as farm roustabout for Virgil and Jade Walker, the elderly New Age hippie gurus who owned the property and dazzled clients from around the globe with their peppy mysticism. Evenings, he bunkered with a case of cheap beer, or, if feeling sociable, went hell-raising in town. In the manner of the ancient Greeks confronted with an epic dilemma, I knocked on his door to seek his wise, albeit booze-soaked counsel. I explained my worries—physical and spiritual.

He shrugged and said my chickens were coming home to roost. Quote, unquote. I grumbled about the enigma of cornpone aphorisms.

"Consult the foolproof Getting Old Checklist," he said. "Has your dick stopped responding to commands? Do you moan when leaning over to fetch a beer from the fridge? *Cluck-cluck-cluck,* amigo."

"The goths and the decadents had it one hundred percent correct," I said. We sat on the porch, watching snowflakes gather in the dusk. A storm was coming; a storm was always coming.

"Which ones?" He sipped a beer and patted my dog, who sat between us, panting contentedly. She was blanketed in pine needles and dead leaves from romping after rabbits in the nearby woods.

"Poe, Baudelaire, Camus. The usual suspects."

"They think we should spend that dough too?"

"They think a man is going to suffer no matter which way he jumps."

When I thought of the treasure, all I could picture was the Croatoan's gangrenous features welded to the mask he'd worn while slaughtering all those mobsters, prostitutes, and hapless jerks who'd stumbled across his path.

"Are you okay?" Lionel studied me intently.

"Meg stopped what she was doing and stared at me, like you're staring. She said, 'You've changed.'"

"Was it a compliment?"

I didn't know.

CHAPTER TWO

Seventy-two hours before the Feds brought the hammer down on Badja Adeyemi, a right bastard of an ex-NYPD cop, he summoned me to his cabin on Elkhorn Lake. He offered my day rate and some Glenrothes 18 to hear his spiel, so I cleared the decks and made the hour drive upstate from my residence in the hinterlands of New Paltz and Rosendale.

The call intrigued me on its face; the offer of scotch and money didn't hurt. A man with his clout had access to every detective in the book. We weren't acquainted and my agency was in the Catskills bush league. Yet it was doubtful that he picked my name out of a hat. What I said about nature having a plan counts here too. The machinery of the universe is always grinding. Now and again, we fleas intersect with the gears' teeth.

Normal people hadn't heard of Adeyemi; however, if you were a criminal, political junkie, or partial to tri-state high society, the name likely rang alarm bells. Hop a time machine back a couple decades on the mean streets of

New York, where Adeyemi toiled as a patrol cop, detective, and lieutenant, respectively, and you happened to operate on the wrong side of the law, his size thirteen jackboot might well have trod your face in the name of justice. His latest résumé highlights included ex-bodyguard and majordomo to a world-renowned business mogul turned politician. U.S. Senator Gerald Redlick, aka Mr. Charisma, CEO and owner of the Redlick Group. Him, everybody knew.

Adeyemi had been holed up in the sticks since August. That summer, he'd participated in the epic public foreign corruption trial of a former Redlick Group CFO. RG specialized in real estate. As with any other heavyweight corporation, its subsidiaries and affiliates extended the mother ship's reach into dozens of techs on multiple continents. Laundering filthy, filthy Russian dough was the key indictment against the CFO. Due to his history with the organization, Adeyemi got tagged as a minor player, although everybody figured he knew more than he'd proven willing to divulge. His cooperation hadn't extended past invoking the Fifth Amendment.

The spectacle ended in a hung jury. News analysts predicted the Southern District of New York would reload and try, try again, this time armed with new information and more pressure on potential witnesses. Redlick was the big fish they wanted; this was known. It beggared credulity to assume anything had transpired at the corporation without his say-so. Problem for the DOJ was, the senator had cunningly insulated himself as a matter of course; he'd placed the majority of his holdings in a blind trust upon assuming office. Critics alleged that he'd orchestrated certain aspects of his business with a wink and a nod, as a mafia don might. Redlick's former CFO declined to flip on the senator, immunity deal notwithstanding. Apparently, the exec was more terrified of vengeful Russian oligarchs (and likely Redlick himself) than doing five to ten in a federal prison.

Adeyemi was likely to be the player without a chair when the organ stopped playing. His prize? An unlucky recipient of the government's full attention. The Feds reasoned that a longtime bodyguard, driver, and confidant would possess mucho dirt on Redlick. Surely said bodyguard, driver, and confidant had been corrupted by proximity. Surely he possessed a weak spot that the Southern District of New York could exploit to force his testimony.

Redlick, a rumored deviant and scofflaw long before this current scandal, had cause to be mightily worried. He was the first New York Republican elected to the U.S. Senate since the 1990s and the odds were stacked against another term. Whatever his legal and political jeopardy might entail, and amid a chorus of fellow GOP senators calling for him to quit his office, Redlick exuded his trademark smugness at every press conference. He was either a man with nothing to fear, or a man who feared nothing.

I got on the road.

Late November had stolen upon us, robbed the trees of their autumn splendor, and bruised the fields with brown and gray. The long, brooding nights of winter were certain to prick a guilty man's conscience with dread, if not introspection.

■ ■ ■

I arrived at the cabin and parked next to an SUV with dried mud on its New Jersey plates. The spot overlooked a beach and a chilly stretch of lake. An early snow had dusted the upper Hudson, with another storm predicted to slam us before the weekend. Fallen leaves had crumbled to dust, opening big spaces between the white poplars and paper birches. Adeyemi stood at the far end of a dock, hands stuck into the pockets of a windbreaker. He wore a .38 police special in a shoulder holster. Invisible under the windbreaker, but I'd gone over the news footage and knew it was there all right.

He watched me exit my old pickup and then slouched in my direction.

Once upon a time, Adeyemi had been as photogenic as a menswear model with those broad shoulders and Dunhill suits. Sixty-eight and sliding fast, his trademark brush cut had thinned to wisps. Lines etched his gaunt face. Lively and mean, those eyes of his. Some might have mistaken his posture for geniality. Not I. Cruelty and evil age like wine.

We shook. His hands were carved from hardwood. The power in his grip reminded me of a video wherein he casually grasped a protester (a kid waving a sign outside of Redlick Tower, natch) by the scruff and flung him over the hood of a car. Here was a man born in the wrong century. He would've been right at home as a broadsword-swinging Dark Ages knight mowing down hapless peasants in the village square.

"Hello, Isaiah Coleridge," he said.

"Hi, Lieutenant. Thanks for the invitation. I haven't had the distinct pleasure of meeting an NYPD Medal of Valor recipient until today."

"You're welcome."

"By that token, I've met my share of cops who'd sweat their own mother. We'll call it a wash."

He was pleased rather than offended.

"Flattering that you've read the stats on my baseball card. I've read yours too."

"What's the line on me?"

"A natural hard case who twisted many an arm and no doubt fitted a few mooks with concrete shoes. Got fired from the Outfit and lived to fight another day. Some trick. I bet your boss was sad to see you go—he invested in college education, finishing school. You've reinvented yourself as a PI. Another neat trick. My hunch is you're a lucky guy. 'Lucky is superior to good' is a rock-solid aphorism."

"My confidential file isn't so confidential."

"This is the era of Big Brother. Anyway, I have pals in DC. That and a few bucks greased the skids." His wink intimated there'd been more threats than bucks involved. "Certain circles, you're as infamous as Sammy the Bull. Except *you* never ratted."

"Never got caught."

He snorted.

"Me neither. We buried more bodies in the Barrens than any of you mobster fucks. Guaranteed."

"No contest, Lieutenant. Pigs run the largest, meanest gang in the world."

"Ouch. Keep it friendly, hey?" He edged closer to me. Mr. Intimidation. He smelled of aftershave and meanness. In his segue to civilian life, he'd shed the cop pretenses of protecting and serving and retained the brutishness, the villainy.

"This is me in friendly mode," I said. "My eyes aren't glowing red yet."

"A laconic brute with a sense of humor. I bet the rubes took one look at you and spilled their guts. When it comes to alleged hard cases, you don't know who'll squeal, not for certain. I mean, I've a nose for it, a dependable intuition. Don't *know* until you try. People surprise you."

"Every minute of the day," I said.

"We did what it took to get confessions out of our perps. Whaled the soles of their feet with billy clubs. Slapped them in cuffs and a ball gag and shot soda foam up their noses. The nervous system thinks it's drowning. Tightened their cuffs until their hands swelled like balloons. My favorite? Ram your pinky down real deep into a guy's eardrum till he hollers. Smart money says it would take ten men and a boy to crack a character such as yourself."

"Might have to use your thumb."

He guffawed and waved me inside.

CHAPTER THREE

We sat at a wooden table. Rude, concave, and stained like a sacrificial altar. He poured two glasses of single malt and shoved one my way. We clinked glasses and drank. He poured again. I surveyed his abode. Not much to see. Exposed timber and plank, a scuffed throw rug, barrel stove, and a loft. Fly rods and bear-paw snowshoes in the corner, a faded tapestry of the Catskills on the far wall. Nothing of a personal nature— no photographs or postcards. Spartan to the bone.

"Elkhorn Lake?" I said.

"Used to be lousy with elk. Ages ago. Conservationists tried to reintroduce them in the early twentieth century. Didn't take."

"Might've worked if sport hunters would stop shooting everything that moves for five minutes," I said.

"Uh-huh. How do you like your steak? Rare? Don't feel too sorry for Mama Nature. She gets her own. White Elk Preserve is over yonder hill. Summer or two back, a wildlife photographer ventured in there and recorded a deer licking salt excretions from the mummified remains of some local hermit. Nobody realized the hermit had gone missing until the authorities carted him to the morgue. You're in the boonies, friend. Unfriendly, remorseless. Remind you of home sweet home?"

"It's pleasant not to have icicles hanging from my nose."

"Must befuddle the wiseguys, you going legit. The Italians are taking the long view. Otherwise, enemies keep piling up."

"Great men have detractors."

"So do assholes." He splashed another generous shot of scotch into my glass. "No offense, big fella. I wanted to take your temperature. Done and done. You'll do. You'll do fine."

I donned my poker face and waited for him to divulge his secrets.

He pulled aside the drapes a smidge and peered into the yard. More a bank-robber-on-the-lam move than that of a salt-of-the-earth cop enjoying his well-deserved retirement. One acquires certain habits when one forges nefarious associations.

"The SDNY wants to clamp my family jewels in a vise before they take another shot at the Redlick Group. Immunity if I testify; a boatload of felony charges if I decline. Ha! I'm not gonna sing."

"Too bad Redlick won't believe that. Or the Russians. Or anybody."

He actually preened.

"Gerry does. He knows I'm stand-up."

"You're hard as nails, I totally get it," I said. "Rock on

with your bad self, et cetera. You don't owe Redlick, though. Testify and go loaf someplace warm under a brand-new identity. Why risk having polonium-210 sprinkled on your toilet seat?"

"The FSB? Those weasels aren't involved. Rent-a-thugs sent by one of the Russian oligarchs Redlick was in bed with, yeah, possibly. It isn't beneath Redlick's cronies either. Fuck 'em. I don't care."

"Hiding in the woods, scanning the perimeter for Russian mobsters? Marvelous retirement plan."

"The game was over in August," he said. "It was over when the DA brought charges. I'm running out the clock on my own terms. *Farmers' Almanac* says everything north of Kingston can expect a deep freeze by Christmas. Bailing for Florida tomorrow. Any bastards want to arrest me, or whack me, I'll be beachside, sipping margaritas, my arm around a cabana girl."

"I bet the senator would love to go with you and leave his worries behind. Reelection campaign starts next year. He can't be happy with this flak."

"Forget next year. The machine is already grinding."

"What's the early forecast?"

"The polls are shaky as a dry drunk."

"Hard to be a conservative in New York."

"Walking a knife edge."

"You'd think a man in his position would be kissing more ass," I said. "Yours, particularly. Despite you being 'stand-up' and whatnot."

"Redlick doesn't operate the way regular people do," he said.

"That's evident. Dear senator kicked you to the curb after he took the other guy's concession call. Loyalty is a one-way street with him."

"The man had his reasons."

"Such as?"

"His handlers determined that I wouldn't mix well with the high-toned set."

"Your record of brutality doesn't play so well outside of the brotherhood, in other words."

"In exactly those other words."

"Half a decade later, Redlick doesn't call, he doesn't write. You and the rest of the erstwhile band of merry men may take the rap for his misdeeds. Instead of sticking the knife into his kidney for revenge, which is completely *your* brand, you play the faithful servant to the end. Strange."

"There's one item on my ledger I'd be happy to clear, in case the curtain is really falling." Adeyemi uncapped the bottle. "Happy to pawn it off on you, to put it bluntly."

I covered my glass.

"My sister's kid lived in western New York, in Horseheads." He poured my share on top of his own dose. "Emphasis on the past tense. Sean Pruitt. He worked on the Jeffers Large Particle Collider Project. Heard of it?"

The Jeffers Project received significant news coverage in its heyday. A complicated undertaking from financial and political perspectives. I recalled controversy swirling around cost overruns, corruption, and safety protocols. My expertise on the subject could fit in a thimble. In broad strokes: supercolliders, colloquially known as atom smashers, are devices that generate electromagnetic fields to accelerate charged particles at high velocity along underground circuits. Some are pint-size and housed in basement facilities; others, like the Hadron, require miles of specially prepared tunnels to achieve the most dramatic effects. The Jeffers Project had occupied the latter end of the scale. The ultimate goals of such a sprawling and costly undertaking? To create a powerful tool for the furtherance of research of particle physics that would, in turn, spur similar advances in the fields of industrial and biomedical technologies.

"The U.S. version of the Hadron Collider," I said.

"Brainchild of several East Coast billionaires. Gerry spearheaded the initiative and brought a partnership proposal to the government. He was tight with what seemed like half of Congress before he dove into politics. He and the president went way back too. The Feds funneled in a sizable chunk of dough with a minimum of oversight. Everybody on the ground floor was guaranteed a seat at the table when it came time to divvy resources for scientific and commercial research projects. It didn't get that far."

"I imagine there was money to be made for certain parties whether or not it ever reached the finish line," I said. "No part of the buffalo goes to waste when it comes to corporate profiteering."

He nodded along.

"The Jeffers Project represented over forty miles of tunnels and installations at Davis-Bacon wages, baby. Bribery, kickbacks, double-dealing. Something for everybody. You're right. Pockets were getting lined, win, lose, or draw."

"We mustn't neglect infrastructure," I said. "Prostitution and gambling. Drugs. The real support an army of laborers, technicians, and overseers would cherish most." I didn't need to be an ex-mob associate to savvy this truth. I'd lived in a state famous for its oil pipeline, maritime industry, and construction empires. Pimps and dealers can still make a fortune in Alaska.

"I have a good, good feeling. You understand the ways of the world."

"What went wrong besides the stuff in the papers? Infighting?"

"Infighting, for sure," he said. "The billionaires are rivals who set aside differences, but peace didn't last. Place was also cursed as the pharaoh's tomb. Like I said, my nephew worked there. Had a cushy gig in the Special Operations department, counterespionage. Which I kinda sorta arranged after he begged me. Relentless kid. He died on-site."

"Cloak and dagger. It got rough?"

"The job was less glamorous than it sounds. He sat on his ass so much, he grew hemorrhoids."

"What happened?"

"Tragedy, sayeth the corporate overlords," he said. "Sean committed suicide. The site was under construction for eleven years. There were eight fatal accidents before Sean died—trench collapses, vehicle crashes, an explosion or two. A suspicious person might fantasize about a connection between Sean's death and those ac-

cidents. I'm not quite that paranoid, but I can't speak for
your state of mind. Congress said no más and reneged on
their funding pledge. The billionaires weren't willing to
absorb the funding deficit. Project died with a whimper."

"Case closed," I said.

"Nailed shut. Insurance didn't kick about the fact
Sean offed himself. Paid his wife to the penny. Except,
my sister isn't sanguine about the ME's findings. She has
a legit gripe. 'Suicide' *was* convenient for the company.
'Death by misadventure' would've opened them to more
liability."

"And 'misadventure' suggests a whole world of sinister
possibilities," I said.

"Either way, local PD and Feds conducted a shitty
investigation. Wham, bam, thank you, ma'am. Par for
the course, considering nobody wanted to step on corporate toes. But when it's *your* flesh and blood . . ."

"The wife good with the verdict?"

"She gives nary a fuck. Linda got her pot of gold."

"Obviously you checked her finances, made sure there
weren't any outsize withdrawals . . ."

"Yeah, buddy. Nothing. She's super fucking smart,
though. Could have waited until after the heat was off to
move money to an accomplice."

I put a mental pin there.

"Sean's mom doesn't buy the authorized account, but
no one ever listens to Cassandras. She turns to you, the
resident cop. And . . ."

"Let's say, as sands pass through the hourglass, I'm
not sanguine either. Two and two comes out five. It

smells like shoddy policework at best, a cover-up to protect corporate assets at worst. Read the report and rap with my sister."

"Horse, then cart," I said.

"You're trying to figure how the lotto dropped your number."

"Some would note that I'm tall, dark, and handsome. Occurred to me I might be a diversity hire."

"You're tall and dark. As it happens, Jonathan Labrador and I are golfing buddies."

Screw a lottery number, this was the other hobnail shoe dropping.

Labrador, another gold-plated member of the billionaire industrialist club and CEO of the obscenely profitable Zircon Corporation. The corporation's slicker-than-goose-shit media campaigns featured fresh-faced white kids drilling wells in foreign deserts, establishing communication networks to disadvantaged communities, building high-tech infrastructure, and similar propaganda. Maggots wriggled beneath the shiny façade. Zircon and the Redlick Group were peas in a pod—the former wanted to rule the world via high tech, while the latter cleaved to the tradition of owning all the dirt it could acquire.

Jonathan Labrador was no fan of Isaiah Coleridge. He nursed ill will toward me for several reasons, not the least of which being that an investigation of mine stepped on his toes and led to the death of his estranged brother, the infamous Croatoan. I prayed daily that Labrador knew nothing of my hand in his brother's death nor my five-fingered withdrawal of one and a half mil from said

brother's nest egg. Possibly worse for our strained relationship was that I menaced his daughter, Delia, during
a heated confrontation. Delia Labrador was a force of
nature. She and I had since mended fences, kinda-sorta.
Alas, Daddy wasn't sharing the rapport. Then there was
her torrid romance with Lionel. Their affair wasn't popular at the royal court. I imagine the Labradors held me
responsible for him as a freeman landholder might be
expected to control a manservant or uppity serf.

Disowned, maniac relatives notwithstanding, rich-
as-God patriarchs tend to have paper-thin tolerance for
meddling detectives who wave guns and occasionally use
them. Now came the heretofore hidden consequences.
Nothing is ever over. Especially if the nothing is something unpleasant.

"You gamed the system as an alleged lawman," I said.
"Became Redlick's fixer and Labrador's golfing buddy.
Have to admire a man who plays that many angles."

"Can't take full credit—well-connected individuals
came courting after Redlick cut me loose. I just had to
lie back and enjoy the attention. Wound up consulting
for Zircon."

"Labrador pumped you for secrets."

"Well, duh. I made it pay off without burning any
bridges."

"'Consultation' is a refined way of saying, 'I supplied
corporate junkets with hookers and twisted arms of
plaintiffs who wouldn't drop pesky lawsuits.'"

"The Outfit-period Coleridge would approve, I promise. Jonny had an opinion of you and your character. Boy, oh, boy did he ever."

"Choice words, presumably," I said.

"He described you as . . . I'll try to be delicate . . . a bully and a thug. Those are your admirable traits. He also indicated that you have huge stones and decidedly situational ethics."

"Mom always said a pair of big balls and a lack of ethics would get me through any door. However, I'm skeptical if you're suggesting Labrador recommended me for a job."

"Jon didn't recommend you for a goddamned thing. Your name dropped in relation to an entirely different matter."

I laughed reflexively. Of course, of course, the exec wanted my head on a stake. Adeyemi was proficient in headhunting. It's pleasantly convenient when interests align.

"Wild guess . . . Labrador took your temperature about putting a round behind my ear and dumping me in the Barrens. You probably have a spot picked out."

"He *did* ask if I knew anyone reliable," Adeyemi said. "I'm personally too hot to do business. The SDNY bird-dogging me is a serious pain. My boy was drunk and it was more a casual inquiry. I wouldn't sweat it."

"Okay, I won't spare it another thought."

"All's well that ends well. My chat with Jon inspired me to check into your bona fides. And here we are, making nice."

"Which leaves us with the fact you could've engaged numerous heavyweight operators."

"Ah, such as Lancing Brothers or the Woolfolk Agency," Adeyemi said.

"The obvious choices. Impeccable reputations. By the book. Eminently convenient with offices in New York and Kingston."

He nodded over the rim of his rapidly diminishing glass of booze.

"The firm that employed Sean is a subsidiary of the Redlick Group."

"Your long-lost buddies," I said.

"Any of them had a role in Sean's death, or a cover-up, they go on the list."

"What about Senator Redlick? According to my math, he vacated the throne not long before your nephew went to his reward."

He swallowed his scotch. Let the moment stretch. Doubtful he was deliberating so much as managing the effect.

"The big man wasn't involved. He'd recently divested his interest in the corporation. I threw my weight around at the operations level to get my nephew hired. Leaned on a human resource manager with a gambling problem. And the personnel manifest listed Sean as a Pruitt, not an Adeyemi."

I stared at him, unblinking.

"He's my friend," Adeyemi said. "One of the few."

"Humor me."

"Gerry too."

"Yeah, what I figured. Any case that comes within a hundred miles of Senator Redlick may as well have a hazardous-to-health warning on the label. And Labrador? How many of his fingers were in the Jeffers Project?"

"Labrador contributed funds to kick-start the job. Fingers, nothing. He *owned* a double helping of that pie."

"Not even one degree of Kevin Bacon," I said. "I'm going to assume you haven't shared your speculation with anybody who might be in a position to shut you up permanently."

"I've mentioned it to my sister. Nobody else."

"Which, according to the Law of Best Intentions, I'm racing a clock before news leaks. I hope this isn't a scheme to settle a score with your old boss."

"The fuck you care?" he said. "Settling scores is practically your business motto."

"What I mean is, the odds are against me discovering anything new. Neither the cops nor the companies will be eager to reopen a can of worms. They'll resist."

"They resist, they're hiding something."

"Hiding something is a rich person's default mode," I said. "Rich and untouchable."

"Nobody is untouchable," he said.

The problem with rich people and politicians is that even if they're not guilty of a particular incident or crime, they're guilty of something. Something that could be exposed via some clod snooping into their affairs.

"I'd be poking the bear," I said. "Possibly two bears, counting Zircon. That raises the stakes. Toss a senator into the mix and the stakes amount to the family farm."

"Recent history suggests you're stupid enough to take it on despite the hazards. Or because of the hazards. Did I mention Jon thinks you're really, really stupid? My kind of endorsement."

"I'm extremely impetuous. He's raw I got the better of him."

"Opening bell in a title fight," he said with a sneer. "Congratulations. You picked a live one for an enemy. Endless resources. Zero compunctions. Pet name basis with top cops. The family passes down its grudges like heirlooms."

"Way to sell the job. I accept this case, he'll be even madder at me."

"Maybe a skootch madder. A cunt hair madder. You can handle that, bad boy."

I wasn't so sure. And because I wasn't sure, I polished off my drink and waited.

"Impeccable and by the book aren't what I need," he said after a while. "RG plays hardball. So does Zircon. You think they might resist an inquiry. That's an understatement."

"What is it you *do* need, Mr. Adeyemi?"

"I need a bad news sonofabitch with a gun. Somebody who won't be intimidated by corporate mercs, who isn't averse to smashing heads. Somebody who doesn't mind killing if it comes to that." He leaned close, clasped my forearm, and grinned. "Because if some fool is responsible for breaking my sister's heart, I hope it comes to that."

Most detectives maintain a list of things they won't

do. Mine is short, so I memorized it. Adeyemi must have read my mail.

■ ■ ■

I drove home in the gathering dusk, chewing on the pros and cons. Three days later, Adeyemi was cooling his heels in a jail cell awaiting trial. Hell of a lot of difference that it made. He wasn't done with me by any means.

CHAPTER FOUR

The next day, I went to Meg's house and picked her and Devlin up.

She'd been cold with me this past week. A colleague from the library brought her son, Caleb, over to play with Devlin. The boys shared a second-grade class. The kid walked into the hall, where Devlin kept a pair of goldfish we'd bought at the state fair. Tossed them on the floor and watched them die, then slipped the corpses back into the tank. No reason for it besides a psychotic thrill. Meg and the other woman were shocked. Devlin didn't say anything; sat there while the adults gave the little shit the third degree and extracted the whole truth out of him. Caleb had been almost eager to confess. The second the interrogation concluded, Devlin calmly stood and decked the kid. Knocked him flat and gave him a few kicks to grow on. Meg said Devlin's face was ghost-white and expressionless.

Caleb killed Mr. and Mrs. Fishy, he said in the aftermath. *The bastard had to pay.*

Sweetie, violence is not the right way to deal with problems. Violence is never—

It was a human reaction, Mom. Let's ask Isaiah.

This boomeranged on me in a big way. It was I who taught her son to pop a jab and follow it home with a stiff right. It was I who instructed him in the rudiments of slipping a punch and the importance of mercilessly kicking a foe when he's down. Suffer no fools and give no quarter. I may have mentioned while watching a Clint Eastwood western that righteous vengeance is a virtue. He'd taken the lessons to heart.

I'd asked Meg if she was mad at me. Her brittle, icy smile indicated, yep, very mad. Thankfully, the temperature had warmed. Although matters remained unsettled.

Stone Ridge held an art fair for local vendors and visiting artists. The gallery downstairs from my office featured an exhibition on the Holocaust. Meg and Devlin and I took it in toward the end of our afternoon tour. Black-and-white photography presented by the grandchildren of a war correspondent. One photo captured the pain and anguish of humanity's dark hour: a bin overflowing with wedding bands confiscated from murdered Jews. A soldier ran his hands through the rings as if plunging them into grain. Death renders the familiar alien. Death makes a mockery of life.

Devlin had questions. He didn't fully comprehend the gravity of the exhibition. Sharp, intuitive child, nonetheless. He picked up context clues. Meg did the heavy lifting, explaining how one group of people came to power and used that power for terrible evil. She asked him to recall the mean kids in school, and fish-murderer Caleb shot to the top of the example list, and she briefly, deftly, described the concept of hatred for the mere sake of hatred, hatred based on differences perceived and otherwise, and how that led to the rise of the Nazis and the horrors they perpetrated. I contributed timely nods and grunts. He didn't say much; there's never closure in these situations.

Dinner in North Kingston; an industrial neighborhood within a stone's throw of the off-ramp. The restaurant was called the Old Aurora Lounge. Came highly recommended by senior gangsters. I could see why. The ambiance whisked the grayer wiseguys back to the era of Jimmy Hoffa and a perpetually befuddled FBI. Brown furniture, greenish carpet, orange walls, and amber drinking glasses. I was told that before smoking in restaurants went by the wayside, the lounge featured ashtrays heavy enough to concuss a moose. Our server's tag said MARGE. She was old and veiny and could've been hunched over a slot machine in Atlantic City. I've never tasted that much chlorine in a cup of coffee.

We enjoyed our meal, relatively speaking. As I went to pay the bill, a man wearing a Caesar haircut and a polo shirt beat me to the counter. He hit on the girl working the register. She blushed, looking everywhere but directly at him.

I stared at the back of his neck, imagining heat rays. He turned, arranging his wallet.

"Hey, Romeo," I said, adding a bit of gravel.

He paused and looked me over. Quizzical, arrogant, not the least bit intimidated.

"We met?" he said.

Every fiber of my being recoiled at the scent of his aftershave, his Eastern drawl. I also detest polo shirts for irrational reasons. Words formed in my mouth, and died there. Isaiah Coleridge of yesteryear followed this guy into the john, or outside, and pulped his smirking face. What did older, wiser, straight-arrow family-man Coleridge do when confronted by a banal little prick? He stepped aside like a grizzly inexplicably ceding the trail to a cur.

"Have a day." The dude thrust his hips forward as he sidled past my bemused self. Walking back to a woman and two kids at a table, his gait slackened and he rounded his shoulders. From alpha wolf to neutered beagle in less than five seconds. What other secrets did he keep from his loving wife and children?

I held Meg's coat and casually asked if she'd seen him at the library. Possibly I entertained the fantasy of tracking him down and kicking his ass at a more opportune moment.

"The guy in the polo shirt? Yeah, that's Dave something-or-other. He and his wife come into the library and check out videos for their kids. Agreeable family. Well, she's cool and he's kind of a dweeb, I suppose. Why?"

"He looks familiar. No worries." I *was* worried. Worried I'd jumped over civilized restraint and into abject domestication.

Apparently, Meg's psychic antenna was receiving a signal, and she gave me side-eye calibrated to dispel any notion I was getting one over on her. She patted my cheek, and a don couldn't have implied greater menace. Her skin transformed in the holiday lights. Red and green and purple. The color spectrum of a holiday mood ring.

■ ■ ■

We were lying in bed. Sleepy, but not ready for sleep. Enjoying the afterglow. Talk segued to my lingering injuries and persistent nightmares. Also reminiscent of the Bronze Age traditions, she, as women tend to do, took my complaints deadly seriously and magnified the stakes tenfold. She'd long sensed trouble, and now her every sneaking hunch was validated. Woman's intuition, or she'd missed her calling as a sleuth. Early on in our courtship I'd made the mistake of congratulating myself on slipping something past her, only to realize, to my chagrin, she excelled at holding her fire until I was vulnerable and exposed.

"You've lived a life of consequence-free violence." She'd lit several candles and the room swam with ceremonial light. Our shadows were the shadows of giants.

I rotated my stiff shoulder and it crackled.

"Wouldn't say it's been a picnic, exactly. Are you even looking at my face?"

"*Consequence-free*, honey. That's changing. Lionel said it. The doctors have said it. Your body is saying it. You won't be able to raise that arm overhead ten, twelve years from now. Won't be able to run on those knees. Your back is probably shot. That misspent youth is a bill due."

She decided it best that I see a specialist.

I hedged.

"A specialist." Sometimes naming a thing robs it of its power. Not this time. "To run even more tests."

"It's what specialists do," she said.

"Sleep apnea, MRIs, rectal exam, or what?"

"Sure, honey. Whatever sweetens the deal."

I took a breath to protest.

"Save it," she said. "I can finagle a referral to a clinic in New Paltz. A friend of mine runs it. Give you the once-over and then we can decide whether you have a few more years or if we should pick out a nice comfy hospice."

"Exactly what kind of clinic? I have a strong suspicion the doorways are strung with beads. Crystals, hemp, rolling clouds of incense, doctors in ceremonial robes . . ."

"The people at General are missing something. I don't trust them."

That made two of us.

"All right, dear. Let me give it some consideration." Still juking and jiving.

"Your body is a ticking bomb. One of these days there won't be a one-of-these-days."

"The Eternal Footman went to fetch my coat," I said. She snickered.

CHAPTER FIVE

Taken at face value, the case of Adeyemi's dead nephew couldn't get any simpler. Sean Pruitt, glorified loss prevention agent, met his fate on an otherwise routine evening in the depths of the soon-to-be-abandoned Jeffers Large Particle Collider. He suffered catastrophic blunt force trauma as a result of falling in excess of one hundred and eighty feet down Maintenance Shaft 40. One detail missing from the report was any real chart of Pruitt's final movements. He signed in for his evening shift and at some point in the wee hours cruised out to Shaft 40 and leaped. The wife claimed he suffered depression, although his action took her by surprise. Coworkers were asked perfunctory questions, but no real interviews occurred. Sloppy policework, indicative of clock punchers working backward from a foregone conclusion.

Even accounting for wading into bureaucratic sloth, I'd earn a princely sum for going through the motions and confirming the ME's findings. The fact it was a closed case meant zero entanglement with the police; always a plus. The problem? In my erstwhile romantic pining to tread the path of a hardboiled PI, I hadn't envisioned taking on elite business concerns or ruthless politicians. I knew what dons could do. CEOs and senators can do worse. Smacking around small-time crooks, tailing cheating spouses, and tracking down low-rent scofflaws was always my intended bread and butter. Perhaps dealing with the occasional stiff. I'd done plenty of tracking, tailing, and smacking over the past couple of years. Just not vigorously enough to make myself whole.

Catch the second? Easy money is seldom by any means easy. The man paying me was a wolf among sheep. Adeyemi's instincts whispered that something was amiss. I paid grudging heed. He'd climbed his mountain the hard way and made every right choice along the path. That took more than stubbornness or dumb luck. His avuncular cruelty was another of nature's not-so-subtle warning signs. This one said WATCH YOUR ASS.

A blue-collar detective is playing a fool's game to delve into corporate malfeasance. Previous encounters with such entities should've taught me to run the opposite direction. Alas, money talks louder than common sense. I accepted Adeyemi's case because I was short on dough, not because I liked the smell of the proposition. Those hospital stays to treat my busted skull and the numerous follow-ups had ripped a hole in my savings. The sound of an MRI motor is the world's loudest cash register hoovering a patient's wallet. Cut-rate health insurance wasn't built to weather this kind of storm. Another mob perk I'd taken for granted—the Family paid for every bump, bruise, and bullet hole incurred in the line of duty.

Except . . . this dead nephew case represented more than a chance to bail my leaky financial boat. I'll admit that pride figured into the equation. I love to challenge authority. Wave a red cape under my nose and I'm liable to react.

Mostly, however, it was about the dough.

■ ■ ■

Lionel appeared on my doorstep, staggering and depleted as the messenger at Marathon. He'd competed in an all-night online poker tournament, stopped to check the news, and beheld the red ticker of woe that the media runs at the top of the page.

The Feds nabbed Adeyemi at JFK airport and whisked him to arraignment. There were many counts. Extortion, witness tampering, and obstruction of justice were the trio that received most of the play-by-play analysis from the network and cable talking heads.

Lionel sat on the couch, beer in hand.

"I wouldn't be rushin' to any conclusions, but I foresee an accident for a certain ex-bodyguard, ex-majordomo-slash-pimp, cum freelance douchebag."

"An accident?" I said. "Like that former advisor to the Kremlin who died in a Virginia hotel room. The dude 'fell' repeatedly and severed his spine."

"What kind of medical examiner signs off on such

bullshit? Two-to-one gets you Adeyemi is sleeping with the fishes sooner or later."

"Adeyemi is an evil sonofabitch. Even the fish won't eat him."

"Amigo, this deal is extra dicey," he said. "Possible corporate espionage. Dirty ex-cops. Russian mafia. A rotten senator. Why the hell did Adeyemi sic you on Redlick anyway? Must've been pissed off at getting the cold shoulder."

"He didn't sic me on anybody. He asked me to double-check the facts."

"Redlick Group and Zircon won't appreciate your due diligence."

"Why do I get the feeling you're worried digging into the corporate side will jinx your canoodling with Delia?"

"The way you blunder around . . . I'm probably shit outta luck. Don't inadvertently ruin my love life, bro. That's all I ask."

"Scout's honor," I said.

"You need the cash," he said. "I need the cash. Who doesn't need the cash? Seriously, Delia says her dad has it in for you. The riffraff on his payroll would have no problem taking a shot if he gave the order."

"Understood. Anything happens to me, certain papers and videos linking Zircon to the Croatoan will surface. Should keep the wolves at bay until a better plan comes along."

"I don't like it." His lip curled like a dog that's scented danger. This meant he actually liked it. He was perverse.

"May not even be a case with this development. I'll have my guy call Adeyemi's lawyer and verify."

"With your luck? The case is on like Donkey Kong."

I changed the subject and jokingly asked if he'd blown his "riding west" bankroll. Over the past months, we'd spoken in desultory fashion of moving on from our half-way house existence—me tying the knot with Meg, him touring west into Northern California.

"The West Coast isn't ready for you," I said. "Wyoming, Montana, maybe Alaska. Be a cowboy, a drifter. They like cowboys in all those bass-ackward states. You'd have to wear a ball cap or a cowboy hat and learn to ride a horse."

"California or bust. Pot growers' mecca over there. Mexican cartels are moving in, putting the clamp on the locals. Getting to be a violent business with traditional growing families on the losing end. Home team could probably use some help. A sniper. A combat engineer. A fuckin' ninja who knows his way around booby traps."

"Do you really, truly, sincerely want to get involved in a guerilla war between pot plantation owners and the cartels?"

He sipped his beer and smirked.

"What about Delia?" I said. The couple were hot and heavy or estranged depending upon the day of the week, the weather, or the alignment of the planets.

Gloom wiped away his smile.

"Don't think she'd be much help setting claymores," he said.

■ ■ ■

I rented an office a few miles northeast of Hawk Mountain. Stone Ridge is a blink-and-you'll-miss-it hamlet located north of the Shawangunks and south of the Catskills. Business had steadily improved (thank the gods or I'd have been a permanent resident in the poorhouse instead of a frequent guest), so I hired a receptionist to answer the phone and keep my affairs organized. Theodora Nowakowski—late twenties, brunette, kind and sweet-natured, but terse in the finest New York tradition. I gathered from the interview that she was a long-suffering Islanders fan who liked scotch on the rocks, dogs, and hiking the Shawangunks. She answered to Ted. Not Teddy, Dora, nor the gods pity the wretch, Theodora. Her dad called her Ted because he'd expected a boy, and that was all she'd say in regard to family.

To break the ice, I asked her to name a favorite fictional detective.

She regarded me blandly.

"I'm thinking Columbo."

Lastly, how did she feel about guns? She opened her purse to flash a petite Smith & Wesson Airweight revolver. I didn't pry into how she'd acquired a carry permit, which is tough to get in New York. After I hired her, she kept the gun in the top shelf of the reception desk during work hours. She hung photos of Ruth Bader Ginsburg and her Bernese Mountain dog, Valentino. Ted stamped her imprint on the office from day one.

I walked in the Monday following Thanksgiving weekend. Primarily to make an appearance, but also to double-check my emergency stash in the office safe. Clear and cool on the heels of the weekend snow. An excuse to tromp around in a fur-lined Levi's jacket and insulated Wellingtons.

"You have a noon meeting with McLaren at the GG." Ted didn't glance up from her monitor. She raised her hand with a piece of memo paper and I plucked it on the way by.

"I hope he's buying."

"He's a lawyer."

"What's that mean?"

"It means, bring your wallet."

A detective's safe should contain a spare gun, unspecified documents, some glossy photos of a dodgy nature, at least two rolls of hundred-dollar bills, and a hideout pistol. I'd hocked the automatic and was down to a fifty and loose fives and ones.

I slipped the fifty into my pocket. Before shutting the safe, I promised the remaining scrabble of cash I'd bring it some company soon.

CHAPTER SIX

Chris McLaren, Esquire, awaited me in Rosendale at the Green Goddess, an upscale dive in the alley-side cellar of a converted church. GG qualified as a speakeasy in the contemporary sense because it blithely ignored state no-smoking laws. Edgar Allan Poe's spirit mingled with clove and cigar smoke. The chef fixed a mean turkey club. I ordered one of those and a bottle of stout.

Red (his nickname when he played offensive tackle for the Orangemen) handled general legal matters for Coleridge Investigations. Mainly that amounted to negotiating contracts, composing threatening missives on my behalf, or apologizing for my behavior, as the situation warranted.

"Okay, yeah, right, so look," he said. "I spoke with the stuffed suit, Tampon, Tamblin, what-the-fuck his name is."

"Adeyemi's lawyer."

"More like executor now that Adeyemi is in lockup and either headed for witness protection, the big house, or the grave. Tambour. Tambour, right. Overeducated chode. His money spends, so fuck it."

"The investigation is a go?" To say I had mixed emotions would be underselling it.

"Adeyemi, being a paranoid motherfucker, planned for this contingency. You are green-lighted." Red wrote several figures in his memo book, tore the paper out, and pushed it across the table. His hands were as big and blocky as the rest of him. "One-month retainer plus basic expenses. Be in your account by tomorrow. Tambour says to hit him with a biweekly report. Run dry on funds, he'll discuss bumping up the retainer. I doubt it, so plan accordingly."

"Okay, tell him I'm on the case."

He removed a thumb drive from his pocket.

"The insurance investigation, police report, and incidentals. A shitload of incidentals."

"Incidentals?"

"Adeyemi included a bucketload of info about the Jeffers Project. Documents are diamond-heist-thorough. Must be swell to have pals in the federal government. Some personal material . . . videos of Sean Pruitt's wedding, public speaking engagements, interviews he did in high school. Off the wall, huh? Help you build a profile."

"Highlights, please."

"Didn't you and Adeyemi go over this?"

"Time to earn."

Red gestured placatingly.

"Right on. The deceased, one Sean Miles Pruitt. Aged thirty-one and getting no older. Youngest of three. Brother and sister live in Canada and England, respectively. Both flew the coop while he was in middle school. Sean graduated Sonoma State U, cultural anthropology with a side of sociology. Two traffic infractions and nary a blip on the radar otherwise. Happily married, on the surface, at least. Bounced around various jobs until he landed a gig with Diogenes, subsidiary of the Redlick Group. Worked his way from their equivalent of the mail room to Special Operations, security team. Three years after that, he's a goner."

Red went on to explain that the toxicology report indicated several active drugs in Sean Pruitt's system. An over-the-counter allergy medication, clonidine for hypertension, a prescription antidepressant, and a synthetic hallucinogen derived from a strain of peyote. The body was clothed in a sweater, linen shirt, linen pants, and sandals. Pathology indicated Pruitt had undertaken a thorough cleaning, possibly by steam, prior to death. His pores and hair contained copious remnants of a mineral oil treatment.

I took the thumb drive.

"Squeaky clean. Dressed, but not for official duty. Under the influence of a hallucinogen and a combo of drugs that could've impaired his ability to function. The ME concludes it's a suicide case from the decedent's use of antidepressants and the fact he drove to a remote site and unlocked the shaft. If his intention wasn't suicide, what else? No mention of a note, though."

"Suicides don't always drop the keys off at the desk when they check out," he said.

"Well, that's kind of dark."

"Our stories gotta end somewhere. Old age, heart attack, a twelve-floor swan dive into the abyss. You don't retain me for my bedside manner."

When a man is right, he's right.

"It'll take several days to lay the groundwork," I said. "I'll organize an itinerary and get myself over to Horseheads first thing next week."

Red queued a video on his phone and set it on the table between us.

"Wanna peek at the prime mover behind the Jeffers Project? The government ponied up a staggering amount of cash, it is a fact. However, it blew my mind when I saw that over sixty percent of the capital was raised by private investors. The Redlick family agitated to build the project, financed the land grab, then hired subsidiaries of their own corporation to provide security and infrastructure. Sweet deal. Ain't America grand if you're a fat cat?"

He pressed the pad and we watched a six-minute infomercial filmed on behalf of the Redlick Group. The narrator who escorted us on our journey of discovery was a relatively young, angular man with shiny helmet-hair and a plastic smile; his motions and expressions were those of a cold, stiff action figure warmed into a facsimile of a human being. Bold script identified him as Thomas Mandibole, Redlick Group spokesperson. I made note.

Mandibole stepped from a helicopter onto the roof of a skyscraper and walked toward the camera. He wore an ivory jumpsuit blazoned with the Redlick logo—a fiery oval reminiscent of a Catherine wheel, except the inner spokes extended beyond the wheel and became spearheads.

Redlick Group: the bedrock beneath your feet. Real Es-

tate. Development. Management Solutions. Infrastructure. Construction. Human Resources. Redlick Group can meet your needs through acquisition, design, attraction, training, supply, building, and staffing, here in the USA and globally. As Mandibole gave his spiel, he strode along heavily populated corridors, glancing at clipboards and signing papers thrust at him by grinning functionaries. After a quick cut, he reappeared in an ivory tuxedo, seated at a banquet table. He raised a toast to an assembly of elegantly attired clients.

Our partners receive nothing less than first-class care, from consultation, through negotiation, and during post-project assessment. He winked and tossed back a flute of champagne into his overly generous mouth. A platinum blonde, baring a stainless-steel smile and most of her torso, poised to refill his drink.

A succession of rapid scene changes occurred—Mandibole dipping the ravishing blonde on a ballroom floor; Mandibole at the wheel of a Jaguar zooming across a plain, trailing a red dust plume; Mandibole golfing; Mandibole, again in the ivory jumpsuit, on a futuristic factory floor surrounded by robots and harried human workers; stars and planets shone beyond a transparent dome, lending the impression that the Redlick Group would soon be opening factories on an alien moon.

The man continued his unctuous patter, bolstered by a discreet yet stirring symphony orchestra.

"So fucking weird," Red said. "A real live song-and-dance man delivers the song and dance. Goddamned repertory theater Fred Astaire."

Redlick Group: the bedrock beneath your feet. Today, tomorrow, the future. A glitch caused the video to disintegrate, Mandibole's voice dragging at reduced speed like the devil emoting in a cheesy '70s horror flick. Dark static flowed and might've gone on forever if Red hadn't shut off the video.

"Well, that's a trip into the uncanny valley," I said. My hackles were hackled.

Red enjoyed my discomfort.

"You're an innocent, hailing from some igloo in Alaska, so let me be the first to give you the scoop—these Redlick peeps are fucking loony." He counted off his fingers. "Redlick Group, Sword Enterprises, Zircon Corp, and Spencer Industries were the main players in the Jeffers Project. Behind the scenes, it's as debauched and corrupt as a Roman court during the crash and burn of the empire. Even got their own Adirondacks annual retreat. Call it the Fete of the Void."

I wondered if Delia had mentioned this soiree to Lionel.

"To be a fly on that wall."

"It's a Northeast version of the Bohemian Grove," Red said. "Twenty-two-foot-tall effigy to some Bronze Age deity; old flabby rich white guys in togas. Lots of booze, lots of filthy secrets. I'm afraid you'd stick out."

"Give me a white jacket and a trayful of drinks. I'd be the Invisible Man."

He pretended to chuckle while casting around for his wallet.

I paid the tab as was foretold.

CHAPTER SEVEN

Twice a year, in spring and winter, I seized a bottle of whiskey and visited Reba Walker's grave at the Pine Hollow Cemetery in Kingston. Granddaughter of Virgil and Jade; my first missing person case and first failure. Recent addition to a lifetime assortment of bitter regrets. I apologized to her headstone, then drank up. Per custom, Lionel fetched me to Meg's to recover.

The night after my graveside vigil was a humdinger. Guilt and residual brain damage make for an inadvisable combination. Add a fifth of eighty-proof and let the horror show commence. Routine nightmares mutated in new and disturbing directions. Achilles, companion dog of my bellicose youth, fell from a mountainside, as he had in the waking world, and dashed upon the rocks. Fire devoured a lush, subtropical forest. Extinct moa birds thundered around me, fleeing the inferno. Dad pursued child-me with an oar raised overhead. The sharp, chipped oar he'd struck Mother with and split her skull. His face boiled and dissolved into an inky well.

Mom floated behind him in silhouette, arms spread, wailing like a banshee. Soundless, though. A slap in the face without the whip crack.

The absolute worst part of this whole deal? My rational side understood the score. A squamous collection of sublimated impulses and fears had metastasized as a thunderhead of evil to hector my subconscious. There was nothing I could do. Refusing to stay put, the interior darkness began to whisper and cajole during waking hours too.

■ ■ ■

Shadows of tree branches flowed across the ceiling of Meg's bedroom. She thumped in the shower. She'd already ushered her son, Devlin, off to school and was prepping for a shift at the library. Minerva lay at the foot of the bed, twitching in her sleep as she gave chase to dream animals. Perhaps moa birds.

Normally some light calisthenics would be in order, and a few rounds at the striking post when I returned to my cabin. Sweat popped onto my forehead at the notion. I lurched into the kitchen and fixed a pot of coffee and waited for the myriad aches and pains to subside. Longer every morning. My left hand, dropper of water glasses, trembled as I poured. Death wasn't even bothering to sneak up anymore—it ambled near with a cheerful whistle.

The house was cold. Meg walked in, sat next to me in a bathrobe, hair piled high in a towel, and placed her hand over mine—the traitorous one. There was much I wanted to say that I didn't.

"What's the matter?"

"I didn't realize anything was."

I appreciated that she tactfully neglected to mention that my hungover self reeked of booze.

"You're giving off the furrowed-brow, heavy-lies-the-crown vibe," she said.

"You know me; I brood."

"No reason to brood. You've done a hero's work. Honest-to-God good-versus-evil shit."

We were going to skip right over my dubious influence on Devlin for the second conversation in a row and that suited me fine. Or it would rear from the bushes like a furious T. rex at an inopportune (for me) moment. That was also fine since it was later.

"Am I in the good-versus-evil business?" I lowered my voice for melodramatic emphasis.

She ignored it.

"Always were. These days you get to be on the right side, sometimes."

"Can a man be bloodthirsty *and* civilized?"

"Do you mean, can a human being be a walking contradiction? Can he or she possess more than one side?"

"Which side is real?"

"Only a rube would ever fall into the trap of thinking any of them are. Your hang-up is you've got imposter syndrome. *I'm a thug, not a REAL detective! I'm no Marlowe!* Neither high intellect, charm, nor finesse are requisites to cracking cases. On the balance, I'd say that going on rampages and scaring the shit out of people works like magic. Face it, sweetie, some of the best detectives were thugs."

"Loving the pep talk, dear."

"The pop psychology question we used to get—if you were a tree, what kind of tree would you be? Different question, same idea. If you were a hero—ancient hero, not a superhero—what kind would you be?"

"Not the nice kind." I was intrigued by mythological figures. Why would a former assassin be obsessed with that crowd? Because Jason, Achilles, Tane, and Thor wore black hats when necessary. Hitmen of the gods.

"Definitely not the nice kind," she said. "Not one from Devlin's comic books or the sanitized version you get in school. His class is reading capsule tales from Norse myth, wouldn't you know? Those are the fake renditions. The knockoff versions. You're the old, Homeric original who wore animal skins and the skins of your enemies and bone and bronze. The kind the gods bestow power and terrible destinies on, and then laugh."

"Baby—"

"They solved problems with brute force and the point of a spear."

"Honey—"

"No powers, only the attitude and the destiny. Yeah, sweetheart, you're a hero. The worst kind. You know what happens to heroes."

"Actually, I'm thinking about Lionel." I wasn't going to admit that death gods and curses were on my mind or that she'd struck half a dozen nerves.

"There's a ball of yarn."

"He rescued a possum stuck under his porch. Now he bunks with a pet possum."

"Where? What?"

"We think a raccoon beat its ass. Missing an eye and an ear. He nursed it somewhat back to health."

"Sure to wow the floozies he drags home," she said. "Possums aren't my bag. Yeah, yeah, God's creatures and whatever. I've only seen dead ones. Maybe that's it. Hard to bond with roadkill."

"Understandable. I think Patroclus Possum may be his new character test for dates."

"How does that work? The possum doesn't approve, no banging?"

"Let's not go crazy," I said. "He rigged a carrier crate setup. Covered it with a floor mat from his Monte Carlo. The possum hides in there and hisses at anybody who gets too close."

"It's like a rehearsal for what he'll do if a woman ever moves in."

"Issue two: He pines for the mercurial heiress."

"Hell yeah, he does. *I* pine for her. She's smoking hot. She's brilliant. And rich!"

"Hence, heiress."

"Don't be a wiseguy."

"I see what you did there. He's hunkered down at the farm and no sign of wanting to ever move on. Fantasies about taking down the cartels don't count. I'm worried that he's done. The cabin is his final bunker. Which is fine, it's his choice. Except, what happens when Virgil and Jade kick the bucket? They're old as the hills."

"Well, you've given the future of Lionel Robard some thought," she said.

"Whoever takes over the property may not be so kindly disposed to a burnt-out war vet tipping garbage cans and propositioning the lady tourists."

"They might not like his varmint either."

"What's the real deal? Headaches? Nightmares?" Meg regarded me with sharpened interest. "Some top-secret bullshit you and Lionel won't share with the wimminfolk?"

"A man offered me a job. He's exorcising demons. The pay is right, though."

"This guy a prick?"

"He is definitely that."

"Now, tell me why you're sitting here under a cloud. The real-real reason."

"Money. What else? That stash we recovered from the serial killer . . . Give me a second." I'd told her a short and severely edited version of the hunt for the beast known by several handles including the Tri-State Killer, and more fancifully, the Croatoan. I admitted to absconding with the bad guy's nest egg, omitting the fact that Lionel and I ultimately located and disposed of him. Few people were aware of the whole story—a few too many, by my reckoning.

Happily, she'd asked several questions in regard to possible blowback and then let it lie.

I went into the living room and fetched a duffel bag I'd tossed into the coat closet yesterday en route to the cemetery. I schlepped into the kitchen and dumped the bag's contents before the love of my life. Roughly a hundred large in tightly bound stacks of C-notes cascaded across that battered tabletop. A couple spilled over and hit the floor. This was a piece of the treasure we hadn't buried. I'm a believer in the power of spectacle to crystallize one's thoughts and foster enthusiasm. Well enough to speak of a fortune in the abstract; quite another proposition to witness it in person and be awed.

"The Croatoan's hoard," I said. "A fraction of the hoard."

"My God."

"Darling, this is where you and your beautiful mind come in."

"If I had a tail it'd be wagging." Meg stared at the money, suspicious and intrigued. "What can I do?"

"Research. The sonofabitch kept newspaper clippings and names in a journal. Some are decades old. I'm thinking you might give his papers a churn, a clue could surface. Before I can commit to getting this money, ah, cleaned, I should figure out where it originated and why a bad man had it socked away in his lair. I have to determine whether it's the Nibelungen."

She leaned over and retrieved a bundle off the tiles, riffling it as one does. Her nose wrinkled as she took in its musky odor. The stink of antiquity and evil. I winced at the notion we'd crossed a threshold—I'd involved her and there were no takebacks.

"Isaiah Coleridge, you better not have stolen the cursed treasure of the dwarves."

"Call me Siegfried."

CHAPTER EIGHT

Ted set appointments for the following week with several of Sean Pruitt's friends and relatives in Horseheads. I planned to call a bunch of other people tangential to the case when I hit town. The Widow Pruitt, who'd reverted to her maiden name of Flanagan, retreated to Northern California shortly after the funeral. Ted's calls to her bounced, so far.

The weather promised to hold. I rented an SUV with snow tires anyhow. My museum-curio Ford was hell on gas. Besides, the staff down at the rental agency looked forward to my appearances—big tipper and such. Obviously, their fondness would ebb the day I finally returned a car riddled with bullet holes. Only a matter of time.

I charted a course south along 209 past Kerhonkson and Ellenville, then west onto 17. The subdivisions of regional New York State are tricky and I hadn't been around long enough to make heads or tails of the nuances. Some folks considered my destination, Chemung County, to be the western portion of the state. Others huffily insisted the region was properly designated central New York. I'd called Ted to ask her opinion as a lifelong resident.

"Well, boss, that's an interesting question. Whoops . . . Someone on the other line." The dial tone buzzed.

A three-hour drive into cow country, taking it easy. Strong winds buffeted the car after I crossed over into Binghamton and paralleled the Susquehanna River past a string of towns—Endicott, Apalachin, and Owego—through Hoopers Valley, and onward. Winter, but not-quite-winter; yellow and brown pastoral vistas patched with ice, like an embalmed corpse of a landscape. Cold to the touch and ready for a permanent shroud of snow. The terrain mellowed the farther west I rolled along the Allegheny Plateau; mountains ceded to long, hilly valleys, scattered forests, and plains. Here was the core of the Southern Tier, bucolic territory bordering Pennsylvania. Breadbasket and erstwhile Christian heartland of the entire state. The Burned-over District, as certain writers of history books would have it known. Lands of the False Revival might be another nickname. None of that concerned me beyond the ticking of a box and filing the data into the niche of my brain captivated by useless trivia.

■ ■ ■

Midafternoon found me in the Chemung River Valley, following the Chemung River, a muddy tributary of the Susquehanna, toward Elmira. Cruising due north, Elmira segues to Elmira Heights and the Heights bleed into Horseheads, which is composed of Horseheads proper, Horseheads Village, and Horseheads North. Twenty thousand citizens dwelling in a mix of modern box and clapboard houses. Neighborhoods are green in the summer and downright postcard-worthy in the fall around Halloween. I felt a pang of sadness to have missed the last of the red and yellow foliage, scruffy lawns, fake cobwebs, and ghosts and jack-o'-lanterns. Christianity and the old gods dance hip-to-hip during the witching season, particularly in historical fossils such as Horseheads. The discomfort this engenders among the upright is a revelation to behold. Contemporary mores erode tradition, year by year. The spiritual blood of puritans and pagans slows to a trickle, yet the ancient heart thumps feebly, not quite dead, only dreaming.

The town was named for the herd of sick and injured packhorses slaughtered upon General John Sullivan's return from his triumphant campaign in the north against the Iroquois Nations in 1779. Natives lined the road with the skulls. Over two centuries later, they referred to the area as the Valley of the Horses' Heads. Picturesque as it was, the region's history depressed me. I already missed the Catskills, which was no picnic either.

Past downtown congestion and rural-fied urban sprawl, hilly farmland spread toward the horizon. I pressed in a westerly direction, proceeding across a vale of retail lots and the regional airport, toward the outskirts of Big Flats, turning north at the last moment. Forest closed in and traffic dissipated. The stripped canopy made a latticework of the fading sunlight. I sailed into gloom.

Sooner or later, the winding secondary roads would've delivered me to Sugar Hill State Forest or the Finger Lakes. Instead, I took an unmarked access lane. Fresh, clean pavement for a mile, straight as a Roman street, then the lane quickly degenerated into a shabbily patched stretch of potholes and swells. Trees thinned and the road broke onto a man-made prairie that butted against a distant line of bluffs and tall timber. NO TRESPASSING signs were posted every hundred yards. A hawk roosted atop a lamppost, ignoring my car, its gaze fixed northward. I passed lattice transmission towers. There were electrical substations in the area. Had the collider been completed, its energy needs would've rivaled that of a large city.

Electric fencing topped with barbed wire blocked forward progress. More placards covered the double gate, each sign warning unauthorized visitors to turn back. A blue metal billboard with white lettering announced this complex to be THE JEFFERS LARGE PARTICLE COLLIDER LABORATORY. Oh, and KEEP OUT. I left the car idling as I walked around the gatehouse, snapping pictures with my cell phone. The gatehouse was silent, its windows grimy. Past the gate lay a secondary fence, then clusters of metal-and-concrete buildings done in beige and gray. I noted an aircraft hangar and a control tower. A windsock snapped in the breeze atop a pole at the near end of a paved runway. Dried weeds and tufts of dead grass thrust upward among cracks in the tarmac.

Aerial photographs provided by Adeyemi's lawyer revealed that this glacial basin extended many miles east and west. Light forest and meadows covered much of the area. Records indicated that necessary tracts of private farmland were purchased via eminent domain. Contractors had bulldozed multiple zones for surface infrastructure. Blueprints meticulously detailed a circuit of particle acceleration tunnels that lay one hundred and eighty feet belowground; dug by giant diesel bores, leaving much of the forest undisturbed. Regarding a composite architectural image of the collider track, it circumscribed a broken ring, a great reversed crescent moon. Most of the track was completed, concrete poured and internal sheathing tube installed; everything except for the laying of directional magnets. Shaft 40 was dead center in the rough, unfinished section of the circuit—several miles of dirt tunnels and wasted potential.

Studying the blueprints sparked an instant of recognition, and I clicked to a gruesome artifact among the Sean Pruitt case files. The autopsy photos weren't for the squeamish. One revealed a tattoo on his right outer shoulder; a stylized sketch of the unfinished supercollider track done as a transistor-board ouroboros with a gap between its jaws and stinger tail. Weird. Weirder yet, both the collider track and the ouroboros tat reminded me of another image that I couldn't quite pin down. Something I'd seen in passing or a fragment of a dream.

The purpose of my mission was to reconnoiter the facilities from afar, not that I expected to gather significant intelligence. I'd mildly hoped for the jackpot of a bored security guard or maintenance worker; somebody to flash my PI license at and slip a few bucks for a quick tour. No luck and I didn't feel like waiting. I suspected it might be a while, or forever, judging by the neglect on display. Breaking and entering was another possibility; I tabled the option. Assuming law enforcement did its job, what would I uncover that the CSI team hadn't?

Also, the property gave me the creeps. A spooky thing happened to reinforce my negative perception—on cue, the SUV engine died. One second it was humming, and the next, conked out. I turned the key and the starter wouldn't even spark. Dead across the dashboard panel. My cell went wonky, cycling on and off with no bars. It was an unpleasant moment. I tried the key one last time and the engine turned over and I was saved.

Haunted Horseheads! Rolled off the tongue with less menace than the reality.

The drive back to town blurred. My attention was repeatedly drawn to the rearview mirror. I experienced a "watched" feeling I'd sometimes picked up on in the Alaskan boonies. That very real sense the land itself wants you gone. Her immune system too reacts to perceived threats by sending agents after you—wolves, bears, blizzards, men deranged by cabin fever, anything handy. What kind of antibodies did this part of the country have at its disposal? Mate a genius locus with a partially constructed supercollider and gods only knew the result. Call me ridiculous and superstitious. I've said the occult isn't my bag, not by that name, anyhow. Nonetheless, after the shit I'd seen pursuing the Croatoan, let's just say my definitions of the possible were malleable.

Argue with the Native Americans who named and ordered the local spirits and lamented the toxic consequences of European incursions. In Alaska, when natives die on the sea ice or go missing upon the tundra, it's occasionally attributed to the malign activity of entities that were here long before men. Who's to say otherwise? Not the mysterious dead. Not me.

I leaned on the pedal. The premonition that the cab of the SUV would shear off, and my head with it, receded as miles passed. Slithered into the tar of my hindbrain and curled up to wait.

CHAPTER NINE

I parked in the rear lot of the Hotel Roan, a Victorian mansion reincarnated to its current state in the 1960s. Everything begins as something else. Plants, animals, people. Even architecture progresses from pupae to imago. The hotel sat back from a quiet street a block west of Newtown Creek. Oak trees scraped the building. The lobby was intimate—a drawing room and bar to the right; an equally modest dining room to the left. The type of accommodations where one would be forced to practically sit in his or her date's lap. Oil paintings of General Sullivan, and the original owner of the mansion, Jedidiah Lark, hung over the reception desk. Paneled windows framed by white drapes let in the muted sunset. I took the stairs to the top, noting that the building indeed possessed the air of a sprawling home rather than a hotel. The kid version of me would've searched for dumbwaiters and secret passages. All the joint needed was a plucky heroine in a nightgown stumbling around by the light of a candelabrum.

More paintings and photographs—the example near

my door was done in murky oils and portrayed a picket of horse skulls planted along a dirt road. The skulls shone dully in purple twilight. A lone cavalry officer, saber in hand, slumped atop a roan mare; the roan's muzzle tilted down and toward the viewer. Her eye brimmed with purple fire, bone white at the rim, and she was Death's mount.

My digs were cozy. The usual amenities, plus a view of Newtown Creek. The tiny parlor featured a rolltop desk and a shelf stocked with clothbound books on regional geography, agriculture, wildlife, and the like. Did anyone ever glance at them besides the maid? I clicked on an honest-to-gods Tiffany reading lamp to bask in the buttery warm glow. Queen-size bed with a thick headboard; chestnut engravings of cavalry horses rampant beneath a full moon. A fifty-dollar-a-night motel would've been sensible. I wasn't in the mood to stare at suspicious water stains or cigarette-burned carpets while sodium lamps fizzed and flickered in a parking lot next to an overpass. The number one reason I chose comfort over utility? Badja Adeyemi was on the hook for expenses.

I showered; changed into a dress shirt and pants, newish Chuck Taylors, and a heavy leather jacket. The revolver went into the room safe. I clipped the jawbone knife to my belt, and the jacket disguised its presence. Then I went downstairs and strolled around the neighborhood to stretch my legs and settle my mind after the drive. I was borderline underdressed for the weather, so I moved briskly.

Deep twilight tinted the sky. The wind tasted of dead grass and moss, mingled with hints of snow and the tang of creosote and exhaust. Car horns blatted south where lights clustered, marking tenements and deserted industrial towers. We used to switch off, back in the dark ages of the eighteenth and nineteenth centuries. NYC is notable because it has never slept and the world once thought its inhabitants mad. Even as late as the 1970s, come sundown, suburbia was a wilderness illuminated by a night-light across most of the U.S.

What attractions drew people here other than business? The National Soaring Museum, Woodlawn National Cemetery, and the Corning Museum of Glass were draws. Elmira and Big Flats hosted various industries. Agriculture, of course. Otherwise? Difficult to reconcile the attraction, although I felt a certain ineffable quality of atmosphere, an electromagnetic current that might hypnotize a vulnerable mind.

My interview with Sean Pruitt's mother was scheduled for tomorrow. I'd arrived early to soak in the atmosphere and to permit my subconscious a jump on the problem. Whatever might be unfolding needed a chance to begin and I thought it prudent to brace for contact. Perhaps a strange concept, considering that Sean Pruitt was in the ground going on four years. The hairs on my neck said, yes, oh yes; be it suicide or foul play, gears were in motion. The Observer Effect might have awakened a dreaming beast. I didn't require a fortune-teller to clue me in to the presence of dark forces. Those sonsofbitches are always lurking.

■ ■ ■

Dinner at a solid Italian restaurant a couple of blocks from the hotel improved my disposition. Probably because the angel on my left shoulder won the argument about saying to hell with my theoretical diet or budget. I called Meg and chatted with her for a few minutes while waiting for the check.

Meg told me about her day. She'd run into an acquaintance and didn't duck for cover before it was too late.

"It was bizarre. Chick wore pajamas at the grocery store. Used to be the fashion, maybe it's back. Her voice, though. Says to me in a little girl's affect, *I bwoke a wibby-wib,* and she did the cry-eye with her fist. Grown woman in a blouse and pajamas on line at ShopRite. We haven't spoken since senior year in high school."

"Didn't duck in time?" I said. "You gotta hone those catlike reflexes." Meg didn't need to hone a damned thing—she'd practiced gymnastics and dance since her youth. I'd seen her press into a handstand from a seated position. She could kick over her head without stretching first.

She laughed and told me to shut it.

All was quiet on the western front; she'd put Devlin to bed and had settled in with *Night of the Hunter*. Minerva was on edge in my absence. The dog paced the house, grumbling at doors, which while not completely out of character, sounded strident tonight. I didn't utter my predictable advice to make sure the place was locked tight; crime doesn't skip small towns, even placid whistle-stops like Tilson, blah, blah. I gave Meg my love and let her get back to that bad boy dreamboat, young Robert Mitchum. I walked to the hotel, naming the constellations as red blinking plane lights crawled beneath them. I also contemplated my luck in finding a woman who properly appreciated Robert Mitchum.

My room was dim except for a puddle of light in the mini-parlor. The silhouette of a woman stood in the corner, where a large window overlooked the rear lot. I caught the slightest trace of ginger. My childhood rushed back. Tepora Coleridge favored a ginger scent and I re membered it from her hugs.

I nearly blurted, *Mom?* like a total rube, and flipped the wall switch. Bright light revealed where curtains gathered and bunched. Tracking right, I spotted a scented candle. Wisps of smoke coiled from its wick. The maid had replaced the towels and folded my discarded clothes. I remained motionless, processing a cascade of emotions and the wider implications.

It had been a while since I'd shed real tears. My throat burned and it was close for a moment. Meg was right; the docs missed something when they scanned my gray matter. An unclosing wound, a tumor, the ghosts of my sinful past.

■ ■ ■

I dreamed I was in colonial times, clad in my skivvies and carrying the boar spear that lies under the bed in my cabin in the real world. A blacksmith in Pawtucket had forged it per my unique specifications. Soldiers hunted me through a forest. Cocked hats, long coats, and muskets. I made my stand in a clearing. An officer on horseback emerged from the misty woods. He wore a crimson-and-bronze high school letter jacket. His face was rigid and pasty—a death mask. The horse's head was skinned to the bone, glistening with blood. It snapped the air in anticipation of tasting mine.

I awakened, sweating, heart racing.

Be careful, Badja Adeyemi said. The laptop monitor faded and brightened, auto-playing a video I'd selected and then fallen asleep watching. Adeyemi whispered his warning to Sean, but the camera microphone caught it just fine. Ghosts, the both of them. Sean and Linda's wedding day as documented by Sean's father, Dr. Alex Pruitt, and his Handycam. Adeyemi, drunk as a lord, had pulled young Sean to the side for some avuncular tips on how to handle women.

Be careful, kid. She's got a wandering eye.

The scene went to black and the speaker hissed.

CHAPTER TEN

June Adeyemi Pruitt lived alone in a historical neighborhood on the edge of town. Many of the houses were stamped with bronze plaques, designating their cultural import to the community. The Pruitt home was done in the Colonial Revivalist style; two stories plus an attic, painted white with lemon trim. It sat between similar houses; one brown, the other forest green. Everybody shared a massive elm that towered over the rumpled sidewalk.

A squirrel cleaned its paws upon a lower branch, in profile, its beady eye fixed judgmentally.

"There's a hawk who'd love to meet you," I said in passing.

June Pruitt greeted me at ten A.M. before I could knock twice. My above-average haircut, very posh suit, and affable demeanor were insufficiently charming. She didn't offer to shake. Her mouth crimped, like she was biting down on pain. Four years may as well be yesterday for a bereaved mother.

Hardwood floors squeaked underfoot as she led me to
the living room. I sat in the center of a couch on a mac-
ramé spread. She remained aloof near the window—
whether an act of unconscious bias or by deliberate
stratagem, I couldn't say. In her teaching role she probably maintained a measure of authority by standing over
her students. Piano to her left, a barrel-shaped floor lamp
to her right. The chipped lamp base was decorated with
faded illustrations of Native American eroticism. She
wore red gemstone beads over a black sweater. No fur or
feathers meant no dogs or cats and an empty home. I
maintain that long sojourns in empty homes are precur-
sors to madness. Her long skirt was black and also her
shoes. Her hair was steel gray. I searched for the resem-
blance to her brother, Badja, and wouldn't have seen any
if I hadn't known they were siblings. Badja Adeyemi radi-
ated wickedness. June Pruitt projected cynicism, the
by-product of barely modulated grief.

We exchanged pleasantries. How was I finding the
Southern Tier? I smiled instead of confessing my dis-
quiet.

"Did Badja mention that Senator Redlick was born
in Horseheads?" She spoke with a slight Northeastern
drawl.

"I'm aware the senator is almost seventy and still
brags about his senior class winning state when he gets
on CNN. What else is necessary to know?"

"He's an avowed UFO nut. He claims SETI and the
Voyager probe are terrible ideas."

"Really? He never mentioned it during his campaign interviews."

"The people who write his speeches edit out that sort of thing. Badja says the guy gets a few drinks under his belt and rants that our attempts to contact alien civilizations are tantamount to ringing the dinner bell—with humanity as the main course."

"Anything else?"

"The Redlicks regard this valley as their fiefdom and the senator is their king. Some claim he's embarrassed by his accent. He retains an elocutionist, a retired actor from the Shakespeare Theatre Company."

"The rain in Spain . . ." I said.

"I'm serious." She looked it.

I cleared my throat.

"The senator hasn't resided here since 1979. He was *Mr.* Gerald Redlick in those days."

"Doesn't discourage him from shooting campaign ads in the old neighborhood with the blessings of the chamber of commerce."

"Your valley didn't become the site of the Jeffers Project by chance. Royalty hath its privileges."

"The Redlick family makes all things possible." The fire of her cynicism brightened the room.

"There are those who fight, those who pray, and those who work." Thus, I demonstrated roughly half of the knowledge I retained from my Western Civ classes. "You work, though you could retire. I admire your dedication. High school English isn't for the weak."

"Well, I pray a bit too," she said, almost pleased. "Alex, my ex-husband, was a state biologist. He retired. This is his house; I'm but a tenant. Alex lives in the village. He couldn't stand to look at this place anymore."

"Your daughter-in-law returned to California."

"Linda went to Healdsburg. Wine country. Fire country."

Despite her stoic demeanor, her evident distrust, June Pruitt wanted to talk. Her cadence, her word choices, the thematic body, were typical of educated people who voluntarily interview with the police and other professional snoops. She'd rehearsed.

"Linda attended USC," I said. "Parents deceased. Siblings in Utah and Montana. She's a color specialist."

"Yes, she freelances for various agencies."

"What is that?" I'd already researched the basic answer. The question was designed to appeal to her intellect, her inclination to lecture.

"It's rather opaque. Let me try. A client owns a fast-food restaurant. Linda helps him choose colors to achieve specific goals. A relaxed environment would feature softer tones. Want people to buy and then move along promptly? Discordant colors. That's a simple example. Linda and her occupation are hardly simple."

"Fascinating. As for your husband, I'd prefer to interview Dr. Pruitt as well. Assuming I could get him on the line."

"Giving you the cold shoulder? That's his way. He considers the matter settled. I'll call him. He needs to participate in this . . ." She absently twisted her wedding band. "My other children live abroad. Sean and Linda never . . ." She folded her hands and I realized that they were nearly as large as Badja Adeyemi's; and then the sibling likeness materialized. "I presume you know what happened—what they claim happened—to Sean."

"I've read the file."

"You've *read* the file." The flatness of her voice matched her expression. "It claims he committed suicide. No reason given. Oh, well, the implication is that he was depressed and mixed medications with some kind of drug—"

"A hallucinogen," I said.

"Yes, a hallucinogen. Then he went to work, drove to a remote area on the site, and . . ." She blinked and swallowed. "And I don't believe that's the whole story."

"Why not?"

"Did the file happen to mention the paramedics or the staff at the medical examiner's office stole his wedding ring?"

"No. The report's a sketchy piece of work, I'll admit."

"Isn't it, though? That's the kind of people I'm dealing with. The kind of people who steal a dead man's wedding ring."

"How long was Sean on antidepressants?" I said.

"Many years. He struggled with clinical depression since his youth."

"Yet you don't agree that he could've committed suicide."

"He didn't. We discussed his condition on numerous occasions; its symptoms, the treatment. He didn't exhibit suicidal ideation. Depression afflicted him like a low-grade fever; always nagging. The worst symptoms manifested as lethargy. At his very worst, his very lowest, he'd lose interest in work or socializing and retreat to his books and papers. Employment proved a challenge. He was a model employee at his best."

"Sean was never admitted for in-patient therapy? The odds of suicide are much higher for in-patients."

"Was he committed or institutionalized? Never. He smoked pot on occasion. Drank socially. Sean was spiritual; a by-product of grappling with mental illness is you tend to excavate the psyche. I assume from his comments he dabbled with LSD, peyote. Conscious-altering drugs. I never knew him to have a problem, though."

"Coke, heroin? Anything like that?"

Her nostrils flared in disgust.

"Not a chance. What did my dear brother say when he sent you here?"

"He told me to ask you."

She studied my face and hands, looking past the scars.

"You're a special kind of detective. The kind my brother *would* hire. Not a cop. He doesn't trust cops."

"Oh?"

"Cops hate black men."

"Cops hate everybody who isn't a cop," I said. "Isn't it a fact the only color that brother cops see is blue?"

"He isn't in the brotherhood anymore. Notice he chose you, a stranger, rather than call upon one of his so-called brothers. He was a popular, lonely man while on the force and plain lonely once he quit."

"Mrs. Pruitt—"

"Do you enjoy speaking to him?"

"Ma'am—"

"In your estimation, is he good or decent?"

"You would agree that as a 'special' kind of detective, I'm the last person to judge him. I'm carrying out his orders, for a price. Cut-and-dried."

"You're ronin, not samurai."

I appreciated her mind the more we spoke.

"That captures the essence, ma'am. Bushido is for suckers."

"I bet he gets a kick out of you, Mr. Coleridge. You're rough. You're rough, and you do what you're told. Badja gravitates toward men of dubious character. Criminals and thugs, and men who disguise their thuggery with uniforms and suits."

I stood abruptly. The movement surprised her like ice cracking underfoot or big, lovable Fido showing his fangs. Her eyes widened as possibilities undreamt of moments ago forcefully presented themselves. While she recovered, I strode to the piano and examined a collection of photographs. Sean, Linda-the-widow, and June's ex-husband, Alex. Badja made a lone appearance in an extended family triptych. There was a handful of the nephews and nieces, professionally posed, and several of Sean beginning in grade school. He played football and basketball in high school. The last shot of him was during the holidays, within months of his death. Frizzy hair, round face, forced smile. His mother's features, though softer. A weary young man ground down by the world;

smiling to reassure his beloveds that he was right as rain, dependable, and happy. One's beloveds are so very invested in one's perceived happiness.

Next to that photograph rested a framed newspaper clipping of Badja Adeyemi as bodyguard, escorting Gerald Redlick into the Redlick Group building in Manhattan. Adeyemi glared at the camera. Reminded me of the hawk roosting atop the lamppost at the Jeffers site. Predators share a particular affect if you catch them in the moment.

"That was his bad cop expression," she said in a shaky voice. "Redlick took a shine to him. Two domineering men with a birthplace in common. They were comfortable because each understood the other. I used to hide that photo in a scrapbook. Now that Sean is gone and Alex has abandoned me, I leave it there as a reminder. Birds of a feather."

"Were Badja and Sean close?"

"Badja made sure he was hired on at the site. I understand Sean hounded him."

"But were they close?" I said.

"Sean admired Badja's courage and toughness. Badja adored Sean. Wouldn't admit it if you had him in thumbscrews. Tenderness is weakness in my brother's world."

"This is a personal question—how was the marriage? Any problems? Tension?"

She didn't hesitate. The disapproving mother-in-law in her pounced.

"The marriage was crumbling. You could detect a chill in the air at family dinners."

"At least you had family dinners," I said. "Is it possible there was another person in the picture?"

"Another man? Was Linda cheating, you mean?"

"That's what I mean."

She gave this some thought.

"Linda never established any significant relationships here. Sean hung around with colleagues at the Jeffers site. From what I understand, he had some of them over to his house for dinner and the like. My husband and I met two or three in passing. No one sticks out in my memory. Well, there was one fellow . . . A tad rough around the edges. Leather jacket and pomade brute. Sean introduced him as D and was eager that we not exchange more than pleasantries."

"Strange, isn't it? Did Sean have reason to fear you meeting his pals?"

"My son was protective of his acquaintances. He dated Linda for six months before he disclosed the fact to us."

"Why is that?" I said.

"Disappointment. One too many so-called friends betrayed him in his youth. Typical kid drama. He was actually popular. However, every child will experience failed relationships. His were sources of shame. He tired of explaining why this boy or that girl was no longer around the house. By his high school years, it was like prying teeth to get anything personal out of him."

"No mother-daughter chitchat between you and Linda?"

June Pruitt laughed.

"Dear God, no. We . . . didn't see eye to eye."

"Socially? Politically?"

"Anything. That's why I seldom visited their home. I wasn't exactly unwelcome, but she kept the red carpet in storage. Easier to let them come to us when they felt social."

If someone had stuck a gun to my head and made me guess, I would've laid money on Sean and Linda's child-less marriage as a bone of contention between widow and mother. Women of a certain age and persuasion want those grandchildren.

"What drew them together? What did she see in your son?"

"That's a hell of a question."

"He had difficulty holding down a job, right?" I said. "Linda's a highly trained, motivated woman. An unequal pairing."

June Pruitt's expression wasn't pleasant. She didn't tell me to jump into a lake, though.

"Were you ever young, Mr. Coleridge?" Her tone indicated she thought I'd rolled out of the womb a certified jerk. "They were different people in college. Sean had big dreams. The passion of a dreamer can be heady as ambrosia. She recognized his potential, an innate brilliance he inherited from his father. It inspired her own creativity. Linda made the mistake many women do; she decided she could 'fix' him. She should've accepted him and left it at that."

"Did she enjoy relocating to western New York? Heck of a transition."

"She didn't hate it. Ringing endorsement, eh? The

state *is* gorgeous. And Sean was getting good pay, for once."

"Long way from California," I said. "Cold winters. Hicks."

"Linda worked from home and traveled when necessary. She wasn't trapped. Have you ever visited Healdsburg? It's quaint. Her property is surrounded by hills and woods. A drier, sunnier version of the hills that border this area."

"You don't buy suicide based on Sean's chronic depression. Fine. Let's consider the possibility there were additional variables. Did you notice changes in his behavior?"

"He was buttoned down around me and his father, so my insight is admittedly limited in certain regards. He didn't handle stress well. The last year, he became scattered, forgetful. His handwriting, which had been fairly neat up through college, degraded. Something weighed on his mind. A bad marriage would account for certain aspects. But I couldn't help but wonder if he was hiding an illness or trouble at work."

I closed my notebook.

"Thank you for your help, ma'am."

"Sorry for my loss, et cetera?"

"Et cetera, et cetera." There were moments I wished that in addition to closing my notebook with finality I had a hat to grab, because hats are often kept near a door.

"What will you do next?" she said.

"What I usually do. Ask nice people rude questions and chase my own tail until something occurs to me."

CHAPTER ELEVEN

The comic store was the last shop standing in a plaza with FOR RENT signs in many of the windows. Devlin's tastes were evolving, but he steadfastly loved the Flash, Wonder Woman, and Green Lantern, so I nabbed the latest installment of each series. The shopkeeper kibitzed as he bagged my selections and talked me into buying a back issue annual of *The Warlord*, a lamentably discontinued series I'd adored in adolescence and then forgotten. *The Warlord* starred an improbably brawny man among men who gallivanted across a Hollow Earth landscape smiting his enemies with a sword and rescuing bikini-clad women from the clutches of evil. What was not to love for a twelve-year-old kid, right? And forty-something kids.

Afterward, I sat in the car, skimming my itinerary, which included in-person interviews with locals who'd known Sean Pruitt. Although what I really wanted to do was ditch my obligations and spend the day reading comics.

I backed out of the parking space and nearly traded paint with a pickup that whipped around the corner. The driver dynamited his brakes and was likely yelling obscenities before he flung his door open. I didn't have an opportunity to ask if he was okay. The driver, an older red-faced hick in a denim jacket and cowboy boots, rushed me with the stated intent to send my "brown ass back to my own country in a box." Less shocking so much as depressing. The righteous racism craze was sweeping the nation.

As one might suspect, my thoughts jumped to the altercation I witnessed between the frat bros and the construction worker at the Kingston traffic light. The angel on my left shoulder encouraged me to reenact the melodrama, but with extra violence. My better angel reminded me of the emotional and legal consequences for resorting to casual brutality. Tough call. Not that I didn't appreciate what my worse angel was laying down, but sort of like pushing aside that last piece of pie because it's the honorable thing to do, I denied my base instincts to maul and maim and used an appropriate level of force. Mr. Denim's punch glanced off my lowered head. Finger bones crunched. I kicked his legs out from under him and he thudded onto his back on the pavement. His breath whooshed. An expression of fear and comprehension surfaced, then was replaced by pain. It's always bad to not realize you're overmatched until after the fight is under way or, in his case, finished.

A worse version of myself would've stomped him in the neck or slammed a heel into his sternum with all my considerable weight behind it. I stepped lightly on his armpit while seizing his wrist, then locked him into an armbar. I calmly requested that he lie still and cool off. He couldn't catch his wind to argue. His buddy came around the passenger side brandishing a golf club. A third guy hovered on the periphery, less gung ho to enter the fracas. Another aging blue-collar patriot with a pomade-slick duck's ass haircut and a leather jacket. I named him Slick.

Golf Pro, white-haired, heavyset, and paunchy, didn't repeat the driver's kamikaze charge, choosing a cautious yet determined approach. His posture suggested he was no stranger to this routine. In addition to experiencing chagrin for doubting that salt-of-the-earth bigots might enjoy nine holes after a hard day in the mines, I marveled at how rapidly the incident had escalated.

I yanked the unresisting Mr. Denim to his feet, caught his collar and belt, and slung him into Golf Pro, who quite understandably didn't conceive what was happening until too late. A man doesn't begin from the premise of administering a beating to some swarthy foreigner to having his two-hundred-pound buddy chucked at him by said swarthy foreigner. Mr. Denim's boots lifted off as I launched him and their skulls collided with a satisfying thump. They lay in a tangle, unconscious. The third man, Slick, bolted.

Vehicles rumbled past on the street. I expected the cops to zoom in at any second. When the fuzz didn't swoop in to clap me in irons, I carried the dudes to their truck and stuffed them inside. I killed the engine and tossed the keys onto the hood. Golf Pro snored through a mashed nose. Mr. Denim's eyes were glassy. A growing lump disfigured his forehead. Breathing sounded normal, if labored. They'd be fine. I advised Mr. Denim to relax for a few minutes and collect his shit. Once he felt okay to retrieve his keys, he'd be safe to proceed.

I wished them many happy returns and briskly departed the scene.

■ ■ ■

While I was initially getting my feet wet in the Hudson Valley, local wiseguys regaled me with a campfire story. A split-level in a wooded neighborhood in Kingston once belonged to a fellow who operated on behalf of the mob; a numbers guy, but also a hitter if the occasion warranted. That nondescript home at the end of the ordinary street proved to be a house of horrors. Numbers Guy and his cronies killed numerous people there and minced them in the basement. Hookers, estranged girlfriends, mobsters, saps who'd pissed them off, et cetera. Numbers Guy ratted to the Feds on the regular, so this continued for years. The minute his usefulness diminished, cops broke down his door in a no-knock raid, expressed shock and consternation at the gruesome revelations, and sent him to the pen for a million years.

Lionel and I once took an opportunity to roll past the murder house. The realtor kept the lawn tidy and the gutters clean in vain; nobody would touch the place with a ten-foot pole. It emanated a psychic stench that caused us to exchange a glance and motor into the sunset. We hadn't spoken of it since, although the experience lingered.

This is pertinent because my tour of Horseheads was characterized by a whiff of ineffable rottenness that came and went with the breeze. The sensation reminded me of that house of the dead, and more recently, the unpleasant vibes at the Jeffers collider site. A stark fact stared hard at me—the universe didn't send me to coincidentally weird, inimical, fucked-up locations; nope, I was finally *noticing* how fucked up the universe and its various biomes are as a general rule.

■ ■ ■

Sean Pruitt's therapist listened to my pitch for confidential information over the phone. I laid it on thick: *Mysterious circumstances, a mother haunted by doubt, corrupt businesses, a possible cover-up, I only have a couple of easy questions,* and so forth. Everything but Connie Chung's why-don't-you-whisper-it-to-me gambit. To no avail. The shrink apologized sincerely, performed the ritual disclaimer regarding patient-therapist privilege, and told me to go fly a kite, albeit more professionally.

Elementary, middle, and high schools; I made the obligatory course of teachers and coaches who'd agree to an interview. Survey said, Sean was a decent student when he applied himself, and a solid if undistinguished athlete. Middling popular due to aloofness, a team player in academics and sports, and that paid for a lot.

Imperfect, yet no troublemaker. Exempting the occasional scuffle, truancy, or belligerent hormonal attitude, Sean was a relatively typical student. Teachers were unaware of the extent of his depression. Sean successfully kept his therapy and medication under wraps with the exception of the school counselor, who, predictably, wouldn't divulge details. Adults are patently oblivious when it comes to the secret lives of children. Sean's classmates might tell a different story were I to get them on the record.

The officers at the Horseheads police station knew the Pruitts. An off-duty sergeant graciously came in to answer my questions. He was a craggy no-nonsense cop who'd been on the scene for a while. We sat in a spare office the size of a broom closet and talked. Yeah, he'd rousted little Sean for smoking a joint at the quarry with a bunch of other kids. *Let him slide with a warning. Quiet, polite. Scored that last-second touchdown against Elmira. Damn shame how he went. Damned shame we lost that atom smasher project. Real money for this town. Damn, damn shame.*

Did the sergeant suspect anything amiss regarding Sean's death? He said no, although he understood why the family might find it difficult to accept. The Redlick Group had steamrolled opposition to the Jeffers Project, helped the government ram through eminent domain, and brought in tons of outside labor. RG tactics divided opinion even during the prosperous early days; once the project cratered, everybody united in an angry front. People were eager to believe the worst, outlandish rumors, and that went double for those who were most hard-done, such as the Pruitts. Damned shame all the way around.

Gonna tell ya, kid, the Redlicks have owned the heart of this town since they were stringing witches from trees. I'm old and I can level with you. This isn't the same as other places. You be as careful as you can.

The sergeant uttered his warning with a placid expression. May as well have said, *Watch out for poison ivy if you wander off the trail. Don't feed the ducks.* He wished me good fortune and sent me packing nowhere closer to knowing anything one way or the other.

■ ■ ■

Wednesday afternoon, I bought lunch at a deli—a Monte Cristo and a large black coffee. The paper cup was blazoned with the shop's horsehead logo. The horse's eyes were X'd out, 1950s cartoon fashion. I ate my sandwich and drank my coffee at a table in a raised garden where everything was dead except for the pigeons who circled and sortied for crumbs. A larger predatory bird wheeled and wheeled, obscured by the moving scrim of clouds. It was a few degrees above freezing. Passersby wore hats, mufflers, and long coats.

My phone buzzed. Dr. Alex Pruitt pleasantly surprised me with a text naming a place and time to meet; nearby and at once. He stressed the latter portion. We'd rendezvous within the hour or not at all.

Hard to say whether this reversal was good news or

one of those ill omens that cropped up with alarming frequency. I wanted to cover the bases with speed and efficiency, write my report, collect the balance due, and mosey on to the next case before the Redlick Group, Zircon Corp, or whoever decided to put the clamps on my activities. Despite a nagging suspicion that the official story didn't hold water, I wasn't thrilled at the prospect of a surprise revelation opening another avenue of inquiry. Sometimes a mystery is wisely left alone, but I'm not one to heed that warning.

CHAPTER TWELVE

Vulture Bluff was the catchy name of my destination. Where there were heaps of dead horses, hungry vultures flocked.

I drove to a gravel lot at the base of an evergreen butte five minutes outside of town. The lot was veiled by thick brush; cracks split across the farthest third of the cratered asphalt. Two other cars were parked—a midsize sedan, brown; and a blue softshell Volkswagen Beetle. A crimson and bronze 1950s Mercury Monterey turned partway into the lot, then reversed and kept going along the road.

I climbed slippery wooden stairs through a tunnel of hemlock and mulberry and emerged into a broad clearing amid more hemlock, pine, and bur oak. An eight-foot-tall fence of warped planks encircled much of the field. From a high-altitude plane, the field might've appeared as a spearhead. Shaggy grass and unraked leaves contributed to the impression of dereliction.

Nearer to me were painted stripes of a soccer infield

bleaching into the pale grass. Toward the far side of the grounds, rotting wooden bleachers canted precipitously. A backstop twined with creeper vines sank into the sod, off-kilter and somehow post-apocalyptic. Scholars cheerfully posit the end of the world will entail clouds of ash, rusted empty towns, and radioactive deserts. I envision a black, endless forest and pregnant silence that elongates into centuries. Mankind's bones lie scattered in mossy graves; home for the meek, scuttling inheritors of the earth.

A man in an overcoat stood at the center of the field, smoking. He controlled a small dark schnauzer mix on a retractable leash in his left hand. The dog described an ever-widening circle, snout focused industriously upon the earth. The man was in his late sixties; medium built under the bulky coat. Wool newsboy cap and glasses.

"This is Franz." He reeled in the dog as I approached. His wedding band appeared to match June Pruitt's. The dog cautiously snuffled my pants and shoes.

"Franz Ferdinand?"

"Boas."

"Ah, the other notorious Franz." I patted the dog. He shied away.

"Alex Pruitt. You're Isaiah Coleridge." The smoke from his cigarette blended with a pleasantly stark cologne.

"I am."

Dr. Pruitt freelanced for several private organizations and traveled frequently overseas. He'd moiled in the dirt as a biologist, transitioned to an office job, and retired with every honor due an overachieving genius. His essays and papers were collected at Elmira College. I'd skimmed the plum examples. One essay snagged my whole attention—his harrowing account of an expedition to a mangrove delta in southern Bangladesh in the '80s. Killer tigers, killer snakes, killer bees, killer everything in that gigantic saltwater swamp. The kind of place a warrior might go to seek a spectacularly gruesome death. It had certainly claimed the lives of woodcutters and poachers. In English, its name translated loosely to the Beautiful Forest, but was referred to by relatives of the aforementioned woodcutters and poachers as the Forest That Eats Men. Which is what Dr. Pruitt titled his essay. Drs. Howard Campbell and Toshi Ryoko, the now-infamous scientists who'd founded the expedition, went on to reap the glory while Dr. Alex Pruitt settled into a more humble and obscure role in the scheme of academia.

I told him I'd read the essay and asked why he hadn't cashed in on a big fat New York book deal. The story was loaded with the good shit American readers crave: sex, violence, and exoticism six ways from Sunday.

"Idealistic, ambitious, stupid. We signed waivers stipulating that Toshi Ryoko and Howard Campbell owned every iota of that expedition. Those raconteurs kept an iron grip on the rights."

"Ah," I said.

"Ever catch the documentaries of the mission?" he said. "The original film is raw and honest, although you'd be surprised how much the camera omits."

"Or a director," I said. I'd screened the cult classic

documentary and a more recent, family-friendly retrospective. "Yeah, I saw it. By the way, ever hear of Anvil Mountain?"

He paused before answering.

"Some in my circle call it the Black Mountain. Why do you ask?"

"Part of a case I worked on recently. This talk of expeditions from days of yore made me curious to see how small the world is after all." In the Small World After All category, Zircon, via a subsidiary, funded multiple research projects conducted by Campbell and Ryoko, beginning with their trip to Bangladesh. More recently, Campbell appeared as a consultant on the Jeffers Project in the fine print section of the credits.

"You've had other adventures beyond Bangladesh," I said.

"Nothing as titillating. I did fieldwork in England. Our department found this enormous Viking coprolite in a marsh. Eleven, twelve hundred years old, fossilized dung. Could split a pot helmet with it. Speaking of helmets . . . We also recovered a chainmail coif with an intact skull. Amazing." He dexterously extracted a fresh cigarette one-handed and lit it with a gas lighter. The sort of fancy doohickey you got as a retirement gift. "Synchronicity that you mention the Bangladesh essay. Sean was a child when I embarked with the doctors on the quixotic voyage. In its aftermath, I worked at a private research facility in Santa Rosa."

"I take it you had a personal relationship with the doctors," I said.

"Yes. June and I rented a house in Santa Rosa and maintained regular contact with Campbell and Ryoko. The men were confirmed bachelors. They doted upon Sean as the child neither would ever have."

"So you saw them often."

"We routinely drove to their house for various get-togethers," he said. "They were nomadic, and the latter 1980s is possibly the longest the duo ever settled in one place. Wherever they reside is akin to a portable museum. Fossils, bones, ancient weapons. Sean was positively dizzy with wonder. He grew rather attached, especially to Dr. Campbell. The feelings were mutual—Howard became Sean's de facto godfather. June and I eventually returned to New York, to our roots. Our children scattered to the winds. Sean attended Sonoma State and made California his permanent home."

"Well, you mention synchronicity. This is more than synchronicity, Dr. Pruitt. I've examined Sean's college essay defending the anthropological work of Campbell and Ryoko. The men exerted a significant influence on him well into adulthood."

"Every step leads a man toward his end."

"It takes a village," I said. "Badja Adeyemi said that Sean pressed him for a position with the project. I note that Campbell and Ryoko are listed as consultants. There's a connection, perhaps?"

Dr. Pruitt nodded.

"Nothing occurs in a vacuum. This valley is rich in folklore, as you can attest. During college, Sean visited Campbell and Ryoko regularly. Became a fixture at the

California villa. Wherever those two reside is known as the villa. He majored in anthropology in homage to their more popular aesthetic. Did nothing with it, sadly. From would-be Livingston to a rent-a-cop."

"Met a girl, got hitched . . ."

"Love snared him. Meanwhile, the doctors traveled extensively, were absent for years at a stretch, and retired to an estate in Massachusetts."

"A bizarre research project, wasn't it?" I said.

"Considering their wingnut record, that's quite a mouthful."

Franz struggled against his leash, determined to investigate a scent trail.

"Come," Dr. Pruitt said. "Let's see where this goes."

■ ■ ■

The dog led us to the perimeter fence, where he victoriously urinated to mark the spot. Reflecting on that last tall cup of joe, I kind of envied Franz.

Murals decorated sections of the fence; accomplished work, vibrant colors muted by the elements and the slow burn of decades. Vaguely Native American renditions of the sun and moon and totems. Some illustrations went darker. Stylized monster birds descended talons-first upon stylized stick-figure men. The grandest and most dreadful of the flock resembled a beautiful winged woman laughing as she brandished a spear. Herds of skeletal black horses stamped and reared and beheaded stick figures. Grotesque skulls (the height of tall trees and disproportionately broad) emerged from mountain caves on stunted legs, waving stunted arms; crowds of stick people bowed in veneration. Seldom-trimmed branches and encroaching brush obscured and defaced the artwork. The fence had struggled to hold off the wilderness for decades and buckled in exhaustion.

"On the ominous side." I indicated a giant monster head. "Your city council had a fever vision in the seventies."

"The Saga of the Terrible Faces. Tourists seldom visit this spot. They are, in fact, discouraged. The mural is for us." He tapped a stickman suspended in the claws of a mountain demon. The demon's maw unhinged in anticipation of its delicacy. "*This* part is you."

"Huh, I look fantastic. What tradition are these illustrations? Seneca? Mohawk?"

"Nothing of the sort."

Several teenagers entered the opposite end of the park. The kids gathered around the backstop. I couldn't discern finer details except that the boys wore crimson letter jackets and the girls wore white and crimson sweaters and bronze skirts; similar to the colors of Valley High, which were red and pale gold. Franz cocked his head. His ears twitched and he growled.

"You live in Horseheads Village," I said to Dr. Pruitt while keeping an eye on the kids. He'd seen them too and was doing his best to pretend otherwise.

"Yes, I rent a studio. June called and said you were by the house. She has confidence in you."

"Kind of her."

"Thank *you* for your civility. My June exhibits the warmth of a freezer."

"She feels similarly about you. What I'm getting at is it's an interesting choice, to meet in this park."

"This is a forgotten place, though it exists in plain sight. No one comes here." He ignored the presence of the high schoolers. "You might profit from the ambiance."

"The ambiance?" I glanced around skeptically.

"Geography shapes the mind. For weal or woe."

"Dickey might've agreed with you."

"Burroughs said of this continent, 'Evil is there, waiting.' Immortal words."

"Those words outlived his wife, no argument."

"I considered anthropology as a major," Dr. Pruitt said. "We are standing upon Vulture Bluff, dubbed for the turkey vulture population's affinity for roosting among the trees." He gestured expansively. "This is the Nameless Field. Native legends aver grass is the only thing that has ever grown here since the Stone Age. It's either a sacred place or cursed."

I didn't inform him I already knew about the vulture part. He enjoyed holding forth, and in that I was sure he and his wife were well suited as a couple.

"Not much of a difference between the holy and the profane," I said. "Although if I were to lay money on who corrupted the scene, I'd lay it on whitey."

"General Sullivan, slaughterer of Indians."

"And equines." I nodded toward the mural's carnivorous black horses. "Was he simply defending himself?"

"Either way, he was a heroic benefactor of the turkey vultures."

"There's an unwelcoming vibe in this neck of the woods."

"You're feeling the oppression of Christian hegemony in conflict with native animism," he said. "Self-righteous, puritanical men seized this land. You're also feeling the eyes of the vultures evaluating the sweet texture of your skin. The eyes of many animals. Animals endure."

"You hate it here."

"I don't hate this valley." He lowered his gaze. "I hate the fuck out of it."

Why did he remain if that's how he felt? Simple—it isn't necessarily love that shackles us to people or places.

"Did Sean and Linda have a strong marriage?"

"Are you asking whether she might've been too eager to collect the insurance money?"

"I'm asking how they got along."

"I'm sure June told you. Sean was a fragile child who grew into a brittle man. No, it wasn't a strong marriage. He left her alone for days at a stretch rather than confront her dissatisfaction. At the end, they fought quite frequently."

"Where'd he go when he abandoned ship?"

"Jeffers Colony," he said. "Seek and ye shall find it on the opposite side of the valley in the hills in the vicinity of Morrow Village."

"I should take a gander. What's there?"

"Deserted houses. Mice. Ghosts."

"Your wife didn't mention it."

"Then it's one more detail of which she remains blissfully unaware."

"She said you adamantly considered his death a closed case. I'm getting a different take."

"I've *never* accepted that Sean's death was his own doing."

His comment caught me off guard.

"Dr. Pruitt, your wife—"

"Believes I'm a coldhearted bastard. We're not *in* love. However, because I love her, I protect her. Try to protect her."

"How do you protect her?"

"Badja paid a man to look around on the QT, two years ago. Detective Griese. He was injured in a street altercation and retired from the investigation midstream. Heavy drinker, I presume. Precisely the kind of thug— no offense—my brother-in-law attracts."

"To be fair," I said, "I don't get the impression many legitimate investigators were clamoring for this job. What happened after Griese dropped the case?"

"Nothing. Badja admonished me to remain patient." He anticipated my next comment. "We didn't inform June or Linda about hiring the detective. The news would've fueled more paranoia. June was erratic, absolutely erratic."

Okay, this might not qualify as a bombshell. It *did* confirm why Adeyemi resorted to hiring me. My detective skills weren't of the slightest concern; he'd valued my potential to play the role of a bull in a china shop. Irresistible force, meet immovable object.

"If I could chat with Mr. Griese—"

"I'll consult my records, forward you the information."

"Thanks. Why didn't you tell your family about the detective? Why conceal your suspicions?"

"This valley and those who own it are capable of terrible deeds when provoked," he said. "June has evidently forced Badja's hand. You're here, conjured, summoned. Pandora's box is opening."

I studied him, gauging his sincerity.

"Is it possible Sean had an enemy? Something not in the file?"

His expression flattened. The sun steadily dropped below the trees and a reddish glow caught in the panes of his glasses.

"I'd be most inclined to scrutinize friends and associates. A seducer, a corrupting influence. Impossible to say if Sean peeked through the keyhole or whether someone, a dweller in the dark, threw the portal wide and ushered him across the threshold." His tone was off. He had definite ideas about who might've "seduced" his darling boy.

"Hit me with names," I said.

He sighed and leaned down and patted his dog. Franz pressed against him, shivering, his gaze riveted on the small crowd. The high school kids had arranged themselves in a line of seven. Four jocks, three cheerleaders. None wore a hat despite the chill. They stood motionless as carvings. The presentation disquieted me because I didn't understand what it meant. It annoyed me because I knew that was the point of the exercise.

Dr. Pruitt continued to dismiss their existence.

"June says that Badja knew what he was getting when he hired you."

"Time will tell, sir. It always does."

I rolled my neck and shoulders and ambled toward the students in their battle line.

"Wait," he said. "You don't want to fool with them."

Oh, but I did.

Franz growled. He barked ferociously. I glanced back; the dog reared on his hind legs, barely restrained, lunging and snapping at the air. The sun was nearly down and the light in the trees congealed. Dusk tightened on the surrounding woods like a lover grasping a fistful of hair.

"Those aren't children," Dr. Pruitt called over the barking and snarling. I *think* that's what he said.

Among my hidden talents is the ability to move quickly without seeming to increase stride. I rushed the group and it broke apart before I'd covered a dozen steps. Five drifted for the gate. A cheerleader and her guy pal stayed put until I'd closed within a few yards. Their uniforms were antiquated and the mascot was wrong—instead of a cartoon horsehead, it was the silhouette of a horse skull, except stretched and sinuous, curving back upon itself, jaws snapping at its own trailing spinal cord. The pair laughed at me, clasped hands, and split. I let them go. Debatable whether I could've caught them anyhow. Fleet as deer.

Dr. Pruitt was right. They weren't kids.

CHAPTER THIRTEEN

American gangster lore delights to depict the mob as an unstoppable force. A capo sends his goons to beat on a guy; they beat on a guy. Capo decides it's curtains for a schlub; the schlub eats a bullet. That's well and good, except not everybody who's gotten crossways with the Family sits around waiting to catch a beating or an ice pick to the spine. People hide. People fight back. More people resist than you might think. Often, it doesn't help much in the end, and yet it happens.

The Buffalo arm of the Outfit took a cut from traffic in Elmira and the satellite towns, albeit haphazardly. So much for the good old days. The mafia foothold in the north had radically declined since 1980. Pressure from the Feds, Russian mobs, and Native American gangs figured into that decline of splendor. The Family concentrated its activities on the City of Lights, the Great Lakes, and smuggling contraband across the Canadian border in cooperation with foreign criminal syndicates.

The Redlicks were the closest thing to a stable organized crime presence in Horseheads, and they had nothing to do with street-level work. Crooked deals went down in smoky back rooms and alleys, same as it ever was, but only a few loosely affiliated thugs exploited the market. Made my task a little more difficult since there wasn't a central authority figure to lean on. So, I leaned on whoever didn't scuttle away before I got my hands on them. Typical PI jobs are tedious because rich dirtbags and average joes require subtler tactics; they're a protected class, as it were. Street- and trailer-park-level scum are cake. Traditionally, I've strong-armed hustlers and pimps with impunity. Who will they complain to in the absence of a syndicate? The cops? City hall?

All week as I interviewed the faculty, I'd scoped the situation at Valley High, on the prowl for the resident lowlifes and drug dealers. Located three blocks south of a dying shopping center, the school occupied a hill overlooking town. The sprawling campus was on the seedy side. It hadn't been completely renovated since the 1950s or '60s; planners kept adding wings and ancillary structures willy-nilly throughout the decades. Kind of rundown, kind of weary, and overcrowded. Budget shortfalls forced frequent school closures, and the bulk of student consolidation fell to Valley High.

Lunch period bell signaled a stream of kids plodding to and from the shopping center. Same spot each day, a blue 2000 Camaro parked on the street near an exit with a clear view and a potential head start on converging security, not that security could be bothered. A bunch of kids visited the driver. He let the more adventuresome girls sit in the car with him as he doled out his wares. I bribed a passing sophomore to fill me in on the details. Confirmed that it was what I thought before rushing in half-cocked. My nerves were still raw from my visit to Vulture Bluff the previous afternoon.

I waited for a lull, then walked over to the Camaro's owner as he sat on the hood, smoking a hand-rolled cigarette. Under thirty, lanky, and built for flight. Spendy wraparound shades NBA stars were promoting. Light insulated jacket, unbuttoned to display his gold chains and tats. Track pants and matching sneakers. Drug-money shoes. The car windows were rolled down and the stereo cranked an eclectic selection of hip-hop and gangster rap.

"Hey, Superfly. Got a minute?"

"No." He dragged and then blew smoke in my face. "You a cop or somethin'?"

"Has life ever been so kind?"

"I don't know you. Don't wanna. Keep steppin'."

I glanced around, sidled in nice and intimate, and showed him the pistol under my coat.

"Well, maybe you've got less time than that."

"You crazy? You wouldn't shoot me, homes—"

I rapped the top of Superfly's dome with my brass knuckles. His shades fell off.

"Why would I shoot you when I can slap you around until my arm gets tired?"

Here's something real: Don't buy the jive about violence as a last resort because *I'm better than that.* No. Violence is only a last resort when it's a last resort. Realistically, it's often a first, second, or middle resort. The Superflys of the world speak the language fluently. Besides, hitting a jerk feels good. It *has* to feel good, or else I wouldn't be able to stomach it. That dopamine rush I'd gotten addicted to in the Outfit was difficult to kick, so I weaned myself slowly.

He struggled to compose himself. Tears streamed from his bloodshot eyes. I left him, reached through the passenger window, and dug around in the glove box until I found some fast-food napkins. I gave him the napkins. Good call—blood trickled down his temple and dripped into his ear.

"Thanks, homes." Superfly rubbed his eyes and blew his nose. He leaned back and exhaled with a full-body shudder. "What can I do you for is what I meant to say."

I wanted to know who ran prostitutes, who ran drugs, who made book. Who'd supplied the Jeffers Project?

"The what?"

"Big hole drilling to China, twenty, thirty minutes north. Are your brains scrambled? Should I hit you again? Second knock in the head usually does the trick . . ."

"Oh, you mean the Dig. Man, that's old news. Place is boarded up and everybody's gone."

"Yet, very much alive in your heart. I guess you must've just missed the opportunity to cash in, huh? You were in school."

"I graduated Valley that summer."

"Wow, you're a Valley High product," I said. "Putting that diploma through its paces too. The alumni committee is undoubtedly beaming with pride. Maybe you met Sean Pruitt. He's the guy who fell in that hole before it was closed."

"Nah, man. I mean, I heard of him."

"Darn it, you're not much help. Where do I go? Who do I speak with?"

Several girls came near, chatting and giggling. Very young. One still wore braces.

"Go on, bitches!" He shooed them. "Bitches, I see you tomorrow!" They moved along with reproachful expressions. "Yeah, I got a couple of names. I don't know what they know. Feel me? I don't vouch for shit. Ask them whatever you want."

He gave up a couple of individuals higher up the food chain.

"Thanks, homie. Another thing." I described the group of "teens" in their archaic uniforms.

"Where did you see them? Up to the field? Nobody ever sees them."

"Vulture Bluff?" I said.

"Vulture Bluff. That's where they go when they . . ." He cast unhappy glances over both shoulders.

"Who are *they*?"

He became squirmier, as if he'd forgotten I could add more lumps to his noggin at my leisure.

"One dude used to be a cop or something. Another ran a construction company. The spooky cheerleader bitches had family money or fat-cat husbands. Did dominatrix shit on the down low. Freaky as fuck."

"You're yanking my chain," I said.

"This is what people say. I bet you won't never see them again. Nah, bro. They're ghosts, urban legends, whatever."

"Yeah? And?"

"And what? Man, this is bullshit—"

I made a fist around the brass knuckles.

"They belong to . . ." He massaged his head, frowning as he searched for the word. "A club? No! A fraternity. Fuckin' fraternity. Called the Mares."

"The Mares?"

"I didn't pick the name, homes."

"Who gets in?"

"The beautiful people. People of means. It's exclusive."

"Not you?"

"Hell no!"

"Sell them dope?"

"Freaks got their own supply. Got their own kicks." By "kicks" he meant perversions. "Hang meat in the woods; bury mason jars of cow's blood. Won't eat the meat until it falls on the ground. Drink the blood curdled by the dark of the moon. Heard it's called greening. The rotten-meat trip. Greening."

"Sounds a bit out there," I said.

"They're into Indian shit. Dancing naked in the woods. Performing rituals. Heap bad medicine." He laughed nervously at his own joke.

"Except it's not native, is it? Bunch of soft white folks

playing games. Fake voodoo. Fake satanism. These parts, it's fake shamanism, huh?"

Superfly was antsier by the second.

"We through here?"

"We through," I said.

CHAPTER FOURTEEN

The bowling alley's crimson-and-royal-yellow marquee had fallen to pieces. OWLING AL Y remained. Good enough. Distinct 1980s vibe and odor. Brick walls that partially absorbed every lackadaisical paint job. Rippled, uneven floors; tiles worn and chipped. Carpet, where it hadn't come untacked, was stained with continental maps of alternate realities. Flat, diffuse lighting. I'm not any great shakes at bowling, although, like most Americans, I've whiled away a few hours down at the lane. In my teen years, it was expressly to hang with the posse and maybe meet girls. Latter days, such as today, found me there because it was the destination of choice for low-rent criminals.

This represented a potentially beautiful shortcut for my intelligence-gathering mission. Mini-kingpins who operate legitimate fronts, such as motels, hotels, restaurants, supermarkets, and bowling alleys, not only swim with the denizens of the underworld, they rub shoulders with everybody else.

Two fogies in baggy shirts and sweats were rolling the rock to mellow pop hits of yesteryear. Neither appeared overly happy to be alive and bowling on a winter's afternoon. Well past lunch, the young guy at the counter said the grill was closed. No dogs, no pretzels, no nachos, nothing. He could pull me a soda, if I wanted. I said I was there to see the Boss Man. The kid said the Boss Man wasn't available as I walked toward a door with an EMPLOYEES ONLY sign.

"Sir, you can't go back there!" He wrung his bony hands. He couldn't have foreseen how lingering in Horseheads after graduation might present such quandaries.

"I do as I please and I do it all the time."

■ ■ ■

On the other side of the door lay a corridor, a tiny bathroom, a closet, a supply room, and a windowless office. Boss Man stoically observed my arrival from behind a surprisingly neat metal desk. A balding fellow in a red and yellow BOWLING ALLEY T-shirt and the weight of the world on his shoulders. To his right was a much older man. Flabby, suspenders, nose buried in the local paper. He didn't get excited when I appeared.

I plopped into an uncomfortable swivel chair. Boss Man waited bemusedly as I studied the plethora of bowling trophies, bowling plaques, and posters and photographs chockablock full of bowlers and bowling teams.

There were a disquieting number of "businessman of the year" and "our school loves this guy" certificates littering the walls.

"Hi," I said when I finished. "Is this really called the Bowling Alley?"

"Sure is. To whom do I owe the pleasure?"

"I'd hope you can guess my name."

That elicited a pained smile.

"Mick Jagger's bag man? A hazard to my health and well-being, is who. Buffalo used to send guys like you to collect."

"You're as close to a capo as this burg has," I said. "Makes you the man I need to chew the fat with."

"Woo."

"I dig those arcade machines on the main floor. Galaga. Galaxian. Joust. Ms. Pac-Man. Space Invaders. Golden oldies. If I had a nickel for every quarter I lost . . ."

He flipped the top on a box of mints and put one into his mouth. He glanced over at Tubby and clacked the lid shut, hard. Tubby folded his paper. He rose with some effort and waddled away.

Boss Man returned his attention to me.

"We got a few more. Those are the popular games. Girls like the claw cranes with the toy prizes. Guys like to pow-pow-pow." He made finger guns.

"Anybody else in town have machines?"

"Quickstop over on Tenth has an Asteroids clone."

"The mall?"

"Video game parlor's gone. Most of the mall is gone.

The theater in there has a couple shit games. I've been here twenty-three years. Got an industry connection. Be a gravy little sideline, but the home console racket is a pain in the ass."

"Basically, this is it if you want to come plug a few quarters into a game and chill." I laced my fingers together behind my head. "Between here and your boy staking out the high school, you've got a monopoly on the teenage dime-bag market."

"*My* boy? Ah, that punk's mouth is so big I'm surprised he doesn't fall in."

"Isn't it the truth? My day, you didn't talk until they chopped the third finger."

Boss Man gave his head a small, warning jerk. I swiveled and saw the counter kid sneaking up with a steel mallet in his hand.

"Jeff, it's cool," Boss Man said.

The kid stopped dead. He pivoted and sailed away like a duck in a shooting gallery when it's dinged. Boss Man rummaged in a drawer. He retrieved a bottle of cheap whiskey and two unsavory shot glasses.

"Apologies. He's on parole. Killer Jeff. Can we skip the brutality and take a snort?"

"Can we?" I said, genuinely curious. He was older, a pillar of the community. He'd have the lay of the land, I hoped.

Boss Man poured.

"To old money and young women. But what do I know? I'm a cash conduit and my girlfriend looks like Christopher Lee in the morning."

"Here's a counter-toast: Stop carrying whiskey glasses with your fingers on the inside, you fucking heathen!"

We drank.

"I'll sing you a tune," he said. "Hell with protocol. I'm not even interested in having the *first* finger chopped."

"We'll see. Sean Pruitt."

"The security guard who offed himself at the collider site. Don't know anything about that."

"Yes, but did you know Sean?"

"He came in here. All the kids do, though." A cagey light shone in his eyes. "That why you're in town? Sean P's suicide?"

"We positive it was suicide?"

Boss Man spread his hands and did an Alfred E. Neuman shrug.

"Told you; I don't know shit from Shinola about that."

"He a customer?" I pantomimed smoking.

"Uh-uh. Not directly. His friends were and he got it from them. He came in here to bowl, grab a burger. The regular stuff. Sweet kid, to tell the truth. I'm sorry he fell into the pit, or whatever."

"Indeed, whatever. Got a theory?"

"I don't have an opinion." He noted the threatening shift in my posture. "Easy, easy. I *know* what it says on the tin—he jumped and took a nosedive. Everybody got paid. Everybody's happy. There's always rumors to the contrary. Conspiracy theories, right? He was suicidal. He saw something he shouldn't have; he was fucking the wrong gal—"

"Or she was fucking the wrong guy and they iced hubby for the insurance money."

"Yeah, I heard that one too. Who wouldn't contemplate snagging a cool million by hook or by crook? Then there's the plain vanilla theory—industrial accidents happen. He tripped over his shoelaces. The end."

"What's your favorite?"

"I tend to believe what's in front of me and doesn't cause headaches. Cops say he tossed himself over."

"Ever meet the wife? Linda?"

"Nope."

"The Jeffers Project," I said, ticking off my list.

"The Redlick Boondoggle. Money was sweet until it dried up. What'd the town get? Clear-cut land and a bunch of rusting shacks. Yeah, and a big ol' hole."

"You have customers on-site when the project was going great guns? A few? A lot? Any of them harbor interesting opinions on the Pruitt matter?"

"Course I had customers," he said. "Goddamned boomtown. Made a shitload of dollars. Man you want to speak with is Lenny Herzog. Batty old guy was in charge of general maintenance at the Jeffers Colony. Herzog is the caretaker. He lives in the hills west of here, past Morrow Village and Buck Springs. Every fella out there has a gun and a dog. Not a man jack of them will like the cut of your jib."

"Let's discuss the Redlicks—"

"Gonna stop you there, chief. Redlicks pay the freight in Horseheads."

"The Redlick Group, then."

"Redlick family, Redlick Group. Difference without a distinction."

As casually as I could, I mentioned the Mares and observed his expression. Less thrilling or revealing than I'd hoped. More surprised than anything else.

"Wowsers. How'd you hear about the Mares of Thrace?"

"Ah, *that's* the whole title. I saw them on Vulture Bluff."

"People born here go their whole lives and not catch hide or hair of those ones. Don't like to be seen. You spot them in costume, it's what they wanted."

"So, give me the lowdown."

"Goofy fuckers."

"Obviously. Any of them frequent your fine establishment?"

He hesitated, weighing his words.

"Three or four years ago, a man and a woman in those throwback costumes they wear came in off the street and wandered around. Five minutes before closing. Place was empty except for me and the janitor. The couple didn't say boo. Just grinned and walked to the trash and dug in there for the spoiled hamburger patties. They chowed down on the way out the door. I recognized the guy from around. He thanked me for the 'provender' and laughed."

"Huh, some of the rumors are true," I said. Superfly had mentioned the "kids" had a penchant for rotten meat and worse. "This is the village temple. What do the peasants make of these folks?"

"You got your Civil War reenactors and dorks who wear chainmail for medieval fairs. The Mares relive their high school glory years while speaking in tongues and sacrificing animals and getting bombed out of their gourds. Religious insanity."

"Greek mythology," I said. "Hercules stole the Mares of King Diomedes as one of his Twelve Labors. Matter of fact, Alexander the Great claimed his horse, Bucephalus, descended from those mares. Probably a goddamned lie, but it sounded bitchin'."

Boss Man gave me a blank look. Classical history wasn't his bag.

"Are members of the society all Valley High grads?" I said.

"Who knows? Not me. Once in a blue moon some tourist asks how to contact them. Gonna be honest. That's fucking unsettling."

He and I were in agreement on that count.

"Admittedly, I don't have much experience in this area. I've watched a ton of Italian giallo and devil movies from the seventies. This kind of shit is never good." I opened a notebook and clicked my pen. "Hit me."

"Listen, chief, this would only be hearsay. It's not like they got a public roster."

"Do your best. I'm easy."

He named names.

"Tom Mandibole?" I underlined the name and glanced up from the notebook. "*The* Tom Mandibole?"

"He works for the Redlick Group. He *is* a Redlick, as a point of order."

"The company mouthpiece? Snappy dresser, grins maniacally?"

"The very one. Rides around in a midnight-black Bentley. Before he went to work for the RG, he did theater and television. Comedy clubs. I saw a video of his comedy act. Wasn't funny." Boss Man lowered his voice in reverence. "He did a ventriloquism routine with a dummy on each knee. Camera pans in tight, and he's slathered on makeup and prosthetics so he's a dummy too. Fucking life-size."

"Back up. He's a member of this society? Mr. Personality?"

"The main man. Tom's busy globetrotting for the RG. Redlicks raised him, although he was in boarding school mainly. Gerald Redlick's dad fostered him as an orphan. No secret there, or anything." He hesitated. "Tom is pleasant. I mean, yeah, pleasant, but weird."

"You think?" I said, picturing Mandibole in pancake makeup and a tight letter jacket. Brrr. "This crowd is somewhere to the right of weird."

"Each to his own. Not mine to judge."

I estimated this interview to have reached the juncture of diminishing returns.

"You're going to rat me out to Mandibole, or whomever, thirty seconds after I leave, aren't you?" It was a rhetorical question. The powers-that-be wouldn't be powers-that-be if a goon could indefinitely schlep around their territory causing a ruckus and not attract attention.

"Dude, I'm making that call before you make it down the hall."

"Be that way. While you're at it, tell whom it may concern I'd like a sit-down."

Boss Man raised his brows.

"Really?"

I placed my hand over my heart.

"It's my fondest wish."

"I'll pass it along."

I thanked him for not making me shut his hand in a desk drawer and left.

■ ■ ■

Tubby had replaced Jeff at the counter. He lowered his paper.

"Hope you got what you wanted."

I laid down a five-dollar bill.

"Every little bit helps. Quarters, please."

"Push and push until you hit a brick wall." He made a small pile of change instead of bothering to stack it. "The brick wall falls on you." He clapped once and made a brush-off motion, like Pontius Pilate's second move.

"Doesn't sound very pleasant."

He raised the paper.

"We'll cover the hole and go about our lives. Always do."

I walked over to the Galaga machine and sacrificed fifty cents into the slot. The screen dissolved from the credits to its game face. Be cool to say that the teen reflexes were there to pair with the thrill of nostalgia. Wishful thinking. Those two quarters were burnt in under a minute. Clink-clank went another pair down the chute and into Boss Man's pocket. I died and I died. Oh, but to be a kid again. That's the advantage of adulthood, though. I no longer possessed the skill, or the extra lives, but I had lots of quarters.

CHAPTER FIFTEEN

The Jeffers Project portfolio was voluminous. Badja Adeyemi had pulled a double fistful of strings to appropriate confidential corporate and government records. I emailed Ted for assistance. We plundered the database until she uncovered an innocuous folder containing the vital statistics of the Jeffers Colony: names and numbers of administrators (no roll of occupants, alas), and, fortuitously, contact information for Lenny Herzog, the caretaker Boss Man mentioned. I asked her to run a background check on Herzog and report ASAP.

Next, I tried contacting Dr. Pruitt. The overeducated shithead obviously wanted me to encounter the Mares of Thrace. But why, unless he thought they had some connection to Sean's death? He artfully dodged my calls and when I stopped by his apartment for a surprise visit, a neighbor informed me the good doctor had jetted off to Europe to spend the holidays with relatives. What timing!

Supper at a greasy spoon, then a phone call to Meg

and Devlin. The boy stressed over a class project due before winter vacation. He denied procrastinating on the assignment for several weeks and informed me I needed to get home pronto to help him put it together. I assured him that I could work miracles with construction paper and glue sticks. Meg got back on the line and said, better you than me, be home soon or else. It warmed my heart that she unconsciously referred to her place, and my being there, as home. I asked how the boy was doing and she sighed and said he hadn't kicked anyone's ass lately. She sounded relaxed, which meant I'd caught her at a good time—the second glass of wine.

After she signed off, I clicked the boob tube for my evening dose. Five seconds later, Dr. Pruitt texted the vitals of the investigator who'd previously quit the case. Rod Griese out of an office in Buffalo. I passed this along to Red McLaren and requested that he huddle with Adeyemi's lawyer and get to the bottom of Griese's dossier, and what, if anything, he'd discovered.

News anchors recited a litany of absurdist tragedy with a familiar refrain—people were shooting one another by the gross; tensions among various countries continued to intensify amid saber-rattling; the world burned, but not to worry, water was rising fast. I cried uncle and went facedown for the count.

■ ■ ■

At Meg's urging to "get in touch with your mother's blood," I'd reacquainted myself with the rich tapestry of

Maori culture and mythology. In the U.S. of A., every youngster learns of Alexander, Thor, and Zeus. Sleeping Beauty, Rumpelstiltskin, and Oberon's court. Kids here are steeped in the cult of Clint Eastwood, John Wayne, and *The Catcher in the Rye*. Having swallowed enough of that for this particular rotation of the grand cosmic wheel, I made it a practice to range farther afield. A humble beginning, yet it awakened a network of sleeping nerves with pinpricks of sublimated awareness.

This renaissance didn't occur in a vacuum. During childhood, I'd visited my Maori grandfather, Hone, in New Zealand and listened to his garrulous recounting of wartime exploits as we reposed in his weedy backyard beneath the stars. Mom had also imparted a bit of the ancient lore upon us Coleridge kids in the guise of bedtime stories; the CliffsNotes version of her heritage.

Mom and her kin believed that souls wander at night. Dreams represent fragments of what the dreamer experiences while roving in astral form. She further held that when some people die, their souls twist and congeal and become inimical to the living. Whether these persons were good or evil in life is of no consequence; it is a matter of fortune and susceptibility. The vulnerable souls become their worst selves, condemned to haunt the earth and make trouble until they slip through a crack and plunge into the Underworld, where the Lord of the Dead waits to eat them.

Such jolly thoughts of darkness and the uncanny haunted me in the wake of my conversation with Dr. Pruitt. They spelled troubled dreams. My soul got a second wind and a-wandering it went. Old gods Papa, Rangi, Tane, and Whiro beckoned.

The dream began as a memory of my childhood. Mom sent me to fetch Dad; we were going to a barbecue at a friend's house. Barbecues and house parties dominated that stretch of my parents' social life. It was predictable as the tides and the phases of celestial bodies. He boozed with his male colleagues while Mom suffered small talk with the women in the kitchen. Sometimes there was an argument and public recriminations. Sometimes he or she would get a tad physical and voices would be raised. Stony expressions and frigid silence on the drive home. I could scarcely contain my enthusiasm.

On this occasion, Dad laired in the garage, sliding a Green River knife across a whetstone.

Is it sharp? I said to show interest; a cub desperate to bond with his grizzled sire.

He delicately tapped the blade's edge. *Yeah, buddy. Sharp enough to split an atom. By the way, and this information will come in handy sooner or later, you happen to get the drop on a fellow, remember there's a major artery in the anus. One poke and a twist, and that's all she wrote.*

I thanked him and said I'd remember. He was a prophet when it came to the bad stuff.

I used to say, bury me in a cave or in a ziggurat. The knife *shicked* back and forth across the whetstone. *Bury me with a two-headed dog who will be my servant in the afterlife. Welcome, my son, to the afterlife. This purple-and-black wasteland is purgatory.* The white light in the window dimmed and clotted. *Beat it, kid. I'm getting this ready for a friend*. He dismissed me, enraptured by the knife and what it could do for him.

Tom Mandibole materialized from a patch of gloom near the furnace. Smooth and plastic-faced, clad in his ivory jumpsuit and smiling carnivorously. He and Dad regarded one another like gunfighters ready to skin their shooting irons. Dad said something in a foreign language and held the big knife loosely in his lead hand, tip in line with the dandy's heart. Mandibole answered with the atonal snarl of circuits scrambling. They rushed to meet in the center of the garage. Dad, charging like a bull; Mandibole, mincing and prancing with the grace of a tarantula.

Rather than reporting to Mom, I chose a different path. A wooden security door led to the yard. In life the door was pale white, but in this place the wood had blackened as if by flames. An elderly Sean Pruitt, dressed in a Valley High School letter jacket, stood at the threshold with the posture of a doorman. He'd plastered pancake makeup and eyeshadow to create a façade of youth. He didn't open the door, but gestured for me to step into a void. Brushing past him, I marked the crimson and bronze colors and the heavy stitching of his jacket, the diabolic horsehead skull that symbolized I knew not what. He wore a class ring forged of iron and set with a ruby in the jaws of the horse skull. The metal ring had broken to form a notch with jagged teeth. Sean Pruitt made a fist. Blood dripped steadily between his fingers onto his tennis shoe.

I passed over. A symphonic gong intoned over the

heat of a low, crackling fire. A choir of sirens sang a lingering note of lust and mourning. The song led me into manhood and the second, worse, chapter of the dream.

■ ■ ■

Centuries before European colonists decreed it New Zealand, New Zealand was named Aotearoa by Polynesian settlers. I strode across a grassy plain, marching inland. The sky was the dark green of pre-industrial reality, and obsidian where it bled into the vacuum. Red light glowed on my flank. Dust and smoke towered above a wilderness consumed by an inferno. Moa birds darted around me, talons churning the earth as they fled for their lives. Farther off, tribal hunters shouted and clashed metal upon metal, driving their quarry onward.

A million flies whined and that whine resolved to a terrible voice roaring my name. It sounded a lot like Badja Adeyemi on an infernal bullhorn. The voice drew my astral self over a despoiled expanse of burnt stumps, toward a forbidding peak, and into the lambent pink eye socket of a titan's skull. I entered the banquet hall of an old-timey stone longhouse. Fire pits, heads on spears, animal skins tossed like throw rugs, and violent murals daubed in red and yellow ochre.

Whiro, dread god of the underworld, reclined at the end of a banquet table. He wore a black suit and a spiked Rolex. His features roiled; a thundercloud constantly reshaping itself. My grandfather's eyes; Dad's hawkish nose; the Croatoan's barbed grin. He inspected platters heaped with human limbs, ears, and eyeballs. Music filtered in from a nearby oubliette; damned souls shrieking.

Welcome to the black kaleidoscope. You can see it all from here. Whiro daintily selected a severed thumb and popped it into his mouth. He chewed. *Dexter Smith, mobster CPA. You commended his soul to my banquet in 1998.* He snapped a radius to expose its marrow. *Nigel Cooper, money launderer, also in '98. Too bad—the punk could've helped you unload that cursed treasure you're sitting on.* He slurped from a clay bowl. *Your blood, Isaiah, is sweeter than the rest. I love your style, kiddo. You make me proud. Truly, don't go changing.*

Charnel rot wafted from the pit. My gut churned.

What do you want? I feared I already knew.

We're peas in a pod, Isaiah. The whine of the flies increasingly tinged his voice. *Flesh of my flesh. A finger-puppet acting out my whims on earth. Your man-at-arms is a savvy fellow. Whip smart. He says you're dead. Dead man walking, perhaps. Angels and devils circle you like vultures. The vultures as well, soon.*

I reached for a weapon, like scratching an itch. No luck—I wore boxers and was empty-handed. Ash smeared my body. Ash clogged my nose and throat. Cherry-bright flakes of ash floated into the longhouse. The moas cried on the wind as they burned.

Whiro's laughter snarled in my right ear, then the left, then both at once.

O, to become an old man bent double by guilt.

Achilles, my loyal hound, crept from the wings and

crouched near the black god's feet. The dog's regal skull was caked in blood and cleft by the impact of a long fall onto rocks. He'd died as a consequence of my negligence, my arrogance. My good boy showed his broken fangs and drooled. Lose the love of friends and family, alas, alack. Lose the love of your dog, you've lost everything.

The floor crumbled; I plummeted through cotton clouds toward a lake. The lake was a shimmering opal. A shadow at the bottom of the lake solidified into my mother, large as a goddess. Half a lifetime ago, Dad brained her and claimed self-defense. Kill or be killed, he'd said. I couldn't be certain of the truth. Both were capable of violence. They'd made me, hadn't they?

The symphonic gong chimed and chimed.

Mom regarded my meteoric descent. Her lips parted into a soundless shriek that boiled the water and engulfed me in a wave of abject rage. The shock wave stripped my flesh to bone, powdered the bone, and I dissolved into the waking world; the world of the unreal and the impermanent.

■ ■ ■

Another day of knocking on office doors and putting the lean on friends, colleagues, and old, tenuous acquaintances of Sean Pruitt. Ted texted the address of Lenny Herzog, custodian to the Jeffers Colony. A relatively short drive, but located in a sketchy rural neighborhood. I tabled that interview and headed home in the midafternoon, grateful for a long weekend, even if it meant glue, scissors, and, God love me, glitter, in service of an elementary school project. That evening, I rubbed Meg's feet and stared at whatever movie played on TV without registering the meaning of the images.

Somewhere along the line, I shook off the stupor and actually processed that it was a news report about the disappearance of Malaysia Airlines Flight 370 and the thousands upon thousands of man-hours of investigation that unraveled certain aspects of the mysterious tragedy while deepening others.

Despite the incompetence and the lies of a corrupt Malaysian government, some semblance of the truth emerged. Forensic detectives, psychologists, intelligence operatives, and armchair detectives played a communal role in piecing together the puzzle. We can imagine that the senior pilot depressurized the plane and killed every passenger and colleague. We cannot imagine why he perpetrated this unspeakable act. Upon going silent, MH370 continued at cruising altitude for over six hours before "presumably" crashing into the Indian Ocean. Ah, but those six long hours she was a ghost plane, for all intents and purposes . . .

I've seen and committed my share of dark deeds. I can't decide whether it's a comfort that the enormity of some actions remains inconceivable, even to a guy who made a career of evil. There's always something worse, something beyond the scope of our experience. This was one.

At the credits, Meg switched to the true-crime channel, where a police detective monotoned the particulars of a case that was proven by science, and twelve inconvenienced citizens, to be a gruesome crime of vengeance. An adolescent boy emptied a handgun magazine into his stepdad's head as retaliation for real or imagined abuse.

She didn't cut a glance at me. I felt the weight of her regard anyway, hot as a branding iron. I'm sure this was firmly categorized as "inconceivable" in her mind alongside the ghost flight. I dared not admit that, yes, the plane crash was a tragedy perpetrated by an evil person, but, baby, I kind of see the kid's point of view.

PART II

JOHN HENRY IN THE PIT

CHAPTER SIXTEEN

I returned to Horseheads on Sunday night and hit the bunk at a reasonable hour, vowing to get plodding bright and early. Hotel Roan was quite pleased to book me into the very same room I'd recently inhabited. I've always been a generous tipper—graft and wanton largesse are the Outfit way—and with a pocketful of Adeyemi's dough, I was practically Daddy Warbucks.

■ ■ ■

The decision of the dreary gray morning: Buttonhole Lenny Herzog or go patrolling the byways of town searching for knuckleheads? Herzog could keep for another day.

Ted called as I sat in the hotel restaurant sipping a second cup of coffee; Buffalo detective Rod Griese waited on the line. Ted patched him through and we chatted. Griese put the T in "terse." Stated upfront this was a courtesy, nothing more because there wasn't anything to tell.

He'd obeyed Adeyemi's strict instructions to avoid the Pruitts unless he discovered anything contrary to the police report, which, due to the infancy of his investigation, he had not. No sense riling Mom or Dad, et cetera, et cetera.

Griese worked on the case for two weeks, mostly by phone. Phase two mirrored my own activities; he visited Horseheads and interviewed several people. The second night, while unwinding at a bar, he scuffled with a guy over a spilled drink. No biggie, or so he assumed. Later, he was crossing the street when a car with its lights off blindsided him. Busted both legs. The driver made a clean getaway. End of detective career, end of story. His new gig as a realtor was boring and safe. Griese said good luck and goodbye.

Onward then.

Boss Man's list of Mares of Thrace members comprised three locations, rather than names. A bakery, a beauty parlor, and an electronics warehouse. The bakery was a burned shell. Somebody left an oven on and poof. Nobody at the warehouse knew anything except that the security guy came in much later. Finally, I asked around at the corner beauty parlor. Forty bucks and a convivial manner secured intelligence on the retired beautician, Nancy. The guy on duty warned me that Nancy was flakier than Grandma's pie crust. I declined the offer of a manicure.

Nancy the Beautician lived in a public housing community not far from a park with a small pond at its center. A spiffy paved walkway encircled the pond. Couples in winter gear strolled, some pushing baby carriages, some walking their dogs. Many of the dogs were decked out in classy sweaters. Hardier people power-walked the circle. Others had the superior idea—they loitered on benches, watching the water, or tossing crumbs to the marauding gangs of pigeons. Nancy the Beautician sat at the end of one such bench while the pigeons strutted around her ankles, fruitlessly appealing for a handout. She was a petite woman, silvery wisps of hair plucked from beneath her shawl by the chilly breeze. Somewhere between a matron and a grandmother. She wore a wool coat. I'd last seen her in a cheerleader uniform in the company of a smarmy middle-aged upperclassman. Her mien wasn't a pallid flat-affect mask today. Her cheeks were rosy and she smiled at me with human warmth rather than the reflexive jaw movements of a predatory animal.

"Hi, Nancy," I said.

"Darn it. You found me." She didn't register any familiarity, nor was she alarmed by the approach of a large, dark man. "Your hair is lovely. So thick and lustrous. It isn't even graying. White people have to sacrifice their firstborn to get hair like yours! You'll keep it until you're very, very old."

"Uh, how kind—"

"But your hands! Your scarified hands! My goodness, those poor ham hocks are positively nicked to bits."

"The Lord giveth, the Lord taketh. Ma'am, I'm a detective. Perhaps you could answer a couple of questions."

"A real detective. Like Angela Lansbury and Tom

Selleck. Where's your fedora? Where's your greatcoat? You don't even have a mustache. May I see your ID, please?"

I passed her my identification.

"Did you know a young man named Sean Pruitt?" I said while she squinted at my card.

"Know him? I coveted him." She relinquished my card. "Sean was a cutie pie."

"Was he your client?"

"Heavens, no. He worked with Frederick. Frederick may have had a thing for him too."

"The Mares of Thrace. Would you tell me what that is, exactly?"

"The Mares? Horses are sweaty, dreadful beasts. Lost my granddaughter to one. Kicked her in the head. Maddened because they eat flesh. Especially the mares."

"You're probably right. What of Sean? Was he a member?"

"Wish I could tell you, Mr. Detective. Would any respectable club have that boy? He wasn't one hundred percent right in the noggin. Saddest boy in town. Clubs want happy people. Not sad sacks."

She reached into her purse and brought forth red lipstick in a silver tube. She applied the lipstick thickly, her eyes on mine as she did so. Done, her lips were blood-red, like she'd rooted in a pile of fresh meat. She smacked her lips.

I gave her a thumbs-up.

"Mr. Detective," Nancy the Beautician said. "Mr. Detective, I certainly hope I helped you." She stood and inclined her head toward me. "Sean is dead, Mr. Detective. Worst kind of dead. The no-comebacks type of dead."

I maintained a bland expression, trying not to let on that my skin wanted to crawl away.

"Do you have any idea what happened, ma'am?"

She made her fingers into claws and lightly kneaded my shoulders through the suit. Her nails were jet-black. Her hands were much stronger than they appeared. Little meat hooks.

"Those are prison muscles. Lose thirty pounds, you wouldn't have to hide that body under a suit." She shuddered and her eyes rolled to the whites and back. She lowered her arms and smirked coyly. "Yes, yes, I can tell the fate of simpering Sean Pruitt. He was dropped down a well. That's how it's done with unwanted children who won't be happy. The leeches drank his blood. The worms had his flesh. His soul was conducted at light speed along the coil. His soul is either in heaven or hell. Same for you, same for me."

"Ma'am—"

"Move along, Mr. Detective. You're wanted in the main house." She gestured. "The hounds are here to fetch you. See? See?"

I glanced around. No one of note. My phone rang and her smile broadened.

"Mr. Coleridge," a man said. "I'm going to give you an address. Lunch is at high noon. We put on quite a spread. Don't be late."

If I knew what was good for me was strongly implied.

CHAPTER SEVENTEEN

If life were a shifting maze in a violent video game, the Redlick mansion was the last zone in Horseheads I'd want to land in. In game terms, it would be the lair of a dangerous beast. Hydra, Minotaur, Cyclops. The founding fathers' quarter of town, behind an ivy-lashed wall and a few acres of cultivated grounds. Old money, old house, closing in on a century and a half of plaster and paint facelifts. Marble pillars, leaded glass bay windows. Dormers and minarets; you get the picture. I'm sure the Olympic swimming pool, squash court, and helicopter pad were out back near the polo field.

I pulled in behind a classic black Bentley. Al Capone–looking gangster ride. A valet collected my vehicle. No one patted me down for weapons. I'd left my tools in the car anyway. He escorted me into the mansion. I was compelled to think of it as a mansion. Far too expansive and casually grandiose to be referred to as a mere house. Chandeliers dominated the vaulted foyer. Exquisitely paneled doors at every turn.

I was escorted to an antechamber and instructed to wait for Mr. Mandibole. While waiting, I admired the décor. A narrow window overlooked flower bushes, a painting of a white man in a frock coat tomahawking a native as two wild horses ripped a soldier apart, and a table supported the crumbling bust of some Roman or other. Excellent light came through a painted window beneath the ceiling beam.

Matching goons entered the room and took up positions flanking the door. The goons were hefty and clean-cut in serviceable suits. Both carried automatics in shoulder holsters. Neither looked at me directly.

A warbling flute trill preceded Mandibole's entrance. I couldn't detect its origin. That it might be an auditory hallucination didn't escape me. Too many knocks to the head. High, shrill, dark side Jethro Tull; the music cut off as he rounded the corner, saw me, and slapped on a huge, bright smile. You've seen the grin in the arsenal of carnival barkers, self-help gurus, and death row psychopaths. His was the same, but emptier.

"Coleridge! Coleridge! Isaiah Coleridge!" He spread his arms theatrically, singing my introduction in a tenor. "Speak the devil's name and he shall appear. Oh, but who's the devil here?" Trained and controlled. A bit twee, a bit obnoxious. Altogether unsettling. Too bad Lionel hadn't accompanied me. He and this creep could've had a Devil-Went-Down-to-Georgia dance-off.

Due to odd pressure changes, I only heard his voice in one ear at a time; defective headphones shorting in and out. The alternating dead ear registered a muffled feedback squeal; eeric fluting, boiling water, an inchoate shriek. I almost stuck a finger in to scrape the wax and barely managed to resist the maddening urge. The longer I stood there, the heavier my body felt, as if my muscles and bones were hardening to lead. The whole scene possessed the overtones of a nightmare, and maybe one I'd already lived through once or twice.

He approached, loosey-goosey boneless, like the King of Pop shuffle-sliding across the marble floor. Cave fish pale and damp. Short; five-five, five-six. Built lithe as a dancer, skin stretched tight across his forehead, cheeks, and knuckles. Close-cropped hair, gelled flat and shimmery. Dark shirt and tailored pants. Shiny black shoes. Our reflections blobbed in those shiny shoes like trapped souls. Tight white suit jacket with a cursive monogrammed pocket square. The monogram was done in crimson. It spelled *FIN*.

He clutched my hand and kissed it with a courtly flourish.

"You are one lived-in sonofagun. Shall we do lunch?"

The ear thing undermined my balance. I almost swooned in sympathy with some dame in a penny dreadful. First werewolves, now gothic heroines. Both were characters who tended to meet bad ends.

■ ■ ■

I followed him a trifle unsteadily and the goons fell in behind. As we walked, the calendar rolled back to the 1920s. Airy and bright with a faint aftertaste of institu-

tional racism and menace. The clouds had burned off;
sun rays lanced through windows and skylights. The effect was dazzling. A labyrinth unfolded around us—
galleries, ballrooms, solarium, parlors. Grand fireplaces
and frescos of rearing black horses painted on plaster and
brick.

"Redlick Manor was constructed in 1846 to a precise
specification," Mandibole said. "Sun phases are captured
over there. Moon, over there. Solar system alignments,
above." He gestured with the expert timing of a tour
guide. Wall panels, ceiling tiles, mantels and lintels were
indeed carved with occult designs of varying subtlety.

"The patterns within the tiles; the eyes etched into
the pillars . . . If you feel you're being watched, that's a
feature, not your imagination. The sundials, the ara-
besques, fitted to a suite of purposes. One purpose." He
inclined his head to regard me over his shoulder. He
touched his hair. "Our friends the Labradors indulge a
different, parallel aesthetic, as do the rest of the elite
families. Our friends and foes. Beneath the surface,
where it truly counts, we share this commonality of purpose." He checked to see if I was nodding along with his
bullshit. I was.

We came to a dining room appointed with gossamer
hangings. The southern wall was covered in a fresco of
black horses rampant to a blazing multi-spoked wheel, or
spiked ring, adorned with skulls—the Redlick Group corporate logo done as a piece of Hellenic religious art. Gerald Redlick's portrait hung at the north end. He wore a
Russian military uniform and a Cossack-style fur hat.

"Remember to toss a sheet over that when *Newsweek* comes in here to do a photo shoot," I said.

"*Newsweek* wouldn't dare cast Senator Redlick in an unflattering light," Mandibole said. "There are rules, my friend. The industry knows which side the bread is buttered on."

The table was set with a sumptuous feast. Cold dishes, steaming dishes, caviar, wine, and coffee. More liveried servants attended our every need. The goons stood beside French doors that let onto a balcony. I assumed the pair were fraternal twins. Or clones indentured to El Presidente.

Mandibole and I sat at either end of the table. Whatever was happening between us was completely and irrevocably on.

Hairless and trembling, an old man in a bathrobe shuffled in and took a chair closer to me. His midnight blue robe was patterned with silvery crescent moons and shooting stars. The way his elbows bowed out from his body lent him an atavistic physiognomy; a Cro-Magnon whose features had gentled and refined down through the eons. His gnarled, shaking hands were far larger than mine. The nails were yellow, stained with bloody filth, and curling back upon themselves. As a kid, I'd seen a black-and-white photo of the man with the world's longest nails in the *Guinness Book of Records*. This was nowhere close, but plenty unusual. His eyebrows were tattooed. He was the magician from a tarot deck and his robe was a wizard's robe. A servant filled his dish with rich burgundy soup. The ancient lifted the dish to his lips and supped. He didn't introduce himself, nor did Mandibole acknowledge his arrival beyond a disdainful flick of a glance.

"Eat hearty, Isaiah." Mandibole kicked one shoe up onto the table and clasped his hands over his flat stomach. "A man such as yourself muddles through life as the primitives explored caverns; a torch thrust forth, and terror in his bowels. You never know if this meal is your last. You never know if you'll be the meal."

I crunched a celery stick spitefully. I washed it down with half a glass of red wine and glared with smoldering menace in case it might help.

"Upon closer inspection, I fear I might have invited a tiger into the house. Try the lamb. It's delightful." He watched me select a chicken dish. "My bodyguards come highly recommended. Do they look tough to you? Could you, a professional cold-blooded killer, take them?"

"They'd be a handful."

"A handful. Well. 'Bodyguard' is too elevated. They're my toys."

"Ornaments," I said. "Isn't that what you mean?"

"Enough about the Corsican Brothers. I'm curious what your research tells you about me."

I opted for the bald truth.

"Your dossier is two double-spaced pages. Next to nothing. I can't find school pictures, old driver's license photos, zip. All updated records are provided courtesy of the Redlick Group. Birth records put you at thirty-nine, forty-seven, or sixty-five, depending upon whether you were born in Greenland, Manitoba, or the Himalayas.

Graduate of a string of private schools and colleges. Multiple degrees. It's impossible to tell what's apocryphal and what's legitimate. The most interesting aspect of your history is that you're the sole survivor of not one, not two, but three major wrecks. Plane crash; train derailment; ferry capsizing."

He cleared his throat.

"Those aren't my only qualifications. The highlights?"

"Sure."

"I am—was—self-orphaned. My talents include four-star fellatio, because gods know high-end clients are numb to anything less than Hoover suction. Two disciplines of hypnotism; regression is my specialty. Close-up magic; card tricks, sleight of hand, and so forth. Eidetic memory. Ventriloquism. Throwing your voice is so much fun it should be illegal. I can sing, dance, and talk super fast."

"It's evident the Redlick Group prizes your oral skills." I leaned toward the old man, whom I'd stared at the entire meal, and introduced myself. No response.

"The Magician isn't chatty," Mandibole said. "His name is Mr. Foote. Heard of him? No? Foote is an old name, a discredited name, buried under the dust in the dustbin of history."

"Good to meet you, Mr. Foote," I said. On closer inspection, I realized the mottles and blemishes on his face and exposed wrists were bruises. Purple, brown, and yellow.

Mandibole looked on with patronizing indulgence.

"Be wary. He's a dangerous being. His cursed house

was once a mortal foe. Foote served their court in a ca-
pacity similar to my own. Long ago, after the conclusion
of a feud, he came to the manor as a political hostage.
The truce holds and here our guest remains with a large
sword hanging over his bald head."

The ancient wiped his mouth with the tablecloth. A
servant removed his bowl. A different servant delicately
set a joint of roast before him. The ancient regarded the
roast without expression. As if summoned by his very
concentration, through the French doors, a black cloud
enveloped the sun. The light in the room dimmed; vel-
vety blue, chromatic blue, laced with veins of deep red.
No one moved to flip a switch. The chandelier hung; a
cold mass of crystal. The Magician's cheeks were sunken,
his mouth puckered and evidently toothless. Tears leaked
from his eyes and glistened as diamond-bright snail
trails. He licked the roast.

My grip tightened on my glass.

"Is this necessary?"

"Feeling pity for him is a waste of your emotional resources," Mandibole said.

"It's not pity, Tom. It's disgust at petty cruelty."

"Sweet summer child. Look closer. The wretch is duly
equipped. There are serpents who fold their fangs until
needed. Behold one who goes on two legs as if he were a
man."

The Magician tore into the meat and gulped it down
in several bites.

"See what I mean?" Mandibole said.

"The Ur serpents possessed legs," Mr. Foote said,

faint and rusty with the blood dripping from his mouth. "The Ur forged an empire. The Ur ruled Gondwanaland. Before the Aztecs, before Aborigines, and Christ. Humans are an invasive species. The Ur were men, you twat."

"The degenerate speaks," Mandibole said. "A rare occasion."

"Our day of reckoning edges nearer," the Magician said.

My appetite had dissipated. I laid my left hand on a steak knife anyway.

"Now the second course." Mandibole clapped twice.

Nancy the Beautician and several friends filed in and took their seats.

I recognized three of the gentlemen as the racist yahoos who'd assailed me on my previous visit to town. The bruises I'd given the two beefy guys were at the sunset stage and damned impressive. Mr. Denim wore a hand cast, due to breaking his fingers on my skull. The duo was even worse off than the Magician and that made me glad.

"You folks take your cosplay seriously," I said.

"Hello, Mr. Detective," Nancy said in a breathy voice.

CHAPTER EIGHTEEN

The women dressed in crimson-and-bronze sweaters and skirts; the men wore Valley High letter jackets. The silver-stitched motto read EVER LIFE, which seemed at odds with Mandibole's monogram. I assigned them nicknames based on impressions. Nancy the Beautician, Mr. Denim, Golf Pro, Slick, Ichabod, Veronica, and Betty. These worthies regarded me with stoic malice. Mr. Denim and Golf Pro itched for a rematch if I knew anything about mad dog glares.

"The Mares of Thrace," Mandibole said. "A shy lot. I managed to coax these forth in honor of your presence." Hardly shy. They were poised in their seats, intent upon me. He said, "Our motto is Ever Life. While flesh and bone are susceptible to the degradation of time and gravity, a youthful spirit is always attainable by dint of meat, drink, and the nourishment of spirit. Ours is a philosophy of dark hedonism. Currently, the Mares manifest the Aspect of Day. This aspect is what the humdrum world sees. Would you care to witness their transformation into the Aspect of Night?"

"No, thank you," I said.

"Thank me later." He inclined his head toward Nancy and her comrades.

The Mares bowed their heads, concealing their expressions. The air thickened. A static charge built and goosebumps dimpled my skin. The Mares straightened and lowered their hands. Their faces were grotesque smudges in the murk. "Flat affect" was the medical term— rigid, semiflexible masks; about as lifelike as four-color comic book caricatures. Weirdly, the closer I looked, the less it seemed that they'd applied traditional makeup as a foundation. It was as if they'd smeared modeling plaster on, let it harden, and done the final touches with thick eyeshadow, blush, and lipstick. Twenty feet away, passable for human. Up close and personal? The results were dubious. Nancy especially unsettled me. Her eyes glittered yellow as they caught a fleck of bloody sun.

Special-effects makeup? Autohypnosis? Was I hallucinating?

"Mr. Coleridge, recently you physically abused two of my servants who were in the Aspect of Day." Mandibole referred to Mr. Denim and Golf Pro. "A word of warning: Pray you never test them when they manifest the Aspect of Night. Their physiological threshold and neuromuscular reactivity are heightened by an influx of natural chemicals, including extreme levels of adrenaline. While in this state, they can quite literally rend you limb

from limb. While in this state, they would love the opportunity to rend you limb from limb."

"We're all friends here." My mouth was dry.

Mandibole glanced toward his coterie.

"None of you will utter a word. Is that clear, Nancy?"
He waited for her to bow her head in deference. "Mr.
Coleridge, anything you intended to ask my friends, you
may ask me. I do not promise to answer fully, truthfully,
or at all. Do commence."

"Sean Pruitt," I said.

"Dead. Nancy the Chatterbox already bent your ear.
A tragedy, seeing as it was the grain of sand on the railroad track that derailed the Jeffers Project. Many lives
were irrevocably altered by the loss."

"Time and perspective lead some to speculate that not
all accidents are equal and not all suicides are voluntary."

"The facts are established. Looking for a scapegoat?"

"Answers will do."

"Gravity and a sudden stop are the culprits," he said.
"A lifetime of poor choices. Rumor has it Sean suffered
from mental illness. Absentminded lad."

"I'm interested in the truth, not the gossip."

"The truth. Did he jump or was he pushed? That's
what you're asking after four years?"

"Yes."

"What I say is immaterial. You won't listen."

"I'm paid to listen."

"You're paid to dig. There's a difference, but it doesn't
matter."

"It matters to the people who loved him." I crossed my arms. "Seems perverse to summon me and then yank my chain."

"Summon you? Hardly. You came to our valley. You impose upon our places of business, enter, uninvited, into our lives. *You* demanded this meeting. Best that we cut to the chase."

"A good idea."

"Dead meat attracts carrion scavengers, predators, and flies. You've followed a gamey scent to our doorstep. Conversely, it's understandable. The ring was removed from your nose the moment you quit the Outfit and so you blunder recklessly. Our house could find a position for you. We could offer you direction."

A servant poured more wine. I drank it because I needed it.

"Hard pass."

He smiled pityingly. The Mares smiled cruelly. The Magician sucked and slobbered; maybe he was smiling too. I had a wry epiphany. Amongst the traditional conspiracy theories revolving around faked moon landings, the Kennedy assassination, UFOs, and Bigfoot, a select vintage deals with the conviction that ultrarich folks are a bunch of raving Satanists, mass murderers, and/or closet eugenicists. I'd waded hip-deep into the headwaters of Cuckoo River.

"I've had the dubious honor of mixing in the company of assorted megalomaniacal fuckers," I said. "Sadists. Button men. Capos with delusions of grandeur. Dons consumed by dope habits and untreated venereal disease. Maybe the don read a history book or watched *Caligula* and it gave him ideas. Baby psychopaths pull the wings off flies. Babies grow to be indolent pieces of shit surrounded by yes-men and whores. They remain babies and psycho- paths under the slick haircuts and fancy suits. Their tor- ments are elaborate to the eye. But if you aren't distracted by the illusion, it's only a kid smeared in shit; a brat with a magnifying glass."

The Magician, engrossed in making love to the roast bone, laughed. Mandibole's expression changed for the worse and the Magician shut up.

"Great, important work proceeds phase by phase in our valley," Mandibole said. "Pulling the wings off flies constitutes a meager percentage of my free time."

"Great, important work. Condos? A business plaza? Your stupid abandoned collider?"

"The collider isn't dead. It's dreaming."

"Right on. The Redlicks aren't guilty of hubris if they can make the magic happen. I guess as long as there's money and a bunch of rich assholes willing to shovel it, there's hope."

He pointed behind his head at the portrait of Redlick.

"Shall we be real for a moment? No one cares for your opinions. Your presence is an intolerable embarrassment."

"Me, an embarrassment? Pal, that's the case for some- body somewhere from the moment I put my shoes on in the morning. You guys aren't special. Oh, hold the phone. You have your great, important work. I almost forgot."

"Nature is red of tooth and claw. You are familiar with this idea." He lowered his voice and said it the way a secret agent might relay a code to his contact, probing for verity. "Terrible outcomes are guaranteed should you persist. Against all reason you are fated to persist."

"Yes."

"Mr. Foote? Since you're in a verbose mood, care to grace us with a pearl of wisdom?"

The Magician shut his eyes.

"Rich and poor," he intoned. "Man and ant . . . Darkness surrounds us. Our atmosphere is a veil. The crust of the earth we walk upon is thinner than an eggshell. It's quite useless, this struggle. Struggle we shall, for men are beasts enslaved by their wants and their fears."

Mandibole appeared satisfied.

"There you have it from the lips of an ascetic possessed of dreadful knowledge."

"Let me recap to be certain I've got the gist," I said. "Thinner than an eggshell and very dark. The woods are teeming with wild beasts. Men are beasts and slaves. Beasts die, men die. Ants. The moral is, I don't care."

"Be that as it may," Mandibole said. "I'm sure you comprehend. Who among us doesn't occasionally bow in obeisance to dread and terrible forces?"

"Namely gravity," I said.

The Magician opened his eyes.

"The Kaleidoscope will revolve, soon revolve."

The Mares of Thrace whipped their heads in unison to glare at the ancient. The boys snarled; the girls hissed.

The Magician winked at me.

"To Hades with climate change, with asteroids, nuclear holocaust." His voice began, scratchy and weak. He gained steam. "To Hades with half measures."

"Mr. Foote, if you please—" Mandibole said.

"The Kaleidoscope is the surest method. It will remove humankind from the galactic map and send us back to the Dark Ages. Perhaps a new Stone Age. We would be preserved—"

Veronica shrieked in rage and raked her cotton-candy-pink nails through the tablecloth and into the hardwood. Wood shavings and sawdust piled around her fingers. Slick and Golf Pro leaped to their feet and onto their chairs, visages twisted in hate, spitting curses.

"Stifle yourselves!" Mandibole slapped the table, flashing a bestial snarl like Dracula breaking up a catfight in his harem. The Mares subsided with alacrity. The Magician hunched, staring at his plate and the roast bone.

I gave tempers a moment to cool.

"What the hell do you want, Tom?"

Mandibole rubbed his temples.

"Mr. Foote speaks truly. It is necessary to pay homage to the lesser of evils. Because so much worse is out there in the dark."

"I'll rephrase the question. What do you want, Tom?"

"I wanted to touch you. To shake your hand. To break bread. To show you the futility of your mission, the fragility of your very hypermasculine existence. To remind you that your instincts are correct, but also futile." Mandibole scrutinized me. One moment, he was a real boy; the next, plastic. "I must ask. Are you an agent of the Labradors?"

"The Labradors didn't send me here."

"Good. I don't know if I believe you. But good. My advice? Hop in your car and drive home."

"Trust me, I'd love nothing more."

"Once you leave, never come back here. Not for love or money." He smoothed his pocket square, tracing the letters.

My head began to throb with the onset of a migraine. The business with my intermittently fritzed hearing was exacting a toll. The sun burned a notch in the black cloud; a red eye. It didn't brighten the dining room. I glanced around the table at the leering imposters in their high school costumes, at the ancient who'd licked the meat to bone, then gnawed a hole in the bone itself. The bone was the size and shape of a primitive recorder. Polished to a gloss finish and pointy as a spike at one end.

The Magician put it to his lips and blew a halting, tremulous note. The note gathered power and sharpened to an unbearable pitch that quivered and ceased. He extended his long, gaunt arm and laid the bone upon my empty plate with a soft clink.

"For when it's time to face the music," he said.

Nausea surged into my throat. I rose, gripping the knife so hard my knuckles ached. Would they really permit me to walk out the door, or would this devolve into a reenactment of Julius Caesar's infamous last scene? The goons and the Mares were far less of a concern than the master of ceremonies himself. He impressed me as a spider, coiled and alert, poised to spring upon its prey.

"What lurks in the darkness of interstellar space? The interstellar reaches of our souls? Terror." Mandibole reclined, motionless, hands in plain view, yet his whisper emanated behind my left ear. Then, louder, "The emotion you're experiencing. It's terror. Terror ruled the indigenous tribes of the Valley. Terror motivated the white colonists. Of course, men fear the wilderness, the natural features of the land. That's why men deface it at every opportunity—burn it, bulldoze it, hack it to stumps, and pound it to gravel. They desire clear lines of sight."

I disliked how he said "they" in reference to humanity.

"Goodbye, Tom. Let's do it again in the next life."

"Some heroes are compelling because they represent the little guy," he said to my back. "She or he *is* the little guy, and everybody roots for him or her to rise up, for the worm to turn."

I made it to the door, then wended my way down the intricate maze of passages. Neither Mandibole nor his Magnificent Seven Freaks had moved to pursue, yet his voice carried eerily and slithered after me as I made good my escape.

"Some heroes are compelling because they're invincible badasses," he said. "Demigods. Both kinds are worthless. Prostrated before the approaching shadow, worms are worms. Demigods are puny, weak, ineffectual. In the face of towering evil, they wither and are consumed."

I nearly stiff-armed the valet aside in my haste to get the hell out of there.

■ ■ ■

Back at the hotel, I guzzled a bottle of the five-dollar water because there wasn't any whiskey, and stared into my bloodshot eyes in the mirror. My expression was the same as after waking from a three-day bender. I showered with the spray set to strip paint and replayed the events of the day so far. Ventriloquism may as well be black magic to me. I questioned the scraps I *did* know. When a ventriloquist throws his voice, are you supposed to feel his breath in your ear?

Standing in the center of the suite, towel wrapped around my waist, slowly coming down from the extreme emotions of the past hour, I contemplated heeding Mandibole's advice to get out of Dodge. For a bit of perspective, I signed into my bank account and studied the figures, particularly the pending transfer of Adeyemi's second retainer installment. An eye-watering sum. Adeyemi was moderately comfortable, however by no means wealthy. This financial outlay represented a hell of a noble gesture toward his sister and dead nephew. It irritated me to consider, not for the first time, that the blackhearted sonofabitch secretly hoarded one or two human emotions. I prefer my bad guys to stay in character. They're easier to sort.

I lingered over the sum, calculating how many outstanding bills it would erase versus the very real chance I'd have to go head-to-head with that Horseheads crowd sooner or later.

To paraphrase Beckett, *I can't go on. For this kind of dough, I'll go on.* Money, yes, money. Also, the fuck-you factor.

Changing clothes, I cleaned out my pockets. The Magician's bone dropped onto the carpet.

CHAPTER NINETEEN

A quarter past eight on Tuesday morning, Lionel walked in and joined my table at the Plowman's Diner. That didn't surprise me much. Lionel adhered to strict routines, yet was capable of deviating from the script in surprising fashion. Ezra Bellow, special agent, FBI, slid in beside him. That was unexpected. Lionel wore his safari hat, thrashed camouflage jacket, holey jeans, and Red Wing shoes. He was plainly hungover. Bellow, African American, late fifties, and solemn as a portrait of doomed royalty, wore a gray hoodie and cargo pants tucked into winter boots. Both were carrying.

Bellow operated out of Maryland and DC, although he went where the job took him. Extraneous circumstances, and his unorthodox philosophy, had led to our occasional collaboration. I'd begun to consider us friends. Granted, a former mob enforcer and an upright, uptight Eliot Ness–loving man of the law made for an odd couple. I harbored the suspicion that Bellow was as close to incorruptible as a cop gets. If a tiny grain of that rubbed off on me, all to the good.

I finished my plate of scrambled eggs while the waitress poured coffee. Lionel sipped and grimaced. He covered his face with both hands, hunched forward, and sat that way. Bellow asked for a menu. He unclipped a set of reading glasses and pushed them onto his nose. He scanned the menu like he was proofreading a deposition and eventually ordered eggs, hash, toast, and a glass of OJ. I resisted the urge to ask where he got the specs. I wasn't there yet.

"Three words," Bellow said.

"Go home, Yankee?" I said.

"Senator Gerald Redlick." He waited for me to comment. In vain. "Senator Gerald Redlick, owner, CEO, and fifty-one percent shareholder of the Redlick Group."

"That's more than three words. Didn't he divest, or place his businesses in a blind trust, or whatever politicians are supposed to do while holding public office?"

"Yes. Very well. Let's try two words and a sentence. Badja Adeyemi. A friend of a friend heard it from a little bird that Badja Adeyemi, disgraced former cop who kisses Senator Gerald Redlick's ass and is currently under federal indictment, put you on retainer to dig up skeletons. Corporate skeletons."

I nodded. "Here's a sentence for you: Badja Adeyemi is a client who's paying me an obscene fee to stumble around with my hands in my pockets and ask people about the weather and if some kid they knew years ago, who offed himself in dramatic fashion, was as squeaky clean as he seems on paper. Spoiler alert—so far, the verdict is leaning toward yes, it was a suicide or an accident, and yes, he was a clean, super-chill dude whose mother loved him to pieces."

Bellow pinched the bridge of his nose, a gesture I was positive he'd developed in the company of wet-behind-the-ears agents and recalcitrant grandchildren.

"He banged on my door at four-thirty this morning," Lionel said from behind his hands. "I was in bed for half an hour."

"You should've warned me," I said.

"We wanted it to be a surprise," Bellow said.

"Are you here to cajole me into dropping the case?"

"And interrupt early Christmas vacation to come talk to a brick wall? Nah."

"FBI dudes get Christmas vacation?" Lionel said.

"The good ones do," Bellow said. "SDNY scuttlebutt has it that Senator Redlick's office is anxious that Adeyemi got rolled up. Nobody in Redlick's camp wants to see Adeyemi pressured. The senator's corporation is a safety net for if and when he rolls snake eyes politically. Your poking into its past dealings could be viewed as a threat."

"Can't a guy poke around the tiniest bit without everybody coming unglued? Jeez."

They both chuckled.

"If not to hassle me, why are you here?" I said.

"Because," Bellow said, "my antenna received a signal that you're stepping into trouble. The antenna doesn't lie."

"Your antenna? Meg's got one of those."

"G-man's sixth sense, or whatever. Years of experience."

"Let me get this straight. Your, uh, antenna, quivered and you hopped a plane, rousted Lionel, and tore ass to this scenic rendezvous."

"Essentially, yes."

"I hope the orange juice is freshly squeezed."

Lionel slipped on a set of tinted shooting glasses. He gave Bellow a sidelong glance.

"Why are you schlepping around in the field? Shouldn't you be heading a department or some shit?"

"Fraternizing with us doesn't help his cause," I said.

"My troubles are at an end," Bellow said. "Mandatory retirement this summer. A plaque, a pension, a good night's sleep."

"Oh, boy," Lionel said.

"Oh, boy?" Bellow said. "Why oh, boy?"

"Statistically, you'll croak within five or ten years of retirement," Lionel said. "No reason to carry on the charade."

"TV dinners and syndicated game shows," I said.

"I might travel," Bellow said.

"Cruise ship shuffleboard with complimentary dysentery," Lionel said.

"We'll cry for your exile to sunny beaches and pitchers of margaritas another day." I inhaled and related my adventures with Mandibole and his ghoulish pals at the Redlick estate.

"The antenna was homing in on the good shit," Lionel said.

"Ye gods," Bellow said. "We've heard stories at the Bureau that beggar belief regarding the Redlicks and the Labradors. The Mares of Thrace never registered a blip on the screen, though that handle is as melodramatic as a Greek youth terrorist group."

"Mandibole exercises a tyrannical degree of control over them," I said. "He may as well crack a bullwhip."

"Money and authority can be administered to erode one's sense of self," Bellow said.

"This is Jim Jones and cyanide punch. Bits of the conversation pointed toward a UFO cult. There may be a split personality component. It's weird. I can't explain what I saw, although it's got to be an illusion combined with fanaticism. Feds have task forces devoted to this stuff, don't they?"

"Fanatics and crazies are our bread and butter. UFO cults are gaining in popularity." Bellow rubbed his chin and stared out the window. "You pick the interesting cases."

"Mystery cults were the fad back when the Roman and Greek empires owned the world," I said. "Who could conceive of one arising from a high school in Jerkwater, USA? And there's more. Seems that about two years ago, Adeyemi hired another detective to manage the case. The detective didn't make it far before 'somebody' ran him down in the street."

"Do tell." He tapped the screen of his phone and listened as I gave him a blow-by-blow of my fracas with the three men in the pickup and how I met them again, or their costumed doppelgangers, at the Redlick estate.

"Sometimes the classic methods work best," he said, continuing to search his phone. "Stage events to mimic a run-of-the-mill altercation that leads to a hit-and-run, or a golf club to the kneecap, and some private dick can't walk without a limp anymore."

"Much less be in the mood to ask awkward questions," I said. "Bellow, I've mixed it up with hired muscle. The Mares are exotic. I saw two more traditional contractors at the house." The Corsican Brothers, Mandibole called the pair of lugs who guarded the door. "Nothing special, nothing as sinister as the Mares. Any corporate flack with two pennies to rub together retains a few mercs on staff."

"The Mares might be specialists Mandibole trusts with personal errands the regular security detail won't touch," he said. "They likely did the honors with that other detective."

"These cosplay dudes see you coming and figure once was nice, why not do it twice?" Lionel said. "Their mistake was not running you over with the truck. And then backing up."

Bellow studied his phone with a deepening frown.

"One piece of trivia, and I don't know if it signifies anything: the Redlick Group attracts a disproportionate number of ex-intelligence personnel. CIA, NASA, FBI, DoD. The occasional disgruntled Treasury agent or disenfranchised police detective. A few of the candidates are homegrown, western New York stock. The rest aren't."

"In-house security? Corporate espionage?" I said.

"We don't track them and they don't advertise."

"As far as the case is concerned, I can only go on what I have. Which amounts to a disinterested police report, semi-hysterical family testimony including the hunches of the most corrupt ex-cop in New York, and the cryptic behavior of local fetishists and their creepy patron." I paused to let my colleagues process. "Does *your* scuttle-butt pipeline lead you to suspect there's something to Mama Pruitt's claim her son's death warrants an investigation?"

"No," Bellow said. "A minute ago, I'm chilling with a glass of above-average OJ, convinced the young brother ate a few too many ingredients, was overcome with melancholy, and took a permanent vacation. Occam's razor says look at the available evidence and Occam is seldom wrong. The ME wasn't stellar. Corporations fast-talk and appear sneaky by default. Sprinkle in Mama's tears, and presto—instant conspiracy." He tipped his cup and found it empty.

"A faultless assessment," I said.

■ ■ ■

We were out in the cold, deciding how to proceed. Bellow shifted from foot to foot in obvious discomfort.

"Isaiah, that business in the Redlick house. The unusual things you experienced." He struggled to find the right phrasing. "It's dangerous. And the professional community doesn't understand it fully."

I wanted to mention, but didn't, how my nightmares were somewhat tangentially congruent with unfolding events, if not prophetic. The dream imagery of Sean Pruitt in a Mare uniform; Whiro's mention of kaleidoscopes. This is how the subconscious does its job—it filters a million disparate details like a sourdough panning for gold. The inner mind occasionally speaks with the mystical authority of an oracle.

"Easy, there. I don't buy into hoodoo. Ventriloquism, sleight of hand, yes. Elaborate mind games, yes."

"Actually, that's what I'm getting at," he said. "Your disorientation and the illusory sounds . . . Someone, maybe your old man, affiliated with the clandestine elements would be more qualified. I've had a peek at classified files moldering in locked basement cells. Toe-curling."

Lionel, slumped against a mailbox, raised his hand.

"Amigo, the CIA and the KGB didn't spend hundreds of millions of Cold War dollars on research into mind control, remote viewing, psychokinesis, and the rest for shits and giggles."

"Borderline swamp-dweller hoodoo territory," I said. "No offense, boys. Brainwashing requires a drawn-out process."

"A pro can mindfuck you in short order," Lionel said.

"Coleridge is right," Bellow said. "Suggestion is a short-term possibility. Deep conditioning is labor and time intensive. Depends on a person's nascent susceptibility, receptiveness, whether he's suffered psychological trauma—"

"Thanks, Agent Bellow," I said. "If I start clucking like a chicken, I'll seek assistance. Tell me again what you're doing here?"

"Figured I may as well tag along and hog the glory if there's any to be had."

"Impulsive in your dotage."

"Burning vacation days. If I stay home, my kids and their kids will descend like harpies and I'll never be rid of them. What's the agenda today?"

"I'm going to drop in on a fellow with keys to the kingdom."

"I have no idea why *I'm* here," Lionel said.

"Baby, I told you," Bellow said. "You can drive the car."

CHAPTER TWENTY

We boarded the SUV. Always roll with a rental in unknown, possibly unfriendly territory, given the choice. Bellow had rented a sedan at JFK. He agreed the SUV was a superior vehicle for trolling the back roads. Lionel punched in Lenny Herzog's address and studied the coordinates. The GPS calmly dictated the turns in a dry, professorial tone. He lit a cigarette and lowered the volume.

"As if I'm gonna trust you, you smooth-talking sonofabitch."

Bellow sat in back. He met my eye in the rearview.

"Want me to make a call? Possibly save you a day tramping in the boonies."

"Can't save a man from doing what he loves." Tempting as it was to avail myself of his not inconsiderable resources, he'd come to New York on his own time at his own discretion and not by Bureau mandate. Maintaining a low profile was the smart move. There were worse fates than "tramping in the boonies."

Hanging my shingle in the mid–Hudson Valley didn't mean simply cruising the hot spots and alleys of Kingston, New Paltz, and Newburgh. Much as I relished nursing drinks in the finer bars, I spent plenty of days in the hills, dales, and byways of the Rondout Valley and environs running to ground deadbeats and low-rent criminals who hoped going off the grid would save their hides. Mosquitos and deer ticks were my mortal enemies. I composed odes to the joys of poison ivy and seasonal allergies. Now at least the bugs were asleep.

The directions led west, then north. We skirted the edge of the Jeffers Project into thickly wooded hills. Our computer navigator uttered a series of increasingly conflicted directions, then fell silent. I'd confirmed our destination with an online satellite image, thus the lack of GPS or reliable cell-phone signal only mildly concerned me. In any event, the excursion was on Adeyemi's tab and I got paid by the hour.

"The AI knows she's not wanted in Luddite Ville," Lionel said.

Bellow wasn't having it.

"Outsiders paint Appalachia, the Ozarks, the Everglades, and related cultural regions with a broad brush. 'Hill country' usually means 'poor people live here.' And even that is a suspect conclusion. You can't nail down the culture to a single tradition or a single influence." It was apparent from his delivery, he'd rehearsed the monologue.

Lionel lit another cigarette.

"Special Agent Bellow, you ever see a documentary

called *The Hills Have Eyes,* or *The Hills Have Eyes Two* and *Three*?"

"I've heard the saying, 'Fields have eyes, woods have ears.' Wise counsel."

Lionel abandoned the two-lane highway and hummed along narrow, lumpen back roads. The roads got sketchier and the forest deeper and darker by the second. Soon, there were few roads and fewer houses. We hooked right at a billboard that used to say something before its paint peeled and locals shot the letters off. This neighborhood embodied a theme I thought of as Libertarian Hell. Decrepit trailers flew American flags in overgrown yards. One enterprising resident had mounted the skulls of animals on a tree in a vaguely occult pattern. I kept an eye out for a Pentecostal church with an inverted crucifix.

"Satanic panic." Lionel nodded sagely.

"It completely missed this street," I said.

"Satanic panic. That's all I'm gonna say."

"That's all you're going to say?" Bellow said.

"Yep."

"Really? Are you sure?"

Lionel drove past a trailer boasting a partly charred Dixie banner stretched across the frame. He cleared his throat.

"Well, there may be more."

Bellow pressed his forehead against the window.

"Hey, what about that shutdown?" I said. "Did it affect Bureau affairs?"

Earlier that year, disagreements between Congress and the president led to a monthlong freeze of federal budgets. This had included wages and discretionary funds for FBI operations. Snitches and undercover cops relied on government cash to play make-believe high rollers, drug dealers, and the like. Bellow said it had been hellish. He told a brief anecdote about an asset a colleague in the DEA deployed to infiltrate a high-value narcotics ring. Names changed to protect the guilty, of course.

The asset, "Tito Boniface," called up his handler and related a tale of woe. As the government shutdown went on, the DEA said everybody on the ground was shit out of luck and basically ghosted its operatives. No moola for coke deals, no moola for lavish druggy lifestyles of the rich and infamous. Over cards with the other hard cases, somebody asked Tito why he'd reneged on a promise to acquire a hefty payload of primo dope. And why was Tito so cheap lately with paying for a few rounds? How come they hadn't seen him at the clubs? *It ain't the shutdown, is it?* one chortled. Tito ran a finger under his collar, Rodney Dangerfield style, and laughed it off. But he was sweating bullets.

"That's the inside baseball John Q. Public never sees," Lionel said.

"Pull a thread and the whole hair suit unravels."

"Dude must've been relieved when the freeze ended."

"They fished Tito out of the Potomac forty-eight hours after that conversation," Bellow said. "Evidently, his poker buddies weren't joking."

We parked near a culvert and walked in along a muddy track. Whatever direction I turned, trees and more trees.

Pine and hemlock blocked out the hazy sky. Something I'd learned in the Northeast: Five steps into the pines and you're on the dark side of the moon.

Ted's file on Lenny Herzog was thin—lifelong resident, attended trade school. Employed in numerous custodial and handyman roles, including a hitch with the Jeffers Project. The latter-day Herzogs were descended from a moonshining dynasty and, once upon a time, owned a chunk of the ridge. Lenny Herzog attended Valley High with that generation of Redlicks. I surmised that Gerald R threw him a bone when it came time to recruit allies for the supercollider construction. Another variation on the odd couple phenomenon that wasn't as weird as it seemed. Scheming rich dudes can always find use for a blue-collar man with underworld connections.

Herzog dwelled in a trailer with an A-frame addition. Tar-paper roof, hand-pumped well, deer bones scattered among busted axles and weeds. Smaller bones were strung on wire and dangled from low-hanging branches like macabre wind chimes. His chariot was a rusty Datsun quarter-ton pickup with no hood and plastic sheeting over the passenger window. An aging blue heeler woofed from the porch to announce our arrival. I expected her master to emerge in suspenders, clutching a scatter gun. Wrong—he looked and dressed like a drab family-size garden gnome. Soft white hair flowed from beneath a sock hat to his waist; clean and ironed plaid coat and canvas pants. His glasses were dense enough to burn a hole in paper. The brand-spanking-new Crocs threw me, I'll admit.

"As I live and breathe, it's Tom-fucking-Bombadil," Lionel said to Bellow.

Bellow fake-smiled and told him to shut up. He continued to exude cheer as he scanned the bushes like a scout expecting an ambush.

I introduced my party (discreetly declining to mention Bellow was a G-man) and briefly explained the investigation. Herzog stroked his beard, listening politely. When I apologized for not phoning ahead, he laughed and said the power company cut him off ages ago. He owned a fancy cell that he strategically monitored, answering messages once or twice a week, if it was really important. It was good to keep people guessing, see? Woodstove, kerosene, and a portable radio did him fine.

He sat on a cinder-block step and patted his dog and changed the subject to the weather (Bellow raised his eyebrows at me), geography, and the moribund state of the world. Appearances notwithstanding, he considered his piece of land practically suburbia—neighbors occupied surrounding ridges and a pop-fifty town hunkered in a basin not five miles west.

His ancestral home had burned to the ground. The ruins were farther up the hill and already covered in moss and vines. Nature moves quickly to reclaim her own.

"My divorce was the best thing that ever happened to my dog. Wife almost died in the fire. I snatched up the dog and booked it. Figured it's what the missus woulda wanted. But no, sir. She made it, damn her luck. Covered in charcoal except for her eyeballs trained on me with no small amount of rage." While he monologued, he filled a pipe and got it going. Pipes are supposed to smell pleasant—that and the professorial aura they imbue on regular stiffs are their whole draw. This load reeked of burning moss and cat piss. A cloud of smoke settled above his head and gradually slithered down his collar and the sleeves of his coat. Watching him inhale and luxuriate, I had an unsettling thought born of years touring rural Alaska. Live too long in isolation, and eventually cat-piss-soaked moss set on fire becomes a fragrant treat.

He asked how I was getting along with Horseheads, and I said fine. He said terrific, because the Valley didn't necessarily treat folks well, especially outsiders intent on upsetting the cart, so to speak.

"She's a curious soul, our piece of heaven," he said. "Can be a patch of hell, depending on her mood."

Pleasantries dispensed with, sure, he'd seen Sean Pruitt at the construction site and camp, exchanged perhaps a dozen words. Of course, the Pruitt boy's death weighed on him. He didn't wish an untimely meeting with the Reaper on anybody. The family had his sympathies.

How sympathetic? I asked. My friends and I needed to have a peek at Sean's old quarters and he was the man with the keys.

Herzog said he could see his way clear to providing the information we sought. There was a price, which he enjoyed enumerating, then haggling over. He received a quarterly stipend from Diogenes Security to inspect Jeffers Colony, perform minor maintenance tasks, and report trespassers, be they vandals, thieves, or mere looky-loos. We had to make the admittedly small danger of losing that trickle of revenue worth his while. He figured four bills would square us away. Oh, and a case of Blue Light, a pound of tobacco he favored, and dog snacks. I could fetch his list at a general store on the main road near the junction. He suggested I take my sweet-ass time since digging up the records would be a lengthy, tedious chore. On second thought, since suppertime would come along before he finished, I was welcome to wrangle barbecue fixings—white hots and pop—and he'd do the ceremonial honors.

I agreed to the request. Even Hercules bowed to the inevitable and ran an occasional errand or spit-shined a stable.

CHAPTER TWENTY-ONE

Obtaining the list of goodies wasn't an onerous quest. The store appeared rustic until we went inside and it was mirrored floor tiles, modern coolers, and fluorescent strips, overseen by a college-age girl who didn't bother unplugging her earphones to ring me up.

Since we had time to kill, we visited the Jeffers Project site and admired the double fence and deserted gatehouse. In the course of the forty-five minutes we spent kicking rocks and shooting the breeze, neither security personnel nor caretakers materialized to shoo us away. We drove a circuitous route back to Herzog's cabin.

Herzog unhurriedly performed several routine tasks (pumping water into jerry cans, fueling his portable generator, and gathering armloads of firewood, as the weatherman said it would drop below freezing that night). The day had grown long in the tooth before he lugged several cartons of records from somewhere in the bowels of his shack and got serious. As twilight deepened into full darkness, Lionel made a fire in the barbecue pit and roasted hot dogs, or white hots, as our host called them. Herzog lit a kerosene lantern and hung it from a hook on the eave of the porch. He squinted at the cramped font of what struck me as a jillion and one identical papers, and arranged them in piles on the rickety steps. He refused our offers to assist combing through the stacks.

Upon glimpsing the documents, Bellow asked how he happened to be in custody of sensitive personal information: addresses, social security numbers, and references to medical histories.

"Yah, I stole them," Herzog said.

"No shit," Lionel said, beer in one hand, skewer in the other.

"Pardon?" Bellow said.

I stifled a laugh.

"These are photocopies I made," Herzog said with pride. "At first, I collected documents willy-nilly, no system to speak of. None of it means spit to me, nohow. Don't you worry, though. I'll suss out the address you want."

"What use are these to you?" Bellow said.

"I'd say my foresight is paying me back." Herzog winked and patted his coat pocket where he'd folded my cash bribe. "Knowledge is a big stick."

Lionel added hot dogs to the pile on a paper plate. Bellow stalked to the edge of the yard and turned his back on us. Grandad's patented I'm-counting-to-ten pose.

"I opened mail and wrote it down," Herzog said blithely. "Private doctor stuff, sex stuff too. Carried a camera under my coat. People get up to embarrassing things when they don't realize Lenny is standing outside their window, watching the whole shebang." He laughed breezily and kicked back with a beer. "Shebang!"

Bellow sidled over, abruptly interested in the conversation. His expression was dangerously neutral. I feared he contemplated reaching for his cuffs. Too many law enforcement agents possessed a carefree disregard for citizens' private information. He stood firmly on the opposite side of that line in the sand—constitutional rights were sacred trusts.

It was an inopportune moment for Bellow's elevated moral standards to be triggered by our hayseed pal. I adroitly changed the subject and asked Herzog what he meant about the Valley being heaven one minute, hell the next, and instantly rued the question. A breeze whispered in the branches and the lantern wavered. I'd instinctively edged nearer the lantern as the woods and everything in them merged into a colossal black shape at the uncertain boundary of light.

"The Valley's old and it's mean," Herzog said. He'd drained several beers and it was hitting him hard.

I'd gotten a taste of the prevailing eeriness, its "colorful" characters, and had no desire to see much more of the Valley's fabled dark side. Reason one hundred and one to conclude my investigation and slap a bow on it as soon as possible.

"What's your opinion on the supercollider project?" I said. "Were you sorry to see it fail, or good riddance to bad rubbish?"

"Oh, they're still screwing around over there on the

sly. Seen lights, heard noises at all hours." He sucked on his pipe and belched tire-fire smoke. "Tell you this much: whatever plans were in store for the finished site weren't nice."

"Such as?"

He shrugged.

"I dunno. Redlicks were involved; it was something bad."

"Whoa, there. Aren't you friends?"

"Their company gives me shit money to do a shit job. The way it's always been with our families. Doesn't make us friends, does it?"

"Seems lonely here in the hills," Lionel said. "I mean, it's peaceful."

"Lonely? No. I have my fun too. I play jokes on my dog."

"Jokes?"

"Oh, like I'm dead. Anyway, I've got company. Gracie and the coons and whatever else comes around at night."

"Such as?" Lionel said. "Bear? Deer? Ghost horses?"

Herzog rocked gently on his heels. The lantern light cast a shadow over him and he could've been a wood-block illustration of Rip Van Winkle after that long nap, or Rumpelstiltskin, crouched near a campfire in a fairy-tale forest, gloating that the queen would never guess his name.

"Well, let me tell you." He scratched his dog's ears. "Gracie's a hell of a watchdog. The other morning, she stalked the edges of the yard, whining and growling. I kept my rifle handy. Bear are thick in this area and that was her bear growl. Blackies this time of year want a few last meals before they go to sleep. They aren't normally a threat, but a man can't be too careful. A couple of nights later, Gracie barked her head off. I figured she'd treed a coon or somethin', right there ten feet from the door in that old pine."

We reflexively turned our heads to follow his gesture to the tree in question.

"I shined my light at the crown and saw a man ogling me. Face white as dust, and half-hid among the branches. He hung there, upside down, like a spider. Then he grinned."

"What did you do?" Lionel said. His eyes were wide.

"Ran inside and barred the damned door is what I did," Herzog said. "It had to be Shanks Mathis, a logger. Disappeared one autumn in the nineties. He was cutting the top out of a tree and it corkscrewed. Shanks and the top of that tree were flung into Twenty-Mile Gorge."

"Logging is a hazardous business," I said.

"Rangers didn't recover his body. They brought in dogs and a chopper. Rough piece of country, you know. Now we see Shanks in the woods. People round here leave offerings for him on his jaunts." To demonstrate, he popped the top on a beer and set it on the porch. "If Shanks is passing through, this'll be gone come sunrise."

I was thinking if he turned his back on Lionel, it would be gone in two seconds.

"Why do they call him Shanks?" I asked the obvious.

"On account of his rusty climbing hooks." Herzog pointed at his shin. "Buckle it on like cowboy spurs, except these are yea-long spikes. A veteran climber with hooks and a strap can scamper up a tree faster than a coon." He rose and limped over to the pine and rubbed the bark. "See these gouges where the sap bleeds? Fresh. More of them go all the way near to the crown. Spurs made those marks."

I pointed at a mobile of bird bones dangling from another tree.

"Aren't those charms supposed to keep bad spirits at bay?"

"There's worse than Shanks. That's what them charms are for."

Bellow produced a crumpled pack of Benson & Hedges and drew one. An inveterate smoker since youth, he'd told me he wanted to quit during one of our periodic conversations. As a former brother in bondage to nicotine, I empathized with the struggle. He considered the cigarette and stuck it back into the pack with a forlorn sigh. A quiet demonstration of a man holding on to his temper with both hands.

"Mr. Herzog. Thank you for the story. My blood ran cold. Could you, would you, find that piece of paper we need?"

The old man flapped his hands dismissively. He resumed digging into the cartons. Soon, we had our prize. Herzog scribbled on a notepad and handed it to me. I didn't recognize the names.

"Sean Pruitt is who you want, yeah?" he said.

"Yes."

"He didn't have an apartment. Quarters were reserved

for out-of-towners and supervisors. Pruitt shacked with his buddies when he stayed at the camp. I wrote it there. Robert Thorpe and Daniel Buckhalter."

"You recall anything about them?" I said.

"No, sir. Faces in a crowd."

I checked the names against my phone database. Thorpe's name was on the lengthy list of known associates I'd acquired. An electrician by trade. Late thirties, married with children. Danny Buckhalter, fifty, was born and raised in Horseheads; Valley High graduate. Thorpe lived in Pittsburgh. Buckhalter was currently in the wind—last known address was the Jeffers Colony. He'd gotten in on the ground floor when the project started. After the implosion, he vanished into the ether.

Herzog wrote directions to the Jeffers Colony and said he'd meet us midmorning to unlock the gate and the apartment. We'd have an hour to snoop around.

"Shucks," Lionel said to me as an aside. "This setup takes me home. Almost sorry we aren't crashing for a sleepover."

"I could leave you and nobody around here would notice," I said.

"Something, something about a dog returning to his vomit."

As we made to leave, Lionel huddled with our gnomish host. He shook some of Herzog's tobacco into a baggie and stuck it into his pocket.

Guided by a pale, sickly beam from Bellow's keychain penlight, the three of us walked in the dark along the rugged path to the SUV. Nobody spoke. Though we were packing heat, Herzog had spooked me and maybe Bellow. Lionel not so much. He was the type to challenge ghosts and goblins to a fight.

I took the wheel and headed the rig toward the highway. I'd had my fill of country for one day.

■ ■ ■

Bellow nodded off in the back.

"I think the old guy dragged his feet so we'd hang around and tip some brews," Lionel said. "He misses the missus."

Our headlights didn't shine far. The road and the trees were a throat.

"What did you think of him?" he said.

"He's a coot who'll be fortunate not to get raided by the FBI once Bellow makes it back to HQ," I said.

"Yeah. Crazy ghost story, huh?"

"Considering where we are, could have been crazier. The world is swimming in small, dark miracles. We're jaded; we hardly notice unless one jumps out of a bush at us."

Lionel lit a cigarette and lowered his window a notch.

"Do you believe it?"

"Do I believe Herzog's encounter with the numinous?" I said.

"Yeah."

"I generally believe people when they say they've seen something. Not my job to assess their veracity. Herzog

185

claims he saw a pasty white boy grinning in a tree. Why not?"

"Why not?"

"*You* bought in like you thought the Tooth Fairy was going to tuck a quarter under your pillow. Besides, I've seen enough weird white boys the past few days to easily suspend any disbelief."

"Say you aren't converting into a true believer," he said.

"I'm a devout agnostic. Let Herzog have his tall tales. The stakes are low. It doesn't matter either way. So, why not?"

"When are the stakes ever low?" He wasn't talking to me.

CHAPTER TWENTY-TWO

'd spotted a respectable motel on the edge of town where Bellow and Lionel could bunk until we rendez-voused the next day. I tried to escape while the boys were chatting with the clerk, but Lionel caught me in the lot and insisted on drinks. I told him he'd had plenty of drinks (two of Herzog's Blue plus a six-pack of Genesee) and he said, nonsense, besides, neither Johnny Law nor I had done our share. Hell's bells, amigo, it was scarcely half-past eight. No way were we letting a perfectly fine evening go to waste. What was the name of that village up the road near the Jeffers Colony? Morrow? That settled it; we were gonna see what the locals had for a bar and write it off as recon.

I glanced toward Bellow in an appeal to common sense. He shrugged and said a couple of shots didn't sound bad.

Half an hour later we arrived among a jag of buildings somewhere in another scenic patch of backwoods hill country. Morrow was as old as the surrounding forest;

moss and grapevine threaded street signs and climbed the infrequent lamp pole. Gas station, post office, general store, and a tavern was the sum of Main Street. Bramble reared neck-high to a giraffe between copses of trees. I was sure houses lay hidden farther back. Two drunks stumbled into the middle of the street, yelling at each other. One of the men tripped over a pothole and busted his ass. His buddy shrieked laughter and busted his ass too. I parked under an oak and sat there while the engine ticked.

"This ain't no tourist trap." Lionel gestured toward the sultry allure of a neon silhouette of an hourglass woman who beckoned thirsty travelers to the Black Powder Tavern. Mist crept in from the woods and the electric light of the sign tinted it crimson. "She is what the hipsters refer to as authentic."

"I'm soaking it in." I eyed the collection of 1970s and '80s cars and trucks in front of the tavern. Trans Am, Corvette, a cherry Pontiac Firebird, and some junkyard-treasure pickups. A handful of motorcycles as well. At least two-thirds of Morrow's adult population must've been bellied up to the trough getting plastered. I'd left my brass knuckles at home, more's the pity.

Several patrons smoked near an oil drum. Their cool appraisal made clear we were recognized as tourists. The joint was hopping, but not packed. Low, water-stained ceiling; sawdust floor; a knotty bar, hewn and stained; jukebox and two pool tables; strong odors of booze and sweat. Loud, of course. I snagged a booth in the corner as a pair of woozy dudes in mismatched plaid vacated. Lionel bought a pitcher of something cheap and sudsy.

We finished the beer. Lionel excused himself and chatted with a woman in mirrored Lennon glasses, a halter top, and hip-hugging jeans dithering by her lonesome at the far pool table. He slapped quarters down. She shrugged and they played. A contingent of bikers (bearded, leather-clad, and obstreperous) at a nearby table ended their banter and watched with what I can only describe as sullen amazement. Their expressions of ill humor deteriorated further when a curvaceous blonde detached from the group and joined her friend. This called for hard booze. Bellow said he was in the mood for blended scotch, nothing fancy. I weaved through a small crowd to the bar and ordered doubles. J&B for Bellow; Buffalo Trace for myself. Made it back without spilling. Bellow had settled in, arms spread against the booth back, relaxed as I'd ever seen him. That moment it seemed possible he might defy Lionel's prediction and survive his impending retirement.

"Isaiah, what the hell are you doing?" He spoke genially. An uncle, a father.

I tasted my bourbon. There didn't seem to be any percentage in answering a rhetorical question. But I decided to try.

"You'll have to be more specific."

"The hell I do," he said.

"Trying to make sense of it all. Before it's too late."

"It's four years too late for Pruitt."

"Maybe not for his mother. Maybe not for me."

"Oh, this about you? Is Mom under the mistaken impression detectives actually solve crimes?"

"She is. Everybody is. I'm doing it because the younger me wouldn't have. Because there are people, not so different from those who used to run my life, who emphatically don't want me to do this. And the more flak I receive, the more stubborn I'll become."

The set of his jaw changed. Respect, perhaps. Or amusement.

"You leaning one way or the other?"

"Too early," I said. "Death by suicide appears to be a slam dunk . . ."

"It does."

"Yet it doesn't. My intuition isn't satisfied."

When I'd desperately needed inside dope on the Tri-State Killer/Croatoan files last year, Bellow played ball. He hadn't asked for an update, and wouldn't, for both our sakes. I sensed his curiosity. I had my own questions. Why had he helped me? Perhaps a subconscious acknowledgment that I could travel certain paths into darkness that he was morally and philosophically forbidden. He felt guilty because he hadn't been aiding my cause. Using me like a tool would be more accurate. My impression of the situation, anyhow.

"Your *intuition* isn't satisfied," he said. "I don't knock intuition. There wasn't much of an investigation on the local end, or from DC. I reviewed the files. An agent shined a flashlight around and asked personnel if anybody saw anything."

"Did he shout it down the hole?"

"Probably. From where I'm sitting, that was all the circumstances justified."

"I intend to check the boxes and cross the t's."

"A placebo for June Pruitt's sake. You really are going soft. Proud of you."

"The police won't listen to her and the last guy her brother hired didn't get far."

He looked through me into some bleak distance.

"Early on with the Bureau, I was assigned to a joint taskforce hunting for a serial killer on the Gulf Coast. The search had gone on for a while before I arrived and it went on and on after I was reassigned. Fifteen years of murders, disappearances, false leads, dead ends. The team filled a shipping container with reports, interviews, photographs, and small pieces of evidence collected from the death sites. People graduated from Quantico and joined the case, like me. Agents were reassigned, like me. Agents retired and bequeathed their notes to an ever-dwindling pool of investigators. Marriages, divorces, firings, heart attacks, strokes, suicides."

Bellow swallowed his drink in one go. Didn't even shudder as it hit bottom.

"You pursue a case for years; sludge through marshes, scoop bodies out of rivers, flatten your arches tracking down witnesses; your hair thins and your sanity does too. The faces of victims haunt your nightmares. Finally, a traffic cop in the Midwest pulls the perp over for a busted taillight and cracks it wide open. Instead of relief, you feel emptiness. Instead of elation, there's a nagging sense of disappointment."

"The gist of that story being . . . ?"

"I understand being the next man up. I understand

your stubbornness. I understand irrationality. Chasing
ghosts isn't for people who want to stay in their right
minds."

"Another round?" I said.

"Sold," he said.

■ ■ ■

I brought the drinks and we sipped and watched Lionel
and the women shoot pool. The lady in the halter top
touched her hair and laughed frequently. The blonde
wore Lionel's hat. They took turns chalking his cue and
blowing off the excess dust. Meanwhile, the throng of
bikers reminded me of a dormant volcano grumbling to
life.

"What made you decide to become a cop?" I said.

Bellow held his glass and turned it in the dim light.
Those ghosts he'd invoked swam beneath the surface of
his skin, jostling for primacy, blending, then separating.
His child self, young agent, family man, widower, jaded
professional.

"Ask what made me stay a cop."

"I'll bite."

"It's 1971, I'm at the breakfast table and my dad is
reading the paper. I see a photo with a headline that
doesn't match until I get a chance to read the fine print
later. A black-and-white media shot of convicted murderer Juan Corona. Owned a peach ranch in California.
Maybe you never heard of him. He's in a suit and tie.
Cuffed, but the chain is almost slack. Grinning like a

comedian. He's clowning for reporters. A deputy sticks a
hand in his short ribs, guiding him forward. The cop
scowls in weary disgust, but Corona gobbles the attention as he does the cha-cha-cha toward the prison bus
and a permanent stay at the crossbar hotel.

"I study the photo and think he doesn't look like a
bad guy. Nah, he looks like my dad's pal from work, a
fella we called Uncle Jim. Jim swaggered into the family
barbecue, several margaritas under his belt, and entertained the kids with a slapstick routine. That's how Corona seemed in that photo. He murdered twenty-five
people with a machete, did Mr. Happy-Go-Lucky, Mr.
Vaudeville, Mr. Psychopath. Itinerant laborers on the ol'
peach farm. Dig a hole, plant a tree. In college, I reacquainted myself with his lurid case history in a true-
crime magazine. An inmate welcomed Corona to prison
by stabbing him good and proper. Another disgruntled
con gouged out Corona's eye."

"Render unto Caesar," I said.

"Amen."

"Ted Bundy smiles in almost every photo. Every
damned photo except that candid shot where he's caught
off guard, snarling like a carnivore."

"That bestial face is the last thing thirty-something
women saw before they died," he said. "*Everybody* in
America used to know him on sight. He could've been
on a trading card in a pack of bubblegum. Bundy, Gacy,
Ramirez . . ."

"Corona."

"Corona. Anymore, you invoke those names and you get a blank stare."

It bodes ill for a society to forget its monsters.

"In Japan, oarfish sightings augur ill," I said. "Upstate New York, it's rednecks and eels."

"Seen any eels lately?"

"No, but we have a bumper crop of rednecks. And Redlicks."

"Are you happy with the change of scenery, the new gig? Domestic bliss?"

Happy? I was too introspective to ever fall prey to that breed of complacency. Happiness tends to ricochet off me, as should be the case for people of my ilk. Best-case scenario? I'll die the way Mifune did at the end of *Throne of Blood*—shouting defiant threats from a balcony while a bunch of disgruntled former comrades turn me into a pincushion. Realistically, it'll happen on an ice floe or on the tundra in winter. Ravens will pick my bones. A fortune-teller predicted that I'd die in the cold. Nothing I could articulate to Bellow even though, as a fellow traveler, he might understand.

He saw that I wasn't going to answer.

"Changing the subject. Are those Viking rejects planning to kill Lionel?"

"Kill? Or maim?"

A biker heaved upright. Tall, heavy, and dangerously embarrassed. He glanced at our table, having seen the three of us wander in as a posse. Calculating the odds, no doubt. I gave him an ice-water stare, held it, and waved with my fingers. He looked at Lionel and the women, back to me and Bellow, and sat.

"We'd best retrieve Lionel," Bellow said. "He and his lady friends are on their third round of tequilas. Nothing good happens after the third shot of tequila."

I volunteered to ruin Lionel's evening. He was past walking under his own power by the time I reached him.

"It's later than you think," he said as I lifted him in a fireman's carry and headed for the door.

The ladies pouted. The bikers uttered a muted hurrah with jazz hands.

CHAPTER TWENTY-THREE

Morning came along in a hurry.

I showered, dressed for trudging in the woods, trailer parks, and abandoned towns, then splurged for breakfast on my tab in the enormously expensive hotel restaurant. The plan was to head home that afternoon and table the legwork aspect of the investigation until I'd successfully withstood the holidays.

The boys awaited me at the motel. Decent weather; bright and cold. I presented Bellow a sack of donuts and hot coffee from a chain shop. His eyes were watery and owlish. Otherwise, he was tip-top and raring to charge. Lionel, conversely, looked like he'd toppled off the back of a speeding garbage truck. The motel wall kept him upright until he staggered forward and performed a Chaplin-esque face-plant into the backseat of the SUV.

"He went to bed in those clothes," I said.

"Same clothes, same face," Lionel said without raising his head from where he'd tucked it between his knees.

Two days without shaving and he had the makings of a beard. "Those girls last night. They had an interesting comment about the Jeffers site."

"Don't you puke in here, soldier." I might have gunned the engine and peeled rubber with slightly more exuberance than exiting the motel lot warranted. "You were blabbing about the case with a pair of barflies? Go on."

"Amigo, I was investigating. One of 'em said the collider site gets active after sundown. People see unusual lights and hear odd sounds out there at night."

"Patrols," I said. "Night watchmen doing their rounds."

"The girls said there aren't any night watchmen." He breathed heavily. "I think we got ourselves a Hardy Boys mystery on our hands. *Curse of the Collider.*"

"Lord, he slept in the tub," Bellow said to me under his breath.

"Lucky you," I said. "I've fished him out of the toilet as the bubbles were getting smaller."

"Today will be a day of suffering," Lionel said.

"He happens to himself," I said to Bellow.

"I could use a drink," Lionel said, muffled. "Hair of the dog."

"Lionel, there aren't any fucking drinks left," I said.

"Guys. I may have to execute a Technicolor yawn." He remained in the duck-and-cover position, to my consternation. "Um. What goes down will come up. *Curse of the Tequila Shots!*"

I urgently pressed the power window controls.

■ ■ ■

The fastest route to the colony took me through Morrow Village. The burg was even spookier in broad daylight. Citizens may well have abandoned the area en masse in the '70s. Then hippies, bikers, and scavengers crept in over the years and occupied the ruins. On the downhill side of town where forest ceded to a stretch of marsh, a crater obliterated the road at an intersection governed by a dead traffic light. Obviously, locals had detoured around the crater since forever—I went jouncing and bouncing over a clearing, at a precarious angle along a deeply rutted hillside, and back onto asphalt. Same as everybody else, apparently.

Lenny Herzog proved a man of his word. He threw open the tall metal gate to Jeffers Colony as I pulled in beside his rattletrap Datsun. I suppose every Datsun in existence was a jalopy by definition.

"Unit 435." He stuck his face close to mine and pressed a key into my hand. "One hour, as agreed. Don't get sticky fingers." He gave everybody in the car the hairy eyeball, as though he'd slept on the deal and jolted awake consumed with buyer's remorse.

I assured him we were only here to snoop and maybe take pictures. Contrary to popular mythology, a PI license doesn't indemnify one against trespassing, much less B&E. I wasn't required to observe cop procedures, but neither was I afforded the privileges or authority of a cop. Herzog's permission was a murky area, although Bellow's presence mitigated that particular concern.

"Didn't people pack their shit when they left?" Lionel said.

"Oh, there's treasure to be found here," Herzog said. "Living units for eighteen hundred employees. Movie theater, post office, grocery store, community center. Swimming pool. The whole kit and caboodle. The camp shut down overnight. Residents had hours to pack valuables and scram. Bosses promised everyone could return later. Didn't happen. This gate closed and that was that."

I envisioned him slinking house to house, picking through abandoned "treasure" like a two-legged coyote.

"One hour means one hour," he said.

Bellow checked the rearview after we passed through the gate.

"He's adamant about that one-hour business. What do you suppose happens if we're late?"

"We turn into pumpkins." I estimated how many laws we were breaking and the mandatory minimum sentence range for trespassing on a defunct government facility. It comforted me to have a Fed in the car, for once. Should trouble descend, I'd let Bellow do the fast-talking.

There's a threshold upon which artificial ecosystems begin to collapse. The colony had exceeded this demarcation and proceeded to an accelerated state of decay. At a remove, the modular structures presented a sturdy façade. Closer inspection revealed algae stains, water-streaked windows, and bubbled paint. Rust bled through everywhere. Windows were boarded. Herzog diligently mowed the grass and trimmed the juniper hedges. He'd hastily and incompletely scrubbed graffiti from the post office windows—perversions of the Redlick logo. Stick figures were impaled upon the barbed wheel; stick figures roasted in crimson flames. The graffiti was similar to the artwork at the Nameless Field on Vulture Bluff.

Some street lamps were smashed. Birds decomposed in the gutters. The broken glass and graffiti merely accented the ongoing hostile reclamation of this patch of land. Herzog was fighting a rearguard action that barely tamed the camp's devolution and reversal into primeval darkness. Yeah, the old Beat writer William Burroughs had been onto something: Nature does not want for evil in the absence of humanity. Organized wickedness is exchanged for the insensate craving of a much greater and no less ruthless organism.

"Good grief, look at this vandalism," Bellow said. "Kids? Disaffected locals who were kicked off the job? That had to be an economic mess."

I thought of sullen locals scaling the fence, brandishing cans of spray paint. Then I thought of the group dressed in high school uniforms at the Nameless Field.

"Not kids." I slowed the vehicle to walking speed. The sense of being observed came in waves. "It's a tumor. This camp. The construction zone. The tunnel. Mother Earth is pushing back hard."

"There's a site in the interior of Alaska," Bellow said. "Macintyre Hill. Similar setup for a mining operation. Abandoned and gone to seed. Heard of it?"

"No."

"I'm surprised."

"Alaska is a graveyard of abandoned towns and radar

installations. World War Two bunkers honeycomb the
Aleutians. I poked around inside one on a hill overlooking Dutch Harbor. Haven't seen it all." The late second
act of my life was convincing me of that.

■ ■ ■

Unit 435 hadn't fared any better than the rest of the
decaying houses. The key stuck in the front door lock
and the knob turned grudgingly. Dampness had swollen
the door in its frame. The interior was a bland duplex
model; living room, kitchenette, bath, and matching
coffin bedrooms. Gloomy at midmorning. I flipped the
light switch to test the power. Juice flowed, although
the globes were chock-full of mummified insects and
the effect was ghastly and I killed it after several seconds. Desiccated corpses of mice and bats were strewn
about. Mold spread in blue-green glaciers across the carpet; it had eaten into the drapes and ceiling tiles.

"That's a fuckton of dead rodents." Lionel played the
beam of his flashlight across the floor.

"Pesticides," Bellow said. "Can't you picture the corporate overlords driving through town in trucks, dosing
the neighborhood with gas? That's how they deployed
DDT when my parents were little. Children played in
that poison."

As he spoke, my personal vision of it was a crop duster
with a Redlick emblem bombing the town. Another part
of my inner self worried that the answer was something
entirely worse.

"My advice is don't lick your fingers after you touch anything," I said.

The long-dead fridge contained a nauseating mess of gray fuzz. Cabinets contained boxes of oatmeal and cereal shredded by mice. One of the bedroom windows had shattered inward. Branches of a dogwood choked by bittersweet vines twisted over the threshold and clutched the bedframe. Water had eroded patches of the ceiling. Moldering magazines, moldering clothes, moldering furniture, mouse shit. A common atmosphere pervades abandoned property that varies by age and particular violence, not dissimilar to the spectrum of aged scotch. Standing among ruins is an eerie reminder of mortality. We are meat and Mother Nature must eat.

Herzog wasn't kidding that the residents had vacated in a rush. An occupant must've been busy packing when he received the order to vamoose. His suitcase lay sprung on the bed, trailing socks and pants like guts. Nothing sinister happened to the former occupants of Jeffers Colony. Records indicated they'd transferred to other jobs or returned to local unemployment rolls. This wasn't the scene of a mass disappearance or slaughter, but a snapshot sans context. Even so, it got under my skin. The implication felt unreasonably pointed, unnervingly profound. *Yes, yes, these weak fucks escaped on a technicality. The polar caps are melting, bitches. Prehistoric viruses are awakening as permafrost softens into mud. I'm coming, ape. I'm coming and my jaws are wide enough to swallow you whole.*

Lionel studied a torn poster of vintage Cher in a two-

piece bathing suit. Mold had warped the beloved super-
star into a demonic monstrosity from a medieval
woodcut.

"Friends, what in the blue fuck are we hoping to find
here?"

I hadn't quite thrown in the towel and Bellow was
switched into another mode entirely. He silently and me-
thodically toured the apartment, poking at coagulated
laundry and assorted detritus with a busted broom handle. Scratching on a closet door caught his attention. He
slid the panel aside and a large possum hissed as it waddled backward into the shadow of its lair.

"Don't get any ideas," I said to Lionel. I moved farther into the apartment and checked the bathroom and
a storage closet. The storage area housed a washer-dryer
combo. End of the line. Concentrating, I mentally
cleared away the current mess, focusing on how the unit
appeared during the height of the project. Who, if anyone, surveyed the contents after Sean Pruitt died? To my
knowledge, there might not have been an accounting of
any kind.

Lionel was right; nothing had survived. We wouldn't
be able to separate the routines and lives of men from the
passage of time. The image was corrupted with no chance
to re-create or rehabilitate it. Despite my cynicism, I'd
almost begun to hope I was onto something, that perhaps I'd salvage a clue, an incriminating photo or note,
or a ghostly phone message. Dust, rust, mold, jettisoned
clothing, shredded paper, and tiny animal corpses were
the sum and the legacy of those who'd moved on. The

meaningful lack of evidence compounded the simple math; the ME and cops had performed their due diligence and correctly concluded a suicide had occurred. Sean Pruitt went to Shaft 40 and jumped to his death.

Tidy, except for pesky, nagging details. Sean Pruitt had taken a sauna, scraped his nails, anointed his entire body with mineral oil, and dosed himself with a combination of drugs including synthetic peyote. That sounded like a ritual. How had Boss Man described the Mares of Thrace? Pentecostal, minus the Christianity.

Pensive and annoyed, I gripped my squash ball; twenty-five repetitions with the right, thirty with the left because that hand needed all the help it could get, and as I meditated, a question materialized. When crashing with friends in cramped quarters, where does one sleep? With a kind of dazed apprehension, I went to the couch in the living room and pulled out the cushions. Two quarters, a ballpoint pen, and lint. There was a floor vent near the couch. I lifted the grille and spotted a white smudge in the murk. A wadded handkerchief was tucked into the space. The handkerchief contained a wedding band and a bent photo of Sean Pruitt and his wife, Linda. June Pruitt had mentioned the ring was missing and presumed it stolen. A klepto paramedic would've made for a simpler explanation. Reality bends in strange directions. The photo was similar to the one she gave me; the couple was younger, less careworn in this version. On the back Sean Pruitt had scribbled, *To my darling, Rita: Youth, Looks, and Love Everlasting.* The wedding band was inscribed, *Darling Sean, Love of My Life, Linda.*

I flipped over the photo. Who the hell was Rita?

"Oh, come on," Lionel said upon examining the evidence. "We were almost in the clear. Tell you what, put that thing back and we'll pretend it doesn't exist."

"Tallyho, boys," Bellow said as he ambled toward us.

I pocketed the evidence.

"It's a bust."

Bellow shrugged and continued to the front door. Lionel made frantic bug eyes at me. I shushed him with a throat-slash motion and followed Bellow.

A man would only stash his wedding ring on the way to a rendezvous with fate if he didn't expect to return. That's a man who anticipated doom; either by his own hand or a helpful push from another. I wasn't sure how to feel. Dread was in the lead by a nose.

Sadly, this meant the drive home to the Hudson Valley was on hold for a few hours.

CHAPTER TWENTY-FOUR

I don't travel without tools of the trade: duffel bag containing outdoor clothes (ninja gear, Lionel called this ensemble), dehydrated fruit, canteen, flashlight, matches, first aid kit, two-way radios, et cetera. More pertinently, I'd concealed extracurricular devices in a hollow panel where the rental agency stored the spare tire: Mossberg shotgun, entrenching tool, bolt cutters, hacksaw, plastic ties, coil of rope, duct tape, and so on. I was ready for trouble when I made the command decision to break into the Jeffers Project and have a firsthand look at where Sean Pruitt died.

Bellow watched Lionel and me plastering mud on the SUV's plates. He forestalled my explanation with a curt gesture.

"The less I know, the less I know. Catch you later." He paid Herzog fifty bucks to give him a lift into town. Herzog was raking it in, thanks to us tourists. I hoped the old woodsman bargained for an immunity deal. Off they putted in that wired-together pickup. Convenient.

To my way of thinking, it was best that Herzog not have any notion as to my plans either.

Lionel and I zipped over to the north side of the Jeffers Project site, which lay a quarter mile south of the colony. We parked at the north gate, which had once served as a main entry point for the construction teams. An access road ran between the inner and outer fences, circumnavigating the entire track. Lionel didn't find any evidence of an active camera or alarm. The powers that be probably figured threats of massive fines and imprisonment would deter most trespassers. He cautioned that I should accept his estimation with a grain of salt. It was well within the realm of possibility that a private security company sent random patrols to discourage professional thieves on the prowl for loose equipment, copper wire, and the like. I'd already gotten busy. I snipped the lock with the bolt cutters, shoved aside the gate, and headed the SUV onto the path.

We endeavored the relatively lengthy drive. At roughly half-mile intervals, dinky modular shacks served as access nodes to the subterranean superstructure. Riding from south to north through tall timber, the numbers painted on the sides of the modulars counted down. Soon, as we crossed into the unfinished sector, the shacks disappeared, replaced by scaffolds and placards in bulldozed lots. Forty-two, forty-one, and forty. Berms of rocks, gravel, and black earth formed a semicircle around a ten-foot-by-ten-foot hole sealed by a sheet of pig iron. Orange ticker tape and VERTICAL DROP signs did their duty.

They'd installed a panel hatch in the iron sheet. We cut the locks, and grunting and groaning, lifted it on corroded hinges. Damp odors of spoiled earth and rusting metal wafted from the hole.

"Pruitt's body was discovered at the bottom of this shaft within hours of the fall. He drove here in a jeep." I indicated a spot near the berm. "Security and other personnel had access to a fleet. What brought him this far? He could've jumped into any of the other shafts. What was special about this one?"

"You're latched on to the idea he killed himself," Lionel said.

"Can't uncover a solid reason for him to be out here in the weeds. Wasn't part of his task assignment. I'm not latched on to anything, though."

"Good. This is also a cozy spot for a murder, which could be the reason he was here." He leaned over and spat. "Nothing down there. Bottomless."

"It's not bottomless. It's maybe a hundred and eighty or ninety feet. And behold, a ladder."

"Yeah, I see that shitty ladder." He put his hat back on. "There's a diamond mine in eastern Siberia. Open pit, over three thousand feet in diameter. Enormous, gaping wound; a borehole to hell. The mineshaft creates its own weather system. Choppers won't fly over the pit. The vortex will suck 'em in."

"Hate to ponder how they made that discovery," I said. "Although it sounds apocryphal."

"Reporting the news, bud." He watched as I tightened the Velcro head strap of my miner's lamp. "Wait. What are you doing? Your fat ass is definitely not climbing onto that ladder."

I clicked the headlamp on and off. Its halogen bulb wasn't as bright as the sun. Close, though.

"Kicked pasta last month." I patted my gut. "Lost a pound, easy. Now to reap the benefits."

"Turn around; you'll find it again. Coleridge . . ."

"Yes, Mom?"

"Weren't you the one who said that the cops and CSI already picked the crime scene over? Multiply futility by four years and you get one hundred percent futility."

"If there wasn't a ladder, I'd cede the field to your pessimism."

"But there's a ladder."

"You call it a ladder; I call it a sign. Have you ever walked around a supercollider track? Sean P was so enthralled with the notion, he had it inked on his arm."

"Right on," he said. "The dead guy was a nerd. Nerds and their science fiction tats."

"You were standing there when Herzog said he thought this place might be the new Area 51. Your girlfriends at the bar gave you valuable intel. Suspicious nocturnal activity, the ladies said. Sounds like a clue."

"Sounds like an excuse for you to play Frank Hardy. Difference between today and last night is that I'm relatively sober. People worried that the Hadron Collider would tear open a black hole, or create a parallel universe. Paranoid delusions are the jelly in the PB and J sandwich."

"Told you before, I'm not a Hardy. I'm Jonny Quest. I've never, ever gone caving. What red-blooded private eye would ignore this golden opportunity to go spelunking?"

"One who isn't a big fucking dummy?" he said.

"We only come in fun-size."

"Mandibole wouldn't like it."

"We crossed that line in the sand a few dunes ago."

The goal wasn't to uncover an overlooked clue, although with the crackling aura of kismet, it wouldn't have shocked me to discover a new puzzle piece. This expedition spoke to my identity as a hunter and a man. Once I got going, there was no return until I'd exhausted every lead, turned over every rock, and followed every trail to a dead end. In the Outfit days, I hadn't possessed the luxury of returning to my bosses empty-handed. The mob levies an exponential penalty for repeated failure, so I did my damnedest to succeed, and success generally aligned with perseverance. The habit was ingrained to the bone. Sean Pruitt's wedding band represented the Rubicon. Odds were, I'd find nothing down there except an abandoned tunnel. I had to go see for myself.

I unrolled a bandanna and fashioned it into a mask to cover my nose and mouth like a stagecoach robber. No sense eating any more flakes of rust or grit than necessary.

"Allow me to log my objection, for the record," he said.

If I'd spoken on the record, I would've copped to being terrified at the prospect of leaving the sunlit world behind on what amounted to a double-dog dare issued by the angel on my left shoulder. He'd been damned pushy of late.

"Duly noted. Any patrols or the cops happen along, tell them we're conducting a safety inspection. Should charm fail, casually toss a rock down and I'll double-time it back to the top. Cool?"

"Uncool," he said. "Way, way uncool, man."

■ ■ ■

Lionel was on the money: The situation was maximally uncool. I arrived at this conclusion sixty or seventy feet into the descent. Darkness, heights, and underground spaces weren't generally a problem for me. Combine the three, add a sense of urgency into the mix, and that caused me to reassess. The ladder was relatively sturdy, albeit creaky as hell under my not inconsiderable weight. It wrapped around me in a tubular cage. There was a platform at what I estimated to be the halfway point. I rested. The open hatch and sky had shrunk. Lionel clicked twice on the two-way; I responded with two clicks and resumed the descent. The ladder style changed to skinny rungs. An unsettling shimmy accompanied the ominous creaks of protesting metal.

This was the farthest I recalled ever being underground. Caving isn't high on my list of recreational activities, nor was it something often required to fulfill mob contracts. Water streamed from cracks in the retaining wall and sluiced into the abyss. I'd read that the shelved Texas supercollider project of the 1990s had flooded the tunnels to stave off inevitable collapse. Optimists crossed their fingers in hopes of resuming work one day.

I trod carefully, in no hurry. Imagine my chagrin when the mooring bolts snapped loose as I grasped a rung. My weight precipitously transferred to my feet, and that rung snapped. I had a moment to regret a whole bunch of rash life decisions, including the recent one to climb into Shaft 40. I could hear the exasperation in Lionel's voice as he relayed the bad news to Meg: *Welp, what's another hospital bill on the ol' pile, right?* Of course, it was more likely he'd have to cover his heart with his hat and explain to her the circumstances of my untimely demise and its macabre similarity to Sean Pruitt's.

My reflexes are above average, so I managed to flail in a semi-coordinated manner and catch another rung. Sadly, brackets tore free with a ping of unseated bolts and it was slick from dripping water anyway. This time I toppled backward and downward.

Yes, I screamed. A cartoon caption bubble would've spelled *Aaaeeeiii!*

CHAPTER TWENTY-FIVE

A sudden drop of three feet can maim or kill. Your spine snaps as easily as that rung had. I fell a solid two stories; farther than twenty feet, but less than thirty. Plenty far to constitute a dangerous, possibly fatal impact against solid ground. Whiro, or Satan, or whoever watches over guys like me, stepped in to save my bacon; I was in a semi-chair position when I landed in a pool of drainage water. The impact stole my air and momentarily stunned me as surely as if I'd gotten slugged in the kidneys with a baseball bat; the shock of cold water shooting up my nose brought me around again. I lightly touched the side of the pit and rebounded to the surface by straightening.

Water sloshed against the sides of the tunnel as I clambered to my feet. It was much deeper at the center where workers dug a foundational trench for the vacuum tube and guiding magnets. Near the wall, water came to my ankles. I'd been extremely fortunate to have pitched away from the ladder, else I would've broken a few bones.

Soaked and shivering, I bent double and coughed until my lungs were raw. Dull throbbing in my legs and lower back promised a world of pain once the adrenaline subsided. I caught my breath and shined the light around; grateful it survived the ordeal. Weatherproof and water resistant to one hundred and twenty meters. Thank you, German engineering.

An arched tunnel of exposed rock was shored by girders that curved like a giant's rib cage; the passage traveled beyond my light. New York State isn't renowned for seismic activity, yet a recent earthquake had severely damaged the tunnel and its foundations. A fissure cracked through the rock ceiling, split the wall, and disappeared into the hardpack floor beneath the veil of water. More cracks extended in both directions. This explained the dire condition of the ladder. What if it had come unmoored nearer the apex of the shaft? The tunnel had shifted and separated and sections were uneven. Chunks of loose stone jutted like fangs. There was no estimating how far the crevices descended into the earth; I'd have to step lightly or else discover the answer firsthand.

X marked the spot where Sean Pruitt went splat, to put it indelicately. The ME's report was ambivalent as to whether he'd fallen down the middle, which meant a jump or a push into the shaft proper, or slipped while climbing the ladder and caromed like a pinball. Unfortunate soul; no mud puddle to save him and it wouldn't have mattered since he plunged from a much greater height.

The cell phone was bricked. The two-way made it,

more or less, although the connection sounded patchy when Lionel called. He'd heard me scream and was reluctantly prepping to scale the shaft. I described the situation. After some back-and-forth, we agreed he'd roll to Shaft 41 and wait for me make the hike. While we conversed, I unloaded the .357, dried it and the bullets as best as possible with a wrung-out corner of my sleeve, reloaded, and holstered the gun. Somewhere in the middle of that operation, the radio screeched and gave up the ghost. I was on my lonesome. Of course, when a man is carrying his faithful sidearm, a sharp knife, and the image of true love in his heart, he's never alone.

■ ■ ■

As I limped northwest toward the rendezvous, my feet and shins ached. I'd bumped against the side of the pool with significantly greater force than I'd reckoned during the initial excitement. The entrance fee to life isn't steep. The micro-transactions are what eventually kill you.

I hadn't gone a dozen steps before I noticed the graffiti. Sprayed on the sloping wall with alternating black-and-white paint. Arrows (singles and clusters), quadrilaterals, trapezoids, crescents, and triangles were plain. Infrequent, slashed into rock, directional. Then frequent, degenerative, and splashed onto girders, the ceiling. Neat trick, that last detail, as the roof vaulted nearly two stories high at its apex. Geometric symbols segued to gibberish symbols and these composed a gibberish language.

The headlamp brightened, dimmed, brightened in a nauseating cycle. No phone, no radio, a flaky light source, and weird damn graffiti. A bizarre day kept getting stranger, for which I had no one to blame except Isaiah Coleridge. I congratulated myself that at least the symbols weren't threatening or satanic. Who'd decorated the tunnel? I'd already discounted teenagers and disaffected locals. The scenery changed as I proceeded. Geometric designs and vaguely Nordic runes were superseded by those stickmen I'd seen around town and environs. Stickmen hunting. Stickmen congregating in caves, bowed in worship. Basking in the veneration of the stickmen were variations of the demonic creatures—the prodigious heads with T. rex appendages and gaping jaws—displayed on the Nameless Field mural. These monstrosities squatted beneath black-and-white disks of sun and moon that overlapped like empty Venn diagrams. The sketches were contemporary, yet, as with the other examples I'd witnessed, emanated antiquity. A mind preoccupied with old, old sentiments guided the hand of this artist, or artists.

Herzog's theories regarding the site might not be so fantastical.

Lamenting my inability to snap photos, I vowed to locate and interview Sean Pruitt's buddies Buckhalter and Thorpe at my earliest convenience. Someone with personal knowledge of the site was damn well going to tell me what the Redlick Group and a cabal of government scientists had had on their minds. Atom-smashing, particle physics, and quantum what-the-fuck-ever aside, the multitude of spooky vibes I'd gotten since day one suggested an agenda quite divorced from pop science. Or any science. It stank of alchemy and the occult, which is to say, black magic hoodoo, and like the rest of the bad ideas of ye olden times, the provincial superstition powering those avenues of human inquiry usually portended trouble for everyone outside the inner circle of trust.

Strangeness performed a flying trapeze leap to the outright bizarre. I entered a section of improved tunnel that extended for roughly two hundred yards; here a foundation was poured and a metal sheath inserted. Panels, sockets, and a narrow channel that traveled the floor and ceiling waited eternally to be fitted with circuit boards, lighting fixtures, and the main conducting rails of the particle accelerator. I had a glimpse at what might've resembled a final working product. The whole tube was painted in swirling patterns and recurring motifs of primitive animism. More thunderbirds and terrible faces; more stickmen and contemporary petroglyphs depicting animals and celestial bodies. Alternating tiger stripes of white and black created a disconcerting optical effect of the tunnel revolving. This mural couldn't be considered graffiti by any means. Far too sophisticated. Service doors were slotted intermittently, camouflaged by the artwork. I laid my hand flat against one door and swore it thrummed as if transmitting a faint vibration of heavy machinery. The metal tube ended and I stepped down into watery muck and rudely hacked earth.

I passed equipment wreathed in tarpaulins, stacks of prefabricated wall panels, cement blocks, and pipes. Distant metallic groans interrupted the tomblike atmosphere of the collider track. A seismic shift? Generators kicking in? The groaning morphed into the shrill bellow of a primitive hunting horn, then an air raid klaxon. The ground trembled and its vibration traveled through my bones. The hairs on my body prickled the way they do when you scuff your socks on a carpet. My heart fluttered and I imagined a cartoon version of myself pulsing with an electrical current that caused tiny bright sparks to travel along the contours of my body.

The headlamp blinked out. I remained stock-still, right hand glued to the wall, enduring waves of vertigo while coming to terms with the idea that I'd gotten myself into a bind.

■ ■ ■

The chorus of deep-sea rumbling subsided. Silence resumed except for the gurgle and drip of water oozing through rock. I thumbed the headlamp toggle and hoped my eyes would adjust, but nope on either score. Dark as a mine. Dark as the bottom of a sealed supercollider tunnel. I'd possessed the foresight to carry an emergency all-weather penlight as a backup. One of those dense little steel numbers that fits in the palm of your hand. I got the light out of my pocket and was feeling for the on switch when I heard an odd noise somewhere back the way I'd come. My brain required several moments to reconcile this particular sound with the context of my environment—nearly two hundred feet beneath the surface, alone in the dark. Except not entirely alone. Arrhythmic splashing approached. Someone, or something, was shambling along the tunnel toward my position.

For a long, horrible second, I didn't think the penlight would activate. Its ghostly thin beam powered on, feebly. Much better than nothing; still crappy. I aimed it with my left hand and drew the revolver with my right. It's too embarrassing to catalogue the fevered possibilities my mind conjured as a shadow moved against the backdrop of deeper gloom. Heart rate jacked into the red, pouring sweat, I was a little boy confronted by the absolute certainty monsters lurked under the bed and in the closet.

Something larger than a dog and shaped like a spider broke into view. I didn't hesitate to empty the .357. The revolver kicked in my fist, booming in that enclosed space. Bullets sparked as they pinged the lurching thing's carapace. The object advanced with a herky-jerky, side-slipping gait. No time to reload; I twisted, dove, and skidded behind a pallet of pipes. The dog-spider thing lunged past on segmented legs, off-balance and whipping a pair of spindly, flexible arms that ended in pincers. Its cylindrical body was metal-plated and pocked by bullet holes. Blue and red running lights glowed softly on its carriage, vaguely illuminating the blades of a retracted auger. That last detail would've been hilariously phallic under other circumstances. This mining machine was an updated, highly modified cousin of the militarized robots that soldiers and SWAT teams sent ahead to perform reconnaissance and defuse bombs. Few carried onboard weapons, although rumors of autonomous kill-bots abounded. The aggressive style of its approach and those flexible, telescoping arms spelled lethal prototype at the very least. Was the device automated or was it piloted remotely? Excellent questions for future study, assuming I had a future.

I dropped the gun and the penlight and hefted a six-foot length of heavy steel pipe. To paraphrase Archimedes, give me a mighty enough lever and I'll roll the earth. I put that theory to the test. The robot wheeled, clunky and slow, and I smashed it with all my muscle and all my weight. The reverberation numbed my wrists and elbows. I felt the shock in my gritted teeth. The robot faltered, listing to its side, jointed legs scrabbling for purchase. I walloped it again, aiming for the dent I'd made near its front end, where ports and nodes nested, and, I fervently hoped, a brainbox. I brought that pipe down like fabled John Henry driving a railroad spike. This blow nearly tore my arms out of their sockets. It wasn't lost on me that John Henry fought a steam engine and died. The robot swayed in caricature of a boxer who's gotten stung. Adding to the nightmarish atmosphere of struggling in the poorly lit tunnel (the penlight lay under a couple of inches of water, emitting a pallid radiance), an unearthly grinding whir started somewhere in the machine's in-nards. Had to be loud, because my ears rang from the gunshots. I would've gone for another power swing, but a metal arm interposed, pincers clamped the pipe, and we were locked in a tug-of-war. In a sickening exhibition of brute power, the pipe crimped and flattened under the robot's clamps. I released, instinctively ducking as the other arm slashed my back and shoulders like an iron-corded bullwhip. I stumbled with the glancing blow, grabbed another length of steel from the pile, and circled counterclockwise, avoiding those threshing arms. My saving grace was the machine's slow, ungainly pivoting radius, of which I took full advantage. A critical rule to defeating a bigger, stronger opponent is to either target his offensive capabilities, or cripple his mobility. I hammered the nearest leg at a knobby joint and was gratified to see metal bend, then buckle. Circling, hammering, circling. Once I'd severely damaged three of its legs, I stabbed the pipe under the robot and into the ground and lifted with that fulcrum. Budging that floundering, uneven weight proved a daunting task. Famous strongman Eddie Hall suffered a brain bleed after his world record dead lift. That was on my mind, you bet. Eddie Hall was no regular-issue human being. I kept lifting, straightening my knees. The robot swiped at me and missed. It toppled into the trench at the center of the passage and sank, trailing a rush of bubbles and foam. Its red and blue lights shimmered like reflective stones.

Advanced military hardware was more Lionel's bag. As far as I knew, the damned thing was submersible, self-repairing, and would recover to initiate hot pursuit. A worse scenario by exponential degrees: *other* killbots could be en route. I'd need a hell of a lot more pipe. Fear helped me forget my aches and pains and incipient exhaustion. I scooped up the light, had several nervous moments until I located the revolver, and hauled ass for Shaft 41.

■ ■ ■

A popular Internet video made the rounds of a robot designed in a lab at MIT. The device resembled a dog and behaved in rudimentary doggy fashion, obeying simple commands. The researcher had even programmed the third- or fourth-generation model to play fetch. The Internet lost its collective mind when a scientist, seeking to demonstrate the folly of anthropomorphism, kicked Fido robot over. The robot struggled to right itself and the researcher kept knocking it down. Iteration six saw the robot become sleeker, faster, less clumsy. Model Six righted itself immediately and exhibited defensive postures and behaviors. Model Six varied its locomotion from stealthy crawling to sudden bursts of speed. Model Six successfully manipulated handles and doorknobs. Viewer sympathy melted into distinct unease. Cute, inept robots engender sympathy; the uncanny valley isn't a trip people are willing to take.

I dwelled on that video while escaping the Jeffers Project underground.

Lionel didn't comment when I dragged myself into the daylight, covered in blood and grime, clothes tattered. I had bruises, contusions, and a shallow laceration across my shoulders. He rang Bellow and told him that we were fine and headed home. I'd slumped in the back, indulging in a bit of self-pity. Continuing my resentful thoughts about the MIT robot program, I recalled several of the corporations involved with the Jeffers Project were defense contractors. I contemplated that and the plethora of occult graffiti. I contemplated generators chugging in the depths of the earth even though public documents asserted the joint was shuttered until further notice. The supercollider blueprints might not even be fully updated. Access tunnels stitched the underground, possibly to a heart or central hub, hidden below and clandestinely powering sectors of the structure. Who? Why? Those girls at the Black Powder Tavern weren't lying when they said it was common knowledge that strange things were done by night at ye old Jeffers Project.

"So." Lionel stared at the road. "What did we learn about listening to Uncle Lionel?"

"Nothing that'll stick. I feel poorly." My teeth chattered as I struggled into dry clothing.

"But it was totally worth it. Right?"

"Totally," I said, stifling a moan. The moan was less in response to my considerable physical discomfort and more in regard to how much the physical discomfort was going to cost me. More than I assumed, was how much.

CHAPTER TWENTY-SIX

I jolted from a doze. Instead of Whiro or Dad or flaming wildlife as was usually the case, Meg alighted from a golden cloud and drifted toward me upon voluminous wings of white and black. She was gloriously, radiantly naked except for strategic strands of hair and artful shadows. We embraced. Her sweet lips were warm upon mine—

The SUV frame shifted again. Gravity pressed me into my seat as the vehicle skated around a curve in excess of posted advisories.

"That streak of returning pristine cars to the rental agency?" Lionel glanced back. He wore his shooting glasses.

Dregs of light bled into the black bulk of woodland. Another vehicle trailed ours. Tough to discern the make or model at this twilit distance, only that it had to be moving fast because so were we. It hung there, a glimmering smear of headlights haunting the opposite end of a straight stretch, then gone as we swung behind a hill and climbed around a battered station wagon that seemed to be sitting still in comparison.

"When did you pick them up?" I said.

"They were pulling onto the Jeffers access road as I turned out. Late 1950s Mercury Monterey."

"Are you fucking kidding?"

"Dark red and bronze. Four-door. Fins and everything. I got a decent look at the driver. A buddy riding shotgun. More in the back. Everybody dressed for the sock-hop after the Friday night game."

I got the picture.

"Allow me to repeat: Are you fucking kidding?"

"Assholes were in a hurry too. Pulled a U-turn and came after us like a bat outta hell. Somebody with a stake in that property finally noticed us meddling kids."

Elevation rose and fell and rose with a vengeance. At seventy miles per hour the highway grade was slippery. I didn't recognize any of the winding, bumpy road. The monotone GPS patiently recalculated, no matter how many turns Lionel blew past. Obviously, he intended to keep this encounter off the radar and in the boonies.

"Isaiah, you once told me a rule," he said. "We were drunk as hell, talking about our old lives. The high points, the pitfalls. Shit that civilians don't know, *couldn't* know. You asked, 'What trips a man up in this business?' It stuck with me, what you said next."

"A grizzled killer showed me the light in the darkness."

The grizzled killer in this case was the late, great, and greatly lamented Gene Kavanaugh. Gene K, the Ace of

Spades. The Old Man on the Mountain. A world-class hitter and my mentor. His ghost lingered in the gallery of my conscience. Daily, he had more company.

"'Not knowing the big picture is a leading cause of on-the-job death.' Your words. You were referencing mobsters, but it's got universal appeal. Being kept in the dark is practically a soldier's creed. To similar detriment."

Another straightaway and I made the pursuing vehicle. A classic Mercury, as Lionel had said; probably souped-up. I unbuckled, leaned over the seat, rummaged in the storage compartment, and got ahold of the Mossberg. By then, we'd whipped around a couple more curves and were rumbling atop a saddleback ridge.

I loaded the shotgun.

"'Theirs not to reason why, theirs but to do or die.'"

"Do *and* die. Ain't no 'or' about it," he said. "Tennyson's heroic logic proves mighty convenient for the pricks running the show."

"A man who doesn't know the big picture finds it hard to stay alive."

"Impossible to duck the ax-swing you don't see coming. Amigo, I feel like we're not getting the big picture."

I didn't think he was wrong.

The engine made a throaty growl you won't ever hear unless you push the speedometer beyond ninety. We sailed over dips and tortured the suspension upon each momentary impact with the asphalt. I braced my free arm against the roof to avoid cracking my skull.

The Mercury closed steadily. It careened over a rise and vanished. The road descended into a hollow and ran across several miles of level farmland that spread like a pastoral painting. Smoke coiled above a farmhouse and that was it; even the cows were in for the winter.

Lionel eased off the gas. He feathered the brakes until we'd decelerated to somewhere in the neighborhood of sixty miles per hour, then slammed them, and after continuing to slide forward a few car lengths despite the antilock safeguard, he punched the gas pedal and executed a skidding left turn across the centerline onto a private dirt lane. Clouds of blue smoke billowed around us, accompanying the eardrum-rupturing shriek of abused tires. Cloaked in its own bank of smoke, the Mercury screeched by on the main road, yawing in a controlled slalom as its driver reacted to Lionel's maneuver. The driver jerked to a halt, reversed, and turned onto the farm road; a shark cruising through the spray of pebbles and mud in our wake.

Going by Lionel's description, this had to be a carload of the Mares of Thrace trying to chase us down. What were they to Mandibole and Redlick? Enforcers? Protection details of religious fundamentalists often scribbled outside the lines. The freaky animism-tinged hoodoo I'd encountered in Horseheads was indicative of fanatics. Fanatics are, by definition, dangerous. The notion of squaring off with cultists in the woods was an unpleasant prospect. Considering my wealth of personal experience with getting shot at, I'd assume another team of the bastards was en route. I understood why Lionel had detoured off-road. The SUV was sturdier, more powerful, and a four-wheel drive. Its weight would serve it well in the slop. I worried about the tactic anyhow. Shotgun notwithstanding, if our pursuers ran us to ground and shooting started, we might lose. This assessment altered my personal rules of engagement somewhat, and not in their favor.

One moment a faint, magical crest of golden-red sunset shone from the rim of the world. Then down came the curtain. The Mercury engaged high beams. Blinding glare filled our mirrors.

Lionel had the SUV flying down the private road. Both hands on the wheel, expertly managing its violent wrenches that threatened to catapult us into the ditch with each rock or pothole. He acclimated to the handling and pushed the vehicle. The speedometer needle crept higher. Barbed fence was strung parallel to the road on the passenger side. On the driver's side, a steep bank dropped into darkness. The panorama shook like a stop-motion film. I smiled as the euphoria drugs flooded my bloodstream.

"When I run out of road, I'm gonna have to make a decision." Lionel slipped his glasses into his breast pocket, like taking his hand from the wheel for a couple of seconds was no big thing.

"You won't run out of road." I watched the Mercury. We maintained the gap. The driver had skills, but he or she could only work with the tools at hand. The car wasn't an all-terrain vehicle. "You'll engage four-by-four and *make* a road."

He laughed. We passed a sward of flattened earth and a clutch of hay wagons and tractor blades. Ahead, the road bent toward the flank of a forest. Cottonwood and willow trees promised boggy terrain. The road degraded into a rutted trail. Good news for our team. The worse it got, the better.

It got worse for everybody. The ruts vanished and we plowed into the heart of a thicket. Brush whapped against the windows and tore off the side mirrors. We collided with a tree and the rear passenger door crunched inward. I dropped the shotgun amidst getting flung around. Glass shattered, but I couldn't see where.

Lionel cursed. The SUV launched into a starless void, its engine screaming. We glided for a semi-eternity before crash-landing. Dead stop. The airbags exploded up front. It felt surreal to sit there in the dark with the vehicle idling and the hazards ticktacking, yellow strobes illuminating nearby tree trunks. I'd covered my head; my arms had absorbed the punishment. In the morning, my body would hurt like I'd crawled into a barrel of rocks and gotten pushed down a ski slope. I wiggled my fingers and sat up, grateful that everything was in working order. Lionel swore again as he roused and deflated the airbag and shoved it flat against the steering column.

The Mercury's headlights bounced way back there in the woods. Might as well have been on another continent.

Lionel shifted into 4-LO, or what old-timers referred to as granny, and drove up out of a ditch onto a paved road. The SUV's undercarriage squealed in protest and the whole rig wobbled as it reached cruising speed. But it rolled. He whooped in victory. Frigid wind whistled through a missing side window. Giant ugly cracks starred the windshield. The dome light stuttered, revealing Lionel's face in the mirror caked in gore. Blood poured from his swollen nose. I handed him a loose sock hat and he wadded it into a ball and pressed it tight.

"Some fun, even without a firefight!" he said. And not sarcastically.

I turned in my seat and scanned the darkness. Any second and I'd see the Mercury's lights pop onto the road. That didn't happen. Any second and the laboring engine would conk out, or the axle would snap. Neither of those things happened either. He navigated to the main highway and we headed east, weary, wounded, but alive and grinning like a pair of idiots. Made sense. We were idiots having a perfectly rational response to self-induced terror and trauma.

■ ■ ■

We eventually departed the tertiary roads and traveled the highway until we pulled into a service area. The other calamity I expected to happen, but it didn't, was to get stopped by a state trooper. Lionel pumped fuel. I bought candy bars and bottles of soda. The spike of sugar and caffeine would see us across the finish line. My hands shook as I gulped the soda. The SUV was a surreal hulk bathed in the sodium light. Scraped, battered, and stove in on the rear passenger side, it resembled a surviving prop from the set of a *Mad Max* demolition derby. People glanced at it, then Lionel, masked in blood, and me, leaning against a register in obvious pain. As we prepared to mosey on, he winced and mentioned that he couldn't raise his left arm. Broken collarbone would be the diagnosis at the doc's office a day or two later.

I took control of the tiller and piloted us the rest of the way home.

The visible consequences of the expedition unspooled in predictable fashion. It was several days before my body didn't feel as wrecked as the SUV looked. My favorite rental agency banned me, and yes indeed, those premiums boarded a rocket and zoomed into the stratosphere. These were transient inconveniences. The astonished look on the sales clerk's face when I handed him the keys was priceless. For a moment he looked as if he'd drop to his knees and tear his hair in anguish. I told him, yeah, he was crying now, but he'd laugh about it someday.

PART III

DEATH OF THE STARRY-EYED KID

CHAPTER TWENTY-SEVEN

Minerva and I spent the holidays camped out at Meg's house. I glanced over my shoulder, dreading repercussions that lurked but didn't manifest. All terrible things in their own due course, Gene K used to say with a murderous twinkle in his eye. The hammer always drops.

Ulster County enjoyed a white Christmas and a white New Year. One of those big daddy mid-Atlantic storms that come along once or twice a decade made landfall and dropped a foot of snow from Upstate New York to the northern hinterlands of New England. Then it got cold. Toboggan rides, plush hats, and scarves for everyone. And miles-long traffic jams and cancelled flights. Hot-chocolate-by-a-roaring-fireplace weather. For me, Tom and Jerrys by a fake fireplace with a dog at my feet. No less cozy.

I happily self-medicated with aspirin, extra rations, and sleep. Sleep is the closest thing to a panacea. The swelling in my knee went down within a week, thus I

assured myself that an emergency hospital visit was un-
necessary. Gimping around was absolutely fine. Meg
didn't comment. I avoided taking my shirt off in front of
her for a few days, but she finally caught me stepping
from the shower. She wordlessly regarded my poor battered torso and the bloody, inflamed slash on my back.
Her expression of shock did the talking. This meant
she'd come to accept my lifestyle with the cool noncha-
lance of a gangster's moll or, and more likely, she was
saving her remarks for later.

Between lounging with a drink in hand and entertain-
ing young master Devlin, who pounced upon my extended availability as a playmate, I chiseled at the Pruitt
case, attempting, and failing, to reach Linda, the widow.
I also made a second round of calls to Sean's former
friends and associates. The first person I contacted was
Sean P's colleague Robert Thorpe, in Pittsburgh. He
took my call with an affable demeanor.

*I initially met Sean through my roommate, Danny. The
night Sean died? I pulled a double shift. We were under-
staffed. Everybody in my department was working OT. I
hadn't seen him in two or three days. He had a key, though.
Came and went as he pleased.* Thorpe wasn't aware of any
enemies or debts. *Sean was on the outs with his wife by
then. I mean, that's why he had a key. For those times he
needed a place to crash. Dunno what their friction was.
Except, well . . .*

*Hate to speak ill of the dead, but gotta admit, Sean
changed over the three years or so I knew him. Not saying
he was doing anything wrong. Just that he was different.*

Sometimes was kind of dopey and forgetful. Wore his shirts inside out, flaked on meetings. Nothing serious. Odd. The flip side of the coin was his rougher personality. He acted secretive. His ideas were different. Flower power. Pagan! Yeah, pagan. Hippie-dippie with a black metal edge. A laborer got smooshed in a trench collapse and Sean laughed. He said, Finally! Somebody's giving back! And then he high-fived Danny, who was straight-up fucking morbid. Maybe Danny helped Sean come outta his shell. Except for Danny's love of hunting and excessive boozing, they wound up having a lot in common.

What could he tell me about Buckhalter? My information on the man indicated he was a carpenter by trade, although he'd hired on with Diogenes as a security technician. Similar to Sean Pruitt, he'd spent the vast majority of his shift monitoring cameras and, for a real dose of excitement, cruising the perimeter of the Jeffers site in a jeep, shining a flashlight into the adjacent woods.

Danny's a Horseheads boy. Big-time jock in school back when mullets were popular. Chummy with Sean and Linda. Danny went to their house for dinner a time or two. The Pruitts probably felt pity for him. No family of his own.

Was it possible that the Pruitts' marital problems stemmed from an affair between Linda and Danny?

Shit, never thought of that. Whoa. There was a lot of opportunity. Hate to think they would do Sean that way.

Anything else?

Danny hunted on his days off. Sometimes he took Sean along to "butch him up." Sean bragged he'd eaten raw liver and drank heart's blood as a rite of bad-assedness. Stupid, if you ask me. Everybody says you don't eat wild game north of Horseheads without charbroiling that shit. It's all diseased. Then there was the hard-core partying. Raves and underground stuff. Sean wanted in on some fraternity deal with some of Danny's high school buddies. Danny wouldn't talk about the club or whatever in front of me. Valley citizens only.

I pressed him on that. He hadn't heard of the Mares of Thrace.

Guess it all affected Danny's work. He was in and out of the apartment at bizarre hours; got written up for being late and hungover. Common affliction on a construction crew. Single guys, even older guys, are particularly vulnerable. Wife and kids and a mortgage keep me honest or might've been right in there with him, partying hearty. I figured he'd get canned, but it never happened. We teased him that somebody upstairs had his back. Dude was untouchable. The units at the colony were reserved for out-of-town employees, but he scored a room anyhow. Probably because he lived in a tent or under a bridge before the job came along. Yeah, he was a favored son. Can't say where he is today. Still in Horseheads, I suppose. Might be worth checking with the rednecks. His people, you know?

A tidbit that stuck with me after the call was Thorpe's comment that the Pruitts were friendly with Buckhalter, the lonely single guy. June Pruitt's description of Sean's "rough" friend "D" corresponded to this emerging portrait. D as in Danny? Any cop will tell you: Charity starts at home. Often, so does trouble. Daniel Buckhalter's name got a double underline and an asterisk to boot.

I continued to pressure Sean's dad, Dr. Alex Pruitt, for a follow-up interview and was rebuffed by a wall of silence. Finally, I left a message stating that perhaps I might catch him at home one evening. This elicited a cryptic email response: *You've seen King Diomedes's herd where they frolic. Sean admired and envied them. It would be wise to seek the counsel of Drs. Campbell and Ryoko. Lunatic cults are their specialty. This is the full extent of my knowledge. Don't contact me further. Yours, Dr. Alexander Pruitt.*

I'd maintained a lifelong fanboy interest in Campbell and Ryoko. Now Sean's father had suggested the pair might know something. It bore investigation. I added it to the growing pile. Ted called them at a number we had on file to set up an interview. Whoever responded informed her the doctors declined to participate in phone conferences. Should I opt for an in-person visit, we would need to consult our respective calendars as they were busy, busy men. She promised to touch base with them soon.

■ ■ ■

Last night, a tiger came undetected onto our second raft and abducted a porter. The expedition is well armed with guns and spears. We have retained the services of an expert big-game hunter and guides. Lanterns were lighted. No one heard a disturbance, but we found the man's sandal and his breeches, which were caught on a nail head. His comrades also discovered a quantity of blood. Several ti-

gers have stalked us from the bank over the past five days. We saw one in the river, swimming behind the raft. Wood-cutters wear masks that face backward to frighten the cats from creeping up behind. This strategy doesn't always suc-ceed. Humans are unwelcome here, except as a source of provender. This place is a reminder of our fragility, our insignificance.

In the earliest days, man, or the hominids who predated man, rightfully feared the natural world. The darkness that covered the earth, and what dwelled in the darkness; upheavals and floods; the occulted moon and sun. Later, man imposed himself upon the world, and the darkness that encompasses the world, with metal and fire and dogs.

Man declared himself the chosen of an almighty patron and those earlier fears were subsumed by adoring awe of He who ruled over all creation, and tribalistic antipathy to-ward nonbelievers. Then science came and over time, whit-tled down that patron creator. Science peeled away the illusion and showed us how minute, how alone we are in an unimaginably empty universe. Once again, man is afraid. And it is good.

I opened my eyes at the desk in Meg's spare room. In the absence of guests, we used the room as an office. The Campbell-Ryoko documentary *The Forest That Eats Men* played on my laptop on a loop. I'd fallen asleep for a long winter's nap with it muttering in the background.

Sean Pruitt had worshipped these larger-than-life characters and I empathized. As a teen, I'd seen Camp-bell and Ryoko in numerous appearances on *Nova* and *Wild America,* and occasionally hosting their own specials, delving into lesser-known aspects of the natural world. Their strings of abbreviated titles and honorifics were confounding. They wrote apostate bibles of zoology, biology, anthropology, and several related disciplines.

Eccentric scientists who'd gotten rock-star famous by operating on the fringe during the wild and woolly '70s and '80s, the old boys' prestige had diminished since their glory days. The duo had been categorically dismissed by the legitimate scientific community, and faded light-years beyond career resuscitation. Mainstream science wasn't enamored of a pair of Fortean charismatics who dabbled in "exposing" Cold War black ops programs, Hollow Earth civilizations, cryptozoological secrets, or Illuminati conspiracies. Today, Campbell and Ryoko were closing in on ninety; forgotten except for a handful of scholars and the occasional grad student beguiled by fringe theories and VHS documentaries. Not even the History Channel featured them to wax professorial in its guest sound bites about cryptozoology or ancient alien astronauts.

The current scene occurred at a tropical campsite. Grainy waves of static pulsed through the image of Campbell and Ryoko, hearty middle-aged adventurers in pith helmets and khakis, holding court by a firepit. Dr. Ryoko finished monologuing in response to an innocuous question. No questions were safe from monologues or soliloquies. This was before Campbell had managed to completely drag Ryoko into the mud, academically speaking. It was a work in progress.

Dr. Campbell smiled urbanely at the camera. He adjusted his glasses.

With due respect to my esteemed colleague, we are hardly alone. I posit that Earth may merely serve as the body farm of an extraterrestrial civilization. Should that civilization choose to make war on us? The outcome depends upon several factors, but it can be boiled down to this: Are the invading aliens moderately more advanced than us? Ah, then we'll be eradicated as were the indigenous people of North America and Australia, for example . . . Are the invaders exceedingly advanced? In that case, imagine a family moving into an old, decrepit house infested with ants and wasps. The insect colonies will survive temporarily . . . in the cracks and beneath the ground.

Certainly, the world is an ordinary place. The supernatural exists in the cracks; it presses in against the biodome that preserves mundane reality. Ineffable mysteries confound our sensibilities. Impact craters in South Africa and Argentina are fascinating examples. Paleolithic tribesmen carved images on the walls of the dikes that were formed by lava after the asteroid hit. Petroglyphs of animals inside the dike structures—

Dr. Ryoko interrupted, gesturing impatiently.

Cattle mutilation, extraterrestrial visitors, ancient global conspiracies . . . None of that nonsense exists. Thousands of reports, thousands of misidentifications and hoaxes.

It merely requires a single verifiable incident to be authenticated, Dr. Campbell said, mild and mannered, unflappable. He'd been around this particular maypole on countless occasions. Laurel to Ryoko's Hardy. *One and that's the ball game for the die-hard skeptics.*

Sean would've been a tyke at that moment in history. The kid's later windmill tilting in defense of Campbell and Ryoko might or might not prove relevant. Arguably, these old bastards were the type of kooky anthropologists one might expect to know the details of a cult like the Mares. It slotted perfectly into their Fortean research.

I clicked the remote and aborted the pseudo-academic tit-for-tat. The screen froze; Dr. Campbell's glasses reflected the fire, his mouth skinned wide in laughter. Dr. Alex Pruitt had said geography shaped the mind. I couldn't disagree. Meddling adults shape a child's mind too. I asked myself what went on in Sean Pruitt's mind besides hero worship? What manner of demons had lurked there? Would identifying those demons reveal the truth about his fate?

■ ■ ■

I cyberstalked the Redlick Group, Zircon Corporation, and the Jeffers Project, among numerous related players. Real estate and chicanery are joined at the hip. Recently, two developers who'd brought foreign investment to an impoverished part of Vermont were accused of fraudulently acquiring hundreds of millions of dollars. The money came from more than six hundred foreign investors hoping to get a special visa through the federal EB-5 program. Lo and behold, several companies affiliated with either Zircon Corporation or the Redlick

Group were tangentially involved in the caper. What did the kids say about corporate greed in America? There was no bottom.

For dessert, I dove deep into the folklore of western New York. Meg's connections scored me a sheaf of scanned historical documents detailing cult activity and uncanny incidents in the Southern Tier region. I supplemented my anthropology homework with phone calls to several university professors and a handful of authors. Unlike the typical stonewalling, these people were relatively eager to bend my ear once they got warmed up on the topic. Predictably, only the Valley High administration and school librarian rebuffed my inquiries.

Nobody had much to impart regarding the Mares as such. However, it became apparent that a similar group, or the same group under aliases, had taken root in the Valley during colonial times. Old-world paganism blending with local mysticism and mutating into a different strain. The Mares of Thrace was an evolving society in that every few years it shed its skin and attached to a new thematic identity.

I uncovered instances of the Mares operating as a youth auxiliary of rebel militias during the War of Independence; a Depression-era youth choir of a charismatic church; a Boy Scout troop; and of late, faux upperclassmen of Valley High circa the 1950s. Rumors of violence swirled in their wake, chiefly assaults and a string of murders and disappearances. Violent crime was low in Horseheads proper, but much more pronounced in neighboring towns, such as Corning. It seemed possible that if the Mares indulged in ritualistic violence, they tended to select victims outside their backyard.

What use any of this would serve remained to be seen.

I prepared a report for Adeyemi's lawyer, omitting my own ethically questionable tactics and definitely not mentioning my speculation about occultism, black ops science experiments, or related conspiracy theories. To summarize, I admitted to possessing truckloads of suspicion and zero evidence to suggest foul play. However, I concurred with June Pruitt that Sean's death tilted toward the suspicious side. Adeyemi would need to decide whether to continue the investigation after the New Year. If so, he'd be ponying up for hazard pay.

CHAPTER TWENTY-EIGHT

Despite my best efforts at exemplifying the qualities of a taciturn grouch, the forced vacation proved restorative to body and soul. I'd missed my little family while lumbering around Horseheads.

Christmas Eve dinner was me and Lionel, and Meg and Devlin. After dinner, I watched an animated superhero movie with the kiddo. Devlin leaned into my side and fell asleep while his cartoon played on. It dawned on me that I felt very protective. I carried him to bed, reflecting, as Meg took over to tuck him in, that he'd gotten heavier. Somewhere along the way, I'd segued from "cool uncle" to a father figure. This scared me for reasons I chose not to interrogate.

Because sensitivity isn't one of my finest qualities, I asked Lionel why Delia hadn't accompanied him for dinner. Was our spread too humble for Her Majesty? Was it his face? He said she'd fucked off to Italy on vacation with a guitar player who fronted a famous band none of us listened to. His disinterested tone wasn't convincing anyone. I felt a twinge of guilt for interrupting his time with the Black Powder ladies.

Lionel sat on the floor, sorting packages of toys, and scowling. His left arm was in a sling painted with snow-flakes and candy canes. Devlin had insisted he wear a red-and-green elf cap while attending the festivities.

"Most aggravating part of Christmas is how much of it boils down to *some assembly required! Batteries not in-cluded!*" He'd graduated from rum and Coke to plain rum with corresponding surliness.

"Let us not forget the five Λ.M. wake up call." Mcg glanced at the clock. "Popcorn and a movie, boys?" Bag popcorn and more rum and Cokes incoming.

Counterintuitively, Christmas is the perfect occasion to revel in the horror genre and forget the horrors of the real world. She put on John Carpenter's seminal 1978 slasher flick, *Halloween*. Having seen the film umpteen times, we drank and kibitzed. Michael Myers terrorized the original final girl, Laurie Strode, while Donald Pleasence, in the role of aged Dr. Loomis, plodded the streets of Haddonfield in pursuit of what he termed "pure evil." I don't laugh off such melodramatic pro-nouncements here in the shadow of middle age. The moral core of *Halloween* resonates, stronger and truer, as decades slide by and the world chases its own tail like Sean Pruitt's ouroboros tattoo, or the strikingly similar (if one squinted) Mares of Thrace horse skull symbol.

Meg, who loved critical dissection, had afforded the film's premise some thought since our last Christmas screening.

"When Michael Myers, aka the Shape, kills the German shepherd, you realize he's overqualified for the babysitter massacre. He's hell on wheels and slaughters everyone who crosses his path, yet a young girl and an old man ultimately defeat him. Why is that? To understand, we must examine the two most important members of the dramatis personae. Old man Loomis is a stand-in for Van Helsing of Bram Stoker's *Dracula*. He uses his .38 snub as a crucifix against the ultimate plodding unkillable monster, which is Count Dracula minus the gothic style and barely repressed sexuality. Michael Myers's sexuality manifests as hatred for those he catches coupling, and an inchoate desire for Laurie Strode that he can only act upon through violence. Slasher logic: If you use that pussy outside of marriage, or if you use that pussy for your own pleasure, I will stab you with my steely, metaphorical cock." Note that she repeatedly jabbed my tender biceps to emphasize this last point.

"Stabbing is fucking by other means. I digress. Only Dr. Loomis and the Final Girl have power over the demonic figure. Whether the Shape is an agent of Satan or a similarly aligned god of darkness makes no difference. Loomis/Van Helsing is an emissary of the Church and thus God's chosen warrior; Laurie Strode/Mina Harker is pure, virginal, and protected by the mantle of divinity. Only these two can effectively thwart or harm the Shape because both are instruments of God. The end."

"Damn, girl," Lionel said. He was pretty far into the bag. "I didn't know you got religion. That's weirdly hot."

"I didn't get religion. I know why it's catching,

though." She winked. "On a related topic, I find it interesting that nuns are obsessed with, yet highly resistant to, phallic imagery."

"I hope we can give that subject the attention it deserves next Christmas," I said.

Later, Meg and I were in bed. Since phallic nuns and serial killers were on my mind, I told her Bellow's story about the orchard owner who murdered itinerants and how the creep grinned as the cops carted him to prison. Told her that the killer had been genial and well-spoken. I explained the horror of his capriciousness, his convivial affect.

"It means nothing when a predatory sociopath speaks." Meg knelt on my thighs as she slipped off her nightgown. She was a silhouette, except for where the nightlight hit the wing of hair breaking over the curve of her shoulder. "What you have is a non-reciprocal pattern of noise designed solely to lull or deceive. Mimicry is the whole deal. A predatory sociopath's mouth is emitting sounds about the weather, the stock market, a bad day at the job. It's asking questions designed to disarm, to cultivate a bond: Can you help me? Do you have the time? I seem to be lost. We're the same. Trust me."

She slid her body along mine. It was slightly disconcerting because I couldn't see her face, but felt the heat of her breath, tasted its liquor sweetness when she kissed my lips.

"They aren't thinking of those questions, not even as the necessary mental articulations of a ruse. Their minds are compartmentalized; there's minimal overlap between thoughts and words. What they're thinking is how to sell you that junk car, screw you out of your life savings, or how to kill you and taxidermy the corpse."

"Let me repeat the immortal words of Lionel Robard: Damn, girl. This isn't the sexy talk a man expects on Christmas Eve."

She stroked my hair. Her hands were strong, like the rest of her.

"Do you want to come with me to the Rail Trail tomorrow?" I said.

"Tomorrow's Christmas. You haven't a snowball's chance in hell of setting foot outside."

"The day after?"

"How about I come with you right now?" she said. "The future will take care of itself."

■ ■ ■

The dreaded wake-up call didn't sound until six-thirty A.M. Devlin was just old enough to think diving onto the bed (like he'd done last year) was babyish. He yelled into the bedroom on his way to the tree. I expressed surprise we'd gotten the extra time. Meg whispered in my ear that the cough syrup had done its job well. From the living room, Lionel's snores were cut short by his moan of anguish. Minerva barked her throaty bark, caught up in the excitement that visits a household but once per year.

We came through the other side. Minerva curled onto her favorite throw rug and chewed a dried pig's ear. I got argyle socks and a wristwatch to replace the one that went belly-up in Horseheads. I hadn't mentioned the tunnel to Meg, nor what happened down there. I smiled wide, strapped the sweet new watch to my arm, fiddled with the settings, and thanked her and Devlin. The gift represented a decent chunk of change for a librarian on a budget. I hugged them tight. It was a beauty, it was perfect. It was an omen of doom. The quartz digital display went haywire after lunch, losing time, then gaining time, then producing error messages. By late afternoon the battery was kaput. I hadn't foreseen this development, but it didn't surprise me. My cell phone had been hinky as well; its battery died within a few hours unless I plugged it into the charger twice a day.

Plump roasted goose for dinner with mashed potatoes, green beans, drop biscuits, and pumpkin pie for dessert. Cognac and a cigar for Lionel and me. Meg sipped peppermint schnapps and Devlin went to bed. He was ruddy and exhausted despite petitioning to stay up another hour. Christmas ranks as a banner day when you're that age. I hadn't broached the subject of his left-jab, right-cross approach to diplomacy, choosing to save that unpleasantness until the holidays were done. Now that the moment drew near, I was getting cold feet. Maybe a meteor would hit during the night and I'd be spared the duty.

Lionel slept in the living room as the news tried to balance holiday cheer with the usual reports of global catastrophe. Patroclus Possum, also bunking at the Shaw residence for the evening, slunk from his crate and snoozed on Lionel's feet. Minerva lay in the middle of the room, every bit of her attention laser-focused on the possum. There was a bit of saber-rattling, but honoring the spirit of Christmas, no open warfare. All that was missing from the tableau were some wise men.

I sat with Meg in the kitchen, holding hands as snow piled against the windowsill.

Meg snapped her fingers.

"The mystery money." She disappeared into another room and returned with a manila envelope stuffed with photocopies of newspaper stories. "In 1973, a private train engine, *Fafnir's Hammer,* two passenger cars, and four people disappeared in the mountains between Oregon and California. Poof, gone Johnson. Train belonged to Major Arnaout Wagner, industrialist. His girlfriend, a bodyguard, and a travel journalist were among the missing. There is speculation, unconfirmed, may I add, that he was transporting a heap of money to Los Angeles. His vanishing was a rather big deal."

"One-point-five million. That's my guess."

"For what?"

"How much money was on the train."

"Guess again, Kreskin. Eight million, according to anonymous sources. A lesser percentage was cash. The rest was coins and precious gems. Literal treasure."

"Sealing an investment?"

"Or a payoff. Odds are even. Wagner was an eccentric. Involved in enough tawdry affairs to make Howard Hughes blush."

"Somebody intercepted him and his dough . . ." I

thumbed through the pages. "You weren't kidding. The 'Vanishing of *Fafnir's Hammer*' made a splash."

"The search went on for weeks. Only so many places an engine and two cars can go. Yet, nada. Not a trace to this day. A Great Unsolved American Mystery."

"What makes you think our stash might be part of the Wagner hoard?"

"This caught my eye." She handed me a news photo, circa 1971, of a beaming Wagner, cocktail raised high. One of the other suits laughing along with him was the founder of Zircon Corporation, Matthias Labrador. "There's more. Wagner invested heavily in Zircon. Sat on the board."

"Oh, boy," I said.

"Heck of a coincidence. You working with Delia and that fuss."

Like my daddy before me, I'm not fond of coincidence. Coincidence is the universe's favorite loophole right after destiny. "Loophole" is another word for snare. Snares have a tendency to tighten around one's neck.

I'd known the Croatoan had either stolen the money or received it as a payment for villainous services rendered. That it might be connected to the high-profile disappearance of a rich pal of the Labradors thickened the plot considerably.

"Nibelungen," I said.

CHAPTER TWENTY-NINE

The day after Christmas, Lionel and I were thrown out of the house.

Meg had gone into the library for a partial shift dedicated to repairing the damage done by the staff "winter solstice" party that she hadn't even attended. She returned while Lionel, Devlin, and I were lounging in our underwear, eating cold cereal and watching cartoons.

"Oh, God. Another patron died." Meg hurled her bag toward a chair. She poured a glass of wine and had a go. "Jenny Selznick. Her obituary is in the paper."

"What happened?" I said.

"Breast cancer."

"Was she elderly?"

"Jenny wasn't even sixty!"

I expressed sympathy and surreptitiously put on my pants, as one does.

Lionel sighed morosely.

"Check your tits. Always check your tits."

Fortunately, he didn't meet Meg's death gaze or he would've keeled over, the fat bubbling in his smoking skull. Ninety seconds later, he and I were in the yard, putting the rest of our clothes on. It was bitterly amusing to observe Lionel dressing one-handed.

■ ■ ■

We grabbed Minerva and ventured to the Rail Trail for a hike between snowstorms. The Wallkill Valley section ran from Kingston down into Rosendale. Minerva always went bonkers for a post-storm jaunt—the "pristine" canvas of snow was decorated with an impressionist fresco of rabbit and squirrel piss. Locals, decked in festive seasonal wear, shouted gaily as they skied and snowshoed. An afternoon of good weather dispels wintertime blues more assuredly than drugs. We settled for schlepping along in their tracks. Icicles dripped from branches and songbirds chirped, basking in the burst of sunlight.

A guy in a canary-yellow bodysuit whizzed past, nearly smacking me with a ski pole and causing Minerva to dive for her doggy life. I'd dreamed of Aotearoa, although I couldn't recall the specifics except a sense of green tranquility in a time before the onslaught of humanity. I muttered a dig at the evils of colonization, the pain and suffering that consequently echoed down through the ages.

Lionel waved his good arm in an encompassing gesture. His doctor advised minimal physical activity until the break completely healed. I figured the doc was ahead of the game in that Lionel wasn't performing calisthenics yet.

"Roads, bridges, plumbing," he said. "This cozy, white-bread hiking path. The dirt under our feet. Everything we have, we have thanks to the conniving of murderous shit-head colonizing ancestors."

"So, let's not be hard on conniving, murderous shit-heads?"

"Let's not be hard on ourselves is what I'm saying. Our conniving shitheadedness is a survival trait."

"Nature's plan," I said, more to myself than to him.

"Means we live long enough to pass our shithead genes to a new generation. Can't argue with Nature."

Glancing over my shoulder to ascertain no skiers or snowshoers were within earshot, I caught him up to speed on what Meg had learned of the provenance of our buried treasure and the ties between its original owner, Arnaout Wagner, and the Labradors.

"That's terrific. Is that supposed to be a lead? Let me know when you decide to get serious. Speaking of those rich bastards . . ."

Lionel expressed an intense and recent fascination with crime and punishment, and how it pertained to the Labrador family business, Zircon Corp. The family and its holdings had gotten into legal hot water over the years. Notable were the troubles that befell one Labrador man or another. Delia's uncle Zebulon, for example, had gotten clapped in irons several years ago for brokering arms deals with China and ordering acts of industrial sabotage against corporate rivals. The big Z was liable to die in prison. Lionel trawled the Internet for old news clips of Zebulon Labrador's high-profile federal trial. The man possessed a fantastic aesthetic, although nothing on the good green earth could've saved him from the hammer of justice swung by an irate judge. Even he wasn't privileged enough to withstand the unbridled wrath of a government who'd been cut out of the lucrative black-market weapons trade.

"Where do you suppose all those fancy clothes went?" Lionel said, almost wistful. "Ostrich jackets? Cobra suits? Sharkskin boots? Did the government confiscate that swag? Was there an auction like they do with cars? Is there a fat cat version of Goodwill? A bunch of slightly less obscenely rich dudes going through the obscenely rich dude's shit. *You* get the boots! *You* get the jacket and the pants. That Rolex is mine, bitch!"

"For the love of God, man," I said. "Call Delia. You've got it bad if you're going to ramble on about Uncle Z's damned wardrobe."

"I'm not calling her. She can gallivant around Italy if that makes her happy."

"You're driving me up a tree. Show some resolve. Talk about anything else until we get back to the car. I'll start the timer."

Lionel pushed his shades aside so he could roll his eyes at me.

"Resolve? I've gone thirty hours without itching my balls because I was set up in a blind, waiting for a green light on some Taliban target."

"Yet you can't go fifteen minutes without pissing and moaning about your girlfriend." I said "girlfriend" in a falsetto. "Admit you can't compete with some longhair rocker and his ski pole. Poles. There's no shame in it."

"Oh, Jesus," he said in a tragic voice and pushed his glasses back on.

"At least we're free men."

"Free? The hell you on about?"

"I'm shut of the Outfit," I said. "You're shut of the military and mercenary work, and maybe your maniac girlfriend. Meg is bound to relent sooner or later. Otherwise, we can head to our shacks and kindle a fire and brood like manly men of yore. Be of good cheer."

Lionel was emphatically *not* of good cheer, as I soon discovered.

"We aren't free. The universe gives us longer leashes and lets us run. It can retract the damned things anytime. We've gone through some shit. We know each other pretty well, wouldn't you say?"

"Sure," I said.

"Wrong, bud. No matter what, people remain a mystery. It isn't much different from getting close to a character on a TV show. You know every quirk about that character; you don't know that the actor, the action star, is scared spitless of guns, that he beats his wife, that he's as dumb as a bag of hammers."

"That car wreck really—"

"Car chase."

"That car chase really bothers you," I said. It bothered me as well, although my worry centered on what might result of the encounter, or who would come calling.

"It got me thinking about the close calls I had in the Corps. Should've bought the farm on several occasions. Dumb fucking luck I'm here and intact. But it's on my mind lately."

"Shell shock?"

"Our grandfathers called it shell shock, yeah. These days, some call it post-traumatic stress disorder. It's no joke. Twenty veterans commit suicide every day." He smiled a flat, dark smile. "Gonna lay a secret on you, amigo. I don't have shell shock or PTSD. Don't worry on that score."

"Hey, I'm here to listen."

"It's okay, amigo," he said. "We both have our demons."

"Hearts of darkness. Well earned."

"Nah, whatever darkness lives inside me took root when I was a baby. Once upon a time, SIDS was the terror in every mother's heart. No sudden infant death syndrome for baby Lionel. Death slunk in as I lay in that crib. Decided it liked the view and would stay awhile. As a man, I went to war because I craved mayhem. Recognized that if I didn't ship my ass to a war zone, there'd be hell to pay at home. Thought I could go overseas and either die or burn the devil out of me. Or drown it in blood."

"But you didn't die, or burn, or drown," I said.

"And the devil is still in there."

"Bonus."

"Ain't it, though? The devil is a real prick. He protects and keeps the worst of us, his favored sons."

"That's gospel. What did Billy Joel say . . . ?"

"Leave Billy Joel out of this, okay? Knew a guy whose best years were in-country. Like me, he only got a good night's sleep on patrol in hostile territory. He cashed out. Right away, home life went wrong. He wanted out from under the peacetime regime. Tried to re-enlist. Uncle Sam didn't want him. Attempted suicide. Got drunk and stabbed himself with a pocket knife. His lungs filled with blood; he gasped and faded to black. Woke the next day with a hangover and a knife stuck in his chest. *There's* an embarrassing hospital visit."

The going was sludgy and we rested on a log whose exposed surface was sun-dried and warm to the touch. Lionel dug a bottle of beer out of his coat pocket. I wasn't in the mood, but had a swig to be sociable.

"Provenance," I said. "Fate minus mysticism. Like the song says, where you begin and where you wind up aren't always far apart."

"No shit, it's provenance."

"In a past life, maybe I didn't run around killing people," I said.

"Are all you Coleridges comedians?" he said. "If anything, our past selves probably ran around killing a hell of a lot more people. The bag limits were higher."

"There you go, obliterating my romantic illusions."

Lionel regarded the bottle.

"Me and my wet blanket. It coulda been a christening

gift. The people who raised me were hard-core alkies. Cigarette in one hand, a glass of hooch in the other."

My ears pricked up. He wasn't what you would call an open book when it came to his family.

"Your parents sound like pieces of work."

He precariously clutched the bottle in his left fist and drew a cigarette to illustrate his point.

"I said *the people who raised me*. Hustlers too. Bet on anything. And I mean any fucking thing. Semi-pros, but they never knew when to cash in. Spent half the year in Vegas pissing away their retirement. Rose at the crack of noon, slobbered off to bed at two A.M. and nothing between except sports on the tube, penny ante blackjack, two packs of Winston, and a quart of the cheap stuff. Apiece. I got a real education from that pair."

"What did they eat?" I lit his smoke.

"The light. Time and space."

"You go to Vegas with them?"

"Nah. Well, twice. That went over like a lead balloon. Cramped their style. Rancher friends of theirs ran a spread in the Northwest. Put me to work." He finished his beer. "That was okay."

We watched our fellow travelers slosh and slide past for a while.

"Been turning it over in my mind and I can't understand what's going on at the Jeffers site," I said. "Are we onto something in regard to Sean Pruitt or did those bogeys come at us because we snooped around the facility?"

"What if the answer is A and B?"

"Separate yet connected."

"*Everything* is connected. Then there's the Valley. Place is fucked. The Jeffers site is fucked. While you were down there playing grab-ass in the tunnel, I had a case of the willies. Haven't been that spooked since the war. Man, if some nimrod would've stepped from behind a tree and said *boo!*, I would've put a round between his eyes."

"Ghost stories," I said. "Herzog got into your head."

"Forget ghost stories. Let's not lose sight of the fact there's a security robot crawling around down there. His claim of clandestine fuckery at the site was money."

"For a security robot, it sure wasn't keeping the graffiti artists in check. The joint looked like a New York subway in 1975."

"Excellent observation," he said. "Security is designed to repel or capture trespassers. I have to assume the graffiti artists aren't trespassing."

"Which leads to: Why would scientists advocate wild-ass faux tribal art on a collider track?"

"You tell me and we'll both know."

"Huh. Maybe Shanks Mathis is responsible. Maybe the Redlick Group locked some leftover scientists in a cell. Eggheads are chained down there in the dark, solving for X."

Lionel wasn't dissuaded by my sarcasm.

"The site isn't on the updated maps. I mean, it's recorded somewhere, but not on search engines or the Internet satellite maps. It's acknowledged in Horseheads, yet only in passing and if you bring it up first. Same deal with the Nameless Field—a blank spot on any map you'll find."

"Odd, yes."

"Those women at the Black Powder," he said. "The ones who clued me in to the strange lights and odd sounds at the abandoned site . . . one was from Colorado. She did the blabbing. Her gal pal was a local. Local girl kept mum. As time passes, fewer and fewer people will admit that the site or the colony exist. They'll drive by the access roads and not even spare a glance. Horses in blinders of their own devising."

"Which amounts to what? A collaboration between superstitious locals and the Redlicks? Mandibole referred to the project as 'dreaming.' They might be carrying on the construction piecemeal and on the sly."

"The Redlicks are locals too, and not a bit less superstitious."

I studied the angle of the sun. My knees were tired and my ribs had given some warning twinges. I didn't want the rest of my body to join the chorus.

"Time to head for the car."

"Already? Minerva is enjoying herself."

The dog joyously rolled in a patch of dirt she'd exposed with furious digging.

"A little longer."

"Her life is short, man. We owe her every single happy moment she can squeeze out of this ball of misery. You got no one in your world better than this dog."

That hit me hard. Instinctively, I wanted to laugh it off.

"We see the people and animals we love through a

filter," I said as Minerva gained her feet and grinned the way she only did at me. "They loom larger in the heart than the eye. I've loved humans and I've loved dogs. You're right. Dogs are the superior life-form."

Why dogs are perfect: For them, your companionship is the sum total of their universe. And yet, if I could've explained to Minerva that I would outlive her by many, many years, and go on adventures and pet other dogs, she would wag her tail and say, *I am glad. I love you.*

There were moments since my last dog, Achilles, died that the pain, always present, reached a crescendo and stole my breath. Once or twice, I'd been absurdly tempted to slam my face into a tree and leave bloody teeth embedded in the bark. Just to express the pain, to one-up it. The moment always passed.

I turned my head slightly where he couldn't see, and cuffed myself once, hard. Little birdies and wheeling stars were preferable to the awful melancholy of contemplating the mortality of loved ones.

"Where are we going next?" Lionel said.

"Got to buy a bouquet of roses if I want to receive a dinner pass."

"Think roses will get us back in the house?"

"Roses will get *me* back in the house."

CHAPTER THIRTY

That evening, I opened the door at Meg's to find Delia Labrador standing on the welcome mat, clutching a gift bag and smoking a cigarette you couldn't buy in the USA. She wore a cardigan over a casual shirt, tight velvet pants, and too precious by half snow bunny boots with pink trim and tassels. On another day, it would've been a leather jacket and combat boots fitted with spikes. She was a mercurial woman. Doubtless her father would've preferred she fronted Zircon Corporation the way Tom Mandibole did the Redlick Group. Instead, she served behind the scenes in a titular, albeit inconsequential role, and lived life on her own terms. Jet-setter or mingler-among-peasants as the spirit moved her. Like I said, mercurial.

"Merry Christmas, Delia." My hands were damp from washing a batch of dishes, so I nodded instead of offering to shake. She didn't care.

"A reliable source informs me that Daddy wants you shot."

"Would that reliable source be your father?"

"I put in a word for you. Reminded him you're more useful without an extra hole in your head. Hope it helps." She swept past me into the house.

I was struck once again with her sheer charisma, otherwise known as sex appeal. Blond or brunette, ballroom gown or burlesque and barely clothed, she was a knockout, a 1940s pinup. Her magnetism was the finishing blow. Charming and vicious, sometimes in the same breath. Far too intelligent and far too wily for my good friend Lionel.

"Investigating the Redlick Group? Silly, silly boy." She set the bag on a table.

"A pernicious falsehood."

"Is that a pretentious way of saying it's a damned lie?"

"You got me."

"Too bad. Because if you were trying to reach my father's heart, kissing his ass or giving him lots and lots of money are the surest methods."

"I live to disappoint."

She rubbed her hands to warm them.

"Some insider info you might want—Redlick Group and Zircon have climbed into bed on about a million business deals. Our families knew each other so far back, we didn't even have servants. Indian-Wars-and-dying-on-the-Oregon-Trail depth of history. And who fucking cares at the end of the day; Daddy utterly loathes the Redlicks. We *all* hate the Redlicks."

"And they hate you," I said. "Because what's not to hate?"

"The Lancasters and the Yorks were chummier."

"A cold war. You stick the shivs in by proxy."

"Formality and the bottom line, don't you know? Family delegations will have tea and crumpets tomorrow and attend a state dinner next week. Fake smiles and dagger eyes. Security sweeps for bugs and bombs prior to and after every event."

"Society page had you in Italy."

"Change of plans. I bore easily. Meg mentioned she was throwing a little holiday shindig—"

"Meg invited you for dinner?" Delia had frequented Meg's library for years, so they were on friendly terms. I lifted a drape and surveyed the empty yard. Delia's ubiquitous security detail wasn't currently in evidence. The vanload of Black Dog mercs likely parked up the street and around a corner. "No troglodytes in tow?"

"Just you, big boy."

Lionel heard our voices and came to greet her.

"Oh, my God! Sweetie! What have they done to my beautiful man?" She flung her arms and legs around him. His knots and bruises were receding; that didn't mean he looked good. "Does your face hurt, baby? Because it's killing me!" She burst into laughter, then apologized and kissed him passionately. Their reciprocal affection was veering into R-rated territory, so I cleared my throat.

Delia extricated herself from his one-armed embrace, touched his chin, and whisked onward to rendezvous with Meg in the kitchen.

"You're a halfway cute couple," I said. "She's the cute half."

"I'm so dead." He gazed after her with an expression of mournful epiphany. "This can never work."

"Because she's rich and hot and you're super-duper not?"

He rubbed his jaw and blinked as if shaking off a daydream.

"For a hundred and one reasons. Take your pick. Damn it."

Unprepared to handle the intensity of fear and melancholy radiating from him, I chucked him on his shoulder.

"Buck up. Bad form to throw in the towel until after dessert. Oh, oh, tell her about the car wreck—I mean chase. She'll go gaga with a contact high. Got to be good for one or two rolls in the hay."

"Who says 'roll in the hay'?"

"Your mom. C'mon."

Dinner was leftovers. Not surprising, since I'd been barely able to shove the fridge door closed after storing the remnants of our Christmas feast. Delia perched between Lionel and Devlin. The boys were patently smitten. Devlin shyly asked if she was a movie star. Why did he ask? She looked like a movie star! Delia explained that she sang and danced and had even acted in a few commercials. Close enough for him. Meg fought a long insurgency to pry the kid away after dinner and nip off to bed. Thankfully, he missed Lionel's downing the last of a fifth of rye and subsequent editorial on colonialism. Instead of relying on charm, he amped his yahoo, self-destructive inclination to eleven.

"White man is the enemy!" he said, demonstrating

simultaneously the truth of that statement and also the axiom that we are our own worst enemies.

"Oh, Lionel, pass the mayo," Meg said.

"And the white bread," I said.

"Colonialist-invading, boat-having motherfuckers!" He sloshed what was left of the booze in his glass.

Having missed the inciting event, I couldn't tell whether this was sarcasm or sincerity. Guessing was perilous when it involved Lionel's deeper philosophy.

"Have another drink, babe," Delia said, lacing her boots.

"Leaving?" I said. Redundant as she'd already headed for the door.

She awaited me on the porch.

"Speaking of whitey and the enemy . . . Believe it or not, Zircon are the white hats."

"Compared to whom?"

"Don't be a jerk. Words to the wise, Coleridge. Grain of salt and whatnot. Watch yourself with those people. Watch yourself with that whole family."

"May have to go with, the hell with Labradors and Redlicks alike," I said.

"Oh, to be a child again with a child's solutions to problems large and small. Crying, breaking toys, tantrums—"

"Pouting doesn't go out of style."

"Picking up your ball and running home won't always be an option." She lit one of her chic cigarettes. Somehow, the tobacco scent heightened her allure. "I can't decide if you're really that self-destructive or if patronizing me is a sport."

"Here I thought you came to canoodle with Lionel and score a free meal."

"Some Column A, some Column B. Column C would be to talk you into not getting disappeared."

"This isn't nineteen seventies or eighties Chile and your dad isn't Pinochet."

"It's getting there," she said. "You might be in for a surprise if you ever tested that theory. Drop the funnies and catch a news broadcast."

"Papa Labrador sent you, didn't he? I'm getting whip-lash from his moods."

"Daddy likes options. The shooting-you thing wasn't ever serious."

"Yay! He *did* send you. Right?"

"It was my idea. He went along. Thanks to my bad-gering, he's come around to the notion that you're an excellent pawn. Lethal in the proper circumstances. Cheap and expendable. Then I saw Lionel and my heart got zingy and softened with the spirit of the season."

"Zingy, eh? No comment. As for Papa Labrador, he's made an error in judgment if he presumes I'm going to help him in any damned way."

"Look," she said. "I don't have a clear picture of what you're doing with Senator Redlick's former hatchet man, except that it's about a man who died at the Jeffers site."

I regarded her in stoic silence.

"Daddy owned a chunk of that collider," she said. "The project was extremely important to him. To us."

"Multi-billion-dollar white elephant. I'm sure it made

your cold hearts go pitty-pat until they froze in your chests."

"Coleridge, you mistake me. This went deeper than stocks and profit margins. We shared a philosophy and an ultimate goal that transcended our identities as Redlick Group and Zircon Corp. So did the others who invested."

"You can't reveal the details, naturally."

"Sworn to secrecy," she said. "What matters is that you grasp the unholy fucking importance of this communal goal."

"Well, I grasp that Redlick Group's spokes-douche, Tom Mandibole, is a homer for the project. He scoffed at the suggestion it's dead and buried."

"Him." Delia looked as if she was about to cross herself.

I bit my tongue to resist confiding details of what I'd gleaned in what was becoming a wide-reaching investigation into the seamier side of large-scale construction. I hadn't managed to read anywhere near the entire collection of reports; I nonetheless skimmed until my eyeballs bled. I came across a series of memos. These memos between congressional watchdogs and their agents embedded in the Jeffers Project led me to conclude the government didn't pull support from the collider due to waste or cost overruns. Those bastards calculate corruption into the bid. The government picked up its marbles and went home because a keen mind on the congressional oversight committee realized Redlick and Zircon, and those other shifty industrialists, had a hidden agenda. Late in the game, an independent geologist on the federal payroll produced evidence of previously undisclosed irregular seismic activity. Carefully obscured from the public, a full-fledged report alleged that an unstable fault line disqualified the collider. The Jeffers Project founders pled ignorance and were lucky to dodge fraud charges. Immense wealth is better than Kevlar sometimes.

Intriguing as it might be, Delia's perspective wasn't quite valuable enough to overcome my suspicion of the heiress to the Labrador empire and future holder of the keys to Zircon Corp.

"Does Mandibole have reason to be optimistic?" I said.

"Perhaps," she said. "Certain unscrupulous persons would slit a baby's throat to see the collider resurrected. Why do you suppose Gerald Redlick went into politics? He means to influence the government on behalf of his family, his company, and the grand project. Grand projects yet undreamt of, in fact."

The witch's cauldron of paranoia and unrequited foreboding in the back of my mind began to bubble.

"You're perilously close to telling me something," I said. "Lummoxes are slow on the uptake. If you've a point to make, spell it out in all caps."

"The Labradors and Redlicks no longer see eye to eye about that bloody space-age catacomb. Zircon prefers the project to remain dormant. Redlick and allies desire its revival. You said it—cold war."

"I wish you and yours the best of luck in the feuds to come."

She rewarded me with a wan smile.

"Daddy is aware of your traipsing around where you damned well shouldn't be. The enemy won't come here into our territory. They'll wait to catch you in the open. *Daddy* would encourage you to continue fucking around and do his dirty work by remote control. *I'm* imploring you to walk away. There are worse fates than concrete galoshes."

"Thank you for your concern." I projected calmness. Riding my decades of finely honed bravado into the dirt.

"Merry Christmas and Happy New Year." Delia's boots crunched on a rime of snow and ice as she sashayed down the walk. A luxury SUV, fit for the president or a foreign potentate, glided up. A gorilla in a trench coat helped her inside.

Meg laid her hand on my shoulder and watched the vehicle zoom into the night.

"What was that?"

"God bless me," I said. "I'm afraid it was the ghost of Christmas Future."

CHAPTER THIRTY-ONE

In college, Sean Pruitt had not only defended various assertions by Drs. Campbell and Ryoko, he'd written a paper about the Campbell-Ryoko documentary *The Forest That Eats Men*. His paper cited a particular set of tapes he'd designated the Ring of Darkness. These tapes were a series of interviews and lectures the doctors had begun in the 1970s, carried into the new millennium. Adeyemi's lawyer sent the material to me upon request. Apparently, the tapes were among several boxes of similar files Adeyemi had borrowed from Dr. Alex Pruitt's collection when they'd enlisted PI Griese to probe Sean's alleged suicide. There wasn't any love lost between Adeyemi and Dr. Pruitt, yet they'd set aside their differences and worked together hand in glove. People, including hard-bitten thug cops, had certainly loved Sean.

Some of the Campbell-Ryoko files were stored on outdated technology. Meg dipped into her library resources to finagle an archaic recorder for my use. I fiddled with the settings and got the reels turning. Scratchy and oddly distorted, but sufficiently clear that I discerned Dr. Campbell speaking on his beloved topic, extraterrestrial intelligence and alleged incidents of human abduction:

"—you think it can't be real, it's a dream, a hallucination, because of the crudeness. The rusty tools, the chains, medieval contraptions. Filth and stink. This can't be an advanced species. This can't be a starfaring race." This from the mouth of multiple abductees.

Dr. Ryoko's thoughts on mythology, folklore, and quantum physics:

Seances are not solicitations of mystical beings, nor invitations to the spectral souls. Energy is not destroyed, only reshaped, distributed, or displaced. Astral projection and astral viewing are achieved through a variety of methods and these methods often labor under the trappings of mysticism. Oracular vision is frowned upon by modern religions, unless expressly bestowed by approved sources.

Legends are similar no matter where you wander. Jesus, Allah, Satan, Whiro, Azrael, Kali. The same, all the same. Light and dark. Positive, negative. Two components of reality are responsible for this phenomenon. Component one is mundane: You've mapped one brain and stimulated one nervous system; you've mapped and stimulated them all. Ike and Mike think alike and everybody is Ike or Mike. Two veers into esoteric territory. Reality is a string of beads. Dissimilar beads occupy different positions, but all are connected. Concepts such as "here" and "there" are modalities, terms of convenience. Heroic figures, monsters, angels, devils are exaggerations upon human characteristics.

I could imagine Gene K's take on this insane bullshit

were he around to compare notes. He would've laughed and said, *I told you, kid.*

∎ ∎ ∎

The phone rang at an obscene hour.

"Coleridge, you're one of the last of a dying breed," Badja Adeyemi said. "That lone mustang stallion on the bluff, overlooking his herd of mares. Now it's punk kids."

"It was always punk kids," I said. "We're punk kids with wrinkles. And for the love of everything holy, don't say mares."

"Had a terrible dream last night. You died. You got lynched and used for a piñata. Saw it clear as a vision. Spent the whole day in a funk. Finally occurred to me to give you a buzz. Glad that you answered the phone."

"In this universe, I did. Universes overlap. Bands on a radio dial."

"You definitely croaked in one of the other ones," he said. "Maybe I glimpsed your unhappy future. To be honest with you, your unhappy future is the least of what troubles me as I fall asleep each night. My dreams insist we all have a dark cloud headed our way. An asteroid is gonna level everything. Gets worse too."

"The jailers need to let you out of your cage to exercise more," I said.

"Soon enough, I'll walk through the door, scot-free."

"Why not today? Enjoying the accommodations?"

"It ain't the worst. Anyway, I have a different idea: You're a dead man. Been dead for years. Somebody you shoulda whacked, you didn't. They got you instead. Everything you experience is a fading dream."

"There's a movie like that already."

"Magical indigenous blood flows in your veins, right? Which means you got access to the Aboriginal Dreamtime, or whatever islanders call it."

"Wrong landmass; wrong culture. It becomes clear that you've lost the plot." Sweat trickled down my jaw and under the collar of my nightshirt. Adeyemi wasn't capable of offending my delicate sensibilities. I couldn't deny that his words struck a chord of unease. Even a stab in the dark finds its target occasionally.

"Get a picture in your head. I'm chilling in a deserted rec room in my bathrobe. *The Rockford Files* is on pause on the flat screen and I'm chowing Italian ice cream. A junkyard dog attorney is sitting across the table. He's also chowing on Italian ice cream. My shit is together, Coleridge. Don't ever doubt it. Where are we on the case?"

I didn't care if he had a team of attorneys eating ice cream with him under a cone of silence; I provided an edited-for-television account of my adventures that was essentially identical to the written report I'd turned in, except with more expletives. Considering his status as a prisoner of the federal government, I assumed the conversation was being recorded and transcribed in real time.

"I have to warn you, somebody is trying to wave me off," I said in conclusion.

"Man, that's a lot of beating around the bush," he said.

"It's a big bush. Your attorney and I should get together. We meet in person, I can be more forthcoming."

"Your sitrep nixed accidental death for Sean. You aren't one hundred percent sold on suicide. That's ominous, ain't it? Off the record, have you ruled out murder?"

"No."

"Goddamn it," he said.

"Do you want me to proceed?"

"I'm having second thoughts. Getting fond of you, Coleridge. You push any harder, these people will react. You bebop back to Horseheads, into their yard, they'll sic the whole kennel on you. We both know you'll *have* to go back if you mean to finish this thing." He was quiet for a moment. "Yeah, I want you to proceed. Proceed until your nerve breaks or the wheels fly off the wagon."

"Roger, wilco. I'm going to wait a couple of weeks, maybe a month. Let the situation blow over."

"Need cash? I'll get you cash."

"Cash is always welcome. A flak jacket might be better."

"Valley's rough."

"It is."

"Even in the best of times, the area isn't always hospitable." His tone was sober, devoid of the machismo and mockery he typically wore like armor. Flat and resigned, like his sister. "Horseheads is a shadow world." He waited a beat. "Do you understand? The *Valley* itself is the reason I tucked tail and fled right out of school. I didn't even accompany Redlick on the rare occasion he made a detour to the ol' plantation. Anywhere else on the planet, I was in his hip pocket. Not the Valley. Fuck the Valley."

"Why?"

"Scenic beauty. Rustic charm. All that happy horse-shit is a façade. Tell me your skin didn't crawl. It's got—"

"An aura," I said.

"An aura, exactly. Make the hair on the back of your neck stand up. Everybody gets used to that feeling and stops noticing. In the city you acclimate to traffic noise, or drunks shouting when the bars close. I didn't stop noticing. The woods scared me spitless. The churches. The patriarchal families. Wackos in the hills."

"You're good with patriarchs," I said. "You didn't even give a damn about your own nephew's death until Redlick handed you your walking papers. Suddenly, family became important."

"You and I both have a track record of not giving a shit," he said. "There was a time I counted Gerry Redlick as family. That overrode my common sense."

"A lucrative business arrangement is what overrode your scruples."

"Same as you and the Outfit. We eventually realized the error of our ways, didn't we?"

"We should probably speak for ourselves," I said.

Adeyemi chuckled as if he was tightening the cuffs on a perp he really, really disliked.

"A wise man sees into the darkness and perceives the true shape of things. I've had time to go over every conversation, every eavesdropped comment. My cop brain is reengaged. Whatever this is in Horseheads, it's bigger than my nephew. Visa fraud on some daunting scale. Money laundering. That valley is bad juju, and it brings out the worst in people."

"Your cop brain chiming in?"

"Cursed, haunted, whatever label you want to slap on. The natives were aware. Double for the miserable fucks who tried to build the collider. RG, Zircon, Sword Enterprises, the whole bunch."

"This come from the senator?" I said. "The two of you had many a midnight confab about cabbages and kings and particle physics, did you not? Or did it come from Mandibole? He regards the unusual qualities of the Valley and her denizens as a net positive."

My comment wasn't as sarcastic as my tone indicated. The moment superstition overwhelms a skeptic is a rare and breathtaking event. Adeyemi's words and my own reactions nudged me toward a realization. Some of us who live past a certain age push through cynicism and into a black dreamland that is the negative of a child's wonder. Even old corrupt cops and semi-reformed hitmen.

"It came to me via osmosis," he said. "I could've listened to the same tapes you have. Who gives a shit? I know what I know, and what I know is the billionaire club chose the spot with great specificity. Gerry holds a wacky point of view when it comes to man's place in the cosmos. Wackier than I ever realized, maybe. Once he mentioned how we were all happier before the advent of industry. How we were safer when we were playing with sticks and trying to figure out fire."

I didn't want him to elaborate. He elaborated.

"He didn't confide in me his master plan. What I deduced? The richies were burying that supercollider in the Valley for the same fucked-up reason the Mesoamericans built ziggurats to align with celestial bodies. They didn't care diddly about measuring tiny particles or mass production of radioisotopes. There won't be a sane explanation at the bottom of the rabbit hole. This is about blood, not science."

Blood, not science.

That last bit knocked over a domino in a chain of loosely organized suspicions strung across my waking thoughts, down into my subconscious. What if this was about superstition and not passion or materialism? I almost hoped the authorities were tuned in to this back-and-forth. I sardonically chuckled to consider the transcript getting passed around a briefing room full of starched shirts and constricted worldviews.

After we hung up, amusement faded fast, leaving a chilly unease that gnawed at me like rats.

CHAPTER THIRTY-TWO

The day after Valentine's Day, I saddled Lionel with a list of minor surveillance jobs. Two cases of spousal infidelity and an insurance scam. He'd snap photos of the subjects in compromising positions, show those photos to soon-to-be-aggrieved parties, and deposit the fat checks. These were perfect errands he could run between pitching horse manure and repairing the farm tractor at Hawk Mountain now that his collarbone had healed.

Meanwhile, I packed a suitcase for a trip west to interview Drs. Campbell and Ryoko. Linda Flanagan hadn't seen fit to return Ted's twice-weekly calls. The widow's family claimed to be in sporadic touch. None had spoken to her since Christmas. Since she and the doctors resided in the same time zone, I decided to make a pilgrimage to the mountain, so to speak.

Over recent days, I'd put myself into a criminal frame of mind. The Mares of Thrace and the Redlicks hovered at the top of my suspect list, which skewed the question of motive into unknown territory. These people were twisted. Their motive could be almost anything.

Less glamorous, yet statistically probable, was a crime driven by either passion or money. At great effort, I'd located a recent photo of Sean Pruitt's former schoolmate and work colleague, Danny Buckhalter. Damned if he wasn't a spitting image of one of the guys who'd jumped me in Horseheads; the ducktail haircut dude who'd split while I tuned up his friends. Buckhalter, or Slick, as I'd dubbed him, was a member of the Mares of Thrace and Sean's acquaintance since childhood. This led to the Lovers' Triangle Theory: Buckhalter and Linda Flanagan conspired to murder Sean Pruitt for the insurance money. Who was to say she hadn't taken a shine to Buckhalter at one of their get-togethers? While Sean was barbecuing, wifey and work buddy might've made eyes. Later, the cheating hearts hook up at a motel and hatch a plan that involves a million dollars in corporate payola. One dark night, Sean Pruitt and Buckhalter are at Shaft 40, smoking dope, roughhousing. Buckhalter pushes him and earns a cut of the corporate payout down the line after the dust settles. Buckhalter's lack of profile suggested he was lying low in the hills, possibly canoodling with his equally scarce girlfriend, the Widow Pruitt.

Oh, baby, it fit nicely, satisfying motives of passion and greed simultaneously.

Puncturing that balloon? Logistically, the theory was sexy, and completely wrong. Sean Pruitt had prepared himself for the end. I couldn't figure a way around his

wedding band and the photo. Their existence was the
ghostly arrow pointing toward confirmation of the police verdict; suicide and heaps of misery for his family,
and for me, the dog chasing his own tail. The "why" of
Sean Pruitt's death, rather than the "how," had usurped
precedence in my theories.

The rest of the evidence was tantalizing, albeit incon-
clusive. Sean P's security clearance would've permitted
him unfettered access to a jeep and Shaft 40. According
to an internal memo, the security camera at the main
entrance had malfunctioned the evening of the incident
and three of four evenings prior. A second memo further
stated that the security system, including CCTV, hadn't
received an upgrade since it was installed and frequently
ran dark. This raised the possibly uncharitable point that
Sean Pruitt's friend and fellow security officer definitely
knew cameras well enough to sabotage one, or a string
of them.

By now, second on my wish list to a heart-to-heart
with Linda Flanagan, I'd become eager to meet the elu-
sive Danny Buckhalter.

■ ■ ■

I flew to Northern California out of Albany. Business
class, thank you, Mr. Adeyemi. Six and a half hours'
flight time was more than my back would happily tolerate in coach. They seated me next to an evangelical
preacher with a dirty sense of humor and pristine white
sneakers. I remarked that his shoes were Revelation

shoes because they were so pale. He laughed and paid for my drink.

Somewhere over the Midwest I attended the lavatory, then stood for a few moments at the threshold between classes. A passenger in coach, aisle seat, five rows down, triggered my early-warning radar as he returned from a bathroom trip at the opposite end of the plane. His bearing and movement were different from a regular person's—predators recognize their own kind. He'd made inadvertent eye contact, which caused him to glance away quickly. I chatted with the nearest hostess—who was contractually obligated to pretend an interest in kibitzing with upper-tier patrons—while assessing the man. Lantern-jawed. Long neck and hands. Pale gray long-sleeve dress shirt, chocolate brown tie, gray chinos, and brogues. Ichabod emulated my own ruse and struck up a patently phony conversation with a guy in a Hawaiian shirt in the center seat. Satisfied from Hawaiian Shirt's body language that the men weren't together, I palmed my phone and took a picture. Seated again, I ordered a scotch and soda and emailed the images to Lionel and explained I'd originally met Ichabod at the Redlick estate. Lionel replied almost an hour later that yeah, he might be the guy who'd driven the car chasing us in Horseheads. I downed my scotch and ordered another. That did the trick; I relaxed a notch or two beneath "spring-loaded" and dozed. While traveling, never forgo the opportunity to eat, drink, or sleep.

The plane landed in San Francisco. My layover was an hour and change. I strolled the jam-packed concourse, briefcase in hand, and yes indeed, Ichabod kept pace. He was skilled; one of those ex-spook or FBI agent recruits Bellow mentioned as candidates for the Redlick Group. I wouldn't have picked him up if I hadn't known he was there. Mandibole had inducted him into his little cult, which was a chilling detail.

I bought a soda at a kiosk. He pretended to ponder magazines at a shop across the way. I walked into the men's room, hoping he'd be stupid enough to follow. He wasn't. Fine; I urinated in peace.

Happily, I controlled the field. I exited the main concourse and headed for ground transportation. What could I reasonably assume? Mandibole, and by extension Gerald Redlick and the Redlick Group, were supremely interested in my movements. Ichabod might or might not have known about my connecting flight. Either way, unless he was part of a detail and able to execute a handoff, he couldn't chance me slipping into the city. Which meant he'd be likely to stick close. A nice lady at the information desk relayed the news that all private car services were rerouted inside the domestic parking garage. I checked my watch—a windup—to gauge whether I had time to spar with my shadow. Frankly, there's always time for yanking the chain of one's opponents.

He tailed me into the massive central garage. I feigned answering phone calls, gesturing freely to convey the impression of distractedness. What was his plan were I to climb into a car and zoom into the sunset? Stop me? Too dramatic. Photograph the license plate and report the situation to his handler? More plausible. He'd expected me to either catch a connecting flight or beeline for a taxi. Now he wouldn't be quite sure where I was headed. Off-balance and off his game. Vulnerable.

I dallied and phoned Lionel. After a quick rundown he promised to drop everything and keep a discreet eye on Meg and Devlin. Delia's cryptic prediction that no one connected to Redlick would come after me or mine in the Hudson Valley was reassuring as far as it went. An ex-hitter turned private eye is expected to undergo hazards to his health. I was fair game for kidnapping, shooting, or getting run over in a parking garage. Conversely, messing around with innocent civilians tempted the fates and risked drawing heat that corporations, shadowy or not, preferred to avoid. Meg and the boy were, in my estimation, ninety-nine percent safe. One percent represents too great a number when it's our beloveds. I was relieved that Lionel would assume the role of watchdog.

Foot traffic thinned as I crossed the garage and turned a corner and saw a bank of elevators opposite a descending stairwell. The stairs were blocked with construction cones and a sign: CLOSED FOR MAINTENANCE. My shadow would be forced into his second fateful decision of the past few minutes—let me go, or sprint to catch up and join me on an elevator, hoping I wouldn't make him in his fancy suit. He sprinted. The soft thump of his footfalls drew near, then slowed. If anybody stepped off the elevators, I'd smile and nod and abort the plan. But the timing was perfect.

Ichabod moved into view. I snatched at his necktie. His face contorted in horror. He was damned fast, slap-

ping my arm and darting away with a yelp. Well and
good, except I'm damned fast too and he committed a
tactical error in raising his hands defensively instead of
making like a jackrabbit.

My initial intent was to give him some lumps and send
him home, tail tucked. Matters escalated the moment we
locked horns, unfortunately. The primary rule for a street
fight isn't much different than military or police doc-
trine: During combat, you don't try to match a foe's skill
or aggression; you respond to resistance with overwhelm-
ing force. I lunged, grasped his belt and yanked, pivoting. He flew past me, an astronaut tumbling in zero g,
hit the landing on his ass, and caromed off the far wall.
Should've been game over right there. It wasn't. He went
ragdoll-limp like someone who's trained in judo or ju-
jitsu. That was fine. I bounded down the steps and clob-
bered him with my briefcase as he struggled into a
crouch. The man deserved his props; he slipped the worst
of my overhand smash, rolled to his left, got his palms on
the floor for leverage, and scuttled backward like an ac-
robat down another flight onto the next landing. Dim-
mer here, lit by emergency amber fluorescent strips, and
more intimate, removed from the view of passersby. I
closed with him on the fourth or fifth step, drove the
briefcase edge-first into his midsection, and when he par-
ried it aside, punched it at his neck. He twisted his body
out of line, caught my wrist, and wrenched downward
with all his weight, performing a deep knee bend. I knew
that trick and what it meant for my spine. I went slack
with the momentum, dropping to a knee, and lost the

briefcase. We remained tangled for a moment, awkwardly counterbalanced. He was well-groomed and smelled of cologne and adrenaline. Roughly my height, rawboned, muscular, and desperate. Even so, I out-massed him by forty or fifty pounds, which, all else being equal, was an insurmountable advantage. Ichabod obviously understood that the physics of our contest were unfavorable to his survival, because he released my wrist, clasped his hands together, and hammered my nose, then my jaw on the return stroke. It hurt. It also pissed me off. Blood rushed down the back of my throat. Blood doesn't taste like much of anything if you're preoccupied with not getting hit in the mouth again. It burns like a real dry vodka. I raised my arms in an X and blocked the next swing. Red light flooded my vision. The light of fury and murder. The light that increases my power threefold and strips my Homo sapiens mind to its scales and fangs. He leaned backward and snap-kicked me in the head as I began to rise. I rotated and instead of knocking my eye out of my skull, his foot glanced off my temple. When I simultaneously whipped my fist up and under his chin for what I intended to be, in that instant of berserker rage, an internal decapitation on par with car crash whiplash trauma, the blow struck his rib cage. Bones caved under my knuckles. My fingers opened into claws, seeking to dig inward after his spine, but he'd already accelerated away. The force of the impact catapulted him off the steps. Less of a ragdoll this time, and more of a gangling dummy full of sand and flailing helplessly. Ichabod slammed into the wall, bounced laterally, cradling his busted ribs. He passed his right hand over his face, fingers splayed, pressing in with the heel of his hand. He was the same, except different, after the pass. Pale, red-lipped, diabolical. He raised himself fully upright, ribs forgotten; laughed and growled deep in his chest; and lurched through a big metal emergency exit door. The door clanged shut behind him.

A wave of dizziness staggered me and the moment to give chase passed. I gulped for air until the roaring in my ears subsided and I was sane again, or trending in that direction. Pain wasn't what shocked me sober. A glimpse at the unmasked face of evil and a thimble of common sense did.

CHAPTER THIRTY-THREE

I pulled myself together in the men's room. Splashed my face with cold water, staunched the bleeding, and carried myself with sufficient aplomb to skate through security, all the while hoping that whoever manned the CCTV cameras in the garage hadn't noticed anything unusual. I proceeded without incident and hopped a shuttle for the Charles M. Schulz–Sonoma County Airport. It's a tiny facility. Quonset-hut-type hangar/boarding area and a concourse so short you can stroll the entire length in under sixty seconds. Mid-February is generally a pleasant time to visit the region if you're escaping a wintry clime, such as the Midwest or Upstate New York. My timing was bad; forest fires engulfed large tracts of the coast and areas abutting Napa Valley. The inferno was on everybody's mind. I stood atop the steps at the airport entrance, sniffing the acridness of the distant, steadily encroaching smoke. The dizzy spells were fading, although my right eye blurred and I squinted to keep the world in focus.

Linda Flanagan resided in a bungalow twenty minutes northeast of the airport and past Healdsburg among dusty

hills. The land of vineyards. The rental agency offered me
its last car, a dinky economy job. I squeezed in and zipped
along 101 until the turnoff, where things got slightly complicated with the looping, winding blacktop byways and
the thickening pall of smoke that drifted in through the
vents and irritated my eyes and throat. Her house sat on a
hill in a shady patch surrounded by maple and oak trees.
The driveway was steep; a stream trickled under a shaky
plank bridge near the base. The bungalow must've been
built in the 1960s; humble and compact, yet elegant and
expansive with ski chalet dormers and a wooden deck that
hung out over a ravine. Unkempt yarrow flowers splashed
yellow, red, and pink in terra-cotta pots.

I walked around the house, knocking on doors, banging on the walls, and peering into windows. Nobody
stirred. The property extended farther along the hillside
into the forest. There were a couple of small buildings—a
shed and a metal cargo box—and a cute mother-in-law
cottage. Squirrels and birds darted across my path. My car
was the lone vehicle in the yard. The pall of smoke and
bits of swirling ash made it difficult to discern whether or
not she'd been home recently. Highly unlikely she'd return with Napa Valley on the ragged edge of combusting.

Debating my options, I rang the Campbell-Ryoko ha-
cienda and got the recorder. I said I was en route and
hung up. My phone buzzed ten seconds later. A man
with a gravelly voice identified himself as Beasley. He
asked where I was and I said Healdsburg. Okay, drive up
to Mendocino, 128 to 101, to Shoreline Highway, and
follow it home. Under no circumstances was I to ap-

proach the doctors' house until I received an all clear. Get a room at the Blue Shell Motel. Call him back when I arrived. He hung up before I could say, yeah, see you in a couple of hours.

I headed north and out of the inferno.

■ ■ ■

Ash blackened the hood of the compact. I stopped at a ramshackle gas station between Philo and Navarro, squeegeed the windshield and headlights, and topped off the tank. The proprietor was a weathered man with a heavy beard who, judging by his accent, had emigrated from somewhere north of the U.S. border. A steel-gray conure with a red crest and red cheeks hopped atop the spinner racks and cocked her head at me. The proprietor said the conure's name was Zora; she'd flown into the shop during another long-ago firestorm and decided to stay. He asked where I'd come from. I said New York. I poured coffee from a pot and fixed it the way I liked. News of the disaster cycled nonstop on the crummy television jammed on a high shelf. He went to the door and gazed south, where an orange-and-black charcoal smudge wavered over the mountains.

"The East gets snow in winter. We get fire."

He obviously noticed my black eye and swollen cheek, but didn't comment. Had I ever been all the way up the coast to the Pacific Northwest? I shrugged noncommittally and he explained how he'd lived there for a few years after bailing on the scene in British Columbia.

Zora alighted on my shoulder. She nibbled my ear.

The proprietor accepted the twenty-dollar bill I gave him and put it in his pocket without offering to make change. I tried to escape. He segued into the epic recounting of a monstrous forest fire suffered by his hometown in the "Territories." Wildfires burned for a week. Several days after they'd cooled to blown ash, brown bears came down from the mountains and shambled among the charcoal hulks of the buildings, foraging.

The shop phone rang and I was able to shoo his bird and hoof it to the car while he answered. A green four-door sedan was parked on the shoulder fifty feet before the turnoff. I placed my hands on my hips and glared. The car crept into the road, executed a three-point turn, and disappeared around a bend. The conure glided out of the shop, circled me twice, and flew after the car.

"Oh, no," I said. I went back and told the owner the bad news.

"It's okay, it's okay," he said, the phone pressed to his ear. "Zora's chasing off evil spirits."

"What?"

"Some dog breeds catch rats; my bird catches spirits. She always returns. You should hurry up and move on. Sometimes she brings one back."

■ ■ ■

The lights of Mendocino were glowing in the dark when I arrived. The Blue Shell Motel occupied a rocky terrace with a view of the town and the ocean. Doubles were all they had left. I told the clerk I wasn't picky and booked one at the far end of the main building. An alley separated the wall of my room from a locked shed with an ice machine on the side. Thoughts of Ichabod and his buddies waiting in the wings, maybe tooling around the countryside in a green sedan, were on my mind as I called Beasley and then turned off the lamp and watched the parking lot and the highway through slightly parted drapes. This move put me in the same category as Badja Adeyemi hiding on Elkhorn Lake, waiting for Russians in ski masks to sneak through the trees. At least Adeyemi had been loaded for bear. California didn't reciprocate my PI license or weapon permits. I hadn't even packed a folding knife.

Beasley said he'd meet me in ten. It was closer to twenty when he pulled up beside my rental in a salt-eaten Jeep Cherokee, climbed out, and knocked on the door. Were I compelled to summarize Beasley in a pithy sentence, it would've gone something along the lines of: Professional beach bum commando moments before a killing spree. A bruiser in a dark T-shirt and jeans, and steel-toed boots that had carried him through years of hiking. Buzz cut, thick neck and shoulders, huge thighs. Hard-bitten, half-tanned, and half-sunburned. At home in the arctic or Saharan desert. Ten to fifteen years on me, but moved as if he comfortably jogged five or six miles every morning before eating razor wire and guzzling lye for breakfast. A webwork of minor scars, plus a couple fit to start a party conversation. An almost handsome mug that appeared to have been used for soccer ball kicking practice. He wore a military-brand fighting knife on his belt. If it came to a tussle, this was the sort of character you immediately tried to cripple or kill; pain wouldn't faze him.

We sized each other up. He rested his hand on the knife hilt. Wound tight from the events of the day, I stood in an interview stance, ready to punch him in the throat before he got the knife free of its scabbard. That was the hope, at any rate.

"Hey," I said. "Anyone ever mention that you resemble Race Bannon's meaner cousin?"

"Who? Really? Bannon kicked ass. I loved that cartoon."

"Loved? I watch Jonny Quest in syndication every chance I get."

"Know what?" he said with a wide smile. "You're fuckin' A-okay. I like you."

I smiled back and it was three-quarters genuine. Still wished I was carrying.

"Well, I like you too, Beasley."

"You got a nice shiner, huh?"

"I've had nicer."

"Hungry?" he said. "I could eat the ass end of a rhino. There's a swell spot up the street. Fish and chips are the best around."

I was disappointed he didn't say rhinoceros.

■ ■ ■

Beasley brought me to a "less touristy" restaurant with a nautical theme and real wood tables with real knives and real glasses. We took a spot with a view of some plants and a void that would've been a fine vantage of the Pacific during daylight hours. The fish and chips were as good as promised. Decent tap beer. This Beasley fellow drank with Lionel's enthusiasm, except to no discernable effect besides a moderate decrease in his stoic scowling.

"You want to bend the doctors' ears about Sean Pruitt?" he said.

"Dang it, man, you were doing so well. Belaboring the obvious counts as a party foul. You heard the messages."

"New York. San Francisco. Healdsburg. Mendocino."

"My itinerary," I said.

"Right. You ran into some trouble with banditos on the road. Unless a telephone pole fell on your head."

I pinched my thumb and forefinger together.

"*That* much trouble."

He returned the sign. Then widened the gap between his blocky fingers.

"These deals start small. They don't stay small. Only two types come sniffing after the docs anymore. Tabloid journos or troublemakers. You ain't a journo. Fuck knows if you can even read."

"Some guys are following me," I said. "Green sedan; unknown number of occupants. The people who sent these guys might also be friends with the doctors."

"Sounds like a personal problem. The docs aren't in contact with anybody from . . . before."

"I'm thinking there's enough trouble for everyone."

"People in the green sedan been on you since when?"

"The flight from New York."

"The opposition has a solid idea where you're headed then," he said. "One or two tails. A second unit could be in any woodpile between here and San Francisco."

"They *could* be watching the restaurant."

"Hope they enjoyed me stuffing my piehole."

"You're surprisingly cool for someone who might be in the crosshairs of a sniper as we sit here digesting supper."

While we ate, he'd scanned every patron who'd walked in. As had I, albeit with more tact. My comment caused him to glare around, a klieg light sweeping for infiltrators.

"Doesn't help to whine," he said. "Ain't like I'm ready to throw a party, though. The docs are in seclusion. Boring as hell. Perfect, in other words. I'd rather beachcomb than brawl with ne'er-do-wells or hunt for ninjas around the house. Yeah, they hired me to deal with the goons, but cripes, I thought it was finished."

"You thought wrong."

"I've had a good look at you. Christ, this is serious, huh?" He pushed back from the table and went to pay the lady at the counter. We walked out to his car. "Here's what we'll do. We'll get your bags and go to HQ. See what happens in the morning."

"I'm fine at the motel."

"You ain't fine at the motel." He clunked the Cherokee into reverse. "Place is a death trap."

"But you suggested it," I said.

"I changed my mind for now."

CHAPTER THIRTY-FOUR

Per my research, Campbell and Ryoko had spent a few years in New England conducting a mysterious research project. When that ended, they returned to California and permanently retired from the world. The world didn't miss them. Their cliffside residence north of Mendocino was a loaner from the cinematographer who'd gotten his break filming the Bangladesh documentary. The cinematographer was a Hollywood wheel; unless my memory for celebrity trivia failed me, he too had made himself scarce.

"The dude has five or six houses scattered across the globe," Beasley said. "He's true-blue. When the situation in New England fell apart, he said we could camp here until Howard and Toshi kick the bucket. Haven't heard from him in a while. The lights stay on, so everything must be hunky-dory."

I mentioned that Campbell's name appeared in connection with the Jeffers Project. Campbell and Ryoko

consulted on a million projects, Beasley said. I asked
what sort of research had they pursued in New England.
He turned on the radio and adjusted the dial until Jimmy
Buffett started blaming a woman for a lost shaker of salt.
He pushed in the dash lighter and lit a cigarette when it
popped. Pall Malls. He confided that he scored them in
bulk from the reservation.

The house was locked behind an electric gate at the
end of an elevated, curving driveway. There were only a
couple of lights on, so I could tell it was a classic split-
level Malibu-style beach house, in this case shaped like a
pile of blocks with lots of balconies and windows, and
that was about all. I carried my suitcases, hesitating a
moment on the flagstone walk to appreciate the clean salt
breeze. It tasted sweeter than creosote and ash. Inside,
the walls alternated through the pastel spectrum of
blue to green to salmon. Granite tiles and reed mats were
flanked by fountains that sluiced over beds of split stone.
Tropical plants and ferns and hanging lamps lent the space
a jungle-at-night ambiance. Too dark to tell whether my
room had a view or not. Clean and a large, firm bed were
the sum of my wants and needs right then. Beasley promised to wake me for breakfast as he departed. I stuck a
chair under the doorknob and fell onto the bed. A tapestry of a Pacific island paradise hung on the wall over
the headboard. That island might be where my soul
wandered for the next ten hours. I don't recall. Gods,
angels, and even Whiro let me sleep in something akin to
peace.

■ ■ ■

Rain slicked the windows when I reentered the land of the living a quarter of an hour past the rosy side of dawn. For the sake of California's citizens and its hapless animal population, I hoped the storm was moving southeast. The accommodations were spacious and on the pampered-playboy side of the tracks. Nobody had lived in the room any time recently; I got a whiff of phantom mildew that seeps into empty, neglected habitations. I showered, dressed in a plain T-shirt and jeans, and sallied forth to explore my surroundings.

The house didn't rival any mansions I'd seen of late; large enough to wander in, to lose one's bearings, though. Daylight confirmed a smashing view of the ocean and that nearly every room, every hallway, was decorated with plants and polished rocks. Scents of frying bacon led me by the nose to the kitchen. Beasley was preparing breakfast for Dr. Campbell. A cozy yet roomy space, brimming with muted gray light.

"Hey, I was fixing to come kick your bunk." Beasley toiled at a range loaded with frying pancakes. "Sit, eat. Dr. C, this is our guest, Isaiah Coleridge. The detective."

"Poseidon requests bacon and eggs," Dr. Campbell said. "Best hand it over before he tears this place down." The scientist sat rigidly upright; his features and hands were stiff as sun-scarred leather. Heat boiled from the range, yet he wore a Norwegian sweater and wool pants and appeared comfortable. His glasses were an anti-

quated horn-rimmed model popular during the Apollo
Space Program era. Everything about him screamed
black-and-white TV, unfiltered cigarettes, and nightly
news broadcasts crackling through the speakers of a
Philco AM radio.

Beasley poured coffee and slid a plate of hotcakes in
front of me.

I dug in.

"I've watched you on TV since I was a kid. You're bigger in person."

Dr. Campbell watched me eat. His eyes were as shallow as a bird's.

"Everyone remarks on that. The mind is a camera.
The camera lies." He said this last bit with special emphasis.

I detoured right to the heart of the issue.

"Some of your old friends aren't keen on me nosing
around your godson's death. They seem extremely agitated that I've flown here to visit you and Dr. Ryoko."

"Friends? No. Former associates. Yes. Are you surprised at the resistance? You're stepping on the toes of
unscrupulous individuals."

"I expected a reaction, but not quite so volatile," I
said. "Let's say it raises a number of questions."

"Enjoy your breakfast, Isaiah. Recuperate. Later,
Toshi will join us and you can ask your questions. The
disposition of Sean's case was settled long ago. Tearing
open the wounds can wait a few hours."

Instead of answering, I shoveled in another forkful
and gulped coffee. Beasley could've put many a short-

order cook on notice. He shut down the range, took a seat with a lumberjack stack of cakes, and went at his breakfast with grim efficiency. I empathized. When you're on call twenty-four/seven, you don't stand on ceremony, and you don't dally once the chow bell rings.

"Where is your partner?" I said to Dr. Campbell.

"He's in the salon, communing with the celestial lights. Beasley, has he evinced any signs of stress?"

"Nurse said he had the makings of a bloody nose," Beasley said. "We're good."

"Thank you. Leave him for a while longer. He's projected far beyond the Second Meridian. Watch for a hemorrhage or a seizure." Dr. Campbell pushed his glasses up and peered as if finally seeing me clearly. "You don't—you aren't well."

"Pardon?" I said.

"Your eye . . . Good lord."

"Oh, this?" I touched my cheek below the shiner. "I'm not walking around with a black eye, then I haven't gotten out of bed."

"Young man, you have a potentially serious medical problem. Beasley?"

Beasley went away and returned with a penlight and a black medical bag.

"Lean in a bit, yes, hold there. Follow the light." Dr. Campbell shined the light into my eyes from right to left and I tracked the motion. "Well, this can't reveal any grand truths. Beasley, we should put him in the scope."

"He wouldn't like the scope," Beasley said.

"Who does? I'd wager the farm he's been irradiated or

subjected to—" He clicked off the light and studied me gravely. "I'll need the box. First the box, then we'll decide."

"I'm not getting in the scope, whatever that is," I said.

Without comment, Beasley handed him a palm-size ovoid device with a yellow lacquered enamel shell. Dr. Campbell shakily passed it over my head and torso like a security tech with a wand. The device ticked and emitted an occasional electronic squeal.

"Is that a Geiger counter?" I said, aware that it wasn't. General stress eroded my composure. I was getting jumpier and more irritable.

"No. Please remain silent or you'll disrupt the survey." Dr. Campbell finally set the device aside. "Mild concussion. Courtesy of the blow to the head you've taken in the last twenty-four hours. Your watch is a cheap manual windup. Did your digital watch malfunction? It did, of course it did. Power drain. This is a recent development. You're investigating Sean's death, which presumably means you've ventured near the Jeffers site. Explain what transpired."

I told him about the supercollider track, the sounds of klaxons and motors, and the sensation of a wave of electricity passing through my body.

"You were in the unfinished sector. Rest assured, there are almost certainly a multitude of subsections, some capable of housing equipment and conducting experiments far from prying eyes."

"The locals who'll talk believe black ops are ongoing," I said.

"This was not your first encounter," Dr. Campbell said. "An electromagnetic wave accounts for much. Don't fret; the side effects of your exposure will dissipate in due course. Other readings are mystifying. You either resonate on a variable frequency intrinsically or some trauma is the cause. Has anyone subjected you to hypnotic regression? Have you been bombarded by infrasound?"

"Infrasound. A year ago."

"Projected by a human or animal? Was it acoustic—a fabricated device or a naturally occurring phenomenon such as wind moving through a sound garden of porous stones?"

"An Aztec death whistle is the closest object I can compare it to. It emitted an almost human shriek." Then I explained it was a weapon employed by the Croatoan.

"The serial killer?"

"The same."

"In the days of antiquity when I consulted with Zircon Corporation, their R&D department kept close tabs on the police action in Vietnam. Rumors persist that this 'Croatoan' was created in partnership by our intelligence services and military contractors. What were the effects of his device?"

"Paralysis. Terror. I've heard it's capable of more severe effects."

"Loss of bowel control? Hemorrhaging? Hallucinations?"

"Narrowed vision. Yes, intermittent hallucinations."

"Infrasound can inflict long-term damage," he said. "Subsidiary effects may present months or years following the initial trauma. Properly calibrated, the ongoing damage can be intensified and manipulated along a behavioral spectrum. Conditioned response at the benign end, progressing to various stages of mind control, including triggerable implantation. The practical applications are endless. The military-industrial complex is infatuated."

"Someone may have attempted hypnotic suggestion," I said hesitantly, reluctant to receive more unpleasant news.

"Elucidate, please."

I described the strange aural effects I'd encountered at Redlick Manor.

"Distressing," Dr. Campbell said, not remotely distressed.

"Mandibole was a stage performer, a ventriloquist—"

"Young man, I've consulted with the Redlick Group. Its staff is known to me. The Redlick patriarchs, past and present, are known to me. To my detriment, to my shame. I am intimately aware of Thomas Mandibole's credentials. I am aware of his nature. I am aware of his capabilities." Dr. Campbell's tone reminded me of Delia's naked antipathy toward the Redlick Group frontman. "He is the herald of House Redlick and a supplicant to abominations. Neither a petty magician nor a ventriloquist, rather an anathema who poses as a common charlatan to lull his enemies."

"A herald?" I said, ignoring the rest of it for the moment.

"A representative in the ancient sense when kings dispatched emissaries to foreign courts. The corporations and the families behind them regard one another in terms of ritualized protocol. Since their commercial interests often align, their political opposition is balanced so as to avoid open warfare. The heralds, or spokespersons, if you will, serve a crucial function. They are ceremonial interlocuters between the families and other entities."

"These heralds perform the families' dirty work as well?"

"I'll leave that to your imagination. You should, under no circumstances, take tea with Mandibole, nor his coterie." He raised his hand to head me off at the pass. "I know little of the Mares of Thrace except by reputation. Their gleeful subservience to the Redlicks is demonstrative of vile temperament. Although . . . I'd hazard a guess that the Mares' own development may be related to the Croatoan's."

I bit down a shudder.

"So Zircon and Redlick Group and the Jeffers Project amount to powerful men fucking with things better left unfucked?"

"Succinctly stated."

"'Malignant' is a unique characterization of Mandibole," I said. "Granted, I had a generally unfavorable impression. 'Malignant' connotes plague. Cancer . . ."

"By Jove, he's catching on," the scientist said to Beasley.

"Okay, then. What's the verdict?" I nodded toward his scanning device.

"Death isn't imminent. You're in excellent physical shape, discounting the superficial wounds and probable cerebral trauma. I assume you pursue a daily exercise regimen? Go forth. The skies are clearing. Walk the paths. Breathe in the fresh salt air. Its healing properties are understated."

It was reassuring to hear him say death wasn't imminent. A man likes to hear that now and again.

CHAPTER THIRTY-FIVE

The storm gods heeded my imprecations and moved south. Rocky hillsides above and below the beach house gleamed blindingly as sunlight fractured into splinters. Puddles of rainwater spread like a trail of fire. Beasley acted as my guide for a short excursion along a footpath that skirted oceanside cliffs. I asked if he'd known Sean well. He lit a cigarette. Yes, of course. Ever since the kid was in elementary school. Beasley had taught him to drive a Range Rover, had to stack phone books on the seat so he could peer over the steering wheel.

We rested at the edge of a cliff. Seagulls drifted below. Clouds scudded and mist parted to reveal blazing diamond patches of ocean. A fresh line of thunderheads built in the north.

"How long have you worked for the doctors?" I said.

"Forever. There were some gaps. Did a spell in the hospital counting ceiling tiles. Thought I was in L-O-V-E for a torrid summer. Eloped to the Bahamas. Found out

I was mistaken. 1 miss those islands. The beaches. The tropical moods. The potcake dogs who snuffled around my porch."

"I was speculating how long it takes to migrate from a rational worldview to nodding along with the craziest whoppers a pair of eccentrics can dish."

The jab bounced off him.

"Dude, I was sitting two feet away, listening to your conversation with Doc Campbell. You met Tom Mandibole and his satanic Mouseketeers' club. Had to be a disquieting experience."

"To put it mildly."

"Ever think maybe what you know, what you've seen in your flea's span on this planet, might not be the whole picture?"

"I dig legitimate explanations," I said. "Makeup, sleight of hand. People are double-jointed." I said this, thinking of Ichabod's mini-transformation in the airport garage. "People can dislocate limbs or alter their posture. The mind plays tricks. I don't understand the desire to pin shit on the supernatural or the extraterrestrial. The world is plenty fantastical."

"A kewpie doll to you, Amazing Randi, master of skeptics. Each and every solitary day, we dwell in the shadow of a cosmic mystery. My faith in the docs doesn't rely on their gurudom." He lit another cigarette. "Regular scientists hide the welcome mat whenever the docs come calling. It's a shame, because nobody really has a handle on what's what. Astronomers studying data from telescopes monitoring deep space have discovered galaxies are moving away from us faster than we'd predicted. Kicker is, either dark energy is fucking shit up, or we're gazing back in time to when galaxies expanded more rapidly, or there's an undiscovered subatomic particle capable of near light speed. The community is great at guessing because it guesses a lot. The docs are certain about fringe theories and the community doesn't tolerate that kind of conviction. They're in exile, academic Siberia. Somebody has to defend them. Doesn't mean I'm a disciple."

"Then what are you?" I said.

"Been with the geezers on a dozen major expeditions in jungles and deserts and godforsaken tropical murder nests where everything wants to eat you, down to the vegetation. Got trapped inside a tomb in a rain forest in South America with a gaggle of porters and a guide. Twenty-ton slab of rock toppled and sealed us in. A trap for tomb robbers. Water rising, snakes and spiders slithering and creeping. Flashlights going dead. While the rest of us stood around, dicks in hand, Ryoko and Campbell did what eggheads do at times like these—they worked the problem."

I wanted to ask how the doctors miraculously saved the day, but he plowed ahead. A beast of a man whose thought processes mirrored his physicality.

"Sean was scarce until he came back into our lives for his college years. Same bighearted kid at nineteen as he was at nine. Starry-eyed little fucker." A shadow crossed his face. "I wish the docs hadn't relocated to New England. If we'd stayed here, near him and Linda, things might've gone another direction."

"I can't find Ms. Flanagan. You think she was bad for Sean?"

"Changed back to her maiden name, huh?" He exhaled. "He's gone. Linda got a million bucks richer. That's the final score. Too much to not enough."

"There might be an overtime quarter," I said.

■ ■ ■

I left a message for Meg to say I was alive. Women appreciate the little things. Beasley directed me toward the living room, where the doctors awaited.

Black oil canvases hung in the hallway, staggered at intervals and varying heights. I felt seasick traversing the hall. The master canvas occupied an otherwise blank wall in the living room. Six by six feet of pure concentrated negative space. It generated the optical illusion of a portal into a formless, eternal velvet. I mildly hallucinated specks of cosmic dust, the glint of pinprick stars, and the devilish choir in my nightmares that had drawn me through the black door in the family garage. Not dissimilar to the music that preceded an entrance by Tom Mandibole. Vertigo pounced, and I stepped back and glanced elsewhere.

"Who painted these?" I said.

Dr. Campbell adjusted his glasses and stared for a while.

"The owner of the house acquired them." He said it wistfully, head tilted. Listening to the same unearthly music. "He wouldn't name the artist. Would you like coffee?"

"Yeah, I would."

"Beasley!"

I looked past sliding doors and a view of stone steps winding down toward the beach. Palm plants rustled in sea-blue planter boxes and oversize clay pots. Deck chairs and a parasol were folded neatly. The beach lay broad and sugar-smooth, dimpled by seagull tracks. Thunderheads I'd seen earlier piled on the red-rimmed horizon. The deep ocean stained darker out there, spreading closer.

The living area was tiered in an L-shaped basin. We moved to a spot decorated with a plush couch and wicker chairs. Photographs, knickknacks, and trophy stands were displayed through museum glass. A dour nurse in a white hospital coat attended Toshi Ryoko. Dr. Ryoko occupied a motorized wheelchair. Withered and doll-like, he was wrapped in a dark blanket that sort of matched the spooky paintings in the hall. His eyes were wide and luminous as the moon glinting off black water. A white-board and a marker hung from his turkey neck. Some of his hair had stuck around. The color and substance of summer clouds. The nurse kissed his forehead and strode away.

"Hello, Dr. Ryoko," I said.

Ryoko's nostrils flared appreciably. Dr. Campbell squeezed his shoulder and sat adjacent to his colleague on the edge of the luxurious couch. Considering that a Hollywood player owned the house, a sexy couch was mandatory.

Beasley brought in a carafe of coffee, cups, and cream and sugar on a tray.

"You're working?" I said to the doctors.

"Toshi and I are noodling some theories," Dr. Campbell said. "I don't take you for a student of the sciences." He waved aside my demurral. "The ox who pulls the plow has no use for agriculture or blacksmithing. Are you fond of popular culture?"

"Am I!" I aimed for cheerfulness rather than sarcasm.

He bared his caramel-shaded dentures.

"Splendid. Pay attention. There will be a test afterward. In the early aughts, there was an Internet phenomenon—"

"Doc," I said. "My schedule is tight, appearances to the contrary notwithstanding. I want to discuss Sean. He bought into your Fortean philosophy with the fervor of a disciple. I'm not sure what came first, the chicken or the egg. Was he always susceptible to irrational flights of fancy? Or did exposure to you and Dr. Ryoko lower his defenses against whatever is going on in Horseheads?"

"Did we enable his behavior? Did we fill his head with stuff and nonsense? Are we responsible for him losing his way?"

"I'm not interested in assigning blame. Soon, I'll reach the end of my rope with this investigation. No more money, no more time, no more near-misses by a group of psychopaths who are intent upon shutting me down. Sean's family wants answers about why this kid is dead. Good, bad, or indifferent. So do I."

"Very well," Dr. Campbell said. He glanced at Beasley. Beasley fetched a small wooden box of cigarettes. He helped the doctor light one and then stepped back. "You should know that I've dreaded your visit, what it might reveal," Dr. Campbell said after several puffs.

I figured this was as close to nervous as the old fellow ever got. What he'd witnessed in the remote mountains and the deepest jungles, on desert islands and in the eyes of his fellow man, had tempered him. A firecracker exploding behind his head probably wouldn't have made him flinch.

We'd see, wouldn't we?

CHAPTER THIRTY-SIX

The coffee was bitter and good. Would've been better with a finger of brandy at the bottom of the cup. Dr. Campbell smoked. Beasley lurked. My mind circled back to Ryoko's eerie comparison to a child-size mannequin. Mandibole's stage show had featured large dolls. No idea where I was going with that train of thought, but I had goosebumps.

"If you'd be so kind as to indulge a few questions," I said. "You're neither engineers nor physicists. What was your value to the Jeffers Project?"

"Numerous disciplines were vital to the endeavor. Psychology, biology, anthropology. You must realize, the construction of the collider and its subsequent applications were merely pieces of a whole. Layers of experimentation existed, beginning with the historical research and including behavioral studies on the entire workforce."

"Which piece was yours?"

"Toshi and I contributed our unique perspective."

"Doctor, I've followed you and your partner's exploits

since I was in first grade. Your unique perspective covers a lot of ground."

"We confirmed to the planners and key investors the spectacular properties of the site."

"What sort of properties do you mean?" I said. "Gold? Minerals? Fossils? Lost ruins?"

Dr. Campbell chuckled.

"My boy, you really have observed our long and winding journey from respectability to crackpot royalty. That's gratifying."

"I'm partial to folklore. Legends, gallant expeditions. Hacking through a jungle to photograph an ancient temple. You guys were the embodiment of Rudyard Kipling's and H. Rider Haggard's stories. The pulp cliff-hangers on Saturday morning. I loved you."

"To study folklore is to commune with the ancestors." He reached over and patted my arm.

"As for your query. This old, dirty continent is a honeycomb oozing black sap. Proper imaging equipment, such as ground radar, or if one physically ventured deep beneath the subsurface and the tunnels of the Jeffers site, would reveal a marvel."

"A man of your experience doesn't toss 'marvel' around blithely."

"Well, it's merely a theory. The Jeffers collider track, and its network of tributary passages, mirrors an older subterranean structure. The plexus of the Valley."

"What sort of structure?" I said, trying to visualize what he meant.

"An impact structure. Imagine an ancient meteorite

lodged like a spearhead in a heart, encircled by a jagged, irregular ring of fissures and chasms and galleries. Imagine the corrosive alien metals of that fallen rock dissolving terrestrial substrata, creating a vast, suppurating wound. Imagine some heretofore unclassified radiation emitting from the depths of the earth in sporadic pulses. Imagine the potential effects on animals and men across eons."

I couldn't imagine, not really.

"Huh, you're saying that instead of cordoning off the area for all time, Redlick and allies eagerly built a research complex with a giant hunk of radioactive space metal in the basement." I pondered this for several moments before moving on. "Have you gone caving in the Valley?"

The question amused him.

"Have I beheld the cosmic spearhead or the broken ring with my own eyes? Dear God, no. Twenty-five years ago, I sold Gerald Redlick a journal and a map that were originally the property of a collector of antiquarian rarities. The journal detailed an expedition undertaken in the summer of 1798. A small company of professional explorers were alerted by the natives of a cave system that ran beneath the Valley. Twelve went in; three returned, including the leader. He claimed the others were 'swallowed by the void.' A likely euphemism for falling into a pit. The addled survivors had contracted a plague. They repeated 'the rule of nine' over and over as their flesh blackened and their teeth and hair fell out. Their stories end as medical curiosities in a cadaver laboratory.

"Redlick became interested in the journal. Displaying an abundance of caution, his forebears gave those caverns a wide berth. Gerald Redlick is cut from a different bolt of cloth. Incidentally, the Horscheads system possesses similarities to caverns beneath Anvil Mountain in eastern New York. Anvil Mountain is a secret maintained by the Labrador family. I'm sure that the relative proximity of these systems and their unusual properties is the result of a dramatic event—a meteor shower over a vast swath of what is now New York State during a prehistoric era."

"And you got your mitts on this journal how?" I said.

"The usual way. We've forged many connections among the disenfranchised and the discredited searchers after truth. I burned a small fortune and all of my influence amassing an archive of documents stuffed into several warehouses and storage facilities."

I glanced at the blurred photographs, the glass cases of parchments and arcane instruments. Among these latter, a ceramic-handled tuning fork leaned next to a shot of Nikola Tesla at a podium.

"The academic community's garbage was an industrialist cabal's treasure," I said. "Those moldy old-monied families recognized you were the real deal."

"As did the government, in happier times. A contraction of communal imagination has disempowered the American spirit of exploration. China and India are embarking for the moon. Our gaze has turned inward. It is the age of the industrialist entrepreneur who bankrolls private voyages into space, deep-sea surveys, spiritual and scientific research. We may have cause to celebrate. We are more likely to rue this evolutionary phase."

"Our dreams are dead as the distant twinkling stars,"

I said. "Mandibole and a man named Foote used the term 'kaleidoscope' in reference to the Jeffers Project."

Dr. Ryoko stirred from dormancy. He clacked his whiteboard and clumsily drew an infinity symbol.

"The Kaleidoscope is a theoretical quantum engine," Dr. Campbell said. "A figure of speech, really. The concept refers to a subatomic filter to bridge concrete and abstract reality. A figurative telescope that, in addition to seeing through time, could peer into multiple realities."

Trapper of dreams and god-particles, Dr. Ryoko wrote.

"Oh," I said. "Sean couldn't resist attaching himself to the project."

"It was the fulfillment of dreams he'd suppressed after college and his ongoing depression," Dr. Campbell said.

Dr. Ryoko thrust his chin like a snapping turtle poking his head out of his shell, glowered at Dr. Campbell, and tapped the whiteboard image.

"Those tabloid news articles that the Hadron Collider posed a threat to humanity?" Dr. Campbell waited for me to nod. "It might create black holes and parallel dimensions, or destroy the fabric of space-time?"

"Apparently, the scientists were wrong," I said. "Humanity is alive and not swallowed by a black hole."

"The Jeffers Project was *meant* to fulfill one or more of those doomsday scenarios," Dr. Campbell said.

"Where did you hear this?"

"Gerald Redlick. When we were younger, he mistook my distaste for aspects of civilization as tacit approval of his extremist views. An unctuous man. He deceived everyone involved with the Jeffers Project."

"That's zealots for you," I said. "Always agitating for doomsday. Always laying in canned goods for Armageddon."

"Which is why the Redlicks proposed naming the collider after a poet who preferred animals and the natural world to the industry and mores of mankind. Robinson Jeffers was a self-designated anti-humanist."

A hell of a poet, Dr. Ryoko wrote. *Correct about everything.*

"The Redlicks and their allies don't refer to the potentialities of global chaos as a 'scenario,'" Dr. Campbell said. "They consider such an outcome to be a prophecy of salvation."

Dr. Ryoko scrawled the collider.

Broken ring is their altar.

"Do you mean they pray to it?"

"I fear it prays to *them*," Dr. Campbell said.

CHAPTER THIRTY-SEVEN

We adjourned for a short break. Beasley wheeled in refreshments; finger sandwiches, a cheese platter, and ginger ale.

Get on w/it, Dr. Ryoko wrote. He didn't sample the delicious sandwiches or the tepid ginger ale. Evidently, he received nourishment via a feeding tube in his stomach. His dark eyes reinforced the impatience of his words.

"Sean's death was dismissed as a suicide." I nodded deferentially. "Feels wrong, but I can't rule it out entirely. Murder? Well, there's a hundred reasons to kill a man. I'm interested in two."

Nobody in the room expressed a bit of surprise.

Not a suicide? Dr. Ryoko wrote.

Dr. Campbell stubbed his cigarette into a ceramic ashtray. He shook his head at Beasley, who'd taken a step forward, cigarette box in hand.

"To echo my colleague—not suicide? Your theory?"

"Logic says depression overwhelmed him," I said.

"Screw logic. Nothing is logical about this case. My gut and every other part insist Sean was murdered. The insurance payout complicates a simple premise: Some assholes thought a black magic ceremony would benefit a construction project. As you alluded, the collider was more like a temple in their twisted view. I don't see how I can take this to the authorities or give Sean's family closure. My theory falls under the category of preposterous in the mundane universe."

"You are perfectly correct." Dr. Campbell looked at his friend as he spoke to me. "There can't be a happy outcome. Justice will not be done. Sean was an innocent. An uncommon trait among adults. His sense of wonder grappled with profound cynicism and depression. He embraced the ineffable and the numinous. Lamentably, it embraced him as well." The old man gestured. "The boy was an artist with a crayon. Despite our many peregrinations, I kept his drawings among my treasured possessions. Would you care to see them?"

"Jesus God, no," I said.

Why come here? Dr. Ryoko wrote.

"Because a man doesn't know what he doesn't know," I said. "What I've seen, what you've graciously shared, goes into the mill." I touched my temple. "The stone is already grinding."

"Excellent," Dr. Campbell said. "I hope speaking with us has helped crystallize your thoughts."

"The Gordian knot is looser. Do you gentlemen happen to be in contact with Linda Flanagan?"

"Dear Linda. Poor woman withdrew into seclusion."

Find her! Dr. Ryoko wrote. The nurse came and wheeled him to his afternoon therapy session.

Dr. Campbell watched his friend go.

"I can't disagree with Toshi. Linda was at Sean's side during his long decline. I wouldn't guess her to possess a traitorous bone in her body."

"People often surprise you," I said.

"In the worst possible manner. Do find her."

Dr. Campbell and I retired to the kitchen. He smoked three more cigarettes and regaled me with anecdotes of Sean's ham-fisted attempts to woo Linda. As the last cigarette burned toward the filter, he set it aside and took my hand and studied my palm.

"Doc, a lot of things bother me," I said as he turned my hand this way and that. "One nags me more than the rest. Why would Redlick, why would anyone, want to create a doomsday device?"

"Doomsday with a small *d*," Dr. Campbell said. "He is among those who believe apocalypse is inevitable and would prefer to guide the eventual crash. Gerald is also convinced that evidence points toward the arrival of extraterrestrial life in our solar system. Astronomers tracking odd comets and asteroids have publicly speculated regarding that possibility. To put it plainly, he is of the opinion we should shut off the lights and revert to a preindustrial civilization. The hope being that any aliens would stroll past a darkened house. The Jeffers Collider could be designed to knock out power globally."

"Okay," I said. Badja Adeyemi had said something oblique, but along these lines.

"There's more, of course."

"Wonderful."

"A moment, if you'll indulge me." He toddled off and returned with a manila folder sealed with string yoked by fancy clasps. He spread crinkled newspaper clippings on the table. "What do you know about the planet's magnetic field?"

"I know it's generated by superheated iron in the crust of the earth."

"Yes, a vast sea of liquid metal creates a magnetic shield that reflects the worst of incoming cosmic radiation. Every so often the magnetic poles reverse. This last occurred in the neighborhood of the Stone Age. The interval before the magnetic field reverses polarity is fraught with peril for life on Earth. Because the magnetic shield is severely weakened during a partial reversal, our ozone is bombarded with cosmic radiation. During the exceedingly rare full reversal, the threat of an extinction-level event rises precipitously. This has occurred and will again." He patted my hand. "As our wrinkles and scars define us, remnants of an ancient tree in New Zealand serve as an extant recording of epochs of this phenomenon and suggest we are, in fact, overdue for a complete magnetic reversal. We may be experiencing one now."

"Why do I get the notion this is bad for reasons other than the obvious?"

"Unscrupulous individuals are watching, waiting."

"The Redlicks," I said. "Obviously."

"The Redlicks and others of their ilk."

"I understand that Sean was attracted to your research; the wilder, the better. But what does this have to do with him directly?"

He raised three fingers.

"Imprudently wealthy men seek immortality via three primary channels. Replication. Great works. Miracles. The Redlicks have assiduously tracked climate change and the advent of the magnetic field's reversal, seeking to manipulate the effects for personal gain. Tell me, Isaiah, what would be a logical consequence of the ecosystem's increased exposure to gamma radiation, for example?"

"Sickness. Cancer," I said. "Two-headed babies."

"In the natural order of things, those are predictable outcomes," he said. "Imagine what rich men armed with unlimited resources and advanced science could accomplish were they to harness the powers cosmic. Cross that with faith in supernatural methods. Well. I shudder to think. Gerald Redlick and Tom Mandibole accept heroic myth, including religious texts, as veiled accounts of genetic mutation from lesser breaches of the field. DNA altered by radiation to produce a lineage of wonders and horrors. With this belief as a motive force, we arrive at the creation of cults and cultists whose fervor is maniacal, whose philosophy is impenetrable, whose vision is terrifying."

"The Mares of Thrace," I said. "They're . . ."

"Frightful?"

"What are they? Really. It may sound stupid, but I have to ask. Are they, uh, fully human?"

"I would assume so." He smiled in bemusement. "Indoctrination, ritual hypnosis, a unique diet . . . These could lead to aberrant psychology and aberrant physical traits. The Mares are one of numerous cults inhabiting the occulted margins of our rational world. Adherents of ancient rites and beliefs. Feral children of the wood who desire renewed vitality and vigor. Hence the pagan rituals, the rumored suckling of animal blood, the preoccupation with youth. Alas, its members are in thrall to a darker ideology than the petty goal of regeneration. The Mares are merely agents who serve a cabal that venerates the notion of godhead. A cabal that would engineer supermen, angels, devils. The cabal yearns to transcend humanity entirely and introduce a state of being whose very nature relegates Homo sapiens to a servitor species, an expendable resource, a plaything."

What does a man say to something supremely insane yet supremely convincing as it rolls like distant thunder in the hindermost regions of his mind?

"These lines in your palm are like rings in a tree," he said. "The Redlicks are imbued with power that derives from immense wealth and venerable status. For all that, they've misjudged your mettle. You were an unexpected variable. The situation is spinning out of control."

"All the bees and none of the honey," I said. "Doc, if the situation in Horseheads is such a clusterfuck, why did you allow Sean to accept that job at the site? You could've steered him away."

"Don't you think we tried? By the time we heard he'd returned to New York, it was practically a fait accompli."

"You turned your back?" I said it harshly, hoping to rattle him, to keep him honest, or as honest as he was capable of being.

The doctor raised his hands in defense.

"My own influence paled in comparison to the forces that held him in their sway."

"Why Shaft 40?" I opened the Jeffers Project schematics on my phone and brandished it accusingly. "Why does X mark that spot?"

"There is occult significance to the geometry of the collider and its unfinished portion where he died."

"What significance?" I said.

Dr. Campbell touched the map at Shaft 40.

"This is where the jaws would be if the ouroboros represented a fracture in reality. Sean's blood poured into that symbolic maw."

"Doc, this is more than I bargained on."

"Your instinct is to divest yourself of this burden and flee." He said this with sympathy for my plight. "The Mares killed Sean. Probably to enact a blood ritual to appease the alleged gods of the valley. The scale must be balanced."

"Proving it is another matter, Dr. Campbell."

"Proving it in a court of law may be impossible. *Vengeance* doesn't require proof. It requires the will and the courage to act. I'm too old. June is too good. Alex is a pacifist at heart. Badja lacks the character and is incarcerated, although he might be convinced to strike in other ways were you to provide evidence of murder. I ask, who else but Isaiah Coleridge?"

I didn't have a retort handy.

"For what it's worth, I'm prepared to ride farther. See where the trail ends."

His parting words were sober as a prayer.

"Light and dark, you are always you," he said. "The time that came before this time? The time where you stood? The place where you stood? It is a memory. The machinery of fate has brought you forward from darkness into light into darkness. You stand somewhere different now. You must be ready . . . for the terrors to come."

That got under my skin. I'd assumed the terrors were already here.

■ ■ ■

A bigger, badder storm hammered us during the night. Lightning scorched the ocean. Huge waves smashed the shore. Winds came shrieking and we lost power. Flash! Mom sat in the darkness at the foot of the bed, leather wings partly unfurled. Flash! Achilles prowled beside me, jaws dripping gore. I opened my eyes. Morning light had sneaked into the room. Roof tiles were flung across the lawn and the driveway. Beasley got a chain saw and cleared a palm tree that had fallen outside the main gate.

I headed south for Sonoma after breakfast. Beasley insisted on tailing me the whole way to the airport in case Mandibole's henchmen tried anything cute. During the night he'd gone out onto the porch and spotted a car sitting in the drive with its lights off. He went to fetch his rifle. The car eased on down the road.

Radio news reported that the wet weather and shifting winds were slowly bringing the fires to heel. No sign of the green sedan or the presumed bad guys.

I landed in Albany in the dark. Lionel idled his Monte Carlo at the curb. He didn't ask questions. Halfway home, it began to snow.

PART IV

RAH, RAH! SIS, BOOM, BAH!

CHAPTER THIRTY-EIGHT

March came in like a lamb and I knew what that meant. The roads and the houses were filmed with grit. Fields and lawns lay skinned. Snow gleamed its dirty face among the haggard trees. A man could walk around in a windbreaker during the day before the sun dropped behind the Catskills and frost breathed against window glass.

I made an ear-numbing amount of calls. One of them was to Adeyemi's lawyer, who set up a conference call on a "secure" line. I kept the update brief and any conclusions to myself.

Adeyemi asked what I'd learned, and I said not enough, which was more or less the truth. I had feelers out for Linda Flanagan and Danny Buckhalter. If I heard something, I'd report. Neither of us mentioned extending the retainer. Any further effort on my part would be itemized and passed along to his lawyer. His thinking was obvious: I'd poked around at some risk to my person, chased promising leads that went nowhere except into brick walls. It was the beginning of a slow, awkward breakup.

He thanked me for my efforts in a subdued tone. Prison wears on weak and tough alike, and tends to knock the starch out of the best of them. He'd held at least a meager hope that someone might be made to pay for his nephew's death. That little match twinkling in the darkness had seemed like a blaze now that it flickered, pitiful and wan. There were select details I might've shared, a plan I might've laid out for his approval. I withheld my intentions primarily because my last shot was aimed at the moon. It seemed cruel to revitalize his optimism and then dash it completely in the likely event of yet another dead end.

■ ■ ■

The universe, in its boundless perversity, signaled less than a week after that phone conference. I'd gotten ahold of the Jeffers Colony caretaker, Lenny Herzog (who really did check his messages weekly at most), and paid him a tidy sum to act as my eyes and ears in Morrow Village. I allayed his wariness by explaining that all I wanted was a bead on Danny Buckhalter or Linda Flanagan—two people he didn't actively associate with personal danger.

Who knew a lonely, doddering coot would jump at

the chance to play detective? I sent him a photo of Linda and said to buzz me if he saw her or Danny. I promised a hefty cash reward in addition to what I paid him to linger at the likeliest bars in or around Morrow, swilling booze as he'd probably intended to do anyhow. It would be fair to rate my expectations as low. But the phone rang around midnight and Lenny cheerfully related that he was sitting not twenty feet from the woman. She looked sort of awful and was carrying on with a tableful of fellas, one of whom resembled Buckhalter, although he wasn't sure. The two were more hands-on with each other than a pair of octopi. I asked if he knew where Buckhalter lived. No, but for a hundred dollars he'd follow the couple when they left the bar and report back. I told him that was a great idea.

I gave Lionel the rundown and he smirked at my ruthlessness. I reminded him that as an avowed Peeping Tom, Herzog brought skills to the game. Then he said, yeah, but what about the dog? I said if Herzog disappeared or got it in the neck because he didn't know how to tail someone discreetly, we'd go find Gracie and bring her to Hawk Mountain. Lionel, despite the impracticality of the scheme, was satisfied.

Several hours passed and I admit to a pang of regret as my imagination concocted gruesome fates for Lenny H. Then Herzog called in with an address and a demand that I email his PayPal account with the agreed-upon payment. It wasn't lost on me that I was as amazed that this flea-bitten hermit availed himself of online banking

as I was that cultists were prancing through the woods
in varsity duds.

What a world.

■ ■ ■

I'd gotten my hands on a 1980s Dodge cargo van for
cheap. White and rust with two bucket seats up front.
My buddy at the salvage yard reinforced the bumpers
and installed a winch mount in the front. Unable to pre-
dict how events might unfold, we prepared for the
worst; loaded the van with an array of tools and equipment, then covered them with a tarp.

Meg asked how long I'd be gone. She'd grudgingly
grown accustomed to me languishing at the house four
or five nights a week, licking my wounds and poring over
curious and quaint volumes of forgotten lore. As we
talked, she supervised my efforts to reattach a section of
gutter that sprang loose during the last heavy snow. Me
on a shaky ladder had us both pondering mortality.

"A few days," I said. "Or forever."

"Oh, sweetie, you aren't killing the comedy."

I could never quite tell when her dry wit was referencing something serious (my former life with the mob, for
instance), nor what response was expected. I did what all
guys learn to do, if they're savvy—I improvised. I fell off
the ladder.

She kissed me and made it better.

"I hope I don't ever die," I said.

"Oh?" she said.

"Yeah. I'd miss you."

■ ■ ■

I borrowed the Monte Carlo. Lionel drove the van. We departed Hawk Mountain at different times and traveled separate routes. Weeks had passed since my California vacation and there were no signs of surveillance. Some of Mandibole's people might've been ex-intelligence, which was a concern. However, the logistics of monitoring my activities and those of my associates over a prolonged duration would require a much larger team and support staff. Could the Redlicks theoretically afford a full-blown surveillance operation? Yes, a small chance existed. Could a small, under-supported team function effectively and without tipping their hand? The odds dwindled to near zero. Horseheads was the real danger. Once I showed my face in town, the fuse would be lit.

I cruised into a golden late-winter morning. On the way, I listened to audio from the Campbell-Ryoko files. These pieces were the last in my possession. I was slightly nostalgic to think we were at the end of our journey. I played them several times.

The first piece was a somewhat recent excerpt of both men discussing their research into social media and the Internet as a lurking threat to civilization:

Dr. Campbell:

Memes, the relentless onslaught of data on social media.

MTV and quick-cut photography changed the brain chemistry of a generation of viewers. Try an experiment. Immerse yourself in a few hours of contemporary thrillers and action films, then try to sit without squirming during Angie Dickinson's escape from the apartment of her one-night stand in Dressed to Kill. *You'll fail.*

Dr. Ryoko:

So, have we retired into senility, you ask? Are we working, you ask? Dare we? YES! We're investigating the parallels between weaponized social media and traditional organic disease vectors. Some esteemed colleagues have long posited that a synthetic virus can be developed and transmitted through a digital medium. Seizure disorder, hypnosis, hypnagogic or fugue states, mind control. Programmers and spiritualists alike suspect the data stream to be capable of sentience that will evolve and propagate. Such an enlightened data stream might infiltrate and hijack the minds of its human consumers. It could manipulate them, control them. Wouldn't such a transaction resemble demonic possession? Is there an appreciable difference between machine behavior and the predatory behavior of animals or plants or fungi?

Dr. Campbell:

Early in the new millennium, an Internet phenomenon emerged. Prosaic images overrun by inky blackness. Digital kudzu. Bizarre, unwholesome text, and blackness oozing from eyes and mouths of popular animated characters and real-life celebrities. The manifest power of an entity known as Zalgo. Seldom seen, always felt. A corruptor to exceed the abominable purview of Satan Hisownself. The phenome-

*non was revealed to be a parody of pop culture created by
Dave Kelly, an e-zine writer. Powerful and disturbing despite its innocuous provenance. It lingers like a stain in the
mind's eye. I consider whether the Zalgo craze was the initial stirring of a non-organic superintelligence, an amal-
gamation of projected thought and the echo of that thought
given substance. Someone, somewhere in a basement, or
bunker under the forest floor, has gazed through the Black
Kaleidoscope, heedless of Nietzsche's maxim. Now the entity
tests its limits.*

The final excerpt was the oldest material. It felt enig-
matically crucial; the answer to a riddle on the tip of my
tongue.

A muffled voice asked Campbell to discuss the Redlicks
and Labradors. Campbell claimed familiarity with both
families dating to his youth. The interviewer joked about
the order of Freemasons and the founding of Redlick
Manor. Dr. Campbell chuckled darkly and said:

*Communities of any size husband secrets. Secrets span
generations. Secrets corrode and deform. They persist like a
tumor because most people who come into contact with them
choose, or are encouraged, to look away, if not forget . . .
Redlick Manor is an edifice in service of occult arts. Naturally, to seal the pact with* [garbled] *the Redlick patriarchs
sacrificed the architect and his army of master carpenters
in an elaborate ritual at the Wendigo Stone in the woods.
Laborers were taken to another location, the mausoleum,
perhaps, and buried alive . . .*

The interviewer interrupted with a garbled comment.
Campbell continued:

I condone nothing, sir. I observe and I theorize. This was, 1896? 1897? Sacrifice is an ancient custom. Constructions of . . . power must be consecrated in blood, else all this effort comes to naught and the spirit of the forest turns a blind eye to the supplicants' travails.

The doctor went on at length. Unimportant at that moment. Dr. Campbell's words echoed and reinforced what Adeyemi said to me. *Blood, not science.* I'd begun to entertain the wild idea that both men were right.

CHAPTER THIRTY-NINE

Sneaking around Horseheads would've been the safest course. We could've staked out Linda Flanagan and her beau and pounced at an opportune moment. We probably could've done it without alerting anyone to our presence. To what purpose, though? Nobody was going to roll over and confess his or her role in a murder. Nobody would help me wrap my case in a pink ribbon. Adeyemi and the doctors said something that stayed with me—whatever Redlick and associates were up to with the Jeffers Project was bigger than one man's death.

When conflict is inevitable, take the fight to the enemy. As far as I was concerned, conflict was absolutely inevitable.

I ate supper at the Hotel Roan, my home away from home. I wore an okay suit and comfortable shoes. Gun, knife, and my grandfather's jade war club. Wireless lightweight two-way radio. The idea was to be seen. The *FIN* on Mandibole's pocket square bobbed to the surface of my consciousness.

The Hotel Roan restaurant did a better-than-average T-bone steak. Bloody with a baked potato, salad, and a pitcher of ice water. I savored the meal, then stepped into the lounge for a drink. Four tables on the cramped floor, four stools at the bar, and a window booth. Behind the bar was a mirrored alcove shaped like an altar to a scant yet discerning selection of bourbon, scotch, and liqueur. Toward the tippy-top of the alcove perched a signed photograph of Donald Sutherland aping his iconic spine-chilling doppelgänger pose at the end of *Invasion of the Body Snatchers*.

The bartender switched the channel to boxing.

Two fighters bludgeoned away at center ring in some grimy overseas arena. I didn't recognize either of them offhand. Harsh lights splashed upon tattered posters and partially whitewashed graffiti. Men and women in sock hats and wool coats yelled encouragement. Chilly venue, wherever it was. Steam mantled the boxers—a heavyweight from the Republic of Congo and a Russian built like a tree. The middle rounds had arrived and the Congolese fighter was intent upon chopping the Russian down. The Russian had no answer for his opponent's left jab or short, clubbing right. He circled, threw an occasional haymaker that was easily slipped, clinched, and lost every exchange. He gulped and flailed like a drowning man. A drowning man who received a punch to the snout every time he surfaced for air.

"It's the straight right that puts you to sleep," the bartender said, watching the action. "He needs one to put him out of his misery."

I couldn't disagree.

"You fight?" He glanced at my hands. He was a grizzled gentleman with small, bruised eyes and a gin-blossom nose.

"See these pretty ears? Not enough cauliflower."

"You got some cartilage in your nose, still." Back to my hands again, unconvinced.

"Broken, never squashed."

Between rounds eight and nine, I texted Meg and told her how much I loved her and Devlin and wished them good night and sweet dreams. I put my phone away and returned to the bout, which only got worse for the Russian. His face was marbled like a slab of raw meat.

Lionel boxed in the military. We frequently discussed the squared circle and the octagon and lamented that Greco-Roman wrestling didn't enjoy much popularity in the States. Lionel laid money on the more important bouts, although he laid money on practically anything. My admiration for the sweet science was purely aesthetic, and a touch envious because fighting and boxing are closely related but utterly incomparable.

I'm drawn to the revelation of character that occurs when two peak athletes spend upward of forty-five minutes beating each other to a pulp. Fighters in the championship rounds are seldom the same men who begin the bout. Their inner selves are revealed blow by blow, given and received, like sculptors carving blocks of granite. Men are equals when fresh and full of hope; by smashed noses, broken ribs, lacerations, contusions, exhaustion, and fear is truth revealed.

My favorite boxer? Of the heavyweights, it has to be David Tua. Toward the end of his career he was whaling on a beefy white boy; whacked that patented left hook into the opponent's body so hard his whole rib cage buckled. White boy dropped; he couldn't breathe, much less continue fighting. If we're talking middleweights, I love Tommy Hearns, but pound for pound, Marvelous Marvin Hagler was among the toughest human beings who've ever laced on gloves. I watched him battle Mugabi in 1986, at a bar on a large screen with my dad and a gaggle of his air force buddies. Mugabi swung a wrecking ball. Hagler absorbed hideous punishment and each knock in the chassis caused him to shift into a higher gear and punch harder. That contest and the gruesome match between Ali and Foreman in Zaire in 1974 are testaments to the obdurate, bellicose disposition of man. Those performances molded my disposition on a fundamental level in a way all my dad's tough love never could. Street fighting and boxing are supremely contrasted. Dad taught me close quarters combat from a bag of World War Two dirty tricks; the champion boxers instilled within my soul a love of tactics and the courage to see them through.

The already cozy bar started to fill up. Besides me and the bartender, a young lady in a green velvet dress muttered into her phone, and two men argued heatedly in the booth. Golf Pro and Mr. Denim back for another go at me. The Mares of Thrace wore the antiquated Valley High jackets, but lacked the funky death mask makeup at the moment. Just a pair of dudes reliving past glory until the moment was right to slap on their ghoulish aspect.

Golf Pro removed his glasses, wiped them, and laughed. He called for a round of martinis. Phone Woman was enraptured by her glowing cathode. For me, another double Auchentoshan to neutralize the lingering aftertaste of dinner. A young, beautiful couple wandered in and ordered cosmos. He wore a tux, and she a white Cinderella gown. They were past their limit and made an adventure of navigating to a table.

The televised beating continued. I nursed the scotch to the bitter foregone conclusion. The referee visibly considered stopping the show in the eleventh. The Russian, slumped, eyes swollen, survived to watch the Congolese get his arm raised in a unanimous decision.

Mr. Denim and Golf Pro observed a moment of silence before resuming their conversation. The beautiful couple were drunk in love in addition to being drunk-drunk, and too busy mooning over each other to register the human tragedy on the screen.

Phone Lady swore. She snapped her fingers and demanded a vodka neat.

"I'm dead," she said to the phone or to herself. "He's going to fucking kill me."

"Good." The bartender poured her a vodka. The woman stared at him, flabbergasted. He reflected her stare, a dishrag draped over his forearm.

Thunderclouds gathered.

I texted Lionel to alert him, then pinned a few bucks on the bar with my empty glass and headed for the exit.

Mr. Denim and Golf Pro patently ignored me as I moved past. Their martinis were virtually untouched. I detest guys like them. Guys who pretend to drink. The thunderclouds caught me as I went through the lobby doors.

Come on then, I said. *Come on.*

I'd parked the Monte Carlo in a slot across from the entrance. Nancy the Beautician leaned on the hood. She was in costume and smiling evilly. A cheerleader transported from an alternate history Cold War America. Inebriated partygoers were cutting up in the loading zone; laughing, snapping pictures, and waving an open bottle of champagne while an exasperated taxi driver looked on.

Nancy beckoned, perhaps hesitant because of the crowd. "Mr. Detective!"

Ghastly pale in brutal contrast with her red, red lips. Ancient and vital. Her seams and wrinkles were armor. As I approached, she sprang off the hood and grabbed my arm. The movement was like a crocodile lurching from tall grass, jaws agape. Her perfume stung my nose and throat. I'd gotten a whiff of her scent in the past. This was magnitudes more potent; the reek of chemical burning, of rancid meat, black horses milling in a stable, whinnying as they tore at one another, hooves churning.

I reacted violently.

The war club was out of my belt and into my fist. Gagging, I raised the club, then brought its calcified knob down in a savage tomahawk stroke that caught her above the eye. Her skull dented; the eye likely destroyed. She slumped, dead weight, claws yet sunk into my arm. I shoved her down.

"You animal!" Nancy shuddered with an electric current. She began to rise. Blood decanted in a rivulet from her forehead and covered her face. "You animal! You animal!" She raked blindly at where I'd been.

I was in the car and reversing. Fast, but not too fast. Making a getaway wasn't the goal. Here came the crimson and bronze Mercury Monterey screeching rubber around the side of the hotel. A blaze of chandeliers in the building's bay windows illuminated Ichabod at the wheel. Golf Pro and Mr. Denim ran out the front doors and piled in. I whipped onto the road and accelerated away before I could see in the jittery rearview whether Nancy joined the posse. Oh, I dearly hoped so. I wanted them all together.

■ ■ ■

Fortune favors the bold. Fortune also favors the prepared. Lionel and I were both. We'd studied maps of a small area north of Horseheads and toured several roads earlier that day. Marking bridges, turnoffs, blind curves, and the like; scoping the possibilities. This encounter could've unfolded along any number of trajectories. So far, it was breaking our way.

I made it a shade over a mile before I realized my arm was leaking. Suit fabric had shredded. Muscle was gashed deep where dear sweet Nancy had latched on. The wound pulsed blood with every beat of my heart. I yanked off my tie and used my teeth to cinch it around my arm as a tourniquet. The Monte Carlo slewed all over the road as I made the emergency repairs.

Meanwhile, the Mercury zoomed up, high beams blaring. Ichabod drove like a maniac to catch me, and now he attempted to pass on the outside lane. The predictable offensive moves would be to either force me into the ditch or zip ahead and block my path. I swerved across the line and cut him off twice. Each time, he dropped back, regrouped, then gunned the engine for another run. On the third attempt, I hit the brakes and roared down an off-ramp into a maze of country roads.

Winding, narrow, generally deserted. Ichabod closed the gap, tailgated, eased off, faked passing, eased off, and repeated the cycle, headlights splashing my mirrors. The Monte Carlo was beefed up and it handled well, but Ichabod was a better driver, no contest. Barring divine intervention, he would've eventually prevailed and crashed me.

Thumping across a girder bridge, I clicked the two-way.

"Ten seconds."

We climbed a long grade and then were hauling ass through broken terrain. My pursuer pressed more aggressively. I doubt Ichabod or his homies noticed Lionel ease out from a dirt road as we roared by. Same stealthy maneuver cops use to nail speeders. His van would be running dark, slightly beyond the range of the Mercury's taillights.

Ichabod knew the landscape better than I did. For example, he was probably familiar with the T in the road a few hundred yards ahead. That fact didn't save him. I waited until the last possible moment, braked, and

turned left. It was ugly and I would've sworn to corner-
ing on two wheels. I made it and that's what goes into
the record book.

Ichabod coasted to the intersection. No hurry; after
the past few miles of sparring, he would be confident that
he could catch me at will. I whipped over onto the edge
of the road and turned my head precisely as Lionel, still
running dark, rear-ended the Mercury. The collision produced a metallic crunch as the van's reinforced bumper
and battering ram of a winch mount burst the Mercury's
trunk. The car was shoved through the intersection,
sparks pinwheeling from where its front end scraped asphalt. It plowed over the embankment, ricocheted off a
tree, and vanished. Not quite a sheer hundred-and-fifty-
foot drop into a ravine. Really damned steep, though.
We'd paced it that afternoon and decided the killing descent would suffice. I'd estimate the Mercury performed
two or three endos before pancaking in a shallow creek
among some rocks.

The van sat crossways in the center of the intersection.
Headlights blinked on as it reversed, then rolled forward
and parked, angled in my direction. Lionel, dressed in
coveralls and a ski mask, emerged and waved. He carried
an automatic rifle in his other hand.

"Going to verify casualties," he said over the radio.
"Rendezvous at Farmer Brown's in a bit?"

I double-clicked, put the Monte Carlo into gear, and
proceeded with the itinerary.

CHAPTER FORTY

The farmhouse Lenny Herzog had told me about lay well up in the hills. I parked beside a blank mailbox. I didn't know who owned the place, only who I hoped to find in the lair. Fallow pastures and thick copses of trees. Private, although not far from a heavily traveled road. The house was a homely panel-and-timber construction enslaved to rural agrarian traditions of the last century. Empty pens, empty barn; every structure collapsing. On this ground, generations of men had slaughtered sheep and cows. Chopped chickens in the neck. Gelded horses. A place of feeding and dying. Its vibe rivaled that of the infamous Kingston Murder House. Human bones rested beneath the potato patch. Always room for one more.

My woozy brain gradually sobered. I busted into the first aid kit and did what I could as quickly as I could. Alcohol, gauze bandages, and twenty yards of tape stabilized the bleeding. I bound my arm like a mummy, downed a few aspirin, and declared it a fix. Should I wait for Lionel? Yes. I didn't.

It was a beautiful night to be on dire business. North and east, a bulwark of raw, primeval darkness held sway, and it enforced a zone of scarcely fathomable stillness that, for several moments, reeled my listening soul back to an epoch when a single mighty forest blanketed the mountains and the plains. Birds of prey glided silent as death; wolf packs yipped warnings to their rivals; a breeze rustled the canopy. During that misty stretch of prehistory, men wisely hid themselves after sunset. My soul strained to decipher the message of this beckoning quiet. The jawbone knife on my hip knew it well, had persisted through eons along an axis of immutable blood. Wild animals were yet animals in this digital age. Only we toolmaking primates had radically evolved, and, for our pains, edged an inch or two nearer annihilation every day.

Significant blood loss and the presence of death elicits my maudlin tendencies.

Light shone from a porch window, revealing a station wagon. I walked along the driveway, sticking to the shadows. Once I got close, I saw a woman in a sweater moving around inside. Her hair was long and blond. No dogs. She was alone. The doorknob turned, so I walked in.

Linda Flanagan froze. Very surprised and very afraid. Hey, if I saw me coming into the room unannounced, blood spattered, at night, in the woods, I wouldn't have liked it either.

She sat on a couch near the fireplace when I asked her

to. The interior lived down to my expectations: a main room sparsely decorated with dusty furniture, tube TV, and no phone. The kitchen was several feet of counter and stove space against the wall. A narrow staircase led to the second floor. Grimy windows. Lamps in the front and rear corners provided illumination. The air was strong with the odor of unwashed bodies and spoiled meat.

I introduced myself twice. She calmed down as it became apparent that I wasn't necessarily there to murder her. She mentioned Danny was out with a friend; they were certain to return at any moment. Liquored to the gills and heavily armed too.

"Been back to Healdsburg since the fire?" I said. "Or is the boondocks version of Castle Dracula your new home?"

Linda was tan, athletic, and vigorous in the photos. Haggard now. Bloodshot eyes and matted hair. Shoeless, dirty feet. Her arms were sinewy and tough, though. I'd have to hit her fairly hard if she panicked and tried to bust a move.

"Yes, I have. The house stands," she said. "The trees were singed. You were there?"

"Looking for you. But just to talk. It's about Sean."

"I—would you care for tea?"

"Relax, I've got it."

I went to the gas stove, one eye on her as I opened cupboards. I found instant coffee, a box of tea, and a .41 revolver hanging from a hook inside a cabinet. I pocketed the bullets and hung it again. She watched me get a kettle boiling on the stove. She then watched me dither, rearranging items, handling them as if I were the Farmhouse Pantry Inspector. Pretty soon we had steaming cups of tea.

I sat opposite her in a rocker with my back to the hearth.

"Aren't you afraid of bumping into June Pruitt? She's only a few miles away."

"What for?" Linda said. She was cooler now that she'd gotten her feet under her.

"It might be uncomfortable. I don't know."

She coughed dryly.

"This is another world, Mr. Coleridge."

I sipped the tea; gave it a moment, then started in on her.

"Sean behaved erratically over the last few months of his life, didn't he?"

"He was argumentative."

"Forgetful?"

"His depression was exacerbated by stress. He could be extremely scatterbrained."

I set Sean's ring and the photo of him and Linda on the coffee table.

Linda's face softened.

"Where did you get these?"

"Who's Rita?"

"I—" She examined the back of the photo. Her brow furrowed.

"Rita was a golden retriever," I said. "His dog in high school. This caused me to go over my interview notes

with his coworkers, to call a few back and probe for anecdotes."

"You're right. I totally forgot Rita. He used to cry
over her on her birthday."

I'd watched a video of Sean as a child. Backyard barbecue; shaggy golden dog and the boy romping in the grass,
Dr. Pruitt blasting them with a garden hose. The home
video camera operator followed Rita's exploits. She jumped
into the pool, causing a ruckus. She stole a piece of cake off
the picnic table and ran away with a slobbery grin. More
ruckus. More shouts of, *Rita! No! Bad dog!* Rita didn't
mind; she got the cake.

"Signing the photo that way," Linda said. "Sean was
confused, very confused, toward the final weeks of his life.
More than I realized. We weren't speaking much. And
when we did, we were really only yelling past each other."

"I'm confused too. Was sleeping with Danny Buckhalter a fringe benefit of that generous insurance settlement?"

Her eyes widened and became teary. She dabbed them
with her wrist.

"God, people talk."

"People talk in towns like Horseheads. People really
talk in hamlets like Morrow. People flap their tongues
like ceiling fans when they're living cheek by jowl in construction camps. Nobody in authority asked those questions. But I did. A neighbor saw you and Buckhalter
sharing a milkshake with two straws at the soda shop.
The cleaning lady spotted you slow-dancing at a club.
His car was parked outside your house while Sean was at
work. Whatever, you got made. Classic."

The truth was, I'd decided to run a bluff and see how it went. This was her opportunity to deny, to retort with righteous outrage, or to flee the interview. The moment stretched. She exhaled four years of tension.

"I loved Sean. We had issues. I fucked Danny because I needed someone to fuck."

"Past tense? Isn't this his home? The stars seem to have aligned for you two. Melts my cynical heart to see a hardworking country boy get the girl and the cash."

"Are you implying that I seduced him to harm my husband in a money scheme?" There was more weariness than anger in her voice.

"That would be the path of least resistance. When in doubt, look to the spouse. I'm suggesting Danny Buckhalter seduced both of you. Manipulating Sean was always the main goal. He was the chosen one. The ninth of nine."

"Chosen?" she said. The furrow in her brow reappeared.

I did my damnedest to summon the literary specters of Holmes and Mason; Poirot and Fletcher.

"Were you aware that nine deaths occurred at the Jeffers site over an eleven-year span?"

She shrugged.

"Yes, vaguely. I worried for Sean, so I tried not to focus on the hazards."

"All were attributed to human frailty or acts of God. A trench collapse and a small explosion took out five. Another worker was struck and killed by a car. Somebody was electrocuted. Another guy fell down a shaft. Sean jumped. So they say."

Her expression vacillated between puzzlement and extremely wary puzzlement.

"Construction is dicey," I said. "Dams, tunnels, nuclear reactors, atom smashers, are *high-fucking-risk business*, to put it in the vernacular of a buddy of mine. Badja Adeyemi also said something I can't shake. He said the collider was constructed in reverence to blood, not science."

"Badja is a devil," she said with a not unreasonable trace of fear. She sipped tea and immediately broke into a hacking cough that went on longer than it should've.

I was implacable.

"Nine deaths, including Sean. My darker nature whispered of a pattern. That less chivalrous part of me knows without reservation what happened to your husband. Because the pieces were right there, waiting to assemble their ugly picture. See, there's a historical precedent. The colonial expedition that first explored the caverns beneath the Jeffers site numbered twelve. Nine died in the caverns. Died or disappeared. Two and a half centuries later, nine workers perished during the construction project. What an amazing coincidence!"

"Okay," she said, drawing it out.

"Sean was friendly with a group in Horseheads," I said to change gears. "A society or club, if you will, called the Mares of Thrace."

Her eyes flickered the way an amateur card-counter's will when she's doing the math.

"Sean mentioned a clique."

"And what a clique! The Mares of Thrace are animists dedicated to the genius loci of the Valley of the Horses'

Heads. They're a blood cult. Live longer, live better through murder. Add a dash of UFO-ology, and we've got real winners on our hands. Too melodramatic?"

"It's melodramatic," she said.

"Christians subscribe to a risen lord and foist original sin on a serpent talking some chick into biting a magic apple. For some reason, that's mainstream."

"I don't quite know how to respond. What do you want me to say?"

"You never interacted with the Mares?"

"Not at all."

"Danny B and his cronies weren't interested in your husband as a friend. Sean was marked for death. That's my theory. It gets worse. What if Sean was only the last in line? What if some, or all, of those accidents at the Jeffers site were orchestrated? Ritual sacrifices. Same as the Aztec priests and the Celtic druids. A lunatic's notion of consecration."

She laughed in a short, harsh burst of incredulousness.

"That's crazy."

"Craziest motive for murder I've ever run across. Yet, here we are. Nothing new when it comes to innocent folks paying for the insanity of a grasping few." I nodded at Sean's ring on the table. "I've struggled with why he stashed these sacred items in a floor vent at his buddies' apartment prior to his death. He was disoriented and brainwashed. A part of him clung desperately to sanity. The part that realized he'd gone down the path of no return. I spoke with a medical professional who provided an off-the-record diagnosis. Sean exhibited signs of early-onset dementia. There's another explanation. A person who consumes quantities of tainted animal matter—rotten meat, for example—is at risk of contracting blood-borne illnesses. His autopsy didn't screen for bovine spongiform encephalopathy, but I'd bet my bottom dollar he had mad cow disease, or a related virus. Slow, insidious, and terminal."

Linda massaged her forehead.

"No."

"I strongly believe your husband intended to join a secret society. The night he died was to be his initiation. He came to that pit of his own free will, a supplicant seeking transformation. The Mares prefer the stench of black blood and green meat, but the sacred offering to the spirit of the Valley had to be pure. So, Sean was cleansed and anointed with oil and dressed in linen garments. He was escorted to Shaft 40 in the dead of night and thrown in. Danny Buckhalter and the others deceived him. They stole his life."

Linda covered her mouth and coughed that dry, ratcheting cough while I spoke. She lowered her hand.

"Mr. Coleridge, I don't know much. Except colors. I can wax rhapsodic about color theory. Hue and texture. The joys of and dangers of saturation. Value, tone, and mood. The color of genius. Of sorrow. Fury. Your color isn't pleasant. You're a mess."

"Linda, we're both a mess. Have you done a spit check lately?"

Over the course of my grilling, her features had sunk

in exhaustion and beleaguerment. She was made of stern stuff, though. She glared and dug deep to fight back.

"Detectives don't solve this kind of case."

"We don't?"

"Detectives hunt down lost kittens and deadbeat dads. Detectives shoot pictures of cheating spouses in flagrante delicto."

"Oh, no, lady," I said. "That's what I do on a good day. Tonight, I'm not that kind of detective. Not to say I don't empathize with your predicament. I'd bet my bottom dollar the insurance money is mostly spent and you don't want to hear how you, perhaps unwittingly, contributed to a murder. Who would? Bad news is, there's always something worse. I've got worse."

The glint of righteous anger kindling in her eyes made me thankful she didn't have a weapon within reach.

"June and Badja are behind this, aren't they? That harpy won't accept anything less than a villain's head on a plate."

"One could make the argument it's the least you and your boyfriend owe the lady." I glanced at my watch. I fervently hoped Lionel would signal he was on the property. My earbud remained silent.

"Oh, fuck her, and fuck you too," she said. "This is ridiculous."

Teatime was over.

CHAPTER FORTY-ONE

Oh Danny boy, the pipes are calling." I said it conversationally, unholstering my .357 and resting it on my knee.

An older man in gray long johns finished creeping down the stairs. Didn't so much as squeak a board. Danny Buckhalter in the flesh. I'd surmised from the station wagon, and the occasional upward flick of her glances, that he lay in wait. The case I'd presented to Linda was as much for his consumption as hers.

Buckhalter, or Slick, as I'd come to think of him after our brief encounters, stopped when he reached the foot of the staircase. Same ducktail haircut I remembered. Brutishly handsome. Unshaven. Lean with rough hands. I didn't like the odd, segmented motion with which he'd descended the stairs, nor how he stood at the bottom, tipped forward the way some predatory insects do before they leap. I wondered if I'd made a mistake.

"You've made a terrible mistake," he said.

"Damn, I knew it." I holstered the gun anyway. It was

a necessary risk. He wouldn't behave in the manner I desired if he worried about getting his head blown off at the first twitch.

"How you feelin', big boy?" he said. His voice was thick and languid, as if from a long sleep. His eyes were alert and crackling, however. "You're pale. Lotta blood soaked into those threads. Lotta blood." He licked his lips and sidled a couple of inches closer. His tongue was longish. "Let me . . . have a look at your arm—"

"Danny, I'd love it if you didn't take another step." I stood and casually put the rocker between us. We were about fifteen feet apart. "You're the watchman. Night off from the warehouse?"

"I come and I go."

"Danny," she said. Neither a question or statement. His presence seemed to wilt her further, to sap the brief surge of fight she'd demonstrated.

"Can you see him, Linda?" I said. "Sean presented the symptoms of early-onset dementia. Rare, but there's precedent and it fit his behavior. I believed my theory. My lying eyes were wrong. He was afflicted by something else. Danny knows. Don't you? Danny knows why you're sick and growing sicker. Can you see him now?"

"See what?" she said. Uncertain. Very, very uncertain.

"Yeah, see what?" he said. "See what, Detective? What should she see?" He oozed closer with each utterance.

The light-headedness was back. Waves of pain coursed through my arm. Sweat covered my face. I leaned on the chair and tried not to make my weakness obvious.

"Sean's condition developed when he took up with

your boyfriend," I said. "If you did an inventory, you'd find your symptoms are eerily similar. Mental fragility, mental fatigue. Names slip. Dates slip. Days. Physical weakness. Lingering cough. Most important—you're psychologically vulnerable. You'd have to be to consider this bozo a catch."

"I'm unwell," she said. Looking at Buckhalter. Really looking at him.

I spoke in a soothing tone, coaxing.

"The money is dwindling, so the romance is too. Love and money aren't the only forms of sustenance. There's light and heat. There's whatever animates *you*."

Buckhalter's sneer faded.

"Detective. Detective—"

"Drugs. Psychological warfare. Hypnotic suggestion. When was the last time you changed your clothes? The last time you bathed? Your breath could peel paint. When he hands you a mason jar of deer's blood or a slab of raw meat, does it even register?"

Her gaze went back and forth. Her mouth moved as if she were reading aloud.

Buckhalter trembled. That would be the rage kicking in. He'd seen me handle his partners in Horseheads. He knew he couldn't take me, not without help, not without getting into character. What had Mandibole called the feral side of the Mares? The Aspect of Night.

He made a shushing gesture. A plea.

"Detective. You should stop. I called *him* before I came down. The man is on his way."

"Maybe he's an emotional vampire," I said to her.

"Maybe he pokes a straw into your jugular while you're sleeping and has a slurp. Maybe it's a combination."

"Danny, what is this," she said. Again, a statement. Flat, rhetorical. She'd gained her feet. We formed the vertices of a triangle. The atmosphere hummed with a gathering electrical charge.

"I can't explain how he did it to Sean then or how he's doing it to you now. He *is* draining you. Your husband was meat, and so are you, lady. You've got to wake the fuck up and see him." I said it in the rhythm of a right reverend driving home the psychological dagger. My own attempt at hypnotic suggestion, but in the service of revelation, of tearing away the mask.

Something had to give.

"You want to see me?" he said to Linda. "Bitch, you always knew." He lowered his head and when he raised it, he was a brand-new Danny Buckhalter. Happier. A man comfortable with what was going to happen next.

I thought of Bundy and all those women. This was the last face Sean Pruitt ever saw. A trick. Actor's stage-craft. This knowledge rendered Buckhalter's affect no less terrifying.

Linda Flanagan didn't scream. She didn't protest. She didn't appear to notice her overflowing tears. Her expression was blank.

"Now you see him for what he is," I said. "He wasn't Sean's friend. He doesn't love you."

"Dan. What. What."

"Linda, go." My chest tightened. The fear was almost unbearable. "Get in that car and drive. Don't look back."

A suppressed inner light flickered and ignited in her gaze. Her expression animated with a cascade of dawning emotions—anger, disgust, and horror. Holy texts speak of scales falling from a person's eyes. This was like that. She became instantly more recognizable as the person I'd come to know from a distance.

"Dan," she said, but to me.

"If he moves, I'll kill him. Get your ass gone."

She walked slowly past him without a final glance. She picked up the pace, her body awakening, remembering. She ran out onto the porch.

Buckhalter and I had a stare-down. We listened to the car door clank shut; the engine whine and fail, whine and fail, then catch, then rev, tires on gravel, receding.

Ten seconds. Twenty. Thirty. Forever.

"Dan," I said. "Admit it."

"Well, dick, this is what Sean wanted. Until he didn't." He cracked his knuckles. He rolled his neck. "Are you happy?"

"We're almost there."

Yes, I'd gotten what I wanted. I no longer wanted it. How to put the worms back in the can? Headlights filled the window. The engine's rumble vibrated glasses in the cupboard. A much bigger engine than the station wagon. Car doors opened and shut.

"Oops," Buckhalter said.

Presently came a warbling flute trill that seemed to originate in my left ear and migrate to the right. Vampish cheerleaders Veronica and Betty waltzed in. One blonde, one brunette, flanking Tom Mandibole. Mandibole had chosen a natty black suit.

"Gettin' tired of your shit, Dan." Mandibole imitated a cornpone accent. "You and your granola-chewing druid chick. You and your schemes." He'd discarded the accent and adopted a chiding tone. "You brought this creature to our doorstep." He indicated me. "Where are the others?"

Buckhalter frowned.

"I didn't, I haven't—"

"Be quiet, Dan. They aren't returning my calls. None of them. That's impossible. They're dead. Do you think they might be dead, Dan?"

"I'm sure they—"

"Shut up, Dan. Mr. Coleridge, hello."

I considered going for my gun and decided to hold the thought.

"Evening, Tom."

Mandibole stepped closer and eyed me with vicious mirth. He was a banty rooster. His spurs were honed steel.

"They really *are* gone. My children of the night. You scamp. You unmitigated fucker of mothers." He smiled furiously. His hands opened and closed, opened and closed. "It was a good run. I have the girls and that's not terrible." He swept his arm toward Veronica and Betty. "I can rebuild. We'll terrorize Hicksville again. Same as it ever was."

Meanwhile, Buckhalter's world was falling apart. His killer-jock side had abandoned him. The plaster mask affect cracked and crumbled. Feral power leached from him. He shrank into himself; gray, puny, afraid.

"Call them again!" he said. "Try again!"

"The Mares are a renewable resource. More of an idea. Bodies are replaceable as long as the spirit is willing." While Mandibole spoke, Veronica and Betty slipped in on either side of a gibbering, handwringing Buckhalter. "Fresh start, girls? Fresh start, Dan? Fresh start!"

"I only did what I thought you wanted," Buckhalter said.

Mandibole stared at me, hand raised. He crooked his finger and the ladies seized Buckhalter's arms and made him a wishbone. It wasn't easy or quick. He was hideously strong. There were two of them and they were gleefully determined. I recalled the painting in Redlick Manor of the horses tearing apart a soldier and averted my gaze.

When it was over, Mandibole continued to regard me with mild amusement.

"Keep the car warm, girls."

Veronica and Betty dragged Buckhalter's remains as they went.

"Cunning animal that you are," Mandibole said, "what did you anticipate when you imagined how this evening would unfold? And if I may, you appear to be in need of a doctor."

"We're off script," I said.

And how. I'd fervently hoped to rattle Buckhalter's cage, get the proof I sought, and lacking that, book it without a shoot-out. Best-laid plans, et cetera. My worse angel had probably gotten a cackle at that plan.

Mandibole clapped once and rubbed his hands.

"Well, you won't require medical attention. You have *my* undivided attention." He didn't draw a weapon, and that was surprising. He stepped forward, right hand open and reaching, left hand lowered and crooked into talons.

Maybe he wanted to dance. I'll never know.

The rocker was solid and heavy. Two-brawny-piano-movers-grunting-to-unload-it-from-the-truck heavy. I turned sideways for leverage and flung the chair from waist level. He brushed it past his right shoulder. The chair veered wildly and splintered against the wall. That was okay; as he reacted to the missile, I drew the revolver, my finger tightening on the trigger as the barrel covered his center of mass. The lamps at either end of the house shrieked white hot and the room went black as the bottom of a well and the revolver kicked and spat fire. Mandibole wasn't there. I shot a wall, pivoted right, trying to withdraw my extended arm, but in the next thunderclap he materialized, the top of his head even with my chin, half my mass, and grinning without a worry in this world or the next. He casually gripped the pistol's barrel, twisting, and the bullet missed his eye and bored into the ceiling and he pried the weapon and flung it aside. I let go to avoid having my fingers snapped like a bundle of twigs. People aren't normally strong enough to take my toys.

Sleep, he whispered into my left ear and my left ear faded with feedback snarl.

Sleep, he whispered into my right ear and my body grew heavy, as if I were in the clutches of a centrifuge and gravity had begun to multiply.

Sleep! His whisper was a barbed hook traveling into my brain.

Cold, disassociated, panicked, I screamed down the red light and it filled me with the power to raise Milo's full-grown bull overhead. As the lamps flared to life again, I punched Mandibole's jaw, exerting force enough to knock a hole in a sandbag, to snap a man's neck. He flinched. I grasped his head in both rock-crusher mitts and tried, with all my might and main, to wrench his spine out of his body. If I could've uprooted a tree, I could've budged him. He slammed the heel of his hand into my nose and my nose squished. Made my heart skip a beat. I traveled some weightless distance, winking out of reality, then in, as I pinballed through furniture. My splinter-torn face pressed to the wooden floor; a galaxy wheeled beneath me, hell-bright, eating the boards, foundation, musty, wormy earth. Nebulae hummed a frozen, ethereal tune, calling to me as the Sirens once sang sweet murder to Odysseus while his oarsmen rowed for their lives. I yearned to dissolve into stardust and join the cosmic tide. It was pleasing to recognize every millimeter of my minuteness. Death was nothing to fear. Peaceful.

Mandibole crossed the room in a single stride. He lifted me by my right arm and a fistful of my coat until we were eye to eye. No one had done that to me since my angry, drunken father when I was a child. He probably meant to send me into the afterlife with a quip. Hanging limp at his mercy, knees bent, arm pinned, I couldn't reach my jawbone knife on the opposite hip. And let me assure you, I wanted that knife in the worst way. My left hand went into my pocket and closed on something— the sharpened bone the Magician had fashioned into a recorder months ago and that I'd discarded with revulsion at the Hotel Roan. A mysteriously appearing recorder with a razor-sharp pointy end.

For when it's time to face the music.

I gripped it like an ice pick and stabbed three-quarters of it through his breastbone. Mandibole released me, momentarily befuddled. He screamed. His mouth dropped open, wider than you'd expect. It had a linear, trapdoor quality, like you'd catch in a ventriloquist's dummy if you did a freeze-frame. Blew my hair back with a ripe scent of green-black jungle and something dead and mummified and cuddled in webbing. I couldn't see his teeth or his tongue. But it was dark in there and black spots floated before me. World-eaters. The screaming stopped, mid-breath. Blood squirted from the hollowed bone like a spigot. He sealed the aperture with his palm. Blood seeped and dripped, but it was better.

"Boy, I loathe that guy."

I assume he referred to the Magician.

He turned smartly and walked away. Staggering, I followed him outside. There was an interesting tableau in the yard. Lionel had arrived. He stood near the van pointing his rifle at Veronica and Betty. The ladies dismissed him and continued stuffing Buckhalter's remains in the trunk of the Bentley. He immediately skirted around and joined me on the porch.

We watched as Mandibole strode to his car like a businessman late for a meeting. Betty opened a side door. Mandibole, hand over his heart, nodded at me before he climbed inside. The big engine fired up and the Bentley rumbled into the night. I hoped he'd expire on the way to the hospital. Probably too much to ask of the gods.

■ ■ ■

Once our enemies were gone, I sprawled on the steps, grateful they were there to keep me from sinking into the earth.

"Goddamn it, Coleridge. You fucking love the hospital, don't you?"

"It's a fetish. Blood transfusions and the sound of money flushing down a toilet turn me on."

"Adeyemi's money." He blew a cloud of smoke. "Couldn't wait half an hour."

"I couldn't resist the urge to get stomped by a dancing ventriloquist."

"Anything broken?"

"My face," I said.

"I mean, anything important?"

"I can't tell if the camera is in one piece." I passed him my belt so he could detach the surveillance camera. "I stashed the big one inside in a cabinet." My real worry was that despite the cessation of weird electromagnetic effects (I could wear an electronic watch again), the recording might be spoiled.

He apologized for missing the fight—the van's front tire went flat after the collision and the lugs had proven a real bitch to remove.

"Everything went off without a hitch, eh?" He handed me a rag to sop my bloody nose.

I breathed through my mouth.

"Flawless execution."

"Of the dumbest idea we've ever had."

■ ■ ■

On the way home, I caught my reflection. Now, *there* was a dude deserving of pity. My swollen face looked as if it had blocked a cast-iron pan in flight. The sleeve on my left arm was heavy with caked blood and required an effort to lift. The rest of me was an orchestra pit of pain getting in tune.

All in all, I felt pretty okay for a guy who'd gotten his ass kicked.

We drove into an abandoned quarry. Lionel transferred the equipment to the Monte Carlo's trunk. We torched the van and pushed it over a cliff. The sunrise was bloody as it climbed out of the black masses of trees.

We'd briefly discussed the farmhouse showdown. The reappearance of the bone mystified me something fierce. I said as much.

Lionel lit a cigarette.

"Since you mention it. I thought it was a weird trophy, but whatever; you're a weird dude. You've toted that thing around for months."

My pains were momentarily upstaged by a chill.

"You saw me carrying that bone?"

"On several occasions. The other day, you fished it outta your pocket like car keys. You didn't really acknowledge it. Held the thing for a few seconds, then dropped it back into your coat."

"A long-term hypnotic suggestion," I said.

"I'll buy that explanation."

"Holy shit. That creepy magician at Redlick Manor must've implanted an autonomic compulsion that I carry the bone, to use it as a weapon under the right circumstances." Which sounded ludicrous as I said it.

"Told you those fuckers could mindfuck you," he said.

CHAPTER FORTY-TWO

Badja Adeyemi's legal team wrangled me a personal audience at his newest residence, the Metropolitan Correctional Center in Manhattan. My presence wasn't strictly necessary. That dungeon wasn't on my list of dream attractions either. Adeyemi wanted to see me, and so I reluctantly went. I emailed the case files to his lawyer prior to our security screening. We met in a private room. Adeyemi had lost a few pounds and gained some crow's-feet. I told him the reddish-orange jumpsuit went with his eyes. His lawyer, Tambour, booted a laptop and played the videos I'd recorded at the farm. Adeyemi slipped the headset on. He studied the video, his mouth set grimly.

The footage became, to employ a technical term, janky in spots, and completely degraded a few seconds prior to Buckhalter's murder. I would've edited that shit anyway. However, much of it was clean. Give me a hallelujah. The footage of Danny Buckhalter's Mr. Hyde impression and the audio recordings of most of the debacle would likely be worthless in a courtroom. No smoking gun confession. Luckily, I hadn't risked my life to gather courtroom evidence. The only person in New York whose opinion counted was hunched over the monitor. Adeyemi played it several times. He didn't take notes. He simply finished and stared at the institutional beige concrete wall.

As agreed, the lawyer kept my report and deleted the sensational files. My copies were safe in a secret location.

"I have my opinion," I said. "And that's all I'll ever have. I'm sorry."

"Same," Adeyemi said. He embraced me, which was a surprise. He'd intuited I'd killed some guys, or done something vengeful on his and June's behalf. The fact I looked like I'd been chucked into a running cement mixer was a giveaway of sorts.

"No hugging in prison," I said. "No hugging in prison!"

As I readied to accompany his lawyer out into the fresh air and sunshine, I asked Adeyemi what he planned to do.

"I'm going to ponder."

"Elections coming this fall. I don't know how much it matters to you, that business with the Jeffers Project. If Redlick holds on as a senator, he'll do his damnedest to revive the collider. Off the books. A diversion of resources so the RG or an ally, such as Spencer Industries, can finish the job."

His old nasty-cop persona resurfaced with a derisive snort.

"Be realistic. Gerry isn't satisfied with a seat in the

Senate. He's gunning for the presidency. Joke candidacy? Joke's on us; he'll win."

"Goodbye, Lieutenant."

"Goodbye, hard-ass."

I didn't think I'd ever see him again. I'm wrong all the time, so why not about that too?

■ ■ ■

Lionel and I dug the Croatoan's trove up in the spring. We hauled it to a warehouse on the Hudson near Kingston. Sonny, the former Japanese diplomat, bade us sit in an office cluttered by shipping manifests and milk crates crammed with documents. Old-timey posters of tugboats and capsized barges and stonily aggrieved barge captains set the mood. Serious, serious Japanese dudes in excellent suits paced the dingy hallway. More loitered in the stairwell, passing cigarettes back and forth. A couple carried wakizashi under their jackets. We'd parked in view of the window. As I chatted with our patron, Lionel watched two guys circling his car, eyes shaded so they could look inside.

Sonny the Diplomat was relaxed as he jovially explained why he couldn't offer more than pennies on the dollar. Can't say I listened to the whole spiel.

An astronaut's brain floats in his skull, is the comment I recall from our conversation. *It was in a documentary. Those missions in space that last for months change the astronauts. Their brains float. They come home not the same.*

Seventy-five thousand apiece. We went in lugging several plastic cartons. In the end, my share of the take was neatly inserted into a large insulated envelope.

"Fuck a duck." Lionel flung his envelope into the backseat after we were safely on the road. He lit a cigarette and smoked in anger.

"Moving that amount of weight in ancient currency is a bitch. He has to wash it through I don't want to guess how many third-world embassies and depots. Warlord caves in Pakistan. Iraqi drug dens. He can't run the entire lump into Japan no matter how many bases we've stuck in there since the big war."

He sighed.

"Ah, well. My bookie's eyes will gleam when I check in this weekend. I can get a new engine for my jalopy. And some tires. Surprise Delia with some classy swag."

"Delia already has all the swag," I said.

"Man swag."

"Man swag?"

"She doesn't have man swag."

"Her boyfriend, the famous rock musician, has that covered too," I said.

He lit another cigarette.

"Been thinking my cabin could be more secure. Friend of a friend is trying to unload an M2 Browning. He's got bazookas."

"Anti-personnel machine guns and anti-tank rockets. *That's* man swag."

"You scoff. Keep playing fuck-fuck with evil corporations, military hardware might become a requirement, not a luxury."

"Seventy-five K will get the creditors off my case. Put a down payment on a house for Meg with what's left." I'd perused a handful of listings with no real sense of commitment. Looking, just looking. "Business is steady. I'm stable."

"This is a taste. Taste won't last."

"Nope."

We went a while farther.

"Okay," I said. "You want to go after a bigger score?"

"The rest of the alleged hoard? The Wagner train missing longer than the Ark of the Covenant. How much again?"

"Seven million, plus or minus. Gold, jewels."

"Our cut would be fat. A fence can move that shit, easy."

"Yeah," I said. Nothing, and I mean nothing, is easy. I didn't say it. Why ruin Lionel's moment?

"Must be Christmas again already. Santa clue you in where we can find the treasure?"

"I've logged hours with the Croatoan's home videos."

"Oh, dude."

"There's a clip separate from his snuff films. One that didn't fit with the Anvil Mountain sequence either. We'll have to dig deeper, ascertain the facts. Going by glimpses of terrain, I believe he filmed where the rest of the money is waiting. In the mountains of Northern California. Won't be easy to find. Won't be without peril."

"One of these days, then."

"One of these days?"

"As in, one of these days, we'll retire to the islands and sleep in a hammock."

"Yeah," I said. "One of these days, we'll go hunting for the rest of the Nibelungen. Live like old Germanic kings. Party hard and come to a tragic end."

Lionel smiled.

"At last, something to look forward to."

■ ■ ■

I wasn't flush for long. Meg insisted I visit the neurologist pal of hers; friend prices or not, it wasn't cheap. What did I learn from the battery of tests, scans, blood draws, and general imposition? My body was aging fast due to frequent abuse and my brain emitted the occasional peculiar wave. What could be inferred? What could be done? Not a blessed thing, the specialist said while scribbling a referral to a psychiatrist who might be interested in chatting. However, I had a standing invitation to drop in for further observation, gratis.

I promised to be in touch.

CHAPTER FORTY-THREE

Bizarre, titillating gossip about Senator Gerald Redlick emerged as news stories over the summer and autumn. Worst of them all, from Team Redlick's perspective, was a sordid October Surprise launched in *The New York Times*. Russian oligarchs, Russian prostitutes, and a selection of dubious real estate details brokered by the Redlick Group ten years past got tongues wagging. Meanwhile, Adeyemi walked out of prison a week prior to the election. The judge heard a motion to dismiss on what the legal community dubbed a bogus technicality. Damned if His Honor didn't throw out the case too.

I called Bellow for a chat. He'd taken the FBI retirement package and signed with a small security consulting firm after three ugly weeks of not knowing what to do with himself. He, like everybody, figured the slow drip of anti-Redlick info was generated by Adeyemi as a method of enacting retaliation without actually testifying against his ex-boss. Bellow predicted the various

news stories wouldn't amount to much legally. He also
forecast that Adeyemi would be arrested on new charges
or shot in the back of the head by New Year's. Word on
the wire circulated that Russian tycoons were already
putting in orders for the guy's scalp. Oh, and since we
weren't allowed to have anything nice, I could expect
Redlick to hold on to his Senate seat.

Also in the Can't Have Anything Nice category, I saw
Tom Mandibole on a cable news sound bite defending
the Redlick Group's sterling reputation against "scurri-
lous" and "politically motivated" attack articles. Someone was going to pay, pay, pay! He looked right into the
camera at me and grinned.

■ ■ ■

Redlick won reelection by the clichéd "razor-thin mar-
gin." This caused Meg to remark, *God might be dead,
but the devil is in business.*

A lone sliver of light penetrated the gloom—Redlick's
colleagues grew spines and did what a majority of voters
hadn't: they punished him for the bad press, if not the
bad deeds. He was stripped of his committees and leader-
ship roles and demoted to a rank-and-file sophomore
senator. Bereft of status and influence, he wouldn't be
masterminding a resurrection of the Jeffers Project any
time soon.

Lionel clapped me on the shoulder when the news
broke. The evidence we'd gathered turned Adeyemi
against his friend, convinced him to strike Redlick down

from the shadows. The dead weren't coming back, and as usual, the masterminds eluded justice, but Gerald Redlick was temporarily thwarted in his larger ambitions. I commented to Lionel that this is what winning looked like these days. The angel on my left shoulder laughed. In the greater battle of good versus evil, this is what winning has always looked like.

Bellow called early one morning in mid-December. His sources reported that the machinery was in motion; odds were being made on Adeyemi's life expectancy. Best bet was forty-eight hours. Bellow reminded me that, as with all gambling, the information was for entertainment purposes only.

■ ■ ■

Lionel and I used a junker car with throwaway plates and traveled incognito to Elkhorn Lake. No one, and I mean no one, not even Meg, knew anything about the trip. This was a real New York winter. Last year, I'd been able to drive all the way in. Not this time around. We parked where the road ended and heaps of snow began. Several other snowy cars and a couple of pickups occupied the plowed spot. We walked our weary asses nearly a mile through the woods and over the hills along a slippery path to Badja Adeyemi's cabin. Our gear dragged behind on a plastic sled.

Adeyemi greeted us from the porch with an automatic pistol. Recognition filtered into his deadpan expression. He nonetheless weighed whether or not to blow my head off a tick too long for comfort. He lowered the pistol, invited us inside, and offered us beers.

"Suppose I'm glad to see you," he said. "How'd you know I was holed up at the shack?"

"Where else would you go?" I said.

The lake was frozen to dark, wind-scoured marble. Black and blue storm clouds glowered like a crowd of villains.

I asked whether he'd spotted any bogeys. Because they were inbound.

"Counted two at the market," he said. "Means five."

"It means six or eight," Lionel said. He slipped into his black clothes.

"They could hit us with a drone," Adeyemi said. "Missile comes through the window and kaboom, this shack is kindling."

I shook my head.

"No, your friends will want it to look like an accident. Carbon monoxide poisoning. Heart attack. Outside chance it could be a staged hanging or self-inflicted gunshot. Four men will breach and neutralize. The rest will perform overwatch and lookout."

"Failing that," Lionel said. "Yep, next time it'll be more dramatic." He was mostly dressed and going over his arsenal. The last glimmer of sunlight enfolded him and softened into a full-body halo. It made me imagine the Angel of Death and his choir tuning their axes and singing their arpeggios in anticipation of what must surely come.

I checked the yard for the hundredth time.

"Let's hope I'm right and it doesn't turn into World War Three."

Lionel loaded his rifle. He laid it on the table next to several knives and a 9mm pistol. He picked up the pistol.

"Welcome to the Underworld. Nobody in the real world gives a shit."

"Frankly, my dear, neither do I."

"Let the blood flow, let it flow, let it flow."

"Shitheels might not even come." Adeyemi leaned back in his rickety chair. His expression was as serene as a grandfather content with himself and the world.

"They might not." I unzipped my bags and brought out the Kevlar battle-plated jacket I'd seldom had an opportunity to wear, and began to shrug into the cumbersome sonofabitch. I felt like a ronin strapping on his armor before the battle to end all battles and that squared everything. I tested the fit of my gas mask.

Adeyemi watched disinterestedly.

"If they do come and we manage to win, there'll be another team next week, or the week after, or ninjas jumping out of the woodwork wherever I go. The fuckers will get me. Today, tomorrow, someday." It wasn't a defeatist observation, merely pragmatic.

Lionel grinned, dazzling white through brown and black camo tiger stripes.

"Roger that. But it won't be *these* guys." He hefted his rifle, adjusting the bunting scope cover, working the bolt action before slinging the weapon over his shoulder. "I'll be in the trees. Radio check in five." He slipped away without a goodbye.

I lit a kerosene lamp and hung it from a hook near the stove. We'd pushed the couch and some chairs near the front door without blocking it so that when the bad guys burst in there'd be an immediate obstacle and we'd kill them while they were delayed. Or Lionel would shoot them as they milled around on the porch. Whichever.

"We're in for weather," Adeyemi said. "But we've got wood and we've got brews. I got a deck of cards, if you play pinochle."

"Gin rummy."

I leaned my boar spear against the wall. Its presence comforted my atavistic self. Spears are the single most effective non-projectile weapon in human history. Something can't bite you if it can't get close to you. The Mossberg was loaded and ready for action. I hoped and prayed whoever was en route didn't dawdle. The idea of lounging in that heavy armor for any extended duration was depressing.

He sipped his beer, stoic as a totem. Finally, he spoke.

"My uncle Gage lived in the hills outside of town. By himself in a cabin like this one. Coyote got shot; Gage found him in a ditch a piece down the road. Tweezed the pellets and nursed him back to life. Chomped the ever-loving crap out of his hand too. Coyote made it, though. Recovered and scampered off for the high timber after a few weeks. But he came around every winter, usually when the storms hit in January, and curled up on the foot of my uncle's bed. Ate the cat food, yada, yada. One of the last times I sat with my uncle, he was drunk and muttering about that coyote. His friend. Hadn't seen the critter for a couple of years." He studied the austere vista, shadow and light playing over his leathery face. Mostly shadow. "Said to me, 'Some nights when it's this cold and the wind is howling, I worry for the coyote out there. Dumb. Mother Nature will take care of him. That's her job. That's the way of it. Coyote's a pile of bones on an unmarked grave somewhere in the hills.'"

Adeyemi lapsed into silence as darkness thickened and all we had was that fragile guttering flame between us and the endless void. Really, that's all anybody has. Flames crackled in the barrel stove and the flue moaned softly. I meditated upon the wilderness and animals alone in the dark, living out nature's plan.

Nature has a plan for me as well. An exit into the posthumous life by a silver bullet through the heart or peacefully in my sleep. Maybe, when it's time, I'll return home to the utter North, lie down on autumn tundra beneath the aurora borealis, and commend my spirit to the fields of ancient lights. Whichever way it goes, the worms in the earth patiently abide.

ACKNOWLEDGMENTS

Jessica M.; Dr. Todd Banister and staff at Banister Animal Hospital of Kingston, New York; Yves Tourigny; Christopher Coke; the Langan Family; Paul Tremblay; Phil Fracassi; Stephanie Simurd; Deborah Gordon Brown; James McAlear; Jason, Harmony, Oksana, Julian, and Quinn Barron; Timbi Porter; Jody Rose; and, as always, my fans.

Special thanks to Sara Minnich, Patricja Okuniewska, Bonnie Rice, Madeleine Hopkins, and the Putnam team; William DeMerrit; and my agents, Janet Reid and Pouya Shahbazian.

Extra-special thanks to my colleague Frank Duffy, who understands; and to Gage P. & Tiffany F.